PROJECT STARFALL

BY COLIN ROSS

First published in The United Kingdom in 2024 by Colin Culbreth

First Edition

ISBN: 978-1-0683409-0-1

Printed in The United Kingdom by Colin Ross Culbreth

Official Blue Sky: @colinross.bsky.social
Official Instagram/Threads: colinrossauthor

Dear Reader,

Thank you for choosing to try ***Project Starfall***. I hope it lives up to your expectations and that you enjoy the story I have crafted.

When you finish, please take a moment to write a review. Without your help and support, my work will never be seen. A review on StoryGraph, Goodreads, Amazon, and other popular review sites would be greatly appreciated and will help encourage me to continue.

Please feel free to reach out if you enjoy **PROJECT STARFALL** or for details about my upcoming works.

With gratitude,
Colin Ross

CHAPTER 1

Ally's lungs burned, but she dared not stop. She'd heard adults complain about lactic acid before, but being nine, she'd never really experienced it until now. Every stride was a force of sheer will. Gritting her teeth, she pushed forward, trailing behind her sister, ducking in and out of light and shadow cast by Grace City's street lamps. Except for the sound of their footsteps smacking against the pavement, the streets were eerily quiet. The sky, however, was dark and heavy, and the rumble of thunder that growled overhead seemed to stalk them, drawing angrier with each passing moment.

She flinched as a vicious crack of lightning lit their path before darkness swallowed it again. Thunder erupted and the angry skies above opened, pelting the pavement with sheets of torrential rain. The cool water felt good on her hot skin. She didn't know if it was the adrenaline or the thrill of success, but the two of them had managed to pull it off! Now it was just a matter of getting home before their mother found out.

When her mother let slip what BC was doing, Ally couldn't believe people could do such a thing. The way her mother said it was just the way of things; that there was nothing they could do about it, it tore her apart. *"But they're being experimented on!"* Ally cried.

For a few days, she couldn't sleep. She couldn't eat. Then she realized that as long as people did nothing, nothing would be done. That night, she begged her sister to help her. To her surprise, Emmalee said yes without hesitation, which struck her as odd given Emma was always the more rational of the two. Ally was the impulsive one, the act now-think later type. She wondered if Emma only agreed because she wanted to see for herself what the stone could do. The rumors in the lab were one thing, but actually *seeing* it… that was something else entirely. Personally, Ally didn't care how it worked, only that it did. She could process how she'd somehow phased through that solid wall later—right now, she wanted to feel the joy of running beside Lucky a little longer.

She glanced down at the beautiful beagle trotting alongside her, happy and hopeful. Ally shot a triumphant smile to her sister, but it quickly faded. Emma only side-eyed her. Her face was stoic and cold, almost worried. She knew that look. A nagging thought began to pull at her. *Had she missed something? The guard couldn't have known who they were, could he? Was she still thinking about Beast? How he'd chosen to stay, knowing what that meant?*

Ally bowed her head, trawling over every detail from the last twenty minutes, letting the rhythmic SPLAT-SPLAT-SPLAT of her shoes and her steady breathing pull her back, until she was again racing above the mirrored blacktop, the road vanishing beneath the dark, glassy surface.

*   *   *

Ally marveled as her feet danced between dual skies, above and below, a surreal mirroring she thought only existed in paintings. It was a phenomenon she'd have pointed out, had it not been for the feeling of unease prickling her stomach. "I think we should go back," Ally whined as a gust of wind blew bits of debris across the pavement.

"We're almost there!" Emmalee called over her shoulder. "Plus, this was *your* idea."

"I know, but—"

BOOM! Ally jumped as a deafening crack of thunder shook the ground beneath their feet. The wind whipped through the narrow passage, and they could hear the distant sound of raindrops starting to pelt the pavement at the far end of the block.

According to her research, the rain would likely wash away any forensics and cover their tracks, but she couldn't shake all the ways this little stunt could go wrong: her, prone against the pavement in handcuffs… the inevitable phone call home… the disappointment in her mother's eyes… the angry lectures that'd follow… grounded until Hell froze over.

"Come on!" Emmalee yelled as she ducked through a slit in the exterior fence.

Ally sighed, but slipped through the wire and hustled up to the stone wall beside her sister.

"Oh crap!" Emma huffed.

"What?"

"No! No, no no…"

Ally watched her sister fumble around in her pockets and start patting them.

"You lost it!" Ally cried.

"Got'cha!" Emmalee plucked her hand from her pocket clutching a rough black rock and giggled.

"Don't do that!"

"Oh, pipe down, little blister."

"We're the same age!"

Emma licked her lips and narrowed her brow, focusing intently, her eyes moving uneasily from side to side as she rubbed the stone.

Nothing happened.

"You mean you don't know how it works!?"

"I know how it works!" Emmalee snapped, gripping the stone tightly now and rubbing it between her thumb and forefinger. "I saw one of the lab guys do it."

Suddenly, a vicious crack of lightning ripped through the alley, bleaching the world in a harsh, unnatural light before plunging it back into darkness. Then came the thunder—an ear-splitting boom that rattled their bones, as if the sky itself had been torn open, releasing a fury of torrential rain.

Both girls scrunched up their faces and raised their shoulders, trying to maintain composure as icy water doused them and slid down their necks.

"Well, hurry up!" Ally cried.

"Don't rush me!"

On the other side of the stone wall, harsh fluorescent lights flickered overhead, bathing a sickly glow across rows of metal cages. Inside, dogs shifted nervously, pacing around in uneasy circles as their instincts prickled. The storm drew nearer. They could sense it. As another crack of thunder tore through the night and shook the ground beneath them, all hell broke loose. The room erupted into a frenzy of yelps and frantic claws against steel, until the door was shoved open, echoing like a gunshot as it clanged against the wall.

A guard hovered in the doorway and took a swig from his cola bottle, the sharp tang of alcohol mixing with the pungent odor of wet fur. Screwing the top on, he started forward, the clinking of his keys like spurs with each step. As he made his way down the line of cages, he scraped the butt of his flashlight along the bars, filling the room with dull clunks that seemed to silence the animals, one by one, until only a few uneasy whimpers remained.

Even after his shifts, he could still hear their pathetic yaps, like a bad song that gets stuck in your head. Working the night shift at the Burton Pharmaceuticals R&D Center was only good for two things: boredom and headaches.

As he took a step, the power suddenly flickered out, leaving him in total darkness until a brilliant white light lit up the room. The subsequent thunder rumbled, shaking the framework of the concrete building. Dogs barked and howled in fright as they helplessly paced their cages. The man gave out a little whoop and chuckled as the thunder dissipated.

"You like that, you little bastards?"—he slammed the palm of his hand onto one of the cages—"Huh?" He chuckled again, turning around as another blinding flash of lightning illuminated the room, bringing him face to face with a set of white, slobbering fangs, snapping and snarling. Beast, they called him, lunged at the gate with a fury that made the guard's blood freeze over. He stumbled backwards, skidding on the slick floor, and crashed into the cages behind him with a resounding clang. All around him, the cacophony of feverish barks erupted like a twisted symphony of maniacal laughter.

He shook himself and straightened, still weary as Beast ripped angrily at the floor of the cage. The man slammed the butt of his flashlight against the cage again, but Beast only seemed to bark louder. "SHUT UP, YOU PIECE-OF-SHIT MUTT!" Again, he struck the cage, only this time, the beam of white light fizzled out.

"Damn it!" He whacked it into his palm, but only managed to make it flash on and off for a split second. "Shit!"

Another flash lit up the demonic glint in Beast's remaining eye and the subsequent crack of thunder spooked him. The guard watched the cage rattle and buckle under the physical strength of the large Newfoundland. He admired the determination of the beast, struggling against all odds to break through the damn welding.

"Oh, you think that's funny?" He yelled, finding his courage, and chucked the flashlight at the cage. It clanged loudly and ricocheted to the floor, but Beast didn't let up. His barking was deafening.

"I'll show you something funny!" He took a few steps toward the cage and unzipped his pants, pissing inside. He laughed, whooping as Beast snapped and barked, trying to break free and avoid the stream.

The guard belched and zipped up, then removed an electric prod from his belt and jabbed it into Beast's side. The dog snarled and retreated to the rear of the cage.

"Why isn't it working!"

"I don't know!"

The guard whirled around and froze. The voices had come from right behind him. "Who's there?" He squinted into the blackness, trying to listen over the sound of the deafening barks, but all he saw were shadowy bricks.

"Why isn't it working!" Ally yelled.

"I don't know!"

Ally lightly shoved Emmalee. "You said this would work!"

"Me? This was *your* idea!"—she shoved Ally back—"This is *your* fault! If it wasn't for you, I wouldn't even be here… drowning like a rat!"

"Trust me, it's an improvement!"

"Whatever! Just give me some space." Emmalee rubbed the black rock with her thumb, scowling as the rain pelted the asphalt with unrelenting force.

"Ugh! Let me try!" Ally ripped the stone from her sister's hand. She started rubbing it, trying to mimic her sister's movements. Suddenly, Ally's fingers twitched. She gasped as a jolt of static electricity shot through her fingers. She looked down in amazement as the stone began to glow.

"Uh… Emma?"

A dark purple hue began to build and tiny sparks of light slithered along its jagged edges.

Suddenly, a bolt of lightning struck the ground in front of them, the stone in Ally's hand pulsing with radiant light. The shockwave of thunder then barrelled into Ally, sending her sailing right through the solid wall.

Emmalee gasped in shock. "It worked! It really worked!" She whooped and dashed forward, colliding right into the concrete with a thud.

"OWW!" She pressed her hands against her forehead.

The guard leaned in closer, catching a shimmer like a mirage in the shadows. He squinted—BOOM!—Lightning flashed again, revealing a girl dripping with water; the whites of her eyes glowed unnaturally, as did her skin.

The night guard gasped. He reeled backwards, smashing hard into Beast's cage, then jerked away like his hand had touched a hot stove and knocked himself out on the corner of another cage.

He fell down and didn't move.

Ally gazed down at the man in uniform lying motionless on the floor. She was too frightened to check if he was still breathing. The animal inside was snapping furiously and ripping at the wire enclosure. She locked eyes with it and froze.

"Ally! Ally, you OK?" Emmalee's voice echoed weakly through the stone blocks.

"I'm OK!" she screamed back.

"Open the door!"

Easing her way through the rows of cages, Ally pressed the handle, only to find Emmalee crooning in the entryway with her arms crossed, leaning against the doorframe.

She smirked. "See? I told you it would work." As she stepped inside, her flashlight beam hit the floor and onto the prone night guard. "Holy crap! Did you kill him?"

Ally didn't answer. She and Emmalee had trained in various martial arts forms since they could walk, but she hadn't needed to get physical here. She watched as Emmalee held the beam of light over his face, catching a puff of steam faintly escaping his mouth and breathed a sigh of relief.

"Go find your pup," Emmalee said. "We need to get her out of here before he wakes up."

Ally made her way down the corridor, checking each cage, until she found it. She plucked out the pin and pulled a scruffy mutt into her arms. "I told you I'd come back for you!"

Emmalee watched Ally giggle as the beagle wriggled and squirmed, trying to slime her cheeks with its big red tongue. She sighed and reached out to pet her, unable to stop herself from smiling.

"Look Emma! She's so cute! I'm gonna name you Lucky."

"Ok. We gotta go!"

"What about them?" Ally asked.

Emmalee looked down the long line of cages full of strays. "We can't, Ally. Come on."

Ally took a few steps forward.

"Ally! Think about it. They might not miss one, but if we let them all out… we're screwed."

Ally hesitated. She eyed the long line of cages and listened to the various whimpering tones. Finally, she made a decision.

She marched forward and began unlocking the cages, one after the other, leaving the doors open wide and helping smaller dogs to the floor.

Emmalee sighed and followed her sister's lead, unlocking the cages one by one.

Ally giggled as a barrage of dogs scurried past her ankles to the end of the corridor, barking excitedly. She watched pridefully as Emma held the exit door open, pushing and urging dogs through,

"OK, we *really* need to go."

"What about him?" Ally said, pointing to the last cage labeled: BEAST. Inside, the massive Newfoundland growled and bared its teeth. Lightning struck again, reflecting the sutures over one side of his face, leaving one piercing eye.

"Let's leave this one…," Emmalee replied, backing away.

Ally moved slowly toward the cage.

"What are you doing? Are you crazy? That thing'll eat you."

"You'd be pretty mad, too, if someone stuck you in a cage and tested poisons on you. He deserves a chance."

Ally slowly pulled the cage door open and backed up against the wall, leaving a path to the exit door.

"Ally, what are you—"

Beast jumped from his cage and stood firm, eyeing them both cautiously, still snarling and growling softly.

"Go on, Beast! You're free!" Ally smiled, gesturing with her head toward the door.

Beast gazed out into the night and stopped snarling, like a sudden calm washed over him. His eye softened and he licked his lips. Ally watched him stare into the open air and could have sworn she saw him smile. Then his ears pricked up and he jerked his head back. Behind them, the night guard stirred, slowly lifting his head and sat up.

"Hey! What are you doing?" he yelled.

"Come on!" Emmalee whispered. "He's coming! Let's go!"

The night guard staggered to his feet. "Stop!"

"Come on, Beast! GO!" Ally whispered.

Beast looked to the exit, then to the guard, then up at Ally. Turning his body, he squared up to the night guard, baring his teeth, hackles raised, and growled a deep, guttural growl.

The guard froze. "Nice doggy... nice doggy." He slowly reached out and picked up his heavy flashlight from the floor. Beast snarled and released a deep, guttural bark. Saliva dripped from his sparkling white teeth. His body twitched and jutted forward in warning.

Ally felt a tug on her wrist and Emmalee pulled her through the exit door. She sadly looked back, watching as Beast covered their retreat, and they turned and ran away from the building. Stray dogs barked excitedly in all directions, away from Burton Pharmaceuticals R&D Center, to freedom. Lucky followed in suit, wagging its tail and cooing in excited yips.

Suddenly, from inside, a man's scream rang out. Loud snarling echoed through the courtyard. The two girls turned back as two injured yelps pierced into the night, followed by three deep, sickening thumps. Both sisters felt a lump build in their throats and a sick feeling spread to their stomachs.

"Is he—" Emmalee started.

"Why did he do that?" Ally asked, standing rigidly and staring back toward the open door. "He could have escaped. Why did he do that?"

Emmalee shrugged. "Maybe he knew there was nothing out here for him."

Ally stood in silence for a moment, then set the Beagle in her arms down gently.

"Come on," Emmalee urged.

Together, they hustled down the empty streets, Lucky trotting beside them, jumping playfully through the puddles and enjoying her freedom.

"She looks happy. You know Mom won't let you keep her," Emmalee said.

Ally stopped dead in her tracks. Her head dipped and her shoulders slumped.

Emmalee looked at her sister. "Look, I'm sorry, OK? Maybe Mom will—"

Ally threw her arms around Emma's neck and held her tight. Tears formed in her eyes. "Thank you," she whispered.

"Gross; don't get all mushy on me," she joked, patting her on the back.

"Shut up." Ally wiped the tears from her eyes and playfully shoved her sister's shoulder.

* * *

"Come on!" Emmalee cried, pulling Ally back to the present. She blinked, realizing she must have run a mile in a daze, like when adults drive for hours without realizing it. She shook herself and followed, dashing around the next corner, only to gasp and skid to a halt outside their front yard—two police officers were standing on the front steps.

Ally felt her sister grab her hand and yank her down behind the bushes. Together, they watched as an officer banged on the door. "Police. Open up."

Ally squeezed her sister's hand tightly twice, and was relieved to feel her squeeze back, a silent reassurance that they were in this together, no matter what happened next.

"That's some incredible response time," Ally whispered as she peered over the hedge.

"I don't think they're here for us."

"Is it because we took that rock?"

Emmalee shrugged, watching as the door opened. Their mother stood in the entryway.

Ally strained to listen, but she could barely hear anything over the encroaching rain.

"Sara Reid?" the officer with a Buzzcut asked.

"Yes."

"Good evening, ma'am. My name is Offic—"

Ally's eyes narrowed. She scanned the street, sensing something was off. "Don't cops usually come in police cars?" she whispered. "Where are the cars? The flashing lights?"

"Shh! I'm trying to listen," Emmalee hissed.

Ally frowned and eyed the door.

"I apologize for the hour, but we're responding to a discrepancy made by your employer, Burton Conglomerates."

"*Former* employer," Sara cut in dryly.

The girls exchanged confused glances. Their mother had been working tirelessly for years on a classified project for the government. There was no way she would just walk away. And to *fire* her? That was even stranger! Her mother used to try and explain away all the broken promises and late nights by saying there was no one else who could do what she could.

"Apologies ma'am… *former* employer," Buzzcut corrected. "Nevertheless, there are some inconsistencies with your statement we'd like to speak with you about."

"I'm sorry; can I see a badge?"

Buzzcut and Mustache held up their badges until their mother nodded and leaned back.

"It's late. Can't this wait until tomorrow?"

"Unfortunately not, ma'am," Buzzcut said. "We were more or less ordered to sort this out this evening. We have our superiors, too."

Sara sighed and shrugged. "Fine; what's this about?"

"Is anyone else in the house?"

"No, it's just me."

Both cops glanced at each other, their heads lingering just a little too long. "What about your children?" Buzzcut asked.

Ally caught the stiffness in her mother's eyes, like prey when it senses a predator is near, and a deep sense of unease trickled down her spine.

"They're at their father's."

Both girls looked at each other and made a face.

"May we come in?" Buzzcut asked. "It won't take long."

Ally strained to listen. The rain hadn't let up. Had her mother stopped talking?

"I'm sorry, but it's late. I'm afraid you'll have to come back tomor—"

Buzzcut thrust his hand against the door, his foot wedged into the narrowing gap, preventing it from closing completely. His fingers clenched around the door and he forced his way into the house.

Emmalee suddenly whirled. "Stay here!"

"I'm not staying—"

Emmalee's expression hardened. "You stay there!"

"Wait! Emma!"

Emmalee raced around the side of the house toward her bedroom window.

"Emma! Ugh!" Ally sighed and began to pace back and forth. The muffled voices in the house were growing louder. Were they shouting? She peered over the bush and gasped. Buzzcut backhanded her mother hard across the face and sent her crashing out of view.

Ally's hand flew to her mouth before her body went rigid. She watched in horror as Mustache closed the curtains. He had a gun in his hand!

Ally cursed. "What do I do?" She didn't know what, but she had to do something! Then her eyes went wide. *Emma!*

She raced around the side of the house to the kitchen door and slipped inside. Sneaking across the floor, she inched toward the doorframe hoping to get a better look, but leapt back as a shadow came into view. Fearfully, Ally backed up and slipped into the kitchen cupboard. It was dark except for the beam of light that pierced through a crack in the cupboard door. She pressed her eye to it, just making out the view into the living room.

Buzzcut paced back and forth in front of her mother, now kneeling on the floor. She could only make out some of what they were saying because her heart was thumping in her ears. Then she heard shouting.

"Give me the code!" Buzzcut screamed and pressed his gun hard into her temple.

Ally gasped. Her sweat went cold. Her legs felt glued to the floor.

"You don't understand!" Sara rasped. "If he gets his hands on Quantum, millions of people will die!"

Buzzcut leaned in close, pressing the barrel harder into her skin. "That ain't my problem, lady. But if you don't give me the code, you're gonna die tonight."

"There must be someone you care about," Sara croaked.

Buzzcut lightly shoved her mother's head. He stood upright and cocked the gun. "I'm gonna count to three."

Ally began to hyperventilate. She couldn't get enough air in her lungs. She needed to get out of the cupboard, but she was too scared to move.

Sara's eyes burned defiantly. "No matter what you do to me, Quantum will do worse."

Buzzcut scoffed and tilted his head. "You're pretty tough, aren'cha?" He smiled. "All right. Have it your way." He returned the gun to its holster, picked up his phone and pressed send. A moment later, the phone clicked. "You were right. She ain't talkin. You want me to kill her?" he said gruffly.

A moment passed.

"Understood." He closed the burner phone and placed it back into his pocket. "You're gonna wish I'd pulled that trigger."

Ally watched Mustache pull Buzzcut aside. For a moment, she thought they were coming for her, but they stopped just outside the kitchen. She couldn't make out what they were saying but she saw Mustache's shoulders slump before Buzzcut shoved past him.

A minute later, Ally heard the front door open. Heavy footsteps entered the room and she could see three men. They were big, tall, and hard. Behind them, lighter footsteps sounded on the floorboards. Ally watched a fourth man enter the room, and the big men stilled, watching him as if awaiting orders. Unlike the others, who had short hair and thick beards, this one was clean shaven. His hair was slicked back into a ponytail.

As he stepped more into view, he removed his jacket and Ally saw he had the kind of muscles you don't get from lifting weights. He was tall, lean and muscular like a seasoned fighter. His gait reminded her of the martial artists she and her sister used to watch between their tournaments.

The man casually removed a handgun from his armpit holster, cocked it, and without hesitation, fired a round into her mother's thigh.

The bang made Ally flinch. Her eyes went wide. As her mother shrieked in pain, she desperately wanted to cry out. Instead, she watched in horror as the man squatted down and jammed his index finger deep into her mother's wound. Sara wailed, thrashing and frantically gripping her leg, desperate to remove his finger.

Ally couldn't hold back any longer. She burst through her cupboard door, ready to put all her martial arts training she'd acquired since she could walk to the test. She opened her mouth to scream, but stopped as a war cry rang out from across the living room. "Nooo!"

Ally turned. Emma rushed from the bedroom door, plucked a Samurai sword from the wall trophy, and headed for the leader. One of the bearded men went to grab her, but Emma shrieked and slashed hard, severing the man's forearm. He gasped and fell to his knees, desperately trying to pick up his limb despite blood pooling on the floor.

As a second man moved in, two swings of the sword sliced through his fingers and across his neck. His eyes bugged out of his skull and his hands clutched his gurgling throat. Panicked, he thrashed about, not knowing he was already dead.

The third man managed to grip his handgun in the chaos, but Emma threw the sword like a javelin, pinning him to the wall through his neck.

Emma's head twisted to the lone assassin, who stood observing, almost as if he were amused. She charged toward him, screaming like a Viking warrior, but the man casually pulled a long knife from his belt, turned, and thrust it straight through Emma's chest.

Ally gasped, feeling the world beneath her shift on its axis. She couldn't move. She couldn't breathe. The horrifying scene before her played out in agonizing slow motion, every detail etching itself into her mind like runes on a cliff.

Emma's scream waned, her breath reduced to a sickening whinge as she fell to her knees, gripping the bastard's clothing as she slumped to the floor. Ally saw blood pooling around her sister's body. She saw her fingers twitch. Her lungs gurgled as more blood drooled from her mouth. Ally blinked, her mind struggled to comprehend the unthinkable—her sister's beautiful life, extinguished in an instant.

A raw, guttural cry ripped Ally back from the abyss. It tore through the silence and clawed its way into the depths of Ally's soul. Ally turned toward her mother. She was reaching out in a fit of desperation, her hands trembling, her gaze empty, her heart broken.

A hard shove launched Ally towards her mother. She missed her footing, tripped and landed on the floor. A pair of rough hands grabbed her by the hair, yanked her up and pressed a knife to her neck.

Her mother stopped shrieking.

"I'm going to ask you only once," the man said with a cold calm voice. "Give me the access code, or I'll open your daughter's throat, right here on this cold floor."

Ally watched her mother's eyes go hollow and vacant, like her soul had just broken. Her eyelids relaxed into a faraway look, like a dead woman walking. "Pegasus057371," Sara rasped.

The man shoved Ally's head forward and stood up, leaving her on her knees. He squatted down and used his knife to cut the straps, freeing a computer that hung around a dead man's neck. He opened the laptop. The screen came to life and he typed in the passcode. Satisfied, he closed the lid. He placed it under his arm and screwed a black tube onto the end of his gun. He turned and raised it, aimed at her mother, and fired three rounds—two through her chest and one into her forehead. The sounds were muffled and quiet, like whispers.

Ally gaped in shock. Her mother sat motionless, leaned against the wall. Her eyes were dull and lifeless. Her hands lay curled and still.

"What about her?" Buzzcut barked.

"No witnesses," the leader's hollow voice replied.

Before Ally could blink, Mustache moved toward her and something struck her hard in the forehead.

*   *   *

Ally groggily opened her eyes, but pain surged through her skull. Her forehead throbbed. She felt dizzy. There were loud footsteps inside the house. And the sound of pouring liquid.

She forced her blurry eyes to open and watched from the floor as Buzzcut emptied the last few drops of a gasoline jug onto the floor and tossed it aside. He grabbed Mustache and shoved him out the door. It slammed behind them. Ally winced, the bang ringing through her throbbing head. Despite the pain, she forced her eyes open and sat up, looking for her sister. She was nowhere in sight, but Ally did see her mother slumped near the wall.

She heard raised voices outside, one of them angry. A moment later, Ally flinched as something crashed through the window and shattered, erupting the room into flames that spread rapidly. She could feel the heat on her skin, like needles poking her all over.

"Emmalee!" she feebly called. "Emma!" She coughed as black smoke began to fill the room. A window shattered to her left and she shielded herself from a fireball.

There was no way out. *I'm going to die here.*

Ally blinked. She felt strange, like energy was leaving her body, almost as if she were an air mattress and the air was gradually leaking out. She felt herself growing tired, but managed to crawl her way inch by inch toward her mother.

She looked into her face. She was beautiful. Her eyes were closed and she seemed to be at peace. Ally laid her cheek on her mother's thigh and closed her eyes, listening to the sound of the flames.

She was ready.

Suddenly, her head slid away and bumped to the floor. Something pulled her away. In a desperate attempt to hang on, Ally gripped her mother's hand. The tugging continued and she could feel her strength leave her. She let go and watched helplessly as she was pulled farther and farther away from her. Finally, her body stopped and she heard a dog barking. It licked her face. Then a set of kind eyes leaned over her and told her everything was going to be okay.

Ally blinked. She felt the weight of her eyelids, the pull into darkness. Her head throbbed and a wave of tiredness washed over her. She lacked the strength to fight it anymore. She gave in, letting exhaustion take her.

CHAPTER 2

WELCOME TO *dis*GRACE CITY

It was the same graffiti mural Ally had passed dozens of times. She'd never really paid much attention to it before, but for some reason, it stole her attention tonight, and she found her eyes lingering on the slanted red letters spray painted to its left: disGrace City. It was an apt name. She imagined its founders chose the name 'Grace' to inspire a sense of civic pride. Today, it was more of an oxymoron. A joke. To some, Grace City was a sprawling metropolis, where skyscrapers pierced the sky, and reigned high above districts with personalities as diverse as its citizens. Where laws protected hard working people and facilitated the dream of a better tomorrow. But peel back the surface, and take a look beyond the dense shopping areas and posh restaurants, beneath the grand landmarks and labyrinthine alleyways, past the bustling streets, frenetic energy, car horns and hurried footsteps, and you can see the city for what it truly is: a ***dis***-grace. Look hard enough and you'll find its underbelly. Decayed. Rotten. That's where Ally lived. West of the city, close to the Scrubs, and far from the more affluent neighborhoods. In South End.

Squinting against the bitter wind, Ally turned the corner and made her way into the container park. It was quiet tonight. It struck her then how usually at 4am the park was filled with pockets of laughter and murmurs from its nocturnal residents. But as she passed by a stack of containers, she began to notice just how few people were left. She recalled seeing a few packing up and moving on, but to where, she didn't know—and truthfully, she didn't care. Ally kept to herself mostly. Safer that way. It wasn't because she feared for her life. Though the area had a rough reputation and had been known to attract degenerates, she could handle herself. Perhaps that was her youthful naïveté, but confidence goes a long way in a place like this. No, it was because life experience had taught her *trust* was just a word. It had no meaning for her. Not anymore. Not since the system betrayed her. She only interacted with people now if there was no other choice.

Ally felt a tickle in her nose. It was bleeding again. She shoved the last wad of tissue from her pocket into her nostril and leaned her head forward. Her heartbeat needed to slow if it was to clot, but adrenaline was still pumping through her like a war drum. The soreness from the underground fight earlier was starting to take hold. She grimaced and placed the palm of her hand over her swollen cheekbone. No need to ice it in this cold. She ran her tongue over her split lip and slowed her pace, inhaling a deep, slow breath, wincing from her bruised ribs.

As she approached her container, something stopped her dead in her tracks. She cocked her head and squinted, first in confusion, then in anger as her eyes fell to the door. To the lock. Her cheeks suddenly felt hot.

"What the f—" she hissed, reaching forward and grasping for the padlock that prevented her entry. Then she saw the sign:

EVICTION NOTICE

Dear Miss Allyson Reid,

This letter serves as an official notice to inform you that, due to non-payment of rent, the locks on the premises at Despotes Container Park have been changed as of December 11th. Consequently, you no longer have access to the property.

Your tenancy is hereby terminated, and you are required to vacate the premises immediately.

Any belongings left on the property will be considered abandoned after 7 days from the date of this notice. If you wish to retrieve your belongings, please contact the owner to make arrangements.

Failure to comply with this notice may result in legal action to recover possession of the property. If you have any questions or concerns, please do not hesitate to contact the owner.

Sincerely,
Bill Despotes

"That son-of-a—" she rattled the lock futilely, "—Ugh!" She jerked away and stomped toward the main office. *I'm gonna ring his goddamn neck!*

She banged her fist hard on the door, waited and listened. Impatiently, she banged again. "Mr. Despotes, I know you're in there!" She heard a shuffle inside.

"Office is closed!" a gruff voice called.

"It's me! Ally!"

"Office is closed!" the voice repeated. "Come back tomorrow morning!"

Ally scowled. "We had a deal! You said I had until tonight!"

"Yah! And it's 4am!"

Ally mashed her fingers to her forehead and glowered. She'd thought *by tonight* was more figurative than literal. She didn't think he'd actually lock her out on one of the coldest nights in December. "Come on, Mr. Despotes. Open the door! It's freezing; where am I supposed to sleep?"

"Not my problem!"

Ally's fist pummeled the metal door. "I have your money! All of it!"

There was a pause. "All of it?" His voice had changed. Softer. More human. There might still be a chance.

"And next month's too!" she added quickly.

The viewing window slid open. A pair of aged eyes peered out at her skeptically. "Show me."

Ally reached into her bag and pulled out the envelope of cash, thumbing through what was left of her winnings.

A moment later, the door shut again, leaving Ally standing in the silent cold. Just when she thought he'd left her to freeze, the internal door locks slid away with a loud CLACK and the door creaked open.

Ally didn't wait for him to fully open the door. She shoved past him and about-faced. Mr. Despotes was a man with salt-and-pepper hair, an untrimmed beard, and gaunt cheekbones that put him somewhere in his late 50s, she guessed. "Now Ally, it's nothing personal… it's just business," he said, raising his hands from under the meager blanket wrapped around his shoulders.

She knew that. But that didn't make her any less angry. "How could you do that to someone? It's freezing! I could die!"

He smirked and pulled the blanket around him tighter. "You're too stubborn to die…" He paused and dropped the smile. "What happened to your face? Are you alright?"

Ally shrugged. "I'm fine." *Or at least I will be once you let me back in.* She could feel him studying her, brow furrowed almost like he was concerned or worried. She could feel swelling in her cheekbone and wondered if the bruising was spreading over her face.

"Are you in trouble?"

She shook her head.

"You fightin' again?"

Ally gave him a look.

He raised both hands, "You're right. It's none of my business."

Ally relaxed her glare. With the exception of locking her out on one of the coldest nights of the year in mid December, Mr. Despotes always seemed like a nice man. He'd given her plenty of extensions and put up with her excuses over the last few months. The last time she'd paid rent, her eye was swollen and her face was banged up. Mr. Despotes was so worried that Ally had to explain the injuries were not from muggers or people who wished her harm. They were from Vale Tudo fighting.

"If you're so good, why does your face look like it's been in a meat grinder?" he'd asked.

It took some doing, but she'd finally managed to convince him that she'd allowed herself to be hit. Dropping an opponent too quickly attracts too much attention.

The first time she'd won a fight, bouncers hauled her into a back room. The only thing that spared her a beating was the amount she'd won. They'd reckoned nobody'd fix a fight for as little as $100 and backed off, calling it beginner's luck. But she couldn't shake the feeling that they were watching her. So now, it had to be more of a performance. She had to let the guy hit her.

Ally opened the envelope in her hand and removed the stack of bills. She carefully thumbed out last month's rent and set it on the table followed by this month's rent and laid it crossways, then proceeded to count out more.

"What're you doing? You're all paid up."

"This is *next* month's," she said, holding out the stack of bills for him.

Mr. Despotes reached out and accepted the money, then his face betrayed him and he handed a third of it back. "Ally… sit down."

Ally clenched her jaw. The man looked like he was wrestling with a big decision, and in her experience, that usually meant bad news was coming. She watched him place the money she'd given him into a small wooden jewelry box before sitting down. He gestured for her to sit opposite.

She felt a lump in her throat and lowered herself into the tattered recliner chair.

"How long are you planning on living like this?"

"Like what?"

"Ally, I'm not too prideful to admit that this feeble establishment is derelict at best and inhumane at worst. People don't deserve to live like this. What are you, seventeen? Eighteen?"

Seventeen.

"Don't you have people who care about you?"

Her face hardened and she looked up at him, her eyes burning, as if to say, *watch it, old man.*

"Why don't you give them a call. Get out of this place."

"I'm fine here."

"Ally, look," he sighed and adjusted the blanket around his shoulders, "about 10 years ago, I had a fight with my son. I said some things in anger that to this day, I can't even remember, but he stormed out and I didn't see him for a while. A few months went by, and I heard he was living with some friends and was working in the city. We even saw each other once, but we both pretended we hadn't."

"Where is this going?" Ally demanded.

"Just listen," he looked away, pursing his lips. "A year later I got a call from the police. He was killed outside an ATM machine. Some kind of robbery gone bad. Now, all I have left is my regret." He turned back at her. "Life is too short to hold grudges. You should call your folks."

Ally bit her tongue and stood up. "Look, Mr. Despotes. I appreciate what you're trying to say, and I'm sorry about your son. But respectfully, you don't know the first thing about me." She leaned down and grabbed her bag. "It's been a long night. I need to try and sleep." With that, she turned and headed for the door.

"They're shutting me down," Mr. Despotes called, making Ally stop. She turned, and saw him take a deep breath. "BC offered me a buyout… and I'm taking it."

Ally sat back down. She hung her head a moment, processing what Mr. Despotes had just said. "How long?"

"30 days. After that, they're gonna bulldoze the place. Probably turn it into another goddamn liquor store or casino. Just what disGrace City needs."

"What are you going to do?" Ally asked.

"*I'm* gonna be fine. The buyout will mean I can finally retire and get the hell out of South End. They've offered me enough to practically afford a place in Sterling Heights. I have no idea why, but how can I turn down that kind of money?"

"You can't," Ally said matter-of-factly. She looked up and forced a smile. "I'm happy for you."

"What about you? Is there any place you can go? Anyone you can go to?"

Ally sat quietly for a moment. She didn't see the point in telling him about her life. Everybody had a sob story. No reason to share hers. Besides, being evicted was the last thing on her mind. If the intel she'd received was genuine, tonight could be the end of everything.

She stood up. "Thank you for telling me. I should go." She turned and walked toward the door.

"Wait!" Mr. Despotes called. She watched him fumble around in a metal box and retrieve a silver key. He handed it to her and she nodded, realizing she'd nearly forgotten about the lock.

Ally smiled slightly. "See you around, Mr. D."

She stepped out into the cold night air. The gravel crunched under her boots as she walked across the open lot, weaving between rows of container-like storage units. The paint was peeling in dull, weathered colors, their surfaces covered in graffiti that seemed to glow under the pale light. As the chill nipped at her fingers, she quickened her pace. Reaching her unit, she fumbled briefly with the key, the sound of the lock snapping open breaking the quiet. With a heavy creak, she peeled the door open, and slipped inside.

Pulling the sliding door shut, she slipped into her Oodie and shuffled towards a small folding table set up near the far wall. On it, sat a laptop she'd nicknamed Frankenstein, on account of it being made of salvaged parts, custom circuitry, and software mods she'd written herself. To find a man like Mr. Smith, there was simply no other way than to carve a path through the murk of the Dark Web and learn the rules, bending them, breaking them when necessary. After all, ghosts simply didn't just pop up on Google searches.

Dropping into the chair, she flipped open the screen and the system sprang to life. A faint glow warmed her face as lines of code and encrypted gateways flickered past. She disabled them, and narrowed her eyes on the icon that was her inbox. Displayed was a new message from Prometheus. She swallowed and opened it.

Tonight. 3am.
The abandoned theater in the Scrubs.

CHAPTER 3

Tonight could be the end of everything!

Ally blew a heated breath into her hands, a temporary relief from the bitter cold. It was too late to turn back now. She hadn't spent months feeling around on the dark web, or enduring weeks of surveillance, long nights and dead ends, only to let a little bad weather foil her scheme. To track him down, it took dedication and patience. But she finally found him, *Mr. Smith*, the bastard who murdered her mother and sister. And she was going to make him pay!

She smiled, allowing herself a moment's pause to picture Dr. Wheeler's face choking out a painful apology when this night was over.

She was going to enjoy this.

As the waning light of the sun faded behind the horizon, darkness crept in like a silent predator, encroaching the unfeeling coves of the buildings. Delicate snowflakes descended from the black, placid sky above. They fluttered in the breeze, casting eerie shadows in the ominous amber glow of Grace City's street lamps.

Ally checked the pocket of her Fanny pack. The grenade was still inside. She patted it with her hand, wondering if the local vet would notice the missing anesthesia drugs, but more importantly, she wondered whether she'd gotten the dosage right. Synthesizing the aerosol wasn't easy. It took time and a precise knowledge of Chemistry. Luckily, she had both.

She pulled an orb from the pack and tossed it into the air. Its arms popped loose, releasing silent rotary fans that caught the air. The hover drone now floated in place, waiting for her command. As she tapped the screen strapped to her forearm, the drone chirped and warbled around her silhouette. It painted her body with a thin beam of neon light, scanning and storing every crevice of her form and bending around her muscles and curves. As it neared completion, she heard it: tires rolling over the loose pebbles on the asphalt below.

Ally cursed. *They're early.*

From the safety of the rooftop, she watched four darkly clad figures step out of the black sedan and head toward the long-forgotten theater below her. She turned to the drone impatiently, waiting in agonizing silence as it made its final pass over her body. "Come on!" she huffed in a gruff whisper. She watched the men pull balaclavas over their faces and enter through the dilapidated doorway. Finally, the drone chirped, and Ally snatched it from the air and stuffed it back into her Fanny pack. She dashed to the adjacent wall and slipped through the busted vent on the roof.

Inside, she crouched in the shadows, watching the men from above through the semi-collapsed roof. Moonbeams filtered down revealing the years of neglect that saturated the building. On the ground floor, the derelict remains of cinema seating lay stacked along the edges of the cracked walls, or were left in discarded piles beside the remains of the concrete floor.

Ally followed, careful not to alert them by stepping on rotten sections of the ceiling floorboards, which were just itching to collapse. She lowered herself into a squat, tracking two men in the corridor below her. Their footprints left a visible trail in the new fallen snow as they clumsily cased the empty pathway. One man was about her size. He took up the front position and looked calm. The other acted like every dark corner was waiting to leap out at him. He passed uneasily through the dark, jerking his light from side to side.

Ally exhaled and lowered herself from the crawl space in the ceiling, carefully dropping down onto the balcony level. She took a second to listen, wanting to be sure they hadn't heard her before moving on. Tiptoeing through the shadows, she tested a tattered curtain. When it held, she slid down and landed with a delicate thump behind them.

The little one jerked his head. She watched him creep closer, puffing out hot clouds of steam into the frosty air. She leaned back, trying to conceal her body. Slowly, she took in a large sum of air, and held it, not wanting her breath to betray her position.

"I don't like this, yo," the weedy one called as he waved his flashlight.

"Jesus… not this again..."

"I'm just sayin'… don't you think it's pretty sketchy for a buyer to arrange a meeting way out here? And all for a bunch of dumb rocks?" He gasped and clawed a cobweb off of his face.

"That ain't what I heard. I heard they ain't just rocks."

The weedy one stiffened as the beam caught sight of a rat scurrying across the floorboards. He shuddered, scooting closer to the bigger man. "Yeah? Wha- what kind of rocks are they?"

"I heard they give people magic powers."

"Ok, I get it. Ha ha… real funny. Let's just sell the damn thing and get out of here. This place gives me the creeps!"

The big man turned. "Stop! Don't move!"

The little one froze, the flashlight in his hand started to quiver.

"What is that?" the big one asked, staring in her direction. "Don't!" he cried as the little one went to look.

Ally felt a cold sweat drip down her spine. Her muscles tensed and she suddenly felt exposed. If she had to, she could make her move. But this would mean the plan was ruined and she'd have to improvise.

"There's a huge spider behind you."

Ally furrowed her brow. There was nothing behind him. Nothing except her.

"Can you get it?"

"Oh, shit!" the big man said. His eyes grew wider. "It's a Brazilian Wandering Spider."

"Is that bad?" Weedy asked.

"One of the most deadly in the world. Whatever you do, don't make any sudden movements. They're drawn to movement."

"Like a T-Rex?" Weedy whimpered like a child who'd just scraped his knee.

Ally readied herself in case she needed to leap out and pounce.

"What do I do?"

"On the count of three, you need to run."

"But you said no sudden movements!"

"I'll distract it. One…"

"Just shoot it, man."

"Two…"

"Come on, man, just throw something at it or—"

"Three!"

The little one lunged forward, squealing and skipping through the corridor, back toward the safety of the moonlit stage, leaving the other chuckling to himself.

Ally's eyes shifted to the big man, alone and exposed. From the shadows, she crept up behind him, quickly snaking an arm around his neck and squeezed with all her might. The man flailed in her arms as she dragged him backwards. He jerked his body and tried to resist her grasp, but she managed to hang on.

Suddenly, he launched his head toward the floor, pulling her legs off the ground, and thrust her hard into a wooden support beam. He regained his footing and swung a hard punch, striking the beam with his fist as she ducked.

The man cried out, took a second to cradle his fist, then went for his gun. Ally back-flipped, clocking him right under the chin with her boot and sent him flopping hard onto his back, but not before a single shot echoed through the still air.

Ally froze. A red stain of guts and blood painted the wall behind her. Not her blood. A rat lay curled on the fallen rafter, its body nearly blown in half, blood still oozing from its flesh. A one-in-a-million shot.

Her attention shifted toward the stage. The other men jerked their heads and started toward her, guns drawn.

Shit!

CHAPTER 4

She quickly ripped the coat off Biggie's unconscious body, threw it over her shoulders, and tore the balaclava from his head. She pulled it over hers, picked up the gun, and took a deep breath before stepping out of the shadows, hoping her disguise was enough.

The men jumped. "Damn it, Ajay! I almost shot you!" Muscles yelled as she edged back into the ivory glow.

"What the hell was that about?" Leader demanded, but Ally ignored him. She stormed toward Muscles and Weedy, but Leader stepped in front of her. "I asked you a question."

Ally stood still for a moment, hoping the asshole didn't put his hands on her or look too closely.

Just ignore him. Wait him out.

He gestured with his arms impatiently, unwilling to let it go. She knew if she spoke, it was all over. What she needed was something to shift his attention. Then she had an idea.

She stepped forward, shoving her way past Leader and knocking against his shoulder hard, as she stepped into the dark corridor. A moment later, she returned and tossed the dead rat at his feet. Both Muscles and Weedy chuckled while Leader glared daggers at her.

"What do you gotta be such a—"

Suddenly, loud, confident footsteps echoed through the darkness and snuffed out their conversation. Three men walked into the open space, also wearing balaclavas.

Mercs-R-Us must have had a special.

One was large. Even through his bomber jacket, his muscles pushed out through the fabric. The other was smaller, but looked like he'd seen his fair share of brawls. His hands were tattooed like the Russian mobsters in crime dramas. The man in the center held a large silver briefcase handcuffed to his wrist. This must be him. Mr. Smith. Her target. The reason she'd risked life and limb to be here. Her jaw clenched, and she let Ajay's pistol slide into her hand. The metal felt cool against her hot skin and the rubber grip held her fingers like they were made for it.

"Hudson!" Muscles barked.

So that was his name, the leader. Hudson and the two others raised their weapons and aimed them at the approaching men.

"Tell your men to put their guns away. You won't need them… as long as you've brought me the mineral," Mr. Smith said.

Mineral? Ally's brown eyes shifted, watching Hudson's reaction. *What did he mean, mineral? Was this a drug deal?*

Hudson nodded to his men and each uncocked their guns, tucking them back into their belts. "You got the money?"

The man smirked amusedly and patted the case. "I'll show you mine, if you show me yours."

Ally didn't like it, and judging by Hudson's hesitance, he didn't either. No honor among thieves, eh?

Hudson reached for the satchel at his hip and shifted it forward. Something was pressing through the thin material. It was rectangular in shape, about the size of a Manila envelope. Reaching inside, he slid the rectangular box out and lifted the lid. Ally barely held back her gasp as the contents glittered, sending sparkling shapes around the dark room, like gold bars reflecting off the sunlight in an old western.

Mr. Smith leaned forward, examining the glowing contents. The way his eyes gleamed with cunning, Ally figured he'd seen enough of these objects to know that the strange aura was somehow authentic and not some ordinary crystal.

He clapped his hands together and gave a playful slug to his bodyguard's shoulder. Then he looked up at Hudson and nodded approvingly. "All right," Mr. Smith said. "Let's do this."

Ally was done being patient. This was her cue. She spun and knocked Weedy out with one punch. Then ripped the pin out of the gas grenade with her teeth and tossed it to Muscles. He caught it instinctively, then recoiled as a cloud of mist engulfed his face. He waved his hand through the air and coughed, spluttering with wide eyes before dropping to his knees, choking. He went down hard.

Hudson whirled. She was about to rush him, but the bodyguards had already drawn their weapons. Instead, she dove over the edge of the stage and ducked for cover as bullets whizzed over her head.

"What the fuck, Ajay?" she heard Hudson yell.

She ignored him, retrieved three hover drones from her pouch and set them on the dusty floor. On her forearm, she ripped off the Velcro cover, pressed a button on her control pad and watched with slight admiration, or be it pride, as the preset programming rendered three duplicate copies of herself in a crawl on the floor in front of her. The holographic projections were perfect, identical to her in every way, taken of her earlier when she was on the roof. She made a mental note to store a scan of her wearing a balaclava for future reference.

"Don't shoot!" Ally shouted, casting her voice low in disguise. "I'm coming out!"

With the projections now fully rendered, she slipped the visor over her eyes and was now looking through the drone's camera at herself on her hands and knees. It was trippy.

She pressed another button, causing one of the holograms to stand up with its hands raised and fulfill the preprogrammed display.

"I'm not armed," she said in as deep a voice as she could manage, keeping her head pointed toward the floor.

Ally saw it briefly unfold from Hudson's eyes. Watching who he thought was Ajay reaching up with both hands. She kept her gaze on the floor as long as she could. As she raised her head, her decidedly unmasculine form was fully revealed. She saw Hudson gawking in shock as a teenager stared back at him.

Ally was tall for a woman. It was how she'd managed to impersonate a six-foot man in the first place. As she stepped into the moonlight, she could feel their eyes crawling over her every curve. She'd spent years fine-tuning her body into a sculpted masterpiece until she was in peak physical shape. Her muscles protruded from under her black sleeves. The backs of her hands were snaked in veins, which rippled across her skin. Her legs were shapely and powerful. She looked like an Olympic athlete.

"What the fuck is this?" Mr. Smith yelled, tucking the suitcase slightly back behind his thigh.

"Hell if I know!" Hudson turned back to Ally. "Who the fuck are you?" he yelled.

"He," Ally said, pointing slowly to the man with the briefcase, "knows exactly who I am." Hudson turned and looked at the man with the money. Her heart pounded and she took a hesitant step forward.

"I've never seen you before in my life!" Mr. Smith yelled.

Liar!

"You don't recognize me?" Ally growled. "How about the names Sara and Emmalee Reid? Ring any bells?"

The man's eyes squinted in confusion and he stared blankly back at her.

"Yeah, well, you probably don't remember all the names of the people you kill." Her voice hardened with each filthy word. "But before this night is over, I'll make you remember."

"What?" the man almost scoffed. "What are you talking about?"

He was good, she'd give him that. He was playing the role of confused innocent well. If she wasn't so confident in her research, she might have believed him. There was only one way to find out.

"Take off your mask. I want to see your face!"

Mr. Smith laughed and glanced around assuredly at the three guns pointed at her. "I don't have to show you shit."

"Take it off! Or I'll take it off for you."

"Shoot her," he said with a lack of emotion. The men obeyed, raising their guns and fired, their rounds seemingly punching right through her chest.

At the same moment, Ally pressed a button on her control pad, manipulating the hologram to collapse in a heap and paused the rendering. Mr. Smith flicked his head to his two bodyguards and they shifted their weapons toward Hudson.

"Woah!" Hudson yelled, feeling completely outnumbered. He threw his hands up in surrender, displaying the gun in his palm. "Easy! Everybody just relax. I know this looks bad, but I swear, I have no idea who that was!"

"She came in with you."

"ME? She said she knows YOU! And besides, my guy was with us the whole… time…" his voice trailed off.

"I said I've never seen her before!" Mr. Smith growled.

Crouched safely beside the elevated stage, Ally's rendering ominously climbed to its feet and raised its head, staring right at them.

"Boss!" the bigger of the two bodyguards barked in alarm. The other recoiled and both shifted their guns. Everyone took a half-step back and gawked at her in disbelief.

"That's not possible!" Prison-Tats rasped. "Even with body armor on, that would have been enough to put anybody down."

Ally summoned all her drones, each rendering an identical projection of her.

"Shoot her in the face!" Mr. Smith shouted, this time in desperation.

"I'm afraid that won't help," came Ally's voice from the second drone behind them. The three men whirled in disbelief. They jerked their heads back and forth in a double take.

"She's right," came Ally's voice from the third drone off to their left.

"What the hell is this?" Mr. Smith bellowed. "Kill them!"

The three men emptied their magazines, each aiming for a different target and spread themselves wide on the stage. Finally, clicking sounds echoed throughout the building and the drones converged in front of them. Through her visor, Ally watched the men gasp in disbelief. Seeing their bullets have no effect and passing straight through their targets must have been quite a sight.

From the safety of the dark passage, Ally's maniacal laugh shot through the trio of drone speakers. The sound was so shrill and loud that the men shivered. Then the real Ally leapt out of the shadows and dealt a high kick to the back of the large bodyguard's head. The sound of his body hitting the floor turned the others, but not before she'd hopped off the stage and reengaged one of the holograms to stand near the grimacing man.

The others turned and stepped forward, allowing Ally to engage Prison-Tats, punching and kicking him with ferocity, then finished him off with a Capoeira kick that knocked him onto his back. She pounced on him, hitting him repeatedly until he stopped moving.

Behind her, the big man clawed his way to his feet. He shook his concussed head and rushed her, kicking her hard in the side and sending her flying sideways. Ally used her momentum to roll onto her feet in a crouch, then she stood up, attempting to block the man's punches like she'd trained herself to do, but he kicked her again and knocked her down.

Ally knew she was in trouble. With pain now coursing through her body, and doubt creeping in, all she had was the adrenaline surging through her veins. When the big man went to kick her a third time, she launched herself to her feet and caught his leg. Then gripped and dropped to the ground, using all of her strength to hyperextend the man's knee with a loud guttural snap. He howled and fell to the floor, rocking gently on the ground whimpering.

Ally kicked him hard in the face and stepped around him. Mr. Smith took a step back and ordered Hudson to shoot. He raised his gun and shakily aimed it at her.

Ally studied his quivering hand. "I have no quarrel with you," she said. "I'm here for him." She raised her index finger and pointed it at Mr. Smith. "You let me have him, and I promise, you'll never see me again."

"I don't even know you, you crazy bitch! Shoot her!"

Ally watched Hudson's eyes glance at Mr. Smith. He surveyed the bodies lying on the floor. Then he looked back at her, clumsily wiping the sweat from his brow with his free hand and aiming the gun.

"Think it through. You'll pull that trigger, alright, but your arm's shaking so bad you'll miss. I won't."

Hudson tried to support the gun with his other arm. Moderate effect, and he knew it.

Again, she raised her index finger. "That man murdered my mother! He shoved a knife through my nine-year-old sister's heart! He deserves to die. If you get in my way, I'll kill you, too."

"She's fucking crazy! Shoot her!" squealed Mr. Smith.

Ally felt the last nine years of frustration and anger boil through her skin. "I'm NOT CRAZY!" Ally screamed, her voice singeing through three drones's speakers all around them. Hudson flinched and took a step backwards, reassessing his odds. "I'm not crazy!" she said again, regaining her control. "What's it gonna be, Hudson?"

Hudson narrowed his eyes. Probably not smart to say his name. *Stupid.*

"Shoot her, goddamn it!"

Hudson's face hardened and she watched him pull the trigger.

The gun exploded into thin clouds of smoke, but Ally stood still, glowering at each gunshot. She counted five.

Hudson's eyes widened. He must have thought he'd missed, the poor bastard. Again he tried, squeezing off two more rounds with the same effect.

He tilted the gun and gawked at it in disbelief, then aimed and emptied the magazine, screaming as Ally walked forward.

His eyes bugged out of his skull and he backpedaled. "What the fuck are you?"

Ally struck his extended arm with both hands and disarmed him. "You should really check your ammo for blanks next time," she quipped, holding up an ammo clip then chucking it away. She took pleasure in his confusion as he instinctively felt for his belt. Then his eyes cooled.

That's right, the shoulder bump, she thought. *I swapped your spare magazine.*

In a blink, she stepped forward and knocked him to the ground with a hard punch to the face. Then she turned to Mr. Smith. Finally! Eight years in the making. This was it!

He held up the briefcase as a shield but she smacked it out of the way. "Take off the damn mask!" she ordered.

"O...okay!" he stuttered. Slowly, he raised his hands and shakily removed the balaclava.

Ally's eyes ballooned. Her jaw dropped. "Shit!" Ally huffed in sheer disbelief. It wasn't him! It wasn't Mr. Smith! Three months of research, recon, and effort wasted!

She clenched her fists and let out a primal scream. She didn't care if she was pacing the floor like a child having a tantrum. How did this happen? How did she—"

She froze. Blue and red lights flickered outside. She heard the faint sound of tires crunching on the gravel, followed by the sound of muffled doors opening and shutting.

"I told you she's fucking crazy," Mr. Smith whined in a half-whisper.

"Shhhh!" she hissed, hearing footsteps approaching. Then she gasped. Several flashlights poured through the dark passages and six armed officers sprinted in.

"ARMED POLICE! Don't move!"

Ally sprang into action. She darted back into the shadows and tapped the sensor pad in mid-sprint, bringing the hover drones and holographic projections of herself to life. She tapped the button on the sensor pad, and the holograms headed for the exit, leading away several officers in different directions.

Ally dashed through the dark passage and dove through a busted window. She paused for a moment, concealed by the darkness and slid along the exterior wall until she reached the corner of the building. Peering around the edge, she observed two police officers guarding the building's entrance. Only, they didn't look like police. She couldn't quite tell from her position, but she could have sworn that their uniforms were different. Perhaps they were private security.

How did this happen? She cursed herself. She was sure it was him this time. How could she have been so stupid? She watched as the officers dragged Mr. Smith and his men out of the entrance, demanding compliance. Using the commotion, she slipped from the shadows like a wraith until she reached the rear-most squad car. Carefully, she ripped open the door and leapt into the driver's seat, making sure to shut the door silently.

Then the car's tires let out a deafening screech as it sped backwards. A confused officer spun around and raised his gun, but the hesitation from the commotion blew any chance he had at hitting his target. Ally cut the wheel hard and pulled the emergency brake, sending the car into a 180 degree slide, and she punched the gas.

I'm going to make it, she thought.

In her rear-view mirror, she saw a few officers scramble to their cars and maneuver around clunkily in pursuit. Ally gripped the wheel and willed the car faster. Her entire body felt the rush of adrenaline surging through her. She knew she needed to ditch the car, but first she had to get more distance between her and the cars in pursuit.

Suddenly, her eyes caught the bright flash of headlights up ahead of her. As the car zoomed closer, she saw a white van turn sideways and skid to a stop, nearly blocking the entire road. She smiled; they'd overplayed their hand.

She gripped the wheel and prepared to squeeze through at the rear, until the side door slid open, revealing what looked like a plastic cannon. It was large, clear and had multiple round barrels like a mini-gun. She was so close now that she could see the barrels begin to spiral.

Instantly, the car jolted like an airplane experiencing turbulence. A shockwave of energy oscillated below her like it was coming from the very ground, right underneath her—like an earthquake. The car forcefully jerked again, then went into a spin, hurling her in all directions. She cried out in pain as the seat belt cut into her chest and shoulder.

The car flipped.

Time slowed.

The world blurred around her until her car smashed against the concrete barriers. Glass exploded in all directions and the car's frame crunched into a mangled slab of worthless metal. Panic swelled inside of her now. Through the ringing in her ears, she could just make out sirens growing louder. She only had seconds to make her escape. Slowly and painfully, she managed to crawl out of the driver's window and shakily climb to her feet.

Even though Ally knew everything must have happened in less than a second, to her it seemed like minutes. In a foggy haze, she watched as police swarmed the totaled squad car and pointed their weapons at her head. She considered running, but after taking a step, a wave of nausea swirled around her. She fought it, but her eyes dipped and her head battled to stay upright. When her body gave up, she fell forward straight into an approaching officer's arms. She didn't even have a chance to gain her footing to resist. The officers rode her to the ground and knelt over her back. Cuffs clamped around her wrists and they jerked her up. It was over before it began. She struggled, though she knew it was pointless.

"Let me go!" she hissed, kicking and pulling her muscles tight.

"Stop struggling!" the officer ordered. "Or we'll use force!" But Ally didn't listen. She began screaming, flailing and kicking.

Then a gruff voice barked out into the night. "Night, night princess!"

All Ally remembered before the light faded from her eyes was a guard raising the butt of his rifle and hearing a sickening CRACK.

CHAPTER 5

That's when my boys pulled her out of the car she boosted," Lieutenant Michaels continued, speaking over the faint hum of the digital video recorder. "She's gone too far this time."

Claire stole a tearful glance through the one-way glass at her foster daughter, Ally. She was slouched in the chair, looking detached as usual, her absent gaze boring right through the wall. Claire bowed her head, closed her eyes and pressed a trembling hand over her mouth. She knew Ally's downward spiral wasn't her fault. The ordeal she'd gone through would have traumatized anyone. But that didn't shake the feeling in the pit of her stomach that she was partially responsible.

Claire sighed, her voice shaking. "Did she hurt anyone?"

Before Michaels could answer, the door clunked open and a man in a suit waffled in along with the bustling sounds of the precinct. "Sorry I'm late," he said. "The streets were jammed with—"

"The protesters. Yes, I know," Michaels interjected, making a face. "Goddamn locusts." He sighed and rubbed the bridge of his nose like it had been a long night. He checked his watch. "Mr. Chamberlain, my name is Lieutenant Michaels. This is Mrs. Johnson, the perp's foster mother."

"Claire," she almost whispered, offering her hand.

Mr. Chamberlain shook it politely, then his gaze shifted to Michaels. "Care to tell me who this girl is to you?"

"I'm not sure what you mean, Councilor."

Mr. Chamberlain took a step forward. "Don't bullshit me, Lieutenant. You have enough to nail her to the wall. In my experience, police don't go out of their way to protect a client like *this*. No offense," he said, gesturing to Claire. "Unless… there's a reason."

Michaels sighed, then nodded. "When Ally was nine, she lost her mother and sister in a house fire. A fire that I believe she started."

Mr. Chamberlain furrowed his brow. "It was your case?"

Michaels nodded. "One of those terrible accidents. In her grief, or perhaps in dealing with the trauma… I don't know," he ran his fingers through his hair, "she concocted this *conspiracy* story."

Mr. Chamberlain tilted his head. "Conspiracy story?"

"She maintains that a man was responsible for their deaths… believes an *assassin* killed them. Saw the whole thing, apparently.

Calls him Mr. Smith." He pursed his lips and exhaled through his nose.

"Shortly after their deaths, psychiatrists diagnosed her as delusional. For the past eight years, she's struggled to keep grips on reality. In and out of trouble… but *this* is the worst I've seen her."

Everyone looked through the one-way glass at the teen slumped in the chair.

"So to answer your question, Mr. Chamberlain, it's personal. Now, if you wouldn't mind… I'd like to clock out and get some sleep."

Satisfied, Mr. Chamberlain turned to Claire. "After you."

Claire shook her head. "She doesn't want to see me. It would only upset her." Her voice a low whisper. "We haven't spoken in a while."

Mr. Chamberlain shrugged, gave a final look to Michaels, and entered the interrogation room.

"I really appreciate this, John," Claire said, after the door had shut. "I know you've put your neck on the line for us; thank you."

"If she gets in trouble again…" Michaels started.

"I know," she finished, turning back to the window, "you won't be able to help her."

Ally was drowning, the weight of despair pulling her deeper into the depths of the chair, until it swallowed her. Her thoughts were stuck somewhere in a muted consciousness, distant and muffled, echoing through her brain in a torturous loop.

... crazy... insane... batshit... unhinged... delusional...

"Did you hear what I just said?" Mr. Chamberlain asked, breaking her concentration. "I said there won't be a trial."

Ally forced the memories back down into the pit of her stomach. *I probably wouldn't be fit to stand trial anyway.*

"Come on, did the butt of that rifle knock you senseless? This is great news! Better than we were hoping for!" he said, blinking at her as if waiting for her to smile.

Ally's stoic brown eyes slowly shifted toward her state-appointed attorney and met his incredulous stare. Even if she had three more hours, she wouldn't be able to explain everything coherently.

"Alright, settle down," he said. "Somebody up there must really like you. You know that crate you helped *liberate* from the distribution truck?"

Is that what the cops told you? Typical... force the pieces together until they fit. I didn't even know about the deal until it went down.

"Well, as it turns out, those batteries were scheduled for recycling—" *Wait, hold up. Batteries?* Her mind raced back to the abandoned theater, to the rectangular box containing the glittering crystal, how it seemed to generate its own light in the dark room, the way the buyer's eyes gleamed with cunning. "—so I was able to talk our pals at BC into not pressing petty theft charges. I politely reminded them how corporations bullying poor, crazy, orphan girls of color in open court tends to be bad for PR."

Crazy!? Ally couldn't help it. She flinched, breaking composure.

"Ah, don't worry," he said dismissively, "that's just lawyer talk, like bluffing in a game of poker. I know; am I good, or what?" He smiled and opened his hands like a magician expecting applause.

Ally's eyes glazed over.

"That being said, I'm not a miracle worker. As for the other little stunt? How should I put this… uh, *commandeering* a police car? Well, that's something that the boys in blue take kinda personally… so there's that."

Ally thought back to her getaway, the white van screeching to a halt ahead, her car jolting like an airplane experiencing turbulence, the shockwave rippling beneath her, the loss of control, the seat belt cutting into her shoulder, the car flipping and glass exploding.

"Between you and me," he said, leaning in a bit closer. "I thought stealing the cop car was pretty cool. I mean, ya know, in a Bonnie and Clyde kind of way." He shifted back into his chair again. "Don't tell them I said that." He let out a nervous chuckle and pointed at her with his index finger.

Ally side-eyed him. Knowing how everything had played out, she should have just slipped away on foot. Stealing the squad car was rash and stupid.

Mr. Chamberlain cleared his throat. "Then, of course, there's that pesky little resisting arrest charge, which I also couldn't get them to budge on. You know what these guys are like… pride as big as their egos.

"The good news is, you're a minor, and given the complications of your past"—Ally's eyes filled with fire—"I was able to talk the prosecutors down to, get this: a year's probation and 300 hours community service!

"The State will set you up with a job and some kind of volunteer work. It'll be no sweat and you can probably put it on your résumé when all of this is behind you. Heck, it may even work out in your favor. I mean, this kind of 'I've had an epiphany and changed my life' attitude can really make a splash on college entrance essays."

Ally relaxed and silently scoffed. *I doubt many insane people get accepted to universities, Mr. Chamberlain.*

Mr. Chamberlain stopped talking. He removed his glasses and rubbed the bridge of his nose before resetting them. Beads of sweat glistened on the top of his forehead below a receding hairline. "Alright," he said, somberly. "Well, I'll just file these papers and someone will be along to explain the rest of the process." He closed the file folder, stood up, and hovered by the table. "Hey, uh... try and stay outta trouble for a while, okay? I don't think you understand how lucky you are."

"LUCKY!" Ally screamed. "What part about my life seems lucky to you?"

The man flinched. He looked taken aback. Ally glared at him and sucked air through her teeth. She waited for his spluttering reply, but it never came. Instead, he picked up his coffee mug and headed toward the door.

She watched him walk away deflated and in spite of herself, she felt some dormant emotions crept up inside of her.

Ah, hell.

She managed to clear her throat. "Mr. Chamberlain?" He stopped and turned around. "Thanks."

He flashed her a polite smile and nodded before leaving her alone in the room.

When he'd gone, Ally hung her head. A normal person would be thrilled they'd just avoided prison. But Ally wasn't *normal.* All she could think about was the last eight years, all that time wasted, obsessing over and chasing a goddamn mirage.

She sighed heavily and placed her hands over her face. *What am I going to do now?*

As the door suddenly opened, Ally looked up and her heart sank. Dr. Wheeler was standing with her arms on her hips, her eyes narrowed into slits, her lips pursed into a half-snarl.

Ally squeezed her eyes shut. She felt sick. The lump in her throat was the only thing holding the river of emotions back. She swallowed it.

"I don't know what to say," Dr. Wheeler grumbled. "Everyone warned me something like this would happen. But I stuck my neck out for you. You lied to me. You manipulated me. You made me look like a fool."

Ally's heart began to tremble. She tried to calm it by sucking in a full breath, but her lungs felt compressed. Tingling spread down her arms and into her hands. She felt like she was drowning again.

"You're just going to sit there? You're not even gonna—"

Ally couldn't hold it back anymore. The river burst through. Eight years of pent-up emotion poured through her in deep, sorrowful sobs. Her body convulsed, wracking her body. She hadn't cried this hard since she became an orphan.

After a moment, a gentle hand touched her shoulder, and Ally quickly turned and threw her arms around Dr. Wheeler's waist. She pressed her face hard against her blouse, leaving dark pools on the fabric.

"I'm sorry!" she wailed, choking out every word through hysterical sobs. "I'm s-sorry! I didn't th-think I was c-crazy… but I *am*... I'm f-fucking crazy! I-I—"

"Shhh…" Dr. Wheeler whispered, her hand moving up to stroke Ally's head.

"I'll do w-w-whatever you tell me to… I-I'll take my m-medication… j-just tell me what to do, and I'll do it!" she choked, sucking in short gasps of air.

"Breathe, Ally. Just breathe. We'll get through this." Dr. Wheeler stroked Ally's head until her body eased.

"Come on. Let's get you home."

CHAPTER 6

Ally slowly opened her eyes, letting her senses adjust to the familiar dark of her container. The sounds of the slum rattled through the thin corrugated walls: raised voices next door, a neglected baby's cry, incessant footsteps thumping through the roof above, the distant sounds of construction equipment.

She rolled over and stared at the ceiling, trying to ignore the winter chill that cut through the old blankets on her makeshift bed. For the past year, this squalor had been her home. After she was expelled from her third school, she and her foster mother had a big fight. Ally didn't blame Claire for being upset, but what she'd said was unforgivable. Even now, the words still cut deep: *"I'm glad your mother is dead, because she'd be ashamed to see what you've become."*

After that, Ally stormed out and rented this storage container in South End using some of the money from her mother's life insurance. She'd told Claire she didn't want anything to do with her and gave her an ultimatum: deposit my share of the foster stipend into an account each month or send me back into the system. She was surprised Claire agreed, but it didn't take a stretch of the imagination to see that receiving money for doing nothing was an appealing arrangement, especially given the state of things in Grace City. But that arrangement was nearly at its end; Ally was nearly 18.

She sighed, peeled the blankets off her legs, threw her feet into her slippers, and stood up. Without insulation, the metal container may as well have been a refrigerator. She leapt for her Oodie and threw it over her shoulders just as something soft attacked her leg. Ally looked down and smiled. Piggy mewed loudly and brushed her tail against her pajama cuffs. "Hey, Pigs!" She swooped her arms down and picked up the cat, smothering her with kisses. "You hungry?"

Piggy hated being picked up and much preferred to have her feet planted firmly on the ground, but Ally liked to remind her that she was a cat, and being snuggled was one of her duties. She carried the protesting ratbag to the old wooden cabinet, found in the street like all her furniture, and set Piggy down onto a tattered piece of cardboard. Grabbing a tin of wet food, she peeled back the lid, sending Piggy pacing excitedly while demanding her breakfast. She rubbed her body seductively around Ally's pant leg, practically yelling. She always did this around mealtime. Food was life.

Setting the tin down on the metal floor, Ally smiled as Piggy began gobbling up its contents, snorting a little with each bite. Had Ally not found her, she didn't think she would have been able to make it on her own. Sometimes it felt like Piggy was the only good thing in her life, the only thing rooting her to the ground.

Ally flicked the radio dial and the vexing sounds of the slum lost their edge, fading into the background as the calming music washed over them. Heading into the bathroom, Ally's eyes honed in on the pill bottle resting on the sink. For several long seconds, she stared daggers into her own reflection. She hated being ill, but after nearly killing a man who, as it turned out, *wasn't* the man from her imagination, she decided to take her medication again. She swallowed two tablets and took one more look at herself before heading back to what might be called a kitchen.

Turning back to the cabinet, she stared at the bare shelves. They almost made her miss the stocked cupboards in Claire's house. She sighed, grabbed a can of beans and collapsed onto the one beanbag chair she had. It was ragged, full of claw marks, and might have been more duct tape than chair at this point, but it worked.

Spooning in a mouthful, she relaxed into the chair as the music slowly faded, replaced by an uplifting tone that chimed before a voice delivered the smooth opening line: *"The world doesn't stop and neither do we. This is Globo-News."*

"Good morning. I'm Robert Gamble," a man said with confident swagger.

"...and I'm Gail Robbins," a woman echoed, sounding almost heroic.

"And here's today's top stories," they said together, pausing while the theme music cycled in and out.

"The Blur—vigilante or hoax? You'll never guess who says they saw him," Robert teased.

"Another earthquake in Old Town? More on that in a few minutes," Gail said.

"The court has ruled—do we still have the right to bear arms? And coming up, an interview you won't wanna miss. We have Nicholas Duncan, Vice President of Burton Conglomerates, and will offer him a chance to comment on those gentrification rumors."

"And finally, water shortages... is this the end of beef? All that and more in a moment," Robert paused as the network melody chimed and faded again.

"Good morning everyone. Is there a vigilante running about the city? Mr. Drumpf thinks so. He's the sixth person to come forward this month claiming to have seen some kind of blurry figure running through the back alleys near the projects. This brings the total reported sightings to 89. According to sources, this Blur was spotted last night fleeing a crime scene. Numerous criminals were found by police bound with zip ties, though when we tried to confirm this, the PDGC declined to comment.

"What do you think, Gail? Is the Blur real? Is there a blurry man running around the city?"

"It sounds like Mr. Drumpf is taking his second electoral defeat pretty hard, Robert."

Ally chuckled. The Blur was just an urban legend that probably got started by the police to scare criminals into staying in for the night.

"Now onto our next story. Did you hear about the big earthquake yesterday in Old Town, Gail?"

Ally leaned forward. Earthquakes in Grace City were one of those unexplainable phenomena that puzzled her. Experts interviewed in the past were unable to explain them. So her interest was always peaked.

"Hear it? TriTech practically collapsed on me! I was having my hair done across the street. You know, the one beside their research facility?"

"Mmm hmm."

"Big clouds of dust were blowing through the air. It sounded like bombs were going off. Everyone was screaming and running around. I thought we were under attack."

"Sounds scary."

"I'll say! Luckily, the whole building collapsed into its own footprint. Experts think there might have been a flaw in the mixture of concrete."

"Another corporation trying to cut costs by cutting corners..."

"Looks like it, Robert."

"You know, I think I felt that one all the way out in Sterling Heights."

"Really, all the way out there?" she quipped.

Robert chuckled, then his voice changed to account for the more serious story. *"In other news, after enduring record levels of gun violence throughout the city, it's finally official. The proposed bill by democrats to ban the sale of fully automatic firearms has failed."*

There was a short pause.

"Yes, you heard that right. After weeks of deliberation the US Supreme Court decided that such a measure would be a violation of every citizen's constitutional rights. Thousands of protestors nationwide took to the streets shortly after the decision. So what does it mean for Grace City? Our own Gail Robbins has more. Gail?"

"That's right, Robert. In light of this decision, some corporations have begun taking matters into their own hands. Hal Burton, CEO and founder of the corporate giant Burton Conglomerates, has pledged to help clean up the streets—"

Ally's ears pricked up. There they were again: BC. Her thoughts immediately went to Mr. Despotes, how he had said BC had offered him a buyout. Then she thought of her mother. She'd worked for BC's advanced science division before she…

"—They have stated publicly that they have a plan to save the underfunded Police Department of Grace City from financial ruin and have recently announced they have been buying up all their shares since they went public last month. This makes Burton Conglomerates the majority shareholder of the PDGC.

"I suppose the big question on everybody's mind is... will this new aid help the police combat the record-high crime wave we've been experiencing... or is this just a clever way to aid the construction of Eden Town?

"Here's Nicholas Duncan, Vice President of Burton Conglomerates."

There was a moment's pause for effect.

"Good morning, Mr. Duncan. Thank you for being with us."

"My pleasure, Gail," a confident voice replied.

"*Mr. Duncan, how do you respond to public concern that Eden Town is just another elitist plot to force the poor out of low-income housing?*"

Mr. Duncan scoffed. *"You know, if these people spent half as much time applying for jobs as they did obsessing over corporate conspiracy theories and unfounded rumors, the hardworking people of this city wouldn't have to pay into all these public support troughs,"* he grumbled. *"Hal Burton's vision for the future only requires that local citizens be temporarily relocated until construction has concluded... at which point, they'll be invited to return to their homes if they wish."*

"What would you say to the people who do not want these new housing establishments? That they're happy with what they have?"

"I'd say the people rarely know what they want. That's why corporations exist. Because people need to be shown what they

want. The reason we are rebuilding Old Town is simply because Burton Conglomerates cares about the people. The frequent earthquakes are tearing this city apart and the current structural buildings are not up to code. That's why they keep failing. If people are saying they don't want safer buildings for their families, then I'd ask them why does a man like Hal Burton care more about their families than they do."

"A bold answer. Tell me, can you comment on the rumors that when the people do return to their homes, they will also return to higher prices... prices which will be unaffordable to many struggling families?"

"Burton Conglomerates is committed to the promises it's made to the people of this great city. However, let's not forget that the financial burden our company is shouldering for this project is already one of the largest any corporation on the planet has ever undertaken. Burton Conglomerates is assisting local law enforcement to protect the construction sites of Eden Town, to curb the vandals and allow us to remain on schedule and keep prices affordable."

"Many people might call that a conflict of interest..."

"Burton Conglomerates owns your station, Globo-News... yet here you are, free to conduct honest, investigative journalism."

"Fair point. But you're dodging the question, Mr. Duncan."

Mr. Duncan sighed. *"Look, the good people of this city know better. We are taking care of the PDGC's financial requirements so they can keep the people of this city safe, and that isn't a conflict of interest."*

"Sounds like quite a challenge."

"Hal Burton has a vision, and we aim to see it through."

"Thank you for your time, Mr. Duncan. Back to you, Robert."

"When we come back," Robert said, as the network theme chimed again, *"we'll be discussing how the latest water shortages are affecting meat prices. Don't go away."*

Ally turned the radio off. She looked down at Piggy, now licking her lips and washing her face. A moment later, she strutted over and sat in front of her bed - a yoga mat and some old blankets - and stared into Ally's soul.

"What?" she asked. "I told you. We'll be out of here soon. You and me will find a nice little house somewhere. One with a little backyard for you to play in. Doesn't that sound good?"

The cat strutted over to the blanket and settled down to purr. Ally looked at her. She smiled, giving her one last pat, scratching behind her ears and getting lost in her soft fur and tabby stripes, then left her container.

CHAPTER 7

Ally was told she'd be serving her community service at a troubled youth facility run by a man named Maury, a former mixed martial arts legend turned philanthropist. They'd explained that the program was designed for people like her—troubled, but redeemable. She didn't know why, but being told she was redeemable always pissed her off. Maybe it was the reminder that she was broken, or that her woes were easily fixed. Still, it wasn't the worst probation deal. She could've been sentenced to urban cleanup or some other dead-end gruntwork. Instead, maybe she'd be able to train while working off her time.

As she neared the dojo, she spotted a man in a suit standing on the curb smoking a cigarette. He was tall and lean, his face was weathered and unshaven, and the scowl on his face seemed to radiate disapproval. The cops said someone would meet her at 7:30 am sharp to make an introduction. This must be him.

As she approached, he made a show of glancing at his watch. "You're late." He blew out a plume of smoke and flicked the butt of his cigarette to the curb.

Ally slowed to a stop. "Had to feed the cat." *Not a complete lie,* she thought. But there was no way she could tell him the truth, that the container park was miles away, much further than her foster family's house where she hadn't even lived in over a year.

The man raised an eyebrow, unconvinced, but didn't seem to care enough to press the issue. "My name's Mr. Hanlon. Not Ray, not sir… Mr. Hanlon. I'm your probation officer. From now on, you report to me." He handed her a business card with an office phone number. For the next several minutes, he explained when she needed to check in, what she could and couldn't do, where she could and couldn't go, and what would happen if she broke the rules. She kept reminding herself it was only for another six months. "Come on. Maury's waiting for you inside." He stepped past her, continuing to mutter over his shoulder. "You're lucky, you know. A lot of people would give their right arm to be in the same room as him."

Ally tried not to roll her eyes. She'd heard this speech before. Everyone had made that clear. How *lucky* she was. She didn't feel lucky.

Mr. Hanlon led her to the front entrance, his steps rushed and thoughtless. He didn't slow down or wait for her. He just marched on, leaving Ally to gaze at the way the large stone blocks gave the place a fortress-like appearance, with two arched doorways like some sort of ancient temple. Above the door, a sign read, "PHOENIX DOJO: From the Ashes," with a flaming phoenix logo in one corner. It was a little on the nose for her taste, but the message was clear—this place was for people to make a change, to be reborn.

Mr. Hanlon pushed open the heavy door, and Ally followed. The familiar sounds greeted her like a warm embrace—fists pummeling punching bags, instructors barking out commands, the rhythmic tapping of feet on the linoleum floor, and the whir of jump ropes slicing through the air. It was all like music to Ally's ears. These kinds of places were always her safe place.

Inside, Mr. Hanlon turned to her, his expression becoming cold. He leaned in and whispered, "Don't embarrass me." It wasn't a threat, but it felt close enough. He gestured toward the office at the back of the dojo.

There, a man stood in the doorway. Tall, dark and handsome. He had the gait of a fighter, one that swelled with power and confidence, a presence that commanded attention without needing to raise his voice. His sharp eyes quickly regarded her before a smile broke across his face.

"You must be Ally. Glad you made it." His voice was warm. He said it like she'd come willingly, like she'd been invited. Like she was his guest. He turned to Ray. "Thank you, Mr. Hanlon. I'll take it from here."

"Whatever you say, Mr. Barão." He bowed his head a little too enthusiastically, like hero worship, then gave Ally a final look that said: toe the line. He left without another word.

Maury turned to Ally. "Let's get a few things clear right from the start," he said, his tone calm but firm. "Whatever brought you here—that's done. It doesn't matter now. The only thing that matters… is *today*, and what you choose to do with it." He gestured around them with his head, luring her eyes to follow. "This place is about change, but that change starts with you."

Ally nodded. It was strange, but something about his words gave her comfort, like they were *her* words. And there was something about the way he said it. She could tell he meant what he said.

"We'll talk more later," Maury said, his expression softening. He gestured toward a row of lockers. "Why don't you wait over there. I'll have Curtis show you around and help you get settled in."

She followed his gaze and sat down on a bench, letting her thoughts wander. She didn't know how long she'd been sitting there before she heard someone clear their throat.

"Hey, uh… do ya mind?"

Ally glanced up. A girl was pointing behind her and she realized she'd sat in front of her locker. "Oh… sorry." She scooted aside, far too quickly than she'd meant to, and tried to play it cool.

The girl regarded her as she opened the locker. "You new here? I haven't seen you before."

Ally forced a polite smile. "Yeah, first day."

The girl nodded thoughtfully. "I'm Lana." She held out her hand.

"Ally," Ally said, shaking it.

"May I?"

"Sure."

Lana sat down beside her and took a slurp from a bottle she'd taken from the locker.

"Hey ladies…" a boy purred, wheeling over from the back. He flashed Ally a cheesy grin. "Sup, new kid?"

"Curtis…" Lana chided.

"What? I'm just being friendly," he snapped.

Lana made a face and leaned back, eyeing him suspiciously.

"I'm Curtis. You must be Ally? Come on, I'll give you the virtual tour. Welcome to the Phoenix Dojo." He pointed to a corner of the gym. "You see her? The pretty girl with those two guys? That's Samantha. Don't be making any moves on her, trust me; I've tried. That guy next to her? That's her boyfriend, Tyler. He's alright, I guess. Typical jock. Not much going on upstairs, but he looks pretty with his chiseled features and big shoulders. Probably why Samantha likes him. Anyway, that's Anthony next to him. Not a bad bunch, if you're looking to make friends," he said.

Grunting turned her head. "Ah," Curtis said, pointing toward the center ring, "That's Terrence. He's a dick. I'd steer clear of hat wiener. The kid's not playing with a full deck, if you know what I mean."

Ally regarded Terrence, studying his form as he aggressively kicked and punched his sparring partner with an untamed vigor. He was ruthless. Every punch and kick surged with power.

"And the guy who's training him, that's my uncle, Maury. You'll have a proper sit down with him later."

Ally watched Maury call out commands, which Terrence seemed to willingly ignore. He was good, but as with so many fighters, she could tell his ego got in the way. Fights were not won with power; they were won with skill, endurance and footwork. None of which Terrence had. He was all power. Fighters like Terrence tried to damage their opponent with each strike, thinking that power would break them. But if the opponent was smart, they would wait for the opportune moment and strike when they tired or when their balance was overplayed.

"The boy Terence is smacking around is Henry Lesser. My Uncle Maury lets him come for free. He helps out with various duties and spars twice a week. I know what you're thinkin'… he's small and Terrence is big… well, Maury thought this would toughen him up. Henry's father is an abusive alcoholic."

"Curtis!" Lana barked.

"What? She'd find out anyway," he snapped. "We figure if he learns to defend himself in the ring, maybe it will help him protect himself from his shit father."

Ally watched Terrence land a powerful hit on Henry, who fell into a heap on the floor and doubled over from the pain.

"Get up!" Terrence screamed. "Get UP!" He turned to Maury, who had popped into the ring and rushed to Henry's side. "Come on! Man, this is bullshit! Where do you find these little bitches?" he screamed.

"That's enough, Mr. Fisher," Maury snapped. "There is no profanity in my dojo."

"My bad, coach," Terrence called, smirking like a hyena to his buddies.

Maury leaned down. "Can you hear me Henry?"

Curtis shook his head. "Like I said, I'd steer clear of that weiner."

As Lana stood and stepped away, Curtis leaned in and whispered, "So what do you think of Lana?" Before she could answer, he motored on, "Lana's a *beast*! Check her out!"

Ally glanced over and her eyes went wide. Lana was doing a set of one-armed push-ups.

Curtis leaned in to whisper, "Her ex hit her after a party about a year ago… nearly broke her nose. After that, she started coming to the dojo every day." He laughed. "The next time he hit her, she sent him to the hospital where he had to drink out of a straw for a month. Dick got what he deserved, if you ask me.

"Over there," Curtis pointed. That's Luke Howard. His parents are drug addicts. And there? That's Kenny Pinkerton, but everybody calls him Sloth."

Ally watched a chubby redheaded kid refill his water bottle.

"His parents were taken away by the State when he was just five. Since then, he's been bouncing around from foster family to foster family. Sad, really. He—" Curtis took a breath as Maury walked Henry to the back office for an ice pack. A mischievous smile curled on his lips. "Look... you're good, right? I'll be back, okay? There's something I gotta do." He shot off toward the ring.

Dr. Wheeler told her that Maury's dojo was a safe-haven for many at-risk children. Ally knew the statistics. As is common with rougher areas of big cities, so many kids are groomed by gangs or shady organizations and robbed of having any chance of a normal life. This dojo seemed to be full of these kids, according to Curtis. She began to feel respect for what Maury was doing.

"So, that was Curtis..." Lana said, making her way back over. "He's kind of a cocky little shit, but he's alright. Some might say, an *acquired* taste."

Ally smiled.

"Yo, Big Mike! When you gonna fix the crapper?" Terrence yelled, his mouth curling into a snarl before slapping hands with a few of his buddies.

A big man continued dragging a mop around the floor. He seemed immune to the taunts.

"That's Big Mike, the dojo's full-time custodian. He's sort of like a friendly mascot. Everybody likes him... everybody except Terrence," Lana added.

"Yo, Big MI—ike..." Terrence jeered, his tone rising and falling. "Hurry up... Ben's gotta take a dump!"

"I do. It's true," Ben laughed, grabbing his belly.

Lana scowled. "One day, someone's gonna teach that boy some manners, and it'll be glorious."

Big Mike leaned his mop against the wall and made his way into the boys's toilets.

"What's his problem, anyway?" Ally growled.

"ID.10.T?" Lana offered.

Ally cocked her head.

"It spells idiot," she clarified. "My Tia says all kinds of weird things."

Ally smirked and turned her attention to Henry, now recuperating in the office with an ice pack on his chest. Maury was talking with him and giving him a pat on the shoulder.

Laughter drew her attention back to the center ring. Some kids were watching Terrence get strapped into some kind of weird training suit. He had attachments on his body and arms like he was receiving a sci-fi transfusion of chemicals. On his head, was a strange helmet. If she had to guess, it was a virtual reality helmet like the ones used for game consoles, only it sort of resembled Luke Skywalker's blast shield helmet from Star Wars.

Terrence began swinging his fists at an invisible opponent, dodging left and right. Then he suddenly wailed, behaving as though he'd just been prodded. He frustratingly shook himself, smacked his gloves together and soldiered on. Another wail, making him flailing wildly around.

Ally spied Curtis perched nearby, giggling beside the ring with a few spectators. His eyes were glued to a screen and he was clicking away on a console controller. From where she sat, it looked like he was playing some kind of boxing game. She figured every time Curtis landed a punch, an electric current passed through the attachments connected to Terrence and gave him a jolt.

The incessant whinging was creating quite the scene. A crowd of children now stood idle, gawking and pointing. Even Lana had taken a break from pull-ups to watch the show.

"What's he doing that for?" Ally asked.

Lana shrugged dismissively. "No one wants to fight Terrence."

"Why not? There are better fighters than him."

Lana looked at her like the answer should be obvious. "You're cute," she said, winking at her coyly.

"AHH! Goddamn it!" Terrence screamed. Ally watched him rip the helmet off and throw it against the ground as hard as he could. It sparked and a little puff of smoke puttered out of the wiring.

"What the hell, Terrence!?" Curtis cried.

"That thing was FUBAR! I can't learn to fight from that piece of shit! I need a human being with human reflexes."

"Oi! Language, Mr. Fisher!" Mauricio called out from across the gym.

"You've broken it," Curtis whined.

"It was a piece of shit anyway," he spat, smirking his hyena-like face. "Now, who wants to get up here and fight a real man?"

No one moved, they all glanced around hoping someone would step up so they could pretend they just missed their chance.

"Derek?" Derek grimaced and started rubbing his shoulder. "What about you, Mazzotta? I'd love to go a few rounds with you," he said, licking his lips.

"I don't do men," she quipped.

"Shit. That's a crying shame." He smirked toward his buddies.

Ally caught sight of Curtis sadly cradling the broken helmet in his arms. She watched him look over the device before sadly tossing the whole kit into the trash. He parked his wheelchair against the wall and didn't move.

Ally jumped as her pocket started to vibrate. She reached in, retrieved her phone, and looked at the screen. Her mouth fell open.

Lana must have noticed. "Girl, you okay?"

"It's—" she almost let slip that it was the police. That Lieutenant Michaels was calling. But she caught herself. Nobody here knew about her past. About the murders. Anyone who has ever attended high school knows what children can be like. On the outside, everyone appears to be cool and collected, like they have it all figured out; hard as diamonds. But on the inside, they're just as scared and insecure as everybody else. The last thing she wanted was to become a target. Or worse, receive judgment, pity or to be treated differently. "I gotta take this," she muttered. "Check you later." She hopped off the bench.

"See ya."

Ally headed for the locker room, staring at the screen. Her pulse was racing. Her palms felt clammy. A year ago, Michaels had told her to stop coming in to see him every week, that he'd call her if there was ever any developments in the case. Ally ignored him. But a year passed and still, there was nothing. Now, she saw his office number dancing on the screen. The air felt heavy in her chest. She swallowed dryly, and went to press accept but her shaking fingers hesitated over the button. Then the call ended. The room suddenly felt colder. Ally gripped her phone tightly, throwing down her fists and pacing back and forth. She'd missed it! She couldn't bring herself to answer, and now she'd missed it! *Ugh*!

The phone vibrated again, a pulse this time… a voice message!

Ally stopped and brought the screen back to her face. Dancing on the screen were the words: ***You have 1 new voicemail***. She sat down on the bench feeling like she'd had too much caffeine. Her heart fluttered and she felt sick to her stomach. She took a deep breath and forced herself to press 'Call.'

"You have one new voice message. To listen to your message, press 1… to—"

Ally pressed 1.

"New message from… 'Lieutenant Michaels,'" his dry voice barked, *"Good morning, Ally; it's Michaels."* There was a pause. *"Listen,"* he sighed deeply, *"there isn't an easy way to say this, but I promised to update you on any changes in your family's case. I want you to know I did everything I could, but as there have been no further developments or leads, the department cannot justify allocating active resources to it. The case will remain open, but it will be moved to inactive status until new evidence or leads emerge. I understand this is hard to hear. If you need support or have*

questions, please—" Ally's arm went limp and she dropped the phone.

For a moment, she was numb. She just sat there, dazed, Lieutenant Michaels's words hanging in the air like a cruel echo. Then she smacked an open locker, slamming it hard enough to practically break the hinges. It felt good, the rage. She slammed another, this time screaming, louder and louder until the sterile walls of the locker room burned. It wasn't just a scream; it was a guttural burst of anguish, an eight year release of frustration, pain, and horror.

Tears began to pour down her face. She was bawling, but the rage wouldn't let her stop. She drove her fists into a nearby locker. The dent was far from satisfying. She drove three more hard punches and felt the wire enclosure buckle. Her knuckles split and she could feel the hot blood boil from them like lava.

She launched backwards, tripping over a bench, and crashed to the ground with a thud. Cursing under her breath, she lashed out, kicking the bench and sending it skidding into the lockers. She leapt to her feet and screamed, saliva sputtering from the corners of her mouth. She jerked her head, ready to tear anything in front of her apart, but a face froze her.

Emma? She shook her head; she was losing it. *Your sister's dead!* the angry voice inside her scolded. *It's just your stupid reflection!*

Ally cast her face away in shame, unable to bring herself to stare into the set of disappointed eyes in the mirror.

Now it was Claire's words that echoed through her head: *"I'm glad your mother is dead, because she'd be ashamed to see what you've become."*

Shame enveloped her. But she was still so angry. *Fuck you, Claire!* she screamed in her head, the sound leaving her throat as an untethered roar.

She reached down, picked up the bench with difficulty and heaved it at her reflection like a battering ram, trying to kill it. The glass shattered. Bits of broken shards pinged to the tile floor like her trust in the broken system, fragments of a life forever altered by an unfair twist of fate.

"Ally…"

She spun around. Lana was approaching. Her palms were out in front of her like she was coaxing a wild animal.

"Get away from me!" Ally screamed.

Lana flinched, but didn't recoil. Behind her, Ally could see a girl with blond hair and wide brown eyes glowing in the fluorescent light.

"Ally, whatever this is, I'm here for you. Samantha too."

The blond girl nodded quickly.

"Get out!" Ally screamed.

Lana tilted her head, her eyebrows slightly raised in a gesture of empathy. Tears were filling at the base of her eyelids. "Come here," she continued to walk forward, her arms out.

Ally squeezed her eyes shut, forcing the tears down her face. She shook her head. "Please, just go," her voice begged, softer now, her throat still taut with tears.

Despite her protests, Lana moved with deliberate calm. Slowly and gently, she wrapped her arms around Ally's trembling form and Ally felt the rage leave her. She crumpled in Lana's arms and together, they slipped to the floor, knees to the tiles, and Lana held her while she sobbed.

"Ally," Lana murmured, "let it out. We're here for you."

She felt another hand rest on her shoulder. Must be Samantha's.

Commotion at the doorway brought Ally back. Children, wide-eyed and curious, cautiously stepped inside. Their whispers hushed as they surveyed the destruction. Ally recognized the shock and bewilderment on their faces. Of judgment and disgust.

"Way ta go, She-Hulk," Terrence barked, rousing giggles from the massing crowd.

"Shut up, Terrence," Curtis shot back.

"Oooooh, I think Hot Wheels is *crushing*." Again more giggling. "See? This is what happens when you let *murderers* in."

This time, the crowd of children didn't giggle. The room fell into a silent hush. Everyone seemed to be holding their breath, their eyes fixed on her.

She quickly looked around. Judgment. Pity. Their expressions burned her like acid. Until now, she'd thought her past was her own, a secret. But seeing her secret etched into various faces, she knew. Somehow, it had gotten out.

Slowly, she stood up and wiped the tears from her eyes with the back of her hand. "What did you say?"

"You heard me."

Ally lurched forward, but felt a gentle tug on her arm. "Don't," Lana whispered. "He ain't worth it."

Ally hesitated, reading Lana's worried face, but turned back to Terrence. "You can throw a punch. Henry can attest to that," she said, "But what would happen if you were in a *real* fight, I wonder… probably blame everything on your trainer, right?"

"You got a big mouth; how about I shut it for you." Behind him, two of his buddies stepped forward, sidling up on either side of him. Terrance regarded them, cocking his head and smirking that it was three against one.

"All right. This has gone far enough," Lana said, stepping between them. "Whatever this is, both of you, let it go."

Ally ignored her. "A minute ago, you were bitching about wanting a *real* fight. Well, here it is," she said, leering around Lana's shoulder with both her arms wide. "If you're *man enough* to accept the challenge."

Lana leaned in and whispered. "Ally, you've made your point. But Terrence is Maury's best fighter."

"Don't worry, I'll go easy on him," she answered.

Lana blinked.

She looked Lana in the eye. "I'll be fine," she said without emotion. "Trust me."

Lana tilted her head and raised an eyebrow. She was intrigued.

"*Go easy on me?* Girl, you're funny!" Terrence chuckled, again getting recognition and attention from his friends.

Ally unzipped her hoodie, tossed it aside, and stepped past Lana.

Terrence's angry glare softened like he was sucking on a lemon. "Damn, girl. *You fine!*" he said, seeing her physique for the first time. "Who knew you've been hiding this bumpty lady figure under them digs, eh?"

Some spectators giggled.

Terrence smiled. He started air-punching and waved her forward. "Come on, Murder-Girl," he said, grinning. "Let's see what you got."

Ally snarled and lunged forward, shoving Terrence hard in the chest. He flew backwards and slammed into the lockers behind him. From the surprise on his face, he hadn't expected the shove to be so powerful.

"Come on, Terrence!" a boy in the crowd yelled.

Terrence shook it off, grinned, and charged forward, coming at Ally with everything he had. With blinding speed, she turned her body and delivered a hard blow with her knee straight into the side of Terrence's jaw like a move from Tony Jaa, knocking him onto his back. The locker room fell completely silent. Ally watched Terrence blink in surprise before his eyes rolled back in his head and passed out.

For a moment, no one spoke.

"That was easy?" Lana finally asked, raising her eyebrows and looking at her like she'd just belched the alphabet.

Ally didn't have time to answer. A booming voice shook the locker room. "What is going on in here!?" Maury's eyes surveyed the wreckage, connecting the dots between the broken mirror and the children encircling them. His eyes locked onto Ally and Terrence, who was now stirring on the floor. "Everybody out! Now!"

Everyone scurried away like rodents.

"You two, get him up!"

Terrence's two shadows quickly reached down and pulled him to his feet. Terrence jerked free of their grasp and groggily steadied himself as they dashed away, leaving him with Ally and Maury.

Maury whirled, his eyes fuelled with intensity. He stared at each of them long and hard. "Anyone want to explain to me why my locker room is in pieces? Why my children are circling up for an unsanctioned fight!? You know the rules here and you will abide by them!"

Ally glanced around and hung her head. She wasn't the type to vandalize someone's property. At least, not usually. That wasn't her style. She couldn't explain it. The rage had just boiled over her and took over.

"Well?"

"Ask Murder-Girl," Terrence muttered, rubbing his neck.

"One more remark like that Mr. Fisher and I'll throw you out of here for good! I don't care *who* your uncle is! Am I clear?"

Terrence shot him an angry glare, but quickly dropped it.

"Am… I… clear?"

"Yes," he muttered.

"I'm sorry?"

"Yes, sir."

"That's better. Manners cost nothing, Mr. Fisher. Respect is earned in this life. It is not given." He turned to look at Ally. "Well? Anything to say?"

Ally looked at the floor. The sting of her actions began to chafe.

"Good day, Mr. Fisher."

Terrence got up and hurried out the door. When he'd gone, Ally spoke. "I'm sorry. I'll clean it up. I'll pay you back for the damages."

Maury crossed his arms. "Ally, your probation officer is just itching for a reason to send you to lockup. Why throw away your one chance on a boy like Terrence?"

"I didn't do it because of him. I couldn't care less about that animal."

"So what was it about then?"

Again, Ally looked at the floor.

"Ally?"

She didn't respond.

"Then I'm afraid I have no choice but to speak to Mr. Hanlon." He turned to leave.

"Wait!" Ally cried, letting the tears pour down her face. "Don't! Please!"

"Then give me a reason."

She sank down onto the bench. "They shelved my family's case," she whimpered.

CHAPTER 8

As soon as Ally stepped out of the locker room, she felt it. The weight of several pairs of eyes pretending not to watch her, the sound of hushed whispers and awkward shuffles. A quick glance around confirmed it. This is exactly what she'd been afraid of. Why she hadn't told anyone about her past. Her eyes narrowed and she swallowed hard. With a clench of her jaw, she adjusted the bag on her shoulder and marched out to the street.

"Hey! Wait up," came Curtis's voice. She heard him throttle up his electric wheelchair until he caught up the distance and was rolling beside her. "Hey, you okay?"

"I'm fine."

"No, I mean, did my uncle tear you a new one? Are you persona non grata?"

"Huh?"

"It means not welcome back."

"I know what it means." She dodged a man unwilling to yield any space on the sidewalk, narrowly missing his shoulder. "He said he'll think of a way for me to make it up to him."

"Ooh, that's not good." He laughed. "Hey, so back there… with Terrence—"

"Look, I really don't want to talk about it."

"No, I mean, it was amazing! Knocking him on his ass. Where did you learn to do that?"

Ally side-eyed him. "Here and there."

"Here and there," he scoffed. "Cryptic. So, where we goin'?"

Ally sighed heavily. "*I'm* going to Echo Park."

"Gross. What's in Echo Park?" he asked, continuing alongside her.

Ally stopped and met his gaze. "Look, I don't mean to be rude, but—"

"You're about to be?" he interjected, smiling with raised eyebrows. "Whenever someone says, *I don't mean to be rude*, they always say something rude."

Ally frowned. "Curtis, I've got somewhere I need to be. I don't have time for a chat," she looked at her watch, "I'm already late."

A few blocks later, Curtis was still rolling alongside her. She flashed him an annoyed glance, but he only smiled back at her. She ignored him, assuming he'd get bored, but soon the graffiti-covered bricks and litter-strewn sidewalks meant they'd arrived.

As they neared the entrance, it occurred to her now just how squalid the place looked from the outside. Old bricks, graffiti messages spreading over a dented metal door and cracked window grille saying God-knows-what. No one can ever read graffiti. The sound of distant sirens echoed nearby as they passed under the cliché flickering fluorescent light above the doorway.

As they ascended the ramp together, Curtis frowned at the building's sign, missing several letters and barely hanging on by a single bolt. The Grace City Wellness Institute was a socially funded program and probably got tired of the upkeep with so many delinquents running about.

Inside the lobby, a handful of people occupied the rigid chairs lining the perimeter. The receptionist smiled and nodded as Ally took a seat.

"Don't you need to check in or something?"

"Don't you have somewhere else to be?" she snapped?

He held his hands up and made a face, then began glancing around the room. "You know, it's pretty nice inside. I mean, compared to the outside. Why did you bring me here, anyway?"

"I didn't *bring* you here. You followed me."

"Wellness institute…" he muttered, "isn't that like, code for crazy people?"

A few patrons turned their heads and Ally shifted uncomfortably. "Curtis? Are you gonna like," she paused, her thumb and four fingers moving up and down like a puppet, "the whole time? I need to think."

He nodded. "Sure; you do you."

Ally readjusted herself, sinking deeper into the back of the chair cushion. She was about to see Dr. Wheeler. The last time was when she was arrested. Now that Ally was here, she felt the weight of guilt pressing on her mind. She didn't know what she was going to say or how she was going to say it. *Just apologize. Everything will be fine,* Ally thought, slumping deeper into the waiting room chair. Her knees bounced impatiently as she checked the clock for the third time, watching as the minutes slowly ticked away.

She traced her fingers against the edge of her jeans as the other night replayed in her head like a fractured filmstrip, the flashing lights, the stern voices, the cold metal handcuffs on her wrists. *How do you apologize for something like that?* Anyway, it likely wouldn't come to that. Discussing another notch on Ally's *destructive behavior chart* was more her style. Just another indicator leading to another assessment and another fight against trialing the pharmaceutical industry's latest psychiatric drug. Psychiatrists baffled her; they were always so quick to prescribe medication as treatment rather than deal with the systemic or mental health issues of their patients. To Ally, there was no such thing as a magic pill.

She blinked, her gaze flicking to the muted TV screen on the wall. Images of the earthquake's aftermath, mentioned on the radio this morning, continued to cycle through beside scrolling subtitles. They reminded her of old war photos.

"What kind of stone is that?" Curtis asked, breaking her thoughts. "Obsidian?"

Ally's hand instinctively went to her necklace. Her fingers rubbed against the rough black jewel fixed to its prong. Without hesitation, she found herself answering. "It was my mother's. It's all I have of her."

She scolded herself. *Stop sharing every detail of your life!*

Curtis nodded. "I lost my mom, too." Ally dropped her scowl and looked at him. "Yeah, during Project Starfall, you know, the meteor shower eight years ago? We were in the museum when it collapsed on us. She pushed me out of the way. Well… mostly." He smiled as he gestured to his chair.

Ally grimaced. "I'm sorry."

"It's okay," he said, waving his hand dismissively. "Well, actually, it's not. Why do people always say that?"

Ally didn't know what to say. She dipped her eyes and stared absentmindedly at the table of magazines until a loud bang shattered the clinical calm of the room. A teenager jettisoned herself through Dr. Wheeler's door and headed for the exit.

"Yo, check out Wednesday Adams," Curtis whispered. A girl dressed in black with white makeup, dark eyeshadow, and black pigtails stormed out of Dr. Wheeler's office.

Ally frowned, not able to take her eyes away from the woman who followed. She watched her stride to the reception desk and retrieve a clipboard. A sickening feeling bubbled in her stomach. *Not again.*

"Allyson Reid?" the woman called.

Ally crinkled her nose, groaned, and reluctantly stood, then trudged over to the reception desk.

The woman smiled. "Good afternoon, Allyson. I'm Dr. Hansen. It's nice to meet you."

Ally eyeballed the woman's outstretched hand. "It's *Ally*... I'm sorry; *who* are you?"

The polite sparkle in the woman's eyes dipped slightly. "Did they not tell you?" she asked. "Someone was supposed to… well, I do apologize; I've been assigned to your case."

"Where's Dr. Wheeler?"

Dr. Hanson smiled like the answer should be obvious. "She's on maternity leave. She's having a baby."

"Is that what *maternity leave* means?" Ally asked sarcastically.

Dr. Hansen's eyebrows twitched. The corner of her mouth pursed like she was chewing on her tongue. "You wanna follow me?"

As she followed Dr. Hanson to the office door, Ally wondered how she hadn't known Dr. Wheeler was pregnant. She'd always just assumed the baggy, loose-fitting or layered clothing was a misguided fashion choice. Thinking about it now, the frequent cancellations and mysterious illnesses now made more sense.

Ally plopped down on the sofa and drummed her fingers lightly on the armrest as she quickly surveyed the room. It was so much different than the last time she'd been here: the warmer color palette, the conference-style furniture, the decorative fluffy rug. Diplomas and personal effects were still in boxes. The wastebasket was full of takeout containers and Ally could still detect a faint hint of paint lingering in the air.

Dr. Hansen retrieved a file folder from the top shelf and seated herself in the chair opposite. She crossed her legs and flashed a smile before thumbing through the pages of the dossier. Finally, she let the paper fall back into position in her notebook.

"So, ready to get started?"

Ally opened her mouth, but a tinkling bell stopped her. A cat was lying in a little cat bed under the radiator. It stood up, yawned like a weasel, and stretched its body, jutting out its front paws onto the floor.

She reached her hand down and twiddled her fingers, making kissy sounds. To her surprise, the cat jingled its way over and brushed its head against her knuckles before leaping into her lap. Ally smiled as the cat began to knead with its paws, her rough edges melting away as she stroked the cat's head.

"His name's Jimmy. He seems to like you." Dr. Hansen said. "Do you like cats?"

"Anyone who doesn't like cats can't be trusted," Ally joked as she scratched under the cat's chin.

"Does this mean you trust me?"

Ally gave her a look. "Is this some kind of pathetic attempt to disarm aggressive patients?"

"Is it working?"

Ally gave her another look. *So she has a sense of humor. Wonderful.*

"I'm kidding. He's diabetic. He needs a shot twice a day, and I can't do that when I'm at the office. So I take him with me."

Ally looked down and cupped the cat's head in her hands, making more kissy sounds. Then the cat did what all cats do, got fed up and fucked off. She watched him hop to the window sill and gaze out into the street. She envied the cat a little. Not a care in the world.

"So, ready to get started?" Dr. Hansen repeated.

Ally's heart fluttered and she felt a pre-sweat form on her skin. It was ironic. As much as she hated Dr. Wheeler, she found herself sitting here wishing for her return. Hell, she'd even take Dr. Miller. But the last thing she was going to do was open up to another stranger for the umpteenth time. She felt the all-too-familiar defiance creep up inside of her. She narrowed her eyes and crossed her arms.

"Is there a problem?" Dr. Hansen asked.

"What… I suppose you want me to whine? Do ya want me to tear up? Ask you for a tissue? Tell you a sob story?"

"Do you *want* to tell me a sob story?"

Ally rubbed her forehead. "Ugh, I can't do this again."

"Do what?"

"Relive everything and have my head examined by another *penny*."

Dr. Hansen blinked. "Penny?"

"Two-faced and not worth much," Ally said dryly.

Dr. Hansen's eyebrows went up. "I see. Well, I'm not Dr. Wheeler."

Ally rolled her eyes and shook her head.

"Okay. Look, I can appreciate how you must be feeling. I am technically a stranger, and you don't know me. But believe it or not, I'm here to help you. And the fact is, Dr. Wheeler has passed your case along to me, so what do you say we get to know each other a little better?"

Ally nodded. "What's your first name?" she asked innocently.

"My first name is Abigail."

"I bet your friends call you Abby."

"I guess they do," she replied.

"But you just said your name was Abigail," Ally said, feigning shock. "Abigail is so *formal*. Does this mean we *aren't friends*?" she mouthed bitterly.

Dr. Hansen's face hardened. "You're right," she said after a pause. "I'm not your friend Ally. I'm not your lover, your babysitter, or someone who's going to fill some void in your life. I'm here for the same reason you are."

"You have a delusional disorder, too?" Ally asked, wide-eyed and over dramatically.

"To get better," she said, ignoring the quip.

"You're here to get better? So I'm like, practice?"

"For *you* to get better. Is this all a joke to you?" she asked, changing her tone from caring to authoritative.

Here it comes, Ally thought. She wondered what her file said about her. What Dr. Wheeler had told her. *This girl has had a traumatic past,* she thought, imitating Dr. Wheeler's voice in her head. *You're not going to have an easy time getting through to her. She is stubborn, highly intelligent, and has trust issues. You are not going to get through to her by being friendly. She needs to know that she can't manipulate you.*

"Here's the situation you're in, Ally. You don't have to like me. But if you're as smart as everyone tells me you are, then you know that I'm the only one standing between you and a prison cell."

Ally scoffed, but managed to see Dr. Hansen's head cock to the side. "Do you have any idea how many strings Lieutenant Michaels must have pulled to keep you out of jail?"

Ally shrugged.

"Let's just say, you owe that man a thank you."

"That still doesn't explain you," Ally snapped nastily.

"Okay, let's put our cards on the table, shall we?" Dr. Hansen set her pen down and interlaced her fingers. "The powers that be thought it best I sugarcoat this on account of your *temperament*."

Ouch.

"But I'm gonna level with you." She leaned forward. "Dr. Wheeler is *not* on maternity leave. Well, not yet. And I did not *inherit* your case by chance. I specialize in patients with delusional behavior. After your recent incident with the police, I was sent here to determine whether or not you should be committed to a psychiatric institute."

Ally's face fell. Her blood went cold. All the animosity she had instantly dropped through the trap door in the pit of her stomach. She'd foolishly thought everything was behind her.

"Now… as you are no doubt aware, therapy doesn't work if the patient is unwilling to cooperate. So if I were you, I'd cut the shit, and start taking your situation seriously. Am I making myself clear?"

Ally squeezed her fingers into fists, glaring at the stupid fluffy rug. "Yes…" she muttered.

Bitch.

"Good." Dr. Hansen leaned back in her chair and brushed a strand of hair behind her ear. "Now, let's address the elephant in the room. What happened the other night? Why were you in some abandoned theater in the middle of the Scrubs with armed criminals?"

Ally shrugged. "Wrong place, wrong time."

"Nice try, but I'm going to need a real answer."

"Have you read my files?"

"I have."

"Then you know what I was doing there."

"Uh huh, hunting *Mr. Smith*, I gather. Just your average night out."

Ally didn't say anything; she didn't like her tone. A dull buzzing washed over her, drowning out the sound of Dr. Hansen's voice. There was a foggy echo in her mind, rattling around like a hangover. Like she was underwater, or coming to after a knockout.

"Ally!"

Ally blinked and turned her head. "What?" she asked dully, trying not to let Dr. Hansen know she'd dozed off.

"Are you listening to me?"

She exhaled heavily and slumped in her chair. "Yes."

"So let me get this straight… you somehow managed to track down a man - who you thought was a heavily-trained deadly assassin - to the abandoned theater in the Scrubs, *alone*, and just thought you'd, what? Mosey on up to him?"

Hearing it said like that did make it sound ridiculous.

"Were you going to kill him?"

Ally turned her head, not wanting Dr. Hansen to see the tears forming at the base of her eyelids. "Honestly, I don't know."

Ally heard Dr. Hansen scribble something on her notepad. "The police say you took out five of his armed henchmen - all of which are hardened criminals with rap sheets by the way - and might I add: two were severely injured; one may never walk again. Most were covered in bruises and gun powder residue, yet you don't have a scratch on you. Care to explain that one?"

"Ask them."

"Oh, the police did…. but they aren't talking. Except to say they didn't know who the hell you were. I imagine your fancy lawyer used that one to save you from serious criminal charges. Another person you owe your freedom to. Still nothing to say?"

Ally didn't reply. This woman had the power to commit her. If she said nothing, or lied, somehow she felt Dr. Hansen would know. She was at her mercy, backed into a corner.

"All right, let's start with something easier. What was that device you used… how does it work?

Ally gave her a look. "Well, I would explain it to you, doc, but I'm fresh out of crayons."

Dr. Hansen looked taken aback.

Ally winced. "Sorry, I just meant—"

"I know what you meant; it's *complicated*," Dr. Hansen paused, then checked her watch. "Alright Ally, tell me about Mr. Smith. According to the police report, you believe he no longer exists."

Ally gripped her knees to keep her hands from shaking and took a deep breath, the words escaping her throat like thorns. "He doesn't exist," she affirmed.

Dr. Hansen picked up the dossier and lightly smacked it onto the table, making Ally jump. "Allyson Reid. You never knew your father. You were raised by your mother, Dr. Sara Reid, an esteemed scientist until her untimely death eight years ago on November 10th from a fire-related accident. You were an exceptionally gifted child and like your mother, demonstrated a high predisposition toward science, mathematics, and engineering.

So you have read my files.

"You excelled in school academically despite being expelled from three high schools for what they referred to as *violent, aggressive and disorderly behavior*, yet still managed to graduate a whole two years early. You were awarded a full scholarship to M.I.T., which you *turned down*."

She paused.

"All of your teachers I've spoken with tell me you're a genius. That you may even be a prodigy. I mean, your aptitude tests are off the charts. You got perfect scores on your—"

"So what?"

Dr. Hansen hesitated, her forehead creasing.

"So what? So I know how smart you are, Ally. How do I know you're not just telling me what I want to hear, like you did with Dr. Wheeler?"

"You don't," Ally muttered, stifling a yawn.

"Huh," Dr. Hansen muttered, placing the end of her pen against her lower lip. "You still having nightmares?"

Ally flinched. "No…"

"No?" she returned, lifting an eyebrow.

Ally looked away. She nodded as more silent tears rolled down her face. "Every night."

"Want to tell me about them?"

"Not really."

"Ally…"

Ally sighed. "Fine." She wiped the tears from her eyes and cheeks and swallowed hard.

For the next few minutes, Ally recounted the night Mr. Smith took everything from her, holding nothing back. Every grueling detail exposed: her mother's tortured screams, the man in a dark jacket as he struck her, the stiffening sound of the silencer, the softness of her mother's hand, coagulated blood, the sound of shattered glass and surging flames. She could feel the heat of the fire on her face, even now.

"And then I woke up in the hospital," Ally said.

Dr. Hansen wrote something on her notepad, set it down, and looked up. "Thank you for sharing that with me, Ally. I don't imagine this is easy for you."

Ally shrugged and sunk deeper into the chair. She didn't want to look up, but she felt Dr. Hansen's eyes burning into her.

"Are you ready to tell me what *really* happened that night?"

Ally felt sick. Lieutenant Michaels's voice echoed in her head. *"Death by smoke inhalation, no gunshots, no foreign bodies, no Mr. Smith."*

She wiped her eyes and sniffed. "I must have lit a candle," her voice quivered. "I don't remember doing it, but my mom… she used to always get so mad at me, ya know? But I never listened. I liked the smell. I must have fallen asleep. The next thing I knew, the house was on fire." She wiped more rogue tears from her face. "I made it. They didn't."

Dr. Hansen studied her expression for a moment, then scribbled another comment on her notepad before looking up again.

"And what about Mr. Smith?"

Ally gripped her knees again and felt her thoughts race back to the darkest part of her mind. She peeked through the crack in the cupboard door. Mr. Smith stood directly in front of her mother. She saw his face. It was angular with a square jaw, a large nose, and long, dark brown hair that was tied back into a ponytail. His arms were strong and his hands rested at his sides with an uneasy calm. He turned. Notable were his eyes.

Black as night.

Soulless.

Empty.

Ally hung her head. "There was no Mr. Smith," she said in a half-whisper. "He's just a delusion."

Dr. Hansen furrowed her brow. "Sorry, Ally. I have to ask. Why have you maintained his existence all these years?"

Ally hesitated. Tears rolled down her cheeks. She inhaled a shaky breath. "Because it was easier than admitting the truth," she choked, wiping her cheeks.

"What truth?" Dr. Hansen pressed.

Ally squeezed her eyes shut. It took every ounce of strength to force the vile words from her throat. "That I killed my family." Her face scrunched into a quiet sob.

A moment passed before Dr. Hansen spoke.

"Thank you, Ally." Dr. Hansen held up a box of tissues. "You must feel better, finally getting that off your chest after so long?"

Ally nodded, taking two. She actually *did* feel better, like a weight lifted off her shoulders. It almost felt easier to breathe.

"Are you still taking your medication?"

Ally nodded her head. "I started this weekend. It's time I accepted what really happened. I've let the past control me long enough."

Dr. Hansen picked up her pen and made a final note. Then she closed the dossier. "Okay. Time's up."

"That's it?"

"That's it," Dr. Hansen repeated. "See? That wasn't so bad."

Ally faked a smile. "So what happens now?"

"Well, my job was to assess whether or not you require *alternative* treatment. But from what I can tell, you feel remorse, you're willing to take your medication, you're trying to take responsibility for what happened, you're taking steps to heal. Therefore, in my professional opinion, and assuming you're willing to stick to therapy and medication, I see no clinical reason why we need to seek alternative solutions.

"I am going to recommend you continue bi-weekly sessions, with me or another therapist of your choosing. We can discuss the dosage of your medication depending on how you're progressing, but yeah... that's it."

Ally nodded, her eyes dipping to the floor.

"What's wrong?"

"I kind of thought since I turned 18 in a few days, and since I've accepted I'm crazy, I wouldn't need therapy anymore."

"Ally…"

"I know… you guys don't like that word."

"Can I speak candidly?"

Ally shrugged.

"While you've taken responsibility for the delusions and have accepted reality, there is still the question of the guilt and trauma associated with it. It's going to take time for you to forgive yourself and heal."

Ally looked down sadly and nodded.

"Let's just stay the course and take it one day at a time." Dr. Hansen stood up and pushed the chair back. "Shall I walk you out?"

Ally picked up her belongings and turned to leave, but stopped short. She turned back to Dr. Hansen and held out her hand. "Thank you."

"You're welcome," she said, shaking it.

Ally smiled and turned toward the door. Before she made it three steps, Dr. Hansen called out to her. "Wait, Ally?" She fumbled through the flaps of her wallet and removed a small card. Then picked up a pen from the cup on her desk, scribbled something onto the back of it, and handed it to her.

The card was elegant and sleek. A silver border lined the edges around Dr. Hansen's name and credentials. She turned it over and saw written in beautiful handwriting was a phone number. "That's my cell," she said, "If you ever need anything, feel free to shoot me a text, call or whatever. Anytime, day or night.

"Our past doesn't get to decide who we are, Ally. We are who we choose to be."

Ally didn't know what to do. She was stunned. What Dr. Hansen was doing for her just now, she was pretty sure violated some kind of doctor-patient regulations. The nervous look on her face more or less confirmed it: *I've never done this before*. All she could do was blink.

As Ally left the office, she strode past reception, but turned back when she neared the door. She raised her hand in a wave, and smiled. Then she rolled her eyes. Curtis had waited for her. He waved back and headed toward her.

CHAPTER 9

Emerging from the building, Ally quickened her steps, shooting a sideways glare at Curtis as he kept pace with her at her side. If he was aware of her annoyance, he didn't show it. Silently, she willed him to just get the hint, but if was willing to sit and wait an hour for her therapy session to finish, then he wasn't going anywhere. She was stuck with him. She sighed inwardly.

When Ally was about five blocks from the police station, raised voices thundered through the streets and as they neared, they saw a spirited crowd of protesters. Picket signs read dozens of slogans including: **'dIS**GRACE CITY,' 'END GENTRIFICATION,' and 'SAVE OUR HOMES,' among many others. A line of police in full riot gear stood shoulder to shoulder opposite the crowd.

"What's all this?" Ally asked.

"Have you been living under a *rock*?" Curtis replied. "Burton Conglomerates is buying up all the homes in the area."

Ally stiffened at the mention of BC, the company her mother worked for, and remembered the radio broadcast from this morning.

"They're here to *fix up the neighborhood* and *rebuild people's homes*," Curtis mocked.

"That doesn't sound so bad," she said. "So why is everyone so upset?"

Curtis shot her a look. "Yeah, you're probably right. I'm sure that once they manage to get rid of us *poor folk*, they'll scale-up the housing and welcome us back with open arms. Rich people, stay away!" he laughed and waved his hand dismissively. "Nah, the second they get rid of everybody, they'll fix up the homes, jack up the prices, and call in the rich people. It's gentrification and they're not even trying to hide it anymore."

As they neared the front steps, Ally eyed the rent-a-cops in riot gear. Something bothered her about their uniforms. They were slightly discolored, like knockoffs, like the ones she'd seen the night she was arrested. She wondered if BC was financing the extra help like she'd heard about on the radio.

Together, she and Curtis made their way up the ramp. Once past the rotating door, she glanced around the lobby. A few people were waiting in the chairs lining the edges of the walls, the kind that are so straight up and down you can't get comfortable. From the look of them, they'd seen their fair share of wear and tear. At the center of the room, the state and national flags cradled either side of a large reception desk as if enclosing it in patriotism. An armed guard stood nearby with his thumbs in his belt loops. His eyes followed her as she approached the desk.

"Hi, I'm here to see Lieutenant Michaels," Ally said politely.

"Ally, haven't seen you in a while," the woman said dryly and forced a smile. "I'll let you know when he's ready."

Ally sat down and watched the crowd of protestors through the window.

"So what are we doing here?" Curtis asked, pulling up beside her.

"None of your business," she snapped.

"Okay," he mouthed and glanced away.

She sighed inwardly again. "I'm here to see Lieutenant Michaels. I don't know if you know… but I was arrested on Saturday, and if it wasn't for him, I'd probably be in jail."

"Heavy," Curtis said. "What'd you do?"

She studied his expression, debating how to insult him, but in the end, thought what the hell? "I staked out and infiltrated a shady deal in the Scrubs, took out half a dozen armed criminals with my fists, stole a cop car and totaled it."

Curtis laughed, but his face dropped when Ally held her gaze. "Wait, for real?"

"Ally? Lieutenant Michaels is ready for you now," the receptionist called.

Ally hopped off the chair and headed into the back towards the cubicles and offices. As she neared Michaels's door, she stopped abruptly and bowed her head. She started taking deep, slow breaths. It hadn't occurred to her until this moment that the last eight years of her life culminated from her delusions, that accepting her role in her family's deaths meant saying goodbye to Mr. Smith and the murders, that this whole meeting was rooted in the fictional past, that she'd have to tell Michaels that he'd been right. And apologize. This conversation is gonna hurt more than the car wreck. She was about to knock when a chorus of laughter erupted.

"Why don't you just tell her you're busy?"

"Yeah, I wish. You know she's been coming here every week? Every week!" Michaels repeated. "For six years!"

"Damn," a voice said.

"I mean, take a look outside… like I don't have other responsibilities."

Curtis stopped beside her and they shared a look. His eyes were wounded.

"Every week it's the same thing. I tell her the evidence just doesn't support a murder.

'They shot her, Lieutenant!' he said in a mocking whinge.

"That's not what the coroner's report says, Ally!"

"And she goes, 'then it's wrong! I was there! I watched it happen! I saw it happen!'"

"Ugh! I'm so sick of it. The same shit for six years! And now that the case isn't being reopened, she's on her way right now to make my life a living hell for the next decade."

Laughter filled the office again. *"You know, I half-wonder if she even had a sister..."*

"That's rough, boss. Want me to shoot her?" Another chuckle.

"Right, you guys better get out of here."

"All right, catch you later, brother," an officer said. Then the door opened and two cops froze like a couple of deer in headlights.

"Uh, Lieutenant?"

The door opened wider and Michaels's face splashed with guilt. "Ally, I—"

"Don't!" She glared at him and contemptuously exhaled, jerking her body away and plowing toward the exit. When she made it to the lobby, she stood motionless, glowering at the street. She heard Curtis's electric motor roll up beside her. She braced herself for the inevitable question: *Are you okay?* But it never came. He probably knew it was always a stupid question. She wanted to say thank you, but she knew if she didn't get out of there, she'd lose it.

Pushing through the rotating door, she bounded down the front stairs, leaving Curtis to wait impatiently for the slow electric hinge to open and navigate the maze of the wheelchair ramp.

"Hey! Wait up!"

Ally was fuming. She stomped her way down the streets, nearly slamming into pedestrians in her path. She felt a high pitched ringing in her ears, like tinnitus, and a fiery hot anger bubbling up inside of her.

She dipped into a nearby alley and, all at once, felt herself unleash a primal scream. She threw her fists down and yelled again, stopping to kick a discarded cardboard box until it was in tatters.

She collapsed into a squat and felt tears rush to her eyes.

The faint whine of Curtis's electric chair got louder until he was right next to her. He didn't say anything for a moment. "I'm really sorry, Ally," he finally said. "That guy sounds like a dick."

She didn't answer. Her dead eyes just looked straight past him.

"Ally?"

She snapped out of it. "What! What do you want!?" she screamed, jumping to her feet. She glared at him and snarled. "I don't want to be friends! I don't need friends, okay? Just leave me alone."

Curtis stared back at her with a dull shock. Then he casually turned and left the alley, the whine of the electric motor waning.

Ally shut her eyes and hung her head. She didn't mean what she said, but her heart felt like it had split in two.

The faint whine of the electric chair returned and Ally opened her eyes to see Curtis pulling himself along like a mime with an imaginary rope. She scowled, ignoring him.

Soon, he was back, this time using a single mime-paddle, slowly canoeing past her. Ally felt the corner of her mouth rise into a smile, but her tears choked it short.

She was about to leave the alley when Curtis passed a third time, rolling backwards, holding onto two imaginary oars and rowing his chair past the entrance.

Ally exhaled through her nose and shook her head, then got up and followed him out. "You're a jerk," she jested, punching him playfully in the shoulder.

"I'm glad you decided to come out; I was running out of ideas."

"Thanks, Curtis."

"Race ya!" Curtis suddenly pressed the override button on his wheelchair and sped off.

"I'm not chasing you!" she called, but he didn't slow down. "Oh, hell."

She started jogging and realized that she was now running. *Jesus, his chair is fast!*

"I can do this all day," he taunted, "Or at least until the battery runs out."

It was neck and neck all the way back to the dojo. By the time they reached the building, they were both laughing.

"I guess I won," she gloated.

"Well, I *am* in a wheelchair, you dick," he said, watching her victorious expression fall. "Relax! I'm messing with you," he giggled. "You should see your face!"

"I hate you."

"Well, that's different," he said, his voice softening.

"What is?"

"Most people just push me around and talk behind my back."

Again, Ally's smile faded.

Curtis giggled again and rolled toward the building. "Oh lighten up. It's just a wheelchair joke. You comin'?"

"I think I'll take the side entrance," she said.

Curtis nodded. "Probably a good idea, I mean, considering whose nephew you knocked out.

"Huh?"

"Never mind. He'll probably be too embarrassed to say anything. You should be fine." With that, he went inside and the door closed behind him.

Ally bit her lip, wondering if he was pulling her leg again. Then she turned and entered the dojo through the side entrance.

CHAPTER 10

Ally headed back to the locker room. She saw her hoodie was hung back up on the peg. *Big Mike*, she thought. She slipped it on again, stopped at the door, and breathed in a deep breath before pushing through.

She half-expected to be rushed and bombarded with a hundred questions. She also thought Terrence might be waiting for her to get a jump on Round 2. But he was nowhere in sight. It was hard to miss the twenty pairs of eyes pretending not to watch her in between muffled whispers. Maury must have spoken to them.

Passing the back office, a man was seated inside. He had his briefcase open and laid out on the desk was a series of documents and manilla folders. She scooted closer to the open window and pretended to lean against the wall so she could listen.

The lawyer crossed his legs and gave Maury a contemptuous look. "It's a good offer Maury. More than fair."

"*Mr. Barão*," Maury corrected him. "We're not friends, Mr. Sherman."

"Apologies," the man replied, "*Mr. Barão*."

"I told you before. The place isn't for sale."

Mr. Sherman flashed him a sharp, toothy grin. "Everybody has their price. It just takes a while to find out what that is."

So that's what he wanted. Ally wrinkled her nose. It didn't make any sense. This neighborhood wasn't special. It was a slum. What did a large corporation want with a youth center? Given the commotion near the precinct, she could wager a guess. Some fat cat was trying to buy up the real estate so that this dojo could become another coffee shop or liquor store, like Mr. Despotes said.

"I guess I'll just have to come back with another offer."

"And I'll just throw it back in your face," Maury said with a hint of disgust.

Ally bent down and untied her shoe, still pretending not to eavesdrop while he escorted the lawyer out.

As they walked past, Ally glanced up and locked eyes with Mr. Sherman. He smiled and swabbed the tip of his tongue over his upper canine. It gave her the creeps. She followed him with her eyes until he passed a large poster displayed on the wall, which stole her attention. She didn't know why she never noticed it before, but she was locked in now. It was a comic book-style poster displaying a man in a fighter's uniform standing proudly. The letters at the top of the poster read: 'THE CHAMELEON.'

“Do you know why they called him The Chameleon?” came Big Mike’s voice from behind her. “It’s because when he was in the ring, he would use his opponent’s fighting style against them. Even fighting styles that Maury had never used or trained with before. He would mimic their movements like he could read their minds.

“No one had ever seen anything like it before. They called him The Chameleon because he would adapt and change his fighting style multiple times during a fight. His opponents would get so frustrated that they would make crucial errors and that’s when Maury would take control of the fight. You should’ve seen him in his prime. It was really something.”

“So why’d he stop?”

Big Mike shrugged. “After his wife died, he just wasn’t the same. He took all the money he earned throughout his career and invested it into this place.”

Ally glanced at Maury. He looked in their direction as he spoke to some new members.

“Is he mad at me?”

“Mmm hmm,” he affirmed.

“How mad?”

“Do you know who you knocked out?”

“Terrence Fisher... local D-Bag and poster child for abortion?”

“Yeah, that... and *Andrew Fisher’s* nephew,” he said, looking at her coyly and studying her reaction.

“Wait, what?” Ally asked, but the front door burst open. A stocky man in a suit paraded in followed by two bodyguards. Terrence was between them, grimacing and holding an ice pack to the side of his head. Ally recognized the man… Andrew Fisher. And he brought hired muscle with him. They looked like mercenaries with their tailored suits and prison tattoos.

Maury looked up, gave the new recruits a fist bump, and made his way over to the two men. They began talking, but she could tell that this wasn’t a pleasant conversation. Maury seemed unnerved. She watched him try to invite the man into his office, but the booming voice of Fisher shook the room. “Does someone want to explain to me why my nephew was sucker punched and knocked unconscious?” he barked, silencing the room.

“It was just a misunderstanding, Mr. Fisher,” Maury said. “Terrence just—”

“Who was it Terrence?” Fisher interrupted. “Point them out.” Terrence pointed his finger in Ally’s direction.

“Shiiit…” she muttered.

"Be cool, Ally," Big Mike whispered, sliding his shoulder slightly in front of her. "Just be cool."

Fisher gave Terrence a shove and the two of them marched over with one of his bodyguards at the rear. The other man stayed near the door like he was watching the room.

Ally stood still, sweat forming on her upper lip. She watched as Maury tried to head them off, but Fisher was on a mission. He marched right up to them and got right into Big Mike's face. "This the guy?" Fisher asked, eyeing Big Mike and staring up at him.

There was a moment's pause.

"Speak up, boy!"

"It was her," came a quiet voice.

Fisher turned around and followed Terrence's gaze to Ally. "What?" Fisher asked, thinking he'd misheard him.

"It was *heeerrr*!" Terrence said louder, but with an embarrassed teenage whine.

"Her?" Fisher looked back and forth like he was waiting for the punchline. "Her?" he demanded, looking at his nephew. Terrence's head was bowed low and his eyes refused to meet his uncle's. "You got your ass kicked by a girl?"

Embarrassed tears rolled down his cheeks. He looked like he was sucking a lemon as he held the ice pack to the side of his neck. "She sucker punched me," he whined.

Fisher turned back to Ally, his eyes cold. She probably should have cowered in front of one of the city's most notorious gangsters, but she didn't. She was still pissed about what happened earlier. She stood tall and her eyes burned with indignation.

Fisher glared at her for a moment longer, then let out a powerful laugh that shook the room. He turned to Terrence, still laughing, and chuckled until his eyes started tearing up. Now Terrence was really embarrassed. He shuffled uneasily and scowled. The two bodyguards started laughing too.

"You're just going to stand there? She nearly killed me!" Terrence whined. "You're just gonna let her disrespect me like this?"

Fisher stopped laughing and looked at his nephew, his eyes chilling back over. "You disrespected yourself. How do you expect to make it in my organization if you get your ass handed to you by a girl?"

"But Uncle—"

"Shut your mouth, boy! We'll deal with this later." Fisher turned back to Ally. He eyeballed her again. Then he clicked his tongue. "She any good, Maury?"

Maury made a face and shrugged. “She’s not one of my fighters,” he said. “She—”

“Is it true you knocked him out with one punch, sweetheart?” Fisher asked curiously.

“It was a kick,” Big Mike interjected.

Fisher ignored him, not taking his eyes off of Ally.

“What’s your name, girl?”

“None-ya,” she said, eyes still shooting daggers.

Fisher leaned in closer with a smug smile. “You got balls, kid. I like that.”

“You like balls?” she asked.

The room suddenly went still, as if it was holding its breath. It was a feeling. She could almost sense the panic that spread across the room. Big Mike adjusted his weight as if expecting retaliation. Maury’s eyes watched Fisher’s bodyguard intently like a predator as his hand hovered near his piece. One word from Fisher and he’d probably shoot her.

Fisher stepped forward and glared right into her eyes. Perhaps he was expecting her to flinch, but she didn’t. She locked eyes with him for only a second, but it seemed like ten. Then Fisher chuckled again and smiled. “I like this one, Maury!” he laughed. “Zane,” he barked, snapping his fingers impatiently.

As Zane reached into his jacket pocket, Maury’s hand shot forward and grabbed his arm. There was a silent struggle for a half-a-second before Maury looked down at the contents in the bodyguard’s hand. He’d just pulled out a flier. Maury released his grip and let Zane hand it to Fisher.

“Touch me like that again,” Zane growled, “and you’ll lose a hand.”

Fisher suddenly rounded on his bodyguard, grabbed him by the collar, and practically lifted him off the floor. “Do you have any idea who you’re talking to?” Fisher yelled. “This is Mauricio Baráo, The Chameleon! This man was the greatest fighter in the history of the sport. He made me a fortune! I’d be nothing if it weren’t for this man right here. So you keep your dick in your pants and show some respect,” he said, shoving him back a step.

The bodyguard recoiled. He bowed his head grudgingly and submitted. He wasn’t going to challenge Fisher. Not unless he had a death wish.

Fisher chuckled and extended his arm. Ally accepted the flier and glanced at it before looking up. “Come to this address if you want to make some real money,” he said. “Tell ’em I sent you.” He turned to Maury. "I could always hook *you* up, too. Maybe an exhibition fight? We could turn over a lot of dough."

"I don't do that anymore," he said coldly and gestured for Fisher to follow him to his office.

Fisher put his arm around Maury's shoulder, escorting him to the office in the back. Zane scowled and walked back to stand with the other bodyguard near the entrance.

"What's Maury doing mixed up with a guy like Fisher?" Ally whispered to Big Mike.

"I'll be right back," he replied, following Zane. Ally watched him with interest.

"Hello Darrell," Big Mike said, leaning forward and giving him a big hug

"Hey Mike," he said back.

"I haven't seen you for a while. Everything okay?"

"Mmm hmm," Darrell said. "Been keeping busy, ya know."

"You look good."

Darrell smoothed his tailored jacket. "I keep tellin' you. If you want some of this, I could hook you up."

"I got a job. Thanks, though."

"Shit. You call this a job, Mike? You're a maid."

"It's honest work."

"It's honest alright… and we all know how well honest pays."

"I do alright. I've got everything I need."

Ally turned her head and stopped eavesdropping. Right now, she was more interested in what Maury was doing with a guy like Fisher, a gangster known for arms dealing and illegal gambling establishments.

Through the window, she couldn't make out what was being said. But she saw something that made her skin crawl. Maury opened a safe and pulled out a small manilla envelope. He handed it to Fisher, who opened the end and thumbed through the paper bills. It was a payoff! The envelope must have had at least a few grand inside.

Maury glanced up. She averted her eyes for a few seconds, but couldn't keep her eyes away for long. Fisher slid the envelope into his inner jacket pocket and shook Maury's hand. A moment later, the two made their way out of the office and back toward the main entrance where a crowd of young boys were standing in a semicircle, chatting and smiling. Curtis was also in the group. They were all holding fliers like the one Ally got. Big Mike was standing rigidly and his upper lip was sweating.

When Fisher reached the main room, he greeted the boys in the group. But when he saw the fliers in their hands, he went ballistic. Without a word, he grabbed Darrell by the collar and shoved him hard against the door frame. He turned and backhanded Zane across the face, yelling that these boys were not to be touched. "If either of you ever come near these boys again without my say-so, you won't live to regret it!" he snarled, foaming at the mouth.

Some of the younger boys in the group dropped the fliers like they were on fire and took a step back. Others tensed up, their eyes expanding.

"I'm sorry Maury," Fisher said, turning. "It won't happen again, as we agreed."

Maury nodded.

Fisher looked down and smiled. "You boys be good boys and listen to Sensei Baráo." The children swallowed and nodded while Darrell took his cue. He opened the door and stepped aside so his boss could exit. Fisher took one more look at Ally, creeping her out with his crooked smile. Then he turned and walked out into the street with the others in tow.

As the door slowly began to close, Ally peered out. She could hear Terrence start to whine. "But what about her? You said—"

"Patience, Terrence," Fisher grumbled in exasperation. "What is it with your generation? This is a game of chess, not checkers."

She couldn't make out the last thing he said, as he had ducked into the rear door of their SUV. Through the glass, she could see Terrence sulk to the other side and flop into the back.

It seemed that the whole room sighed when the door shut. Maury began picking up the fliers from the floor and took them from some of the boys's hands. Ally, however, casually slipped the flier into her pocket.

"I don't want to see or hear about any of you *ever* going anywhere *near* that man. You understand me?" he said, tearing them in half. The boys nodded their heads. "Anyone who does, won't be welcome here." Maury looked at Ally, then retreated back into his office.

"All right guys, show's over," Big Mike said, ushering everyone back.

Ally stood still for a moment, watching everyone move around, then watched Maury walk into the back office. *What was a man like Fisher doing in a place like this? Why was Maury mixed up with a gangster? What was the money for? Was it a payoff? Did Curtis know about this? Did Big Mike? Why did Fisher freak when he saw the boys holding the fliers?* Questions surged through her mind until she looked at the clock. It was nearly four.

"Hey, it's Ally, right?"

She turned and a thin blond girl waved at her with a shy smile as she stepped closer. "I'm Samantha. You know… from before, in the locker— um," she shook her head. "A few of us are gonna grab a bite before we head to the soup kitchen. You wanna come?"

Ally glanced behind her. A few guys were taking turns on the bench press. Samantha's boyfriend was pretending not to notice them talking. She followed Ally's gaze and stepped forward. "Look, Tyler can be a dick. But he can also be really sweet."

"Uh huh," Ally smiled.

"No," she smiled and brushed a fallen strand of hair out of her face, "I mean, you should come. Once he gets to know you, he's a great guy."

Ally looked into Samantha's eyes. Kind. Sincere. But the voice in her head was screaming. *You know how this plays out. She's just inviting you to get dirt. She's not interested in you. Once they've had their fun, they'll drop you.*

Ally made a face. "Ah, I can't. I have to pop home and feed the cat. Thank you though."

"Come on!" Samantha grinned. "It'll just be for a couple of hours. I'm sure the cat will be fine. Plus, if you don't come, I'll suffocate in a fog of testosterone."

Ally looked over at the boys barking and slapping hands as one of them racked the weights. She looked at Samantha's pleading eyes and smiled, quieting the loud voice in her head. She was planning on coming back anyway. Plus, Lana said she was cool. And Piggy was used to her irregular hours. "Yeah. Okay. I'll go."

"Yay!" Samantha cheered. "Come on."

"I just need to get my stuff."

"Awesome. Don't ditch me, okay?" She winked and backpedaled to Tyler and his friends.

Ally watched Tyler drape his arm around Samantha's neck and lean in to whisper something. She smacked him playfully, then pointed her index finger at him sternly. Ally wondered if he was teasing Samantha about inviting her. Then she got her answer. Tyler side-eyed Ally, then the group headed over to the barbells.

Ally grabbed her things from a locker, noting that the majority of the mess she'd made had already been cleaned. She hung her head, then headed for the door.

As she reached the main exit, something told her to turn back. She eyed the trash can and stopped. Her fingers twitched at her side and she glanced around. Seeing no one paying her any attention, she reached down and stuffed Curtis's broken VR helmet into her bag. She hesitated another few seconds, then she pushed her way out of the dojo and headed toward Samantha.

CHAPTER 11

The soup kitchen wasn't a building. It was a food truck, one barely large enough to heat up a few items and keep others cool. In poor weather, a canvass cover was usually draped over the outdoor dining area, but today the sun was out. Maury set it up to be an inclusive place, free from judgment. Most of the time it was a pretty chilled space, however today, a group of teens were cooing around Curtis, awing over what had happened earlier.

"Then guess what she said?" Curtis asked with a huge grin.

"I don't know, what?" Samantha asked.

"Do you like balls?" he said, laughing hysterically now. Laughter and gasps erupted at the table.

"No way!" Tyler said dismissively. "There is no way you said that."

"She did too! She looked right at him and said, *You like balls?* laughed Curtis, mimicking her voice. "Didn't you?" he said, waving his hand at Ally.

Tyler and Anthony shook their heads and rolled their eyes, "Whatever."

"Hey Uncle Maury!" Curtis called from the table. Maury smiled as he spooned a helping of potato stew onto a tray and looked up. "Did Ally ask that gangster if he liked balls?"

Maury looked in their direction. He placed both hands onto the serving counter and squeezed, then nodded his head. The entire table burst out laughing again, this time including Tyler.

Ally sat quietly. She smiled politely, enjoying the positive attention, but she knew it wouldn't last. She turned her head to look at Maury. *People always find a way to let you down.* He caught her glance and immediately a look of guilt splashed across his face.

"Ally?" Samantha asked. "Are you alright?"

Ally dropped the far away look, smiled and nodded but wasn't sure if her expression was very convincing.

"I could never do something that brave," Samantha said.

"It wasn't brave. It was stupid." Maury was now standing next to the table. "Ally, can I have a word?" he asked, looking down at her.

"Anything you have to say to me, you can say to the group," she replied, looking up at him.

His gaze swept across the others at the table. "I think it would be better if we could talk in private."

"Private? You mean like you and Fisher?" she asked, eyeing him carefully. For a moment, Maury stood still, just staring at her, not happy with her reply. He opened his mouth, but quickly closed it again. She decided to press the issue.

"I mean, what possible business would a mobster have with a non-profit? Especially one run by a public benefactor... such as yourself, eh Maury?"

"His nephew trains with us," Maury replied. "And I think everyone saw what made him show up today."

"Yeah... there's that," she conceded. "But something tells me he was already on his way."

After a pause, he turned his attention to the others. "That man is dangerous. I don't want any of you discussing what happened in public anymore. It isn't safe."

"Is that what the two of you were discussing in your office?" she asked coldly. "Our safety?"

Maury glanced at Curtis. He was sitting uncharacteristically quiet in his wheelchair. Samantha, Anthony and Tyler sat still, feeling the tension, but pretended not to notice. "There are tables to clean. I suggest a few of you get going. Excuse me," Maury said. "I should get back to serving."

Ally watched him walk back to the serving counter and resume his duties. She had so many questions. Is Maury dirty? Is he working for the mob? Is the dojo some kind of money laundering service? She didn't know. But she aimed to find out.

As she turned her head back to the table, Curtis was glaring at her. Not in a hateful way. It was more like a 'you don't know what you're talking about' kind of way. It made her start to wonder, did Curtis know? Did he have some involvement too?

She was about to start asking questions when suddenly the utensils and items on top of the table began to rattle, slowly at first, then practically vibrated themselves off the table. Everyone stopped talking and stared in confusion. A car alarm broke their silence and everybody jumped. They looked at each other as two more car alarms went off. Then three. Then six. Frantically, everybody looked around, gasping and growing anxious. Then, as if someone had turned off a switch, the reverberating sounds suddenly stopped. A few seconds later, the world seemed to forget all about it and go back to their lives.

The group laughed in relief, letting go of their nervous tension. "That was a big one," Samantha giggled, clinging to Tyler as he groaned in disgust. "What?" Samantha asked.

"CooCoo alert. 6 o'clock," he whispered.

"Great," Curtis grumbled.

A rough looking man with long scraggly gray hair and beard turned away from the serving area holding his tray of food and smiled. He looked to be in his 50s, but could've easily been younger. Living rough tends to age people, she thought. He started toward them and eagerly set his tray down on the table.

"Hiya fellas," he said warmly. "Lovely afternoon, isn't it?"

"Hi Barney," Curtis said with a hint of sarcasm. Samantha, Anthony, and Tyler suddenly stood up and said that they needed to go circulate to other tables. Curtis flashed them a *fuck you* smirk and watched the three leave, smiling.

Ally noted Barney's expression. Though the trio attempted to hide their disdain, Barney definitely knew they were avoiding him. It was written all over his face, though he did his best to plead oblivious. She knew that this was probably a regular thing. Sometimes volunteers didn't like to get too close to people. Some felt helping out was enough. Others went out of their way to make their lives easier by putting them in touch with various services or organizations which could help them further. Very few people actually sat down and talked to them like human beings.

She was glad Curtis didn't leave, though his expression was a cross between annoyed and trapped. It seemed Barney was excited to see him.

"Barney, this is Ally," Curtis said. "Ally, this is Barney Wallace. He writes for the Grace City Whirlwind. It's an online tabloid."

"Nice to meet you," he said enthusiastically, holding out a grubby hand. Ally shook it and said likewise. "You look familiar. Do I know you?" he asked.

She shook her head. "I don't think so."

"I can't place it, but I've seen your face somewhere before." He eyed her up and down. "It'll come to me in a minute." There was a long pause as his eyes drifted from her face, down her torso and back up again. He cocked his head from side to side and even tried closing one eye at a time.

"Barney… you're being creepy again," Curtis whispered. Barney shook himself and slumped back in his seat. He averted his eyes and apologized.

"It's okay. No harm done. Maybe I just have one of those faces."

Barney didn't seem convinced. "Hmm," he said dismissively. He stared a bit longer, took a mouthful of soup and swallowed it, then turned his attention to Curtis. "So? Did you look into it?" he asked with a hushed voice.

"No, I told you before, Barney, that I don't believe in all this conspiracy crap."

Barney's happy expression faded. "Oh, okay," he nodded quickly and went back to his soup.

"What conspiracy crap?" Ally asked.

Curtis began shaking his head slowly, his eyes wide as if trying to warn her. She smiled back at him coyly, finding enjoyment in watching him squirm. Barney seemed like a nice enough guy and she certainly didn't see the harm in listening to someone talk.

Barney's smile returned. He took another mouthful of soup, some of which spilled down the front of his beard, swallowed, and glanced over his shoulders like he expected spooks to jump out of the bushes and tackle him. Then he leaned in close and almost whispered. "What do you guys know about earthquakes?"

"Jesus Christ..." Curtis muttered, rolling his eyes.

"Earthquakes?" Ally repeated. It wasn't the question she was expecting. Usually it was lizard people, Roswell, or the moon landing, but earthquakes? This was a new one.

Barney nodded, very serious now.

"Umm… well, when tectonic plates rub against each other, the potential energy builds up until eventually seismic waves of energy are released and causes the ground to shake."

"Very good," Barney affirmed. "And where do earthquakes typically occur?"

"Around the Ring of Fire in the Pacific Ocean. And along fault lines," she said while Curtis apathetically fiddled with his spoon.

"Correct," he said, looking over both shoulders again. "So do you get it?"

Curtis snorted.

"Get what?" Ally asked, shrugging.

"Why we're having so many earthquakes. Why so many buildings are falling down all over Old Town."

"Umm, because they're *old*?" Curtis interjected.

Now it was Barney who snorted. "Do you see any fault lines around?" he asked, looking in both directions and dramatizing with his hands. "No, you don't. So that begs the question then, doesn't it? What's causing these earthquakes?"

"Earthquakes can happen anywhere, Barney," Curtis said. "Not just at plate boundaries."

"Yeah, but not over and over in the same geographic region!" he fired back.

Curtis sighed heavily again, rolled his eyes, and shook his head.

Ally knew that less than 10% of earthquakes happened away from plate boundaries. She also knew they were rare. Barney was right. She felt her thoughts drift back to the abandoned theater, to the earthquake that foiled her getaway. The one that caused her to lose control and crash. She'd never considered the frequent earthquakes before. Like everyone else, she'd always just accepted them as part of daily life. Now, she was curious to find out what Barney knew.

"What about deformation?" she asked.

Barney chuckled. "It's bugging me, but you really remind me of someone. You sure you're not a seismologist?" he joked.

"Deformation?" Curtis asked.

Barney stopped smiling. "Deformation is like… solid rock distorting, or changing slowly. And when it happens, it can spread out over a much larger area than the plate boundary itself. But no… to answer that question, we're too far away."

Ally shrugged. "I give up. So why are we having so many earthquakes then?"

"Yeah, this'll be good," Curtis sneered, crossing his arms and leaning back into his chair.

"You may not remember this. It was a little before your time, but about 15 years back, an asteroid—a big one—the kind called a global killer, just missed Earth by a few thousand kilometers. I mean, can you imagine that? *A few thousand kilometers!* We're talking about the infinitesimal space above, so a few thousand kilometers is pretty significant. Anyway, this made the governments of the world start talking."

"Yeah, I read about that in school." Ally said. "World leaders met to discuss the possibility of another mass extinction event like the one that wiped out the dinosaurs, but the probability of it happening was so low that the governments of the world wouldn't justify the money needed to build any kind of planetary defense strategy."

"*They* didn't, but *ours* did. Remember when parts of Grace City were bombarded by meteors?"

"No, I completely forgot about that," Curtis said.

"You're talking about Starfall?" Ally clarified.

Barney nodded. "That was them."

"What do you mean, *that was them?*" Curtis barked. "Are you saying the government caused a meteor shower?"

"I know what it sounds like."

"Yeah, it sounds *batshit*."

Barney's expression darkened. "Well, maybe you would understand if you hacked into BC like I asked you to do last time!"

Hacked, Ally thought. *Does he mean Google?*

"I'm not going to commit a felony because some cooky hobo-looking has-been thinks the government is using some kind of earthquake weapon to level clusters of buildings," Curtis snapped nastily.

"Woah," Ally interrupted, leaning forward and holding out her arms as if separating children. "Let's both just take a breath." Curtis reluctantly conceded and Barney grumbled as he spooned another mouthful of soup. "Right, carry on Barney."

Curtis shot her a quick look. *Really*?

"As I was saying, the government teamed up with the advanced sciences department at Burton Conglomerates and together, they built something called the—"

"Quantum Tunneler…" Ally finished. Her memories flooded back to her bedroom. Her mother, sitting beside her, telling her about how there was this mystery particle that would just inexplicably disappear and reappear on the other side of a solid barrier… and that studying this particle would mean groundbreaking scientific advancement. Her mother said she was building a Quantum Tunneler.

Barney looked impressed, while Curtis gave her a puzzled look. "That's… right. A Quantum Tunneler, or in this case, an asteroid deterrent weapon," Barney finished.

"Wait, I have a question," Curtis interrupted. Barney sighed, but gestured in allowance. "How much have you had to drink today?"

"Curtis!" Ally scorned.

Barney scowled and waved his hand playfully at Curtis, making a dismissive noise.

"Come on, Barney," Curtis said, smiling coyly.

Barney shifted in his chair. "Only a few sips…" he said unconvincingly.

"*Barneeeey*?" Curtis crooned, winking and grinning playfully.

"Okay, so I drink… okay? But that doesn't mean I'm wrong."

"It kinda does," Curtis muttered.

"Listen, they attached it to a satellite and put it into orbit so that if another asteroid came along… BLAMO! They could neutralize it. Only get this! It's next to impossible to change the trajectory of massive objects hurtling through space, so this thing wasn't designed to just zap asteroids. It bent the natural laws of physics. This thing was supposed to allow solid objects to pass right through other solid obj—"

"Pass through?" Curtis interrupted. "What do you mean, pass through... like phasing? Like the Flash?"

"Light's got nothing to do with it," Barney grunted. Each interruption caused the frazzled look on his face to grow.

Curtis shook his head. "No, in DC Comics, there is a superhero named The Flash who runs really fast and can vibrate his cells so rapidly that he can phase through solid objects," he explained.

"Right! Exactly like that!" Barney exclaimed. "Yeah, an oversimplification, but yes..." he said, reaching out to Samantha as she walked past and asked if there was any soup left.

"I'll find you something," she winked, glancing at Curtis, who rolled his eyes and shook his head.

"So eight years later, another asteroid was spotted, only this one was predicted to hit Earth. It wasn't a planet killer this time, but it was large enough to cause some major damage. And of course, the government didn't tell everyone because God forbid they'd want people to know about their imminent deaths. No no no. Keep shopping. Capitalism must go on!"

"Barney…" Curtis interrupted.

"Sorry, so they fired the weapon at the asteroid, only its molecular structure was unique, alien. Instead of hopping over Earth, it absorbed the radiation from the weapon's laser. It must have become unstable and exploded."

"And you know all this because…?"

"I had a source…" he shifted uncomfortably again.

"Had?"

"It dried up."

Curtis scoffed. "*Dried up*. See Ally? What's a conspiracy without unconfirmed sources, here-say evidence, fake news—"

"That's enough, Curtis," Ally barked, scowling before turning back to Barney. "Go on."

Barney accepted another bowl of soup from Samantha and thanked her. He took a bite, then continued. "The weapon may have stopped the asteroid from impacting in one location, but hundreds of smaller pieces still peppered multiple cities around the world. Very sad for those people. A lot of people died. But those pieces are worth a fortune now. The laser essentially charged them up like batteries."

Ally's eyes widened and her lips tightened. She stared at Barney, her thoughts drifting back to the theater. To the shiny rock.

Curtis must have noticed the color drain from her face. "What's with you?" he asked. "You look like you've seen a ghost."

"I've seen them."

"Ghosts?"

"No, Curtis! The meteorite fragments… when I got arrested, the police thought I'd lifted some kind of mineral from one of BC's warehouses. Their private security stormed in. But the weird thing is, the arrest report said I had stolen a crate of old batteries that were due for recycling. The charges were dropped. But I saw what was stolen. It was a rock. But it... I don't know... kind of glowed."

"I rest my case," Barney said smiling. "They glow because the Quantum Tunneler altered their molecular state and packed them with radiation. Non-harmful, but the radiation is the most efficient battery technology the world has ever seen. It's nearly perpetual."

"Oh, come on Ally. You can't possibly be buying into this. If what he's saying was real, it'd have been all over the news."

"Well, I guess that depends on if you trust the news reports from eight years ago," Barney said, rolling his eyes.

"You mean the facts?" Curtis clarified sarcastically.

"Yes," Barney agreed.

Curtis nodded at Ally and made a duck face.

"Come on, Curtis, you're way too smart to be this stupid. These buildings are built to withstand… I mean, do you think a perfectly sound structural building just collapses on itself due to normal fire damage? This isn't *Building 7…*" he said, raising his voice a little. "If you had hacked into BC like I told you to, then maybe you would have read up about all the collateral damage!" he argued, pointing to Curtis's wheelchair.

"Wait… wait… stop," Curtis said, taken aback. "Why did you just point at me and say collateral damage? Is that some kind of wheelchair joke? Because only I'm allowed to make those."

"The building that fell on you? It was them, Curtis!"

"Ha! Except you have your facts all muddled up, old man. The satellite which you claim was put into orbit eight years ago was destroyed!"

"Oh, right. I forgot to mention that," he said.

"So you admit it?"

"Of course I admit it. The satellite was destroyed when the asteroid exploded."

"So that means all the earthquakes since *couldn't* have been caused by the satellite then, could it?"

"I didn't say they *only* had a satellite. They probably still have a prototype weapon, most likely housed in some kind of mobile vehicle."

"Oh, fuck off!" Curtis said, waving his hand dismissively. He turned to Ally. "See this is why you can't talk to conspiracy theorists," he blurted, "They have an answer for everything!"

Ally's eyes widened. "Mobile vehicle? Like a white van?" she asked distantly.

"What?" Curtis huffed.

Barney shrugged. "Yeah, maybe. I suppose it could fit in a van." He looked at Curtis. "Ask your father. He'll tell you."

"What's that supposed to mean?"

"He worked for Burton Conglomerates," Barney said. "But after your mother died and you were nearly crushed, BC officially shut down the project. Unofficially, they just relocated and started up again. Everyone was reassigned. Except for your father. He quit."

Curtis looked sick. "Ok, this isn't funny anymore. You need to stop playin'," Curtis barked.

"I'm not," Barney insisted.

Ally watched Curtis blink at Barney through watery eyes. She'd listened to her fair share of conspiracy theories from some of the homeless vets, but this was different. There had to be some truth to what he was saying, right?

"Did somebody put you up to this?!" he yelled? "Cuz it isn't funny."

Barney shook his head. "No… I—"

"So you're telling me that my mother's death wasn't an accident? That my father and everyone close to me has been lying to me for years? Why would they do that?!"

"I, uh—"

"All right, we're going to sort this out right now," Curtis grumbled angrily, "Then we'll see how full of shit you are." He picked up his phone and dialed a number. It rang twice before a man answered.

"Dad? Dad, I need to... Dad! Shut up and listen," he shouted into the phone. "Is it true what Barney said about Mom?"

There was a pause on the line.

"No, I'll be home later. You need to answer me, right now! Did you work for BC? How did Mom die?"

Another pause.

"Why won't you just answer the question?... Because I'm with Barney... Barney!... Ugh, it doesn't matter... Is it true?... IS... IT... TRUE?"

Maury looked up, noticing the commotion coming from their table and quickly walked over.

"Holy shit..." Curtis muttered, dropping the phone into his lap.

"He confirmed it, didn't he?" Barney said smugly. "He said the building collapsed on—"

"Did you know?" Curtis yelled.

Maury looked at Barney, then at Curtis. Then it hit him. He sighed and averted his eyes. It was as good of an admission as any.

Curtis smacked the bowl of soup off the table, sending its contents splashing across the next table, startling some patrons and volunteers. Then he turned his wheelchair around and rolled out of the dining area.

"Curtis?" Ally called after him. "Curt!" He didn't turn around.

"Let him go," Maury said. "He just needs time. Goddamn it, Barney. What did you say to him?" Maury asked.

He shook his head. "I'm sorry. I didn't think he'd..."

"It's none of your business! Do you have any idea what you've done?"

"I think I should go," Barney said and stood up. "Thanks for the soup." He turned tail and hurried away.

CHAPTER 12

Ally slipped the key into the lock and lifted the large metallic door to her storage container. It opened with an all too familiar guttural squeak from the rusty metal hinges. As she pressed on a battery-powered work light and shut the door behind her, she was immediately greeted by a mew from below.

Piggy rubbed her back and tail against her legs excitedly. Ally picked her up and smothered her with kisses.

"I know! I know! I'm sorry. Let's get you some food." She set her down and set a tin of wet food beside her on the metal floor.

Her mind wandered to the news about the earthquakes, how the protestors were marching in front of the precinct and chanting for their homes to be left alone. She thought about what Barney had said. About Curtis. She knew what it was like to have false memories. How the shock of not knowing your past can be a heavy burden to bear. She decided to check in on him.

She picked up her phone and started typing out a text.

You okay?

It was all she could think to send. She held the phone in her hand for a moment until the message indicator showed the message had been read, but he didn't respond. He clearly didn't want to talk. At least not yet.

She checked the time. It was only 10 o'clock. There was no way she could sleep. Since *the incident*, she hadn't slept more than one or two hours per night on average. 'A bout of insomnia,' Dr. Wheeler called it. *Yeah, a lengthy one. Moron.* Then she remembered the VR helmet Terrence broke was still in her bag. Fixing it wasn't anything to do with skill. She knew she could fix it. But what she wondered was whether or not the parts inside were so severely damaged that she would have to replace them. She probably had some reserve equipment lying around her container that she was sure would be compatible if push came to shove. But first she had to take a look inside.

An hour later, she'd not only successfully repaired it, but upgraded it entirely with the same technology as her own holo-tech. Only, instead of external hologram projections, she removed the bulky and heavy casing and managed to fit all the functional components into an old visor she no longer used. Now, the 3D images were simply projected onto lenses, rather than inside a bulky face shield. When she slipped the VR glasses on, the screen came to life, along with the auditory speakers. Satisfied with her work, she removed them and put them back into her bag.

Next, she picked up her phone but set it down again when there weren't any messages. She waited a moment, debating whether or not she should send another one, but instead reached into her jeans pocket and pulled out the flier Fisher gave her. On it was an address and a time.

'Come to this address if you want to make some real money. Tell 'em I sent you.'

She narrowed her eyes, crumpled the flier in her hand, and tossed it beside her bed, then laid her head down on the pillow. Piggy tucked herself in on top of her ankles, curled up in a ball. She never liked to sleep near her face or hands. She much preferred to sleep down at the foot of the bed where she would be least likely disturbed. Ally couldn't blame her. I mean, who can resist petting a cat? It's like a drug.

Suddenly, she felt a wave of tiredness creep in. Rather than fight it, she meant to take full advantage of any sleep she could get. She closed her eyes and within a matter of minutes, she was fast asleep.

*   *   *

Ally's eyes shot open. She thrust herself upright, panting, her body sticky with sweat. The nightmare was so vivid and so real that it took her a moment to remember where she was. Her brown eyes desperately scanned the familiar dark of her container, until the grogginess wore off and she heard the sounds of the slum around her.

She closed her eyes and shook her head, then headed to the bathroom and took her medication. She removed Dr. Hansen's card from the mirror and held it in her hands, tracing the silver outline with her thumb before turning it over. She eyed the number written on the back.

'*Call me if you need anything.*'

Ally sighed, picked up her phone and started dialing, but stopped halfway through. Her thumbs hovered over the screen before she caught sight of her reflection in the mirror.

If I call her, they'll just force me to have alternative therapy.

She placed the card into her pocket and began pacing. *It was a dream. I just need to blow off steam. I need a good workout. That will sort out these delusions and put them behind me.*

She looked at her phone. It was 1:00am and Curtis still hadn't replied.

She took two steps toward the door with every intention of simply going to the dojo to work out. But just as she was about to leave the storage container, a thought occurred to her.

She back-stepped and turned to face the bed. On the floor was the crumpled flier she'd discarded earlier. Then a little smile formed on the corners of her mouth.

Ally wrapped the chain around the container bars and locked it with a padlock. She flipped up the collar on her jacket, tucked her hands into her coat pockets and headed toward the slums.

Angry shrieks rang out into the night as Ally neared the end of the stacked containers. She stopped and listened, hearing a woman yell and multiple male voices barking back.

It's not my business, she told herself. She turned her shoulder and continued her walk.

She made it a few more steps, but a sickening shriek made her freeze. This one was different. It was panicked, helpless.

Ally hung her head and squeezed her hands into fists until her knuckles cracked. Another shriek filled the night air.

Dammit... She turned toward the direction of the sound.

Peering around a storage container, she spied three tattooed skinheads. One had his hand around an elderly woman's throat, pressing her against the wall. She had to be in her late 70s. In the other, he threatened to bash her with a pipe. He was yelling at her to shut her mouth. Inside the container, two others were rummaging around, dumping out drawers and turning over furniture.

Ally turned away and leaned herself against the cool metal. She closed her eyes and quietly thumped the back of her head against it. She had enough trouble.

"Keep struggling," she heard the man grunt, "and I'll shove this pipe so deep inside your ass you'll taste metal."

Ally's eyes fluttered open in fury. She shot around the corner, picked up a piece of tarmac, and stormed right up to the man with the pipe. She struck him hard on the back of the head. His shoulders slumped forward and he fell to the ground with a loud thud.

The other two thugs turned as the metal clang of the pipe bounced on the rocks and dropped what was in their hands. Without a word, they came toward her, stepping ominously through the doorway and stopped at her 10 and 2 o'clock. Their eyes glanced down to their unconscious comrade on the ground, then flicked back to her.

"Shoulda minded yer business, hero," one growled, reaching forward to grab her.

Ally sidestepped and jabbed him hard in the face, sending him staggering back a step. His hand instinctively touched his nose before examining the crimson blood. His eyebrows shot up as his tongue swirled in his mouth. Then he spat a mouthful of blood onto the ground before glaring at her. "Not bad. My turn." He reared back with his fist and swung hard.

Ally dodged his strike and countered with a one-two punch, again sending the man scuttling backwards.

"Quit playin' around," the second man jeered.

The first snarled and rushed her. He swung two punches, which Ally blocked, and kicked her hard in the leg. The blow knocked her off balance, giving him time to slug her in the gut. She doubled over, feeling the wind exit her lungs, and fell to her knees. She felt a hand grab her hair and jerk her up, the other pinning her arm to her back and held tight.

Ally struggled to break free, but stopped when she heard the SHICK of a switchblade. The other man held it up for her to see.

"Fair is fair. Blood for blood."

The man came at her, thrusting the blade toward her stomach, but with all her might, Ally twisted her body, and the man stabbed his comrade instead.

She felt him let go as he cried out.

Ally booted knife-man in the chest, sending him crashing back into the wall of the container, and leapt forward. She landed on him, hitting him repeatedly in the face until she was sure she'd broken both of her hands.

A shadow loomed over her. She whirled just in time to see a bloody knife blade rise and shimmer in the lamplight.

SMACK!

The old woman cracked him on the back of his head with a pipe and sent him to the ground, woozy and concussed. He instantly vomited.

Reeling, the two injured men staggered to their feet, picked up their buddy, and draped him over their shoulders.

"You're dead!" knife-man growled. "We'll see you again real soon!"

They shuffled away, hobbling down the street.

When the men disappeared, Ally looked up at the woman.

"You okay?" the woman asked, reaching her arm down to help Ally up.

Me? Ally took her arm and rose to her feet. "Thanks."

"It's me who should be thanking you. Not everyone would be willing to help in a situation like that. Here, come on inside. I'll make you some tea."

"No, thank you. I'm fine," Ally said politely.

"I didn't ask you," she said. "I insist." She took Ally by the arm and together, they walked inside and shut the door behind them.

Ally looked at what could be called the kitchen. Like her place, the room was desolate and empty. She had a rickety table with two chairs. In the living space, she had a broken chair that was vomiting bits of foam from its cushions. Unlike her, she did have a bed in the corner of the room, but she guessed that it was something she managed to take from the street. It didn't look comfortable.

The woman picked up the table and two chairs the men had knocked over with surprise agility and strength. Then she stepped over some items and reached for a tin. "I don't have any sugar or milk," she said. "I hope you don't mind black tea."

"Black tea is perfect," Ally said.

Sandy nodded happily and flicked the kettle on. She retrieved two cups from the counter, examining them both by running her thumb over each rim. She frowned and placed one cup in front of herself, and another slightly to the side before digging into the tin and tossing a black tea bag into each cup.

"What's your name, darling?" the woman finally asked, turning her shoulder away from her slightly.

"Ally, you?"

"Sandy," she called, removing something from her inside jacket pocket. There was a quiet sound of a metal lid being unscrewed from a container and a splash of liquid dropping into a cup. The woman shoved something back into her coat and reached for the kettle as it clicked off.

She poured the steaming liquid into the two cups. Ally reached out her hand to take the cup, but grimaced as her chewed-up knuckles cracked open again.

Sandy suddenly put down the kettle and grabbed Ally's wrist. She scowled, and opened the freezer drawer. A second later, she wrapped a bag of peas with a towel and placed it over her hands.

"Really, Sandy… I'm okay. I don't—"

"Hush," she said sternly and picked up an old square tin from the floor. Ally watched her remove a stack of letters, a small tube of ointment, and a rag, and set them on the table.

"Give me your hands, sweetie."

"I said I'm—"

She glared at Ally, holding out her shaky palm. Ally sighed and held her fists forward. Sandy tutted, removed a flask from her inside jacket pocket, unscrewed the metal top with the same scratchy sound, and poured it over her knuckles.

Ally winced.

"Don't be such a baby." She wiped her knuckles with the rag and smeared ointment over the cuts.

Ally turned her head and caught sight of the letters on the table. They were eviction notices. Dozens of them.

Sandy followed her gaze. Her face fell a little. "I've survived worse than this," she said. "I'll survive them too."

"Who *were* those guys?"

Sandy waved her hand dismissively. "Ah, it's just corporations fighting dirty."

"Those guys didn't look very corporate," Ally said.

"Yeah, well... men like that are easily hired out."

"Hired by whom?"

Sandy looked at Ally as if studying her. "Let me tell you something honey, I've lived in this city for nearly 70 years. I've lived high and I've lived low. The one thing that never changes around here is that those with power… always fear losing it."

Ally thought about this for a moment. She couldn't really argue.

Sandy set the ointment down and poured the remains of the hot water into her cup. Ally could smell the alcohol as the steam rose.

"So what did they want?"

Sandy shrugged nonchalantly. "I imagine to keep me from paying my rent."

"And why would they want that?"

Sandy took a sip from her tea. "If your eyes are open, you shouldn't have to look very hard to answer that question. Social cleansing isn't anything new. History's ripe with examples, if you know where to look. Now I suppose it's corporate giants facilitating gentrification."

"But that can't be legal."

Sandy chuckled. "When is it ever? Legally they can't force people out, but there are other ways of getting what they want."

"Like paying a band of thugs to rough you up and scare you into leaving voluntarily," Ally finished.

"Now you're getting it," she said, winking a little as she took another sip of her tea.

"So what are you going to do?"

Sandy shrugged. "Fight as hard as I can until they force me out," she said. "Then I suppose I'll have to move on."

"If it's going to happen anyway, you might as well take their relocation money and use it to get out of this shit hole."

Sandy smiled. "You're young. Some things are more important than money."

"But you could have died tonight."

Sandy sighed and set her tea down. "Everyone has a battle to fight. Maybe one day you'll find yours."

The two of them sat in silence a moment.

"Are you going to report them?" Ally asked.

"Report them?" she laughed. "You really *are* young."

Ally checked her phone. Still no text messages.

"You probably have somewhere to be. Don't let me keep you."

"I do. I have a thing."

"At this hour? Honey, no boy is worth that," she laughed.

"Thanks for the tea." Ally smiled and stood up.

"Now wait just a minute, sweetie," Sandy said, rising up off the chair with some difficulty. She rustled around in a cardboard box stashed in the corner and pulled out a piece of bread. She proceeded to slab some butter onto it and handed it to her.

Ally eyed the box. It was her last piece. This was probably her dinner. *Damn it.* She did her best to swallow down the lump in her throat.

"Sandy, I can't—"

"Shhh! Put some meat on those bones," she said, winking.

I'll bring her a box of groceries in the morning.

Ally leaned forward and gave Sandy a hug. "Ice that face," she said, pointing to the bruise forming on Sandy's cheek before setting off for the address on the flier.

"Don't you worry about me. I'm gonna be just fine."

CHAPTER 13

Ally wormed her way through the inner slums until finally, she reached the address on the back of the flier. Nerves were starting to creep up on her, but she swallowed them down. As she raised her fist, she hesitated before banging hard on the metal door. The thumping echoed loudly, making the metal hum at a low octave. At the top, about head height, a small rectangular window slid open and the eyes of a gruff bouncer peered out. "Wrong address," he muttered before he slammed the little door shut.

Ally banged a second time, and again the little door slid open. She held up the flier for him to see.

"Fisher invited me."

He looked at the flier through the little window and cocked one of his eyebrows.

"Go check; I'm happy to wait."

The man raised an eyebrow again, but nodded slowly before the door slid shut.

After five minutes of pacing and trying out different standing positions, the loud clang of three unhinging deadbolts rang out from the inside. The large door swung open and the bouncer waved her in.

Soon, she found herself in a dark and grimy hallway of concrete. A dim amber light glowed from the ceiling about every 10 meters and with each step she took, the sound of a roaring crowd grew louder and louder. It echoed from the distance and she felt like a Roman gladiator.

Reaching the end of the corridor, she stepped into a large concrete room with a makeshift arena at its center. Four large chain-link fence panels were attached together with thick chains, each with a large work lamp at the corners that projected an eerie bluish-white light onto the center ring. It was square in shape, approximately 20 square feet in size, and surrounding the fight arena were dozens of screaming spectators from all different types of backgrounds. She wondered how many of them were desperate and owed money to the wrong people.

Stepping out of the corridor shadows, she walked around the arena getting her bearings. She noted an office toward the back where people in suits were watching the fight from behind bullet-proof glass. She reckoned that if Fisher were here, he would be behind one of those glass panels. Attached to the side, she spotted a little corner room. Inside sat a bookie. She walked forward and tapped on the wire cage covering the window.

"I'd like a fight," she said.

The bookie looked up from his notebook, then resumed his calculations, paying her no mind. He was busy monitoring the small television screen just in front of him and was keeping track of the current fight.

"I said, I'd like a fight," Ally repeated, louder this time and tapped on the cage.

"Sorry honey," he said condescendingly without raising his head. "This ain't the place for ladies. Take a hike… or Bruno here will have to get nasty."

Ally lowered her head and looked further back into the little room. A large man was sitting on a stool in the back. He cracked his knuckles and sniffed, eyes like pure adrenaline.

"Look, unless you would like to explain to Mr. Fisher why his personal invitation was rejected by *Timon* and *Pumbaa*, I suggest you get off your ass."

At the mention of his name, the bookie lifted his head and for the first time really looked at her. "Fisher invited you?" he asked skeptically.

She nodded.

The man picked up his phone and dialed a number. "Put him on the phone."

A moment passed.

"Sorry to bother you sir, but there's a girl here who claims you personally invited her to—"

There was a pause on the line before the bookie's expression changed.

"Could you repeat that, sir?"

Ally studied the man's face. It's tough exterior fell like he was trying to swallow a tennis ball. She watched him slowly hang up the phone and lean on the desk. He stared at the wall in front of him like it was a window, like a dog who just had its leash yanked. Then he snapped out of it. He turned back to her.

"You've got your fight," he said. "You bettin'?"

She nodded.

"Cash?"

Ally reached into her jacket pocket and pulled out a wad of bills that she'd taken from a pipe in the floor of her storage container. It was a third of what was left of her mother's life insurance. She held it up and placed it in the little slit in the window.

"That's a lot of money," he said. "You sure you want to do this?"

She stared at him and didn't flinch.

"Okay…" He shrugged, picking up the wad of cash. He ran it through a counting machine twice, wrapped a rubber band around it, and tossed it to Bruno, who took it into another room behind him. Then the bookie turned to Ally.

"Name?"

"Ally."

"Bet?"

"All on knockout."

He shook his head. "I'll give you 10:1 odds if you make it 3 rounds."

"Knockout," she repeated.

The man smirked. "Kid, with the guy you're fighting, you'll be lucky to last a round."

"If that's true, then you wouldn't mind offering me 20:1 odds."

"20:1?" He laughed and eyeballed her. "Do you know how much money that is? Are you even good for it?"

"I'm good for it," she lied.

He blinked and eyed her. "Do you know what they do to people who don't pay up?"

Ally crossed her arms.

"Look, let's say you're good. And I mean, *REALLY* good… this ain't like the movies. The guys in *here*? They do this for a living. They'll hurt you."

"20:1. Knockout," she said sternly.

"Okay, don't say I didn't warn ya, sweetheart."

"Just have my money ready," she grumbled, glaring at the bookie before she approached the ring.

Two men were fighting. Each was landing devastating blows to the face and abdomen. A red clock timer was counting down until the bell rang and the two fighters stopped and lowered their arms. A referee held up the hand of the victor, though that's not a very apt way to describe them. Both men looked like they'd been through hell.

She watched as they both ducked under the ropes and left the ring. Then she saw something that stopped her.

"What are you doing here?" she asked.

Curtis shrugged. "I thought this would be a good way to piss off my dad and my uncle."

"How did you get in?"

"My uncle used to fight in places like this. I know a few guys.
"

"How did you know I was here?"

"Lucky guess," he said, but Ally could tell he was lying. "Actually, I, uh… I need to ask you something."

"You could have just sent me a text."

"No, this needs to be done in person." He bowed his head, then looked up at her with big eyes. "Before… with Barney… when you mentioned the white van… how—"

A loud bell interrupted them as another fight ended. He glanced at the ring and shuddered. One of the fighters had just been beaten unconscious in less than two rounds. His face was swollen and caved in. "I don't know why anybody would fight here," he said, watching the loser get dragged out by the staff. "I heard there's a guy here… Grzegorz *something…* they call him the Polish monster. He's supposed to be big, I mean, *really* big. I heard he once stepped on a man's skull and crushed it. His brains splattered all over the—"

"ALLY!" the announcer interrupted through the mic. He was waving at her to come into the ring. A second later, the spotlight hit her.

Curtis looked at her in shock. "You're not fighting, are you?" he laughed nervously, "Because that would be stupid."

Ally shrugged and flashed Curtis a coy smile. She stepped through the roaring crowd, ducked under the ropes and climbed into the ring. A few bouncers behind her stepped back into position and guarded the ring.

From the other side, she saw her opponent stomp through the crowd and duck into the ring from the opposite corner. Before her stood a huge man. He was bigger than any man she'd ever seen in her life, like a serial killer on steroids.

Ally looked at Curtis. He pointed, horrified, and mouthed: "Grzegorz."

Ally turned to the giant, then shot a squinted glance toward the VIP area behind the bulletproof glass where she imagined Fisher was watching her. Then the penny dropped. Fighting someone like Grzegorz was not an accident. Fisher had planned this whole thing! He counted on her showing up tonight looking for a fight. This was a setup! A setup designed to get revenge for his nephew.

She turned her head to the ropes. Three bouncers stood at each side. No way out. Grzegorz was laughing at her. He knew exactly what she was thinking.

The referee stood in the center of the ring and called both fighters forward. Ally was tall for a woman. She was 6 feet, but this man, Grzegorz, towered over her. He was easily 7, possibly more, and his body was three times the size of hers.

The referee began laying out the rules, or rather, lack thereof. There seemed to be only one rule... and that was, when the bell rang, both fighters were to stop immediately or the one breaking the rule would owe the crowd their money back.

The referee looked at both fighters and asked one final time if they understood. Both nodded and the referee stepped back and out of the way.

"I hurt you," Grzegorz muttered in broken English. "I beat you until nothing left."

"Awww, you must say that to all the girls," Ally quipped, orbiting him in the ring.

DING.

Grzegorz popped his neck and thundered straight toward her. The crowd was going nuts. They were cheering and screaming and slapping their hands on the edge of the ring. The noise was deafening. She could barely hear herself think, but she willed herself to focus. She knew she would only have one shot at this. At first, she thought she'd keep moving and dodging until he tired, but she knew if Grzegorz were to land even one punch, that'd be it for her.

Grzegorz reared back and swung his right hand with all of his might. Ally dodged and put as much distance as she could between them. He was deceptively quick. There was no way she would be able to tire him. She had to think of something else, and fast.

Grzegorz turned and began riling up the crowd. The sound was so loud, her nerves tingled.

That's it!

She'd studied this before. A few years back. She'd read about a Shaolin Monk who'd defeated his opponent with one move. She'd even practiced this with her holotech, but never on a real opponent.

Grzregorz growled and swung a punch, barely giving Ally time to step left. But she delivered a lightning-quick one-two jab with clenched knuckles to his right arm in two places. She leapt back and prepared for the next swing.

The crowd was still screaming, but Grzegorz took a step backwards and dumbfoundedly stared at his right arm. It was hanging limply at his side. She watched him try to lift it, but it just hung there like a dead arm. He looked down at Ally, snarled, and rushed forward, taking a hard swing with his left arm.

Again, she ducked right and punched, targeting his nerves in two places. Then she repositioned herself again and waited. Grzegorz now stood with two dead arms hanging from his sides. He struggled and struggled but could not lift either of them. She'd paralyzed each nerve by hitting them just right.

Grzegorz was stunned. He had no idea what was happening, which only made him more infuriated. He lunged forward and attempted to kick her in the chest. But again she was ready for him. She kicked his extended leg hard in the calf, sending it rocketing upwards and sending him off balance. He fell hard onto his back and Ally launched herself over him.

The crowd fell silent.

Grzegorz grunted, moaned and snarled. He looked up at her, half-confused and half-enraged. "What you do to me?" he barked.

Ally leaned over. "I beat you until nothing left." She stomped him hard in the forehead, sending the back of his head cracking against the springboard, knocking him out.

Slowly, she rose to her feet. The crowd couldn't believe it. There were a few surprised whispers and quiet sounds of disbelief, but the room was silent. The referee checked Grzegorz's pulse, then held up Ally's hand as the winner.

She glowered defiantly toward the bulletproof glass, but something drew her attention. She felt drawn to a section of the crowd. The hairs on the back of her neck stood up. Among the faces of strangers, was one she could never forget. A face that chilled her to the bone. It was Mr. Smith! He stepped through the arena toward the dark corridor that led to the exit.

Ally leapt to the corner of the ring. A bouncer stepped toward her. "Let me out!" she screamed. "Get out of the fucking way!"

The man stepped aside and she darted out past them, sprinting through the parting crowd and knocking into several people. She scrambled past the bookie counter and into the dark corridor.

When she reached the street, she was frantic. *It had to be him! It had to be!* His face was burned into her retinas. She could never forget his cold, dead eyes.

She raced up and down the street, pressing her face through any car windows in the area. But there was no sign of him. He'd vanished.

She took a step, her vision swirling, and nearly lost her balance. She braced herself on a parked car.

What the...?

She pressed a shaky hand to her chest; her heart was trying to break out of her ribcage. Even through her shirt, her skin felt hot, too hot. She tried to inhale, but her lungs felt like they were closing. She couldn't suck in a full breath.

A drowning feeling was rising inside of her now. She tried to walk, but her body refused to obey. She stumbled, catching her balance on a lamp post flickering above her like a strobe light and doubled over. Again, she tried to suck in air, but couldn't get a full breath into her lungs.

Her vision went blurry. Suddenly, there was commotion all around her. Shouting and crashes echoed nearby like she was at an underwater concert. But her mind would not let her focus on anything except her desperation to breathe.

Did someone drug me?

Someone grabbed her by the arm and gripped her throat. Ally blinked, frantically swatting at the arm weakly, gasping for a mouthful of air. The man shoved her and she fell backwards, cracking her head against the pavement. Pain rocketed through her skull. She saw stars. Dazed, she felt the back of her head. It was wet and her ears were ringing.

"Get away from her!" a voice under the water cried.

Curtis?

She must have been seeing things because when she opened her eyes, she was engulfed in a cloud of smoke. Curtis was looking down at her. His mouth was moving, but she couldn't hear him. Her eyes suddenly felt heavy. She was losing consciousness.

Air...

"Curtis… help…" She choked, reaching out and grabbing for his arm, but a big man pushed his chair out of the way.

Now she must really be hallucinating. A ninja suddenly flew over her, colliding with the big man, and through fading vision, she watched this black figure take on six people at once. Through the smoke, his movements were swift and powerful. Within seconds, this man in black had knocked down ten men and was after more.

"Ally! I'm here!"

Curtis?

Darkness crept in and swirled in her eyes. Then she saw only black.

CHAPTER 14

Ally stirred. A faint rhythmic sound chirped beside her. She could hear the bustling of voices whispering nearby. Slowly, she opened her eyes, but hissed and shut them again. The bright fluorescent lights were blinding. She groaned, recoiling from their intensity. All at once, she felt pressure building in her temples, throbbing and threatening to burst the veins in her head.

"Ally, you're okay," came a familiar voice. "You're in the hospital."

"Dr. Hansen?" she asked, squinting.

"Abby, please," she replied, leaning forward now in the chair beside her bed. Her face was tired and concerned.

"Where am I?" Ally asked groggily.

"You're in the hospital. In the recovery wing."

Ally winced. Everything hurt, like she'd taken a nap in a washing machine. "What happened?" she asked. "Why am I here?"

"The nurses say you had a panic attack," Dr. Hansen whispered. "They say you hit your head."

Suddenly, it all came spiraling back to her. If she had to put words to it, it was a series of rings of light, all surging toward her brain and striking her like waves of energy. It's hard to explain. But she remembered everything. She was standing in the ring. The crowd was still and the face of her mother's killer was staring at her like the room had darkened and a spotlight had lit up his face. She could never forget that face.

"Ally?" Dr. Hansen asked. "Should I get the nurse?"

Ally could feel tears forming in her eyes. She couldn't stop them from pouring down her cheeks. She felt herself growing agitated.

"How did you... why are you...?"

"Your friend Curtis called me. You handed him my card just before you passed out," she said. "I came as soon as I could."

She relaxed a little. She remembered Curtis had been there. That made sense. But she had no memory of asking Curtis to call Dr. Hansen. "What time is it?"

"It's after five," she said. "You've been resting for a few hours. Do you know what happened? I mean, do you know what triggered it?"

Ally's body went rigid. There was no way she could tell her doctor that she was in a shady underground fight club. She didn't know what to say. She didn't know what would make her not sound crazy.

Shit. The money! I didn't collect the money! Ugh!

"It's okay, Ally. You can tell me. You can trust me."

"I don't know if I can. Tell you, not trust you."

"Why not? What's the worst that could happen?"

"Oh, I don't know... my probation gets revoked, I go to prison, you think I'm crazy, you commit me, I start alternative therapy—"

"Ok, point taken," she interjected. "Ally, I know trust hasn't been a luxury of yours. But I promise, you can trust me."

Ally took a deep breath and decided to tell her about Mr. Smith. She was wrong about her before. Maybe she really *could* help. *Probably best to leave out the underground cage fight though.*

"I haven't been fully honest with you, Dr. Hansen."

"Abby," she corrected again.

"Ever since... *that night...* I haven't been able to sleep. I probably only sleep one or two hours on average—"

"Would you like me to prescribe you something?"

Ally shook her head in annoyance, instantly regretting it as pain throbbed through her brain. "The reason," she began again, "is because every night when I do manage to fall asleep, I see *him.*"

"Who?"

Ally looked straight into Dr. Hansen's eyes. "Mr. Smith. Ever since I was nine, people have been telling me that my memories and my dreams were delusions. That he was just something my subconscious made up to help me cope. After so many years, I started to wonder if I really *had* seen him… until tonight."

"What do you mean?"

"I saw him, Abby. He was right there. In the street," she lied. "I know it was him."

Dr. Hansen shifted uncomfortably in her seat. "Ally... this is very common with delusional patients. Do you want my advice?"

Ally felt a wave of emotion rise up in her throat. She pressed her head back in the pillow, sighed heavily and shut her eyes, forcing a tear to roll down her cheek. "See?" she gasped. "I knew you wouldn't believe me."

"Ally, I know what it must have felt like. I know that to you, in that moment, it was indistinguishable from reality. I've been doing this a long time. Delusions can manifest themselves in times of stress. They're like mirages. They look and appear real. You probably just had a temporary relapse."

"I saw him, Abby! He was real. He wasn't a delusion."

"Ok…" Abby said. Her body relaxed. "So you saw him on the street?"

Club, street, same difference. "Yes."

"And I assume you chased after him?"

Ally nodded.

"And when you followed him, did you see him then?"

Ally thought back. Mr. Smith had turned and walked out of the underground room. Through the corridor and through the only door to the outside. To the street. But when she got there, he wasn't anywhere to be seen.

"No," Ally half-whispered.

"You see?" Dr. Hansen replied, "You know it was just a delusion. If Mr. Smith were real, you would have seen him in the street when you chased after him."

Ally considered this for a moment. Dr. Hansen had a point. When she'd made it outside, there was no sign of him.

She wanted to scream.

"So what do I do," Ally asked, silent tears falling down her cheeks. "How do I go on like this? I need these delusions to stop." She began sobbing.

"Are you taking your medication?" Dr. Hansen asked.

"Yes, I took two tablets an hour before it happened," she insisted.

Dr. Hansen pressed her thumb under her lower lip. "Maybe we need to prescribe you a stronger dose, or we could try another brand and see if it has a stronger effect?"

Ally reluctantly nodded. She hated taking pills. But if taking them meant these delusions would stop haunting her, then that is what she had to do. "Will they ever stop?" Ally asked.

Dr. Hansen looked at her sympathetically. "You have suffered an extremely traumatic event. The good news is," she said, "your brain is a muscle made up of cells like any other part of your body. You need to train your brain to rewire itself. Through time, therapy, and medication, you will get better. The only thing is, we cannot say for certain how long a trauma will take to heal. Or *if*...

"I can have a new prescription waiting for you by tomorrow. Why don't you swing by my office and pick it up."

"Thank you, Dr. Hansen... Abby," she self-corrected.

"Don't mention it," she said, placing a supportive hand on hers.

Just then, a nurse walked into the room. "Hi Ally. My name is Mindy. I'm the supervising nurse on the floor tonight. How're you feeling?" she asked.

"Tired... groggy... sore, but alright."

"That's perfectly normal. You had a nasty bump to the head when you arrived. The grogginess you feel is from the concussion and the sedative wearing off."

"Sedative?"

"Yeah, when the EMT's arrived, they had to give you a sedative to help you calm down."

Ally didn't remember that.

"Have you ever had panic attacks before?" she asked. Ally shook her head. "Well, panic attacks take a toll on you emotionally, but they really aren't that physically harmful. If they become a regular thing, we'll figure out a way to deal with them, but typically, panic attacks are triggered from stress. I would advise you to lay low for a few days and rest up. No excitement.

"Well, you're free to go," Mindy said. "Don't take this the wrong way, but I hope I never see you again," she said, setting her clothes on the chair.

"Same here," Ally smiled back.

"I'll send in your visitors now," she said, turning toward the door.

"Visitors?"

A moment later, Mindy returned with Curtis, Maury, and another man who looked very much like an older version of Curtis. It must have been his father, Marcus. Then her eyes hardened. Claire was slinking in the back, looking frazzled, like she was hesitant to enter, but then she moved through the threshold and stood just inside.

"Hi Ally," she said softly.

Ally ignored her. She turned her head and glared forward.

"You look well, I mean, considering the circumstances."

"Gee, thanks Claire," Ally said sarcastically. "Yeah, I'm doing *real* well, thanks."

"I just meant—"

"Hey! Where's the rest of the Johnson crew?" she interrupted. "Let me guess, they said you were wasting your time coming here, right?"

Claire shifted her weight awkwardly. "Maybe I should go."

"Yeah, I mean, you showed up, right? You've done your good deed. Now you've got another mother-of-the-year story to share with your friends at the tennis club," she said coldly.

"Ally..." Maury started to say.

Ally's head whirled. "What the hell do you know about it?"

Maury didn't answer. He just blinked at her. She'd have felt bad, but the truth was, it was none of his business.

"It's okay," Claire said. She turned to Ally. "I'm just glad you're okay."

"I'm great, doing great," she continued sarcastically.

"Please call me if you need anything," Claire said. "I really do mean that."

"Uh huh, will do. Bye Claire."

Claire's face couldn't hide the hurt she must have felt. She forced a fake smile and nodded, then turned to the others. "Very nice to meet you all," she said as she slung her purse over her shoulder and slipped past them.

"Nice to meet you too," they said.

For a moment, no one spoke. The room was left in an awkward mist. Ally scowled and looked at the wall.

"Umm, sir?" Dr. Hansen said, looking at Maury. "You're bleeding."

Everyone's attention turned to Maury's arm. Blood was dripping onto the floor far too steadily to be just a scratch. There was a small pool on the cream colored floor.

Maury shifted uncomfortably. He quickly bent his elbow and raised his arm in an attempt to conceal the wound and change the angle of the drainage.

"I'll wait in the car," he muttered.

"I'll walk you out," Dr. Hansen said. "Feel better soon, Ally; I'll see you later." She smiled and gave Ally's hand a comforting squeeze, then left the room.

When the two had gone, Ally threw the hospital blanket off her legs and stood up. She marched over to the chair near the foot of the bed where her clothes had been laid out and bent down to scoop them up. When she turned to face everyone, she could tell something was amiss. Everyone was awkwardly looking away, except for Curtis, who sat with a stupid smirk on his face. It struck her then why her gown had felt a bit drafty. *Whoops*. She cleared her throat and the room got the message. Everybody started to leave so she could change.

"Dad, can I talk with Ally for a moment?" Curtis asked.

Marcus looked at each of them. "One minute. Meet us in the car," he said. Then he left the two alone.

"Here," Curtis said, handing Ally an envelope when they were alone.

She took it, peering at her returned cash bet before sliding out a solitary piece of white paper. "What's this?" she asked, pulling it out.

"It's a cashier's check. You didn't expect to carry out a duffel bag with 50 grand in cash, did you?" he joked. "You ran off so quickly you forgot to get your winnings."

"Thanks, Curtis," she said, looking at the check. "How'd you get this?"

"My dad pulled some strings. I don't think he knew how much you'd won, or he probably wouldn't have sent me to collect." He chuckled nervously.

"So the two of you sorted things out?" she asked.

He shrugged.

"You in trouble?"

"No more than usual." He smiled.

Ally studied his body language carefully. He was hiding something.

"What did you need the money for?" he asked. "What was worth risking your life over?" Ally shrugged. She didn't want to tell him about her plans to move house. "What's really going on with you, Ally? What happened to you on that street?"

"It's getting late. I need to get home. I've got to feed the cat," she said, ignoring his questions.

He raised his eyebrows in defeat and started wheeling back. "Hurry up and get changed. We'll give you a ride home."

She was about to protest because she really could use the fresh air and time to think, but realized she wouldn't be able to convince them that she'd be safe walking home, especially at night. Plus, the weather report predicted snow tonight and it might actually stick. She didn't feel like walking home a few miles in the snow.

A few minutes later, she reluctantly followed Curtis to the car.

"So where do you live?" Maury asked as she climbed in the back seat. Ally casually looked up and offered him the Johnsons's address. She didn't want them to see where she really lived. But Maury put the car into park, turned his body around and looked at her. "Where do you *really* live?" he repeated.

"What do you mean?" She tried to look and sound confused.

"Look, it's not my business, but when we were in the lobby waiting for you to wake up, Claire mentioned you've lived on your own for nearly a year. She said if I wanted to know where, I'd have to ask you."

Ally turned her head. "That's because she doesn't know."

"Actually, she does. She said she followed you one time. She was worried about you. She said she still checks in on you every once in a while, just to make sure you're safe."

Ally gazed out the window. She honestly didn't think Claire cared. When she first proposed the financial arrangements, she expected Claire to put up a fight. But she didn't. Except for tonight at the hospital, she hadn't seen her or the rest of the family again.

With resignation, she sighed and directed Maury to her slum full of containers. As he drove, she had to make small talk most of the way but eventually the conversation died down and she rode the rest of the way in a comfortable silence.

Laying her hands in her lap, she felt the lump in her pocket. The envelope felt heavy against her leg. She smiled, imagining Piggy bounding around in her new house, somewhere warmer and safer than the converted storage container held together by a botched welding job.

She reached her fingers into the envelope and felt the wrinkled bills, imagining a possible new future. Now that she had tonight's winnings, she thought about all the things *normal* kids would do with it: buy fancy clothes and accessories, shoes... and to be able to actually eat at restaurants again. *Anyone who said money can't buy you happiness obviously doesn't know what it is like to be poor,* she thought. Then her thoughts betrayed her. She thought of Sandy, of the past due rent letters, of the looming eviction.

Ally pulled the cashier's check out of the envelope and signed the back of it. On the envelope she wrote: *For your next battle.*

"Maury? If it's alright with you, I'd like to make a stop first."

He looked back at her through the rearview mirror and nodded. She directed him to Sandy's place. As he drove closer, Ally noticed some red and blue lights flashing in the darkness ahead and she felt a lump in her throat. She'd seen this before. Eight years ago.

As the car slowed, an ambulance and three police cars came into view. She watched in horror as the EMTs loaded a gurney into one of the ambulances. She didn't have to see who it was; she knew it was Sandy.

Before the car had completely stopped, Ally leapt out, but an officer headed her off and held her back. Through flooded tears, she watched the EMTs shut the door. Then a flash drew her attention. A second body was being photographed. A man with salt and pepper hair was lying on his back in a pool of blood. His throat had been cut.

Ally dropped to her knees and cried.

CHAPTER 15

Two hours earlier, atop an unfinished construction platform in a sea of skyscrapers, a strong wind howled through the scaffolding, blowing bits of snow through the metal safety grating. Fisher clutched his coat tightly around himself as he ascended in the slow lift. From up here, the city below looked peaceful, like a storybook about the spirit of Christmas, where tiny flickering lights sparkled like distant stars through black chimney smoke.

"Jesus... it's freezing!" Fisher muttered, flicking up his collar around his neck.

In front of him, stood three men. There was Mr. Sherman, an idiot lawyer in a thousand dollar suit. He stuck out like a sore thumb in the bitter cold, shuffling his weight from one foot to the other. To his left, stood Hal Burton, an elderly tycoon in his late 70s, wrapped warmly in a scarf and beanie, and a coat that likely cost more than Fisher's car. Beside him, was his guard dog. Unlike the other men, the cold air seemingly had no effect on him, a hardened assassin. Fisher had heard him referred to as Mr. Clark, but he was known by many other names.

"Whose cheerful idea was it to meet all the way up here?" Fisher asked.

"You're late," Hal grunted.

Fisher checked himself and swallowed uneasily. He wasn't accustomed to being scolded like a teenager. Ordinarily, he set his own agendas and arrival times for his business affairs. He was Andrew Fisher and not some worthless peon. But this meeting was different. As powerful as he was in his own dealings, he knew that he didn't retain that power here. So he swallowed his pride and checked his ego.

"Apologies. There was another matter that required my attention," he grumbled.

"Nice priorities," came a deep voice.

Fisher turned his head. Felix Overguaard leaned against a support column and blew out a cloud of cigar smoke. His face was concealed by the shadows of the building, his eyes lit only by the red glow of the cigar.

"What's *he* doing here?" Fisher growled.

"We are here to discuss how we proceed," Hal replied.

Fisher squinted his eyes and felt the severity of the situation. He was fully aware of the numbers. He'd lost a considerable amount of money on the last fight. That girl had caused one of the largest upsets in his recollection. He didn't even have enough money in the safe to cover the losses.

"It's being handled," Fisher huffed coldly.

"That's not good enough," Hal said. "Phase 2 is rapidly approaching and we cannot tolerate incompetence at this juncture."

"Incompetence!" Fisher snapped.

Mr. Clark took a half-step forward and Fisher instantly checked himself. His eyes shot to the floor and he bowed his head in submission. He had no intention of challenging a man like Mr. Clark. He'd witnessed his methods before. Brutal and savage. Mr. Clark was the type of man you only hear whispers about. The type that doesn't exist on paper. Corporations sometimes refer to them as fixers, mechanics or economic hitmen. These are dangerous men or women contracted to correct various *agitations* to industry. People without records, allegiances or conscience. He knew if given the order, he wouldn't hesitate.

Fisher swallowed hard. "Forgive me," he groveled. "I'll get the money back."

"See?" Felix said, gesturing at Hal, who nodded in silent agreement.

Fisher narrowed his eyes, feeling like the butt of a bad joke. "See what?" he was forced to ask.

"The disruption to the cash flow is not why we're here," Hal clarified. "You let your ego get in the way of our business arrangements. What were you thinking, letting that girl fight in your club? What if she was killed by the Pole? That is the kind of attention which could have jeopardized the entire operation. The last thing we need is a murder investigation and some idealistic cop sniffing around. I have half a mind to let Mr. Clark throw you off this building right now!" he barked.

Fisher clenched his teeth to remind himself of his place. He knew he needed to be careful here. Any excuse or sign of weakness would turn the tables. "I said, I'm handling it. The club has been wiped. There is no sign we were ever there."

Hal looked at Mr. Clark, who nodded like he'd already inspected it.

"My guys are tying up the loose ends as we speak. You'll have your money back within 24 hours."

Hal sighed. "Maybe what we need *is* stronger leadership." He turned to Felix. "How long would it take you to absorb Mr. Fisher's operations?"

"Not long," Felix replied, flashing Fisher a smirk.

It took all Fisher's strength not to rush him and bash his skull in with one of the tools lying around the construction site. But he knew the consequences of such an act. So instead, he did nothing except look at Hal, praying he wasn't actually considering putting that maniac in charge of his affairs.

Hal finally turned his head. "Mr. Sherman?"

The lawyer cleared his throat. "Uh, she rejected your offer."

Hal narrowed his eyes. "You told me you could handle this."

"I can. I just need a little—"

"Yeah? Then why ain't it done yet?" Felix piped in.

Mr. Sherman looked around nervously. All eyes were on him and expecting an adequate response. "Look, you said you wanted this done quietly, and *quietly* takes time. People have rights. I can assure you, I am pursuing all legal channels."

"I could take care of your tenant problem for you tonight. Just say the word," Felix interjected.

Hal considered his options. He took a deep breath and let it out, then turned to Felix. "Remove the tenant," he said. "Tonight."

"You can't do that!" Mr. Sherman blurted, turning three heads. He swallowed and tried to sound brave. "I won't let you."

"You hear that, gentlemen?" Hal asked rhetorically. "That's the sound of a man who's outlived his usefulness. Mr. Clark, show Mr. Sherman why we *can do that*."

A little spark ignited in the assassin's eyes. He moved toward the lawyer and didn't stop until he had a firm hand on the back of his neck. Mr. Sherman squirmed and struggled to resist but the man wasn't fazed. Mr. Clark walked him right up to the edge of the building and without so much as a push, sent Mr. Sherman straight down to the pavement below.

Fisher heard the man's scream gradually fade until a faint splatter silenced the night again.

"Does this mean I'm still in charge?" Fisher asked, trying to look unfazed.

"Replacing you so near to the coming shipment might complicate matters, so for now, we will continue as planned."

Fisher breathed out a silent sigh of relief.

"I hope for your sake, you can manage to toe the line, Mr. Fisher. Do we understand each other?"

"Yes."

Hal stepped forward and made his way toward the lift, but turned back when Fisher called his name. "Mr. Burton? With your permission, sir, I'd like to remove the tenant myself. It's a personal matter."

Hal considered the request, eyed the others, then nodded. After a moment's pause, Mr. Clark turned, his black eyes boring a hole into Fisher's soul. His eyes said he knew something more than Hal and Felix did. Something that Fisher should know too, but for some reason was holding his tongue. It was almost like a *see you soon* kind of look that made his skin crawl. Then the lift descended.

Felix smirked as he passed and headed down the staircase.

When Fisher was sure everyone was out of earshot, he screamed loudly, picked up a few construction tools and bashed them into whatever he could find. Then he adjusted his tie, smoothed his hair, and took a deep breath before turning and descending the staircase.

Fisher stepped over Mr. Sherman's body, or rather, the stain on the pavement where his body had landed. Some of Felix's men had already made it disappear. But they'd yet to scrub away the blood, brain matter, and bone fragments which now coated the path.

Fisher approached a black Audi parked across the street and Darrell opened the rear door for him.

"Where to, boss?" Zane asked when he'd seated himself in the back. Fisher read out the address and Zane shifted into gear and drove until they pulled up just outside a run-down container.

The rest of the neighborhood had already been vacated. There were just a few more containers on the lot preventing BC Construction from excavating the site. Remains of the meteor shower, which cascaded down all over parts of Grace City years ago, were rumored to be embedded in the soil. Despite multiple attempts to relocate the residents civilly, Fisher now had no choice but to carry out Hal's wishes.

He stepped up to the porch and raised his hand to knock, but the door chain unclicked and the deadbolt slid aside. Sandy was standing in the doorway wrapped in a warm dressing gown and hat. They had hoped shutting off her heating would encourage her to move. But she was harder than they gave her credit for.

"I wondered how long it would be before you'd show up," she muttered, with a surprisingly strong voice.

"How are you Ms. Sutton?" Fisher asked with sincerity.

"I'm cold. And tired," she said grumpily. "Come in, please," she offered. "Would you like a cup of tea?"

"Tea would be lovely," Fisher said and stepped into the house and shut the door behind him.

When the pot had boiled, Sandy set the cup down in front of him, then sat opposite. "I'm sorry, I can't offer you milk or sugar." She held up the bottle of alcohol, overing him a spike.

Fisher shook his head. "Black tea will be just fine." He reached forward and sliding the cup of tea slightly closer to him, then hesitated before taking a sip.

"I must say, you surprise me," he said. "You… *do* know why I'm here..."

"I know," she said.

"So why invite me in? Why offer me tea? Why not get a knife or poison my tea?" he asked.

"How do you know I *didn't* poison the tea?" she quipped.

Fisher smiled and picked up the cup in his hand, then took a careful sip, letting the hot water warm his insides. "Can I ask you a question?" he asked. Sandy shrugged. "Why didn't you just take the money we offered you?"

Sandy took a sip and leaned back in her chair. She thought about it, then after a moment, decided what she wanted to say. "I made a decision. It was as simple as that."

"So you *want* to die."

"I didn't say that. I have chosen to let you in, to treat you with kindness and love, to offer you tea. The choice of whether or not I die, is yours."

Fisher sat for a moment. He didn't mind killing when the adversary deserved it. But this was a woman in her late 70s. It just felt wrong. She reminded him of his mother. Every instinct was telling him to walk away. But he had a job to do and didn't want to drag it out any longer. He'd volunteered to spare Sandy the unpleasant death Felix would have offered her. A death of pain and violence and fear.

With a heavy heart, he retrieved the gun from his holster and set it on the table. "You can shut your eyes, if you want…"

"No guns," she said.

Fisher cocked his head sideways and tried to read Sandy's expression.

"Use your hands."

Fisher couldn't help but blink. This woman had a choice to live, but chose death. She had a choice to die painlessly and quick, but chose to suffer. As he looked into her eyes, he suddenly understood. Strangling her meant he had to choose to take a life and had to commit to that choice for every second of it. A lot of men couldn't stomach it. He didn't know if he could. But felt he owed it to her, as a last request.

Fisher nodded and placed the gun back into its holster. He slowly stood up and walked around the table. Then he raised his hands and placed them gently around her neck.

Sandy's pulse was racing. She was taking loud, quick breaths through her nose, refusing to blink. She stared right into Fisher's eyes.

"Are you ready?" he finally asked.

"I'm ready."

Then she went still and her breathing stopped as Fisher tightened his grip.

"I'm sorry," he whispered softly.

She never took her eyes off his. It took her longer to die than Fisher was expecting. Even when her body began twitching, her hands remained clenched to the arm rests until at last, her body went limp.

Fisher released his grip, placed his hand over Sandy's eyes and closed them. Then he slowly picked up his tea, washed the cup, and placed it into the dry rack. He knew this night would always haunt him.

Satisfied the forensic evidence was taken care of, he opened the door and froze. A bearded man with salt and pepper hair cried out on the threshold and pulled his fist away mid-knock. Fisher blinked.

"Who are you?" the man asked, scrutinizing him. Then he peered around his shoulder.

CHAPTER 16

The next morning, Ally approached her locker, pausing briefly to read the note taped to it. As she scanned the words, a sense of apprehension began to bubble.

Ally,

Please come see me in my office when you get in. We need to talk.

-Maury

Ally sighed heavily. She'd known this was bound to happen. She'd poked and prodded enough to practically guarantee it. So why did she have such an ugly feeling in the pit of her stomach? She turned and made her way to the office.

Maury was sitting at his desk talking with what looked like another lawyer. This man was different. He had a greasy loan shark written all over him. His hair was slicked back and his suit looked expensive.

She was about to leave and come back later, but Maury saw her and held up his index finger. He stood up from his desk and walked over to the door, opened it for the suit, and gestured for him to leave.

The man chuckled, closed his briefcase and stood. "We'll be in touch," he muttered, petting Ally's figure with his pervy eyes as he walked through the door.

Ally noted his shoes and made a face. They looked like gator leather and had some kind of tacky insignia on the toe that reminded her of a hood ornament for a Rolls-Royce.

Maury's sour expression faded and he put on a smile. "Come in, Ally. Have a seat. How are you after last night?"

Ally nodded. "I'm okay. Thanks."

"Last night, you seemed pretty upset. Were you close to them?"

"The man was my landlord. I'd only met the woman the other night. She was…" Ally sighed, "someone I was planning on getting to know better."

Maury nodded. "It's a shame. The police think her landlord killed her over a rent dispute, then slit his own throat after he'd realized what he'd done. Just a sad situation."

Ally thought for a moment. Mr. Despotes didn't seem the type. Ally'd been late on her rent several times and the worst he'd ever done was lock her out. Then she remembered the buyout. *Why would he kill Sandy over money when he was about to be rich?* It didn't add up.

"He wouldn't have done that," Ally said.

"Of course," he said, though she doubted he believed her. Maury walked over to his desk and began tidying, picking up a pile of scattered papers which were sprawled out on the corner and moved them aside. One fell to the floor and Ally instinctively reached down to pick it up. It was a foreclosure letter. Final notice. She stared at it in shock.

"You weren't supposed to see that," he said with regret in his voice and took it gently from her hand. "Don't worry, I have it under control."

Ally stared at him for a moment as a rush of emotions bubbled up inside of her. She'd just started to like this place. And now, like everything else in her life, it was about to be taken away. She couldn't hold back any longer. "Well, maybe if you were paying your bills instead of paying off mobsters you wouldn't be having money troubles."

Maury cocked his head. "What?"

"Oh, don't even pretend, Maury. I saw you hand that envelope to Fisher. How much was in there, huh? And don't try and tell me I didn't see what I saw."

Maury shut the door and paused.

"Tell me this dojo isn't laundering money for the mob," she sneered.

He turned back to her, his eyebrows raised and his face somber. "Is that what you think? That I'm involved with that guy? That I'm dirty or corrupt?"

She shrugged. "I suppose this is when you tell me you're not."

"Ally, you have it all wrong."

"Here it comes…"

"Ally, just listen to me for a second," he began. "Please?"

Ally crossed her arms and glared at him.

"You're right. It *was* a payoff. But not for what you think." He sat down in his chair and took a deep breath.

"Six years ago, my wife and I were walking home after having dinner. We were celebrating. We'd just found out she was pregnant. On the way, a few teenage boys stepped out of the alley. One of them had a gun," he said, tears pooling up in his eyes. "Anisa tried to talk to them... to get them to walk away, but they shot her. Her last words to me were, '*they don't have anybody.*'"

Maury hung his head and went quiet.

"So when I could, I turned my efforts into this place. I promised myself that I would do everything in my power to help at-risk young people and try to be there for them. To see people the way my wife did."

"And the payoff? Did you borrow money from men like Fisher?" Ally asked.

Maury shook his head. "No. I pay him every month so that our boys aren't recruited by his organization. Fisher looks out for them. He makes sure that local gangs don't allow them in. He lets me know if any of my boys's names pop up."

Ally felt a wave of guilt sweep over her. She *did* have it all wrong. "I'm sorry. I didn't know."

Maury waved his hand dismissively. "Anisa died believing that one moment in a person's life didn't define them. Before she died, this was her fight. Now it's mine. I like to think this is what she would have wanted."

"What are you going to do?" she asked. "About the money?"

"I don't want you to worry about that. It's my problem. We always manage. Last night, Curtis set up a GoFundMe page online. People are generous. It's the holidays."

Ally felt like there was something that Maury wasn't telling her. She was getting this feeling a lot lately. "Well, I should probably let you get back to… whatever it is that you were doing."

"Actually, there's one more thing I wanted to talk with you about."

Just then the door opened and Big Mike poked his head in. "You ready, boss?" he asked.

Maury looked at Ally. "You hungry? We could talk over food. My treat," he said, standing up.

Ally shrugged. She couldn't say no to free food, so she followed him out of the office.

Curtis gave one last pointer to a patron before coming over. "Hey Ally. Thanks for fixing my gear."

"What are friends for?" she said, grinning down at him.

His face crinkled. "Stop that; I don't like it," he said, turning to follow Maury.

Ally smirked and shook her head. *Dick.*

When they'd walked five or six blocks, she learned Maury had arranged to take the day off and take them out for a late brunch at one of the greatest breakfast burrito joints on the planet, according to him.

As the three of them passed through the door, they were instantly greeted by Roxanne, the owner. "Hey Maury!"

"How you doin', Roxie?"

"The usual?"

"Make it three," he smiled, holding up three fingers.

"Sure thing."

The three of them made their way to a table and five minutes later, three breakfast specials arrived—three braised tofu-scramble sofritas with the works. Ally's mouth began to water. The smell alone was intoxicating and she found herself inhaling her burrito. Her eyes rolled back in her head. She hadn't eaten like this in years.

After the third bite, she noticed their eyes on her. Curtis hung his mouth around the end of his burrito, and Maury motioned for Roxie to bring over another.

"Good, huh?" Curtis asked, smiling with a mouthful.

She swallowed and nodded, placing the half-eaten burrito onto her plate and slowing down to chew. Roxie brought over another plate and set it in the middle of the table. She flashed Ally a smile and went back to serving.

"Ally, I have a confession to make. I asked you here for a reason. I want you to know that I am here for you if you ever need anything, or need someone to talk to. What you shared with me in my office… I want you to know you're not alone."

Ally's expression fell a little. She nodded. "Thank you."

"After our last conversation, I wanted to offer you my help—" Curtis cleared his throat. "—Our help," Maury clarified. "Will you tell Curtis what you told me? He's a brilliant researcher. If there is anything to find, he'll find it."

Ally considered this, weighing up the pros and cons of sharing these private details of her life. Letting them in was a risk, but if it led to even the slightest chance of finding the truth, she had to take it. She sighed and began to tell Curtis everything. That for the past eight years, she resisted the idea that she was delusional, how she spent countless hours in therapy trying to fight that diagnosis, about the various psychiatric drugs they'd told her would correct her *imbalance*. About the dreams. About the night at the warehouse where she almost killed the wrong man. That, in that moment, she knew she *was* delusional. Last night, when she saw the killer in the flesh, her head was spiraling. She didn't know what to believe anymore.

"And that's what you think caused the panic attack?" Maury asked. "Seeing Mr. Smith?"

Ally shrugged. "Maybe. I don't know… I was sure I saw him. Only, at the hospital, Dr. Hansen said," she paused, "maybe she's right. Maybe all of this was triggered by stress... like a mirage."

Curtis screwed up his face. "That seems like dumb advice."

Ally shook her head. "I've looked it up. Intense trauma can cause PTSD, or in rare cases, delusions. Maybe my memories are just delusions created to cope with the trauma." A hollow chuckle escaped her lips. "I don't know what to do. I'm supposed to pick up my prescription soon. But I can't shake it, what if they're not delusions? What if they're real?"

"If they're real, then maybe you shouldn't be trying to repress them. Maybe you should be trying to let them out," Maury said.

"How? How do I know if I can trust what's in my head?"

He rested his finger on his lip, thinking. "How certain are you that you saw him that night?"

Ally shook her head. "Then, 100%. Now? I don't know what's real anymore."

"Maybe we should go to the police? I could come with you…"

Ally gave him a look. "A girl with a history of delusions claims to have seen an assassin in an illegal underground fight club run by a notorious mobster?"

Maury raised his brows and frowned. "Yeah, you're right... that probably wouldn't go down well," he said, tapping his fingers on the table. After a few seconds, he looked at Curtis, who nodded in affirmation.

"Ally, we'd like to help you, if you'll let us."

"How? I just told you the police don't believe me. Been trying for years."

He shared a quick glance at Curtis. "There are other ways of investigating."

CHAPTER 17

An hour later, Maury dropped Ally and Curtis off about two blocks from the police station. Initially, when they'd offered to help, she thought it was out of pity, but here they were. Curtis said he had a plan but was being very cloak and dagger about it. She hated being kept out of the loop and trusting people wasn't one of her strongest impulses. But what was more annoying was that despite her protests, they were now heading to the one place she said was a dead end.

"This is a waste of time," Ally grumbled. "I told you, the police don't believe me."

"Trust me. I've got a plan," Curtis said.

"And this plan involves *not* telling me what we're doing? Great plan…"

"You just tell the sketch artist about Mr. Smith and I'll take care of the rest."

"Whatever that means," she muttered, rolling her eyes and going quiet.

They made their way past a larger crowd with picket signs, still protesting the acquisition of land by Burton Conglomerates. The size of this protest had nearly doubled. Men, women and children were chanting, yelling and waving their signs and banners wildly in the air. Beside them, a large battalion of riot police carefully stood nearby, watching the protestors.

"Jesus… this is a bit overkill," Ally muttered.

"Yeah, well… doesn't surprise me. All the news has been yakin' about is the inevitable clash, not the message. And police don't have patience with protestors. To them, we're just thugs, rioters or looters rather than people with just cause. The only response they know how to do is show force," Curtis said, pulling up to one of the barricades.

An officer held up his hand. "What's your business here?" he grunted. His movements were quick and jerky like he was strung out on adrenaline. His eyes darted back and forth like he was studying the massive crowd and seemed to barely register the two of them.

"We're here to see a sketch artist," Curtis said. "Child rapist. Big guy, about your height; brown hair, stubbly face… sort of an ugly I just smacked your mother kinda expression. You seen anyone like that 'round here?"

Ally stiffened and swallowed, knowing full well Curtis was describing the cop in front of him.

The officer looked down and seemed to glare at him from under his riot helmet and face shield. His bloodshot eyes then flashed to Ally. Grudgingly, he stepped aside, letting the two of them slip past the line of riot police.

The inside of the precinct was bustling with officers, detectives, lawyers, and various clients. It was far busier than earlier in the week.

"Maybe we should come back another time," Ally muttered.

"No, we're gonna see this through," Curtis replied, moving his way toward the reception desk.

Ally caught sight of a security guard watching them from beside the desk, his hand resting on his side holster.

"At ease McClain," Curtis joked. The guard glared at him, but did eventually remove his hand from the top of his holster and reinserted his two thumbs into his front belt loops. But he never took his eyes off them.

When Curtis reached the reception desk, the receptionist greeted him with a tired politeness. "We are here to see a sketch artist. We called ahead," he said.

The receptionist turned to face the computer screen, tapped a couple keys, and pulled up the appointment. She reached behind her and handed Curtis a clipboard where he was told to sign in. It was a standard form, one that asked about the purpose for the visit, what time they entered, and who they were seeing.

Curtis filled out the form and handed it back to the receptionist. "I'll let them know you're here," she said and picked up the telephone. "You can wait over there," she pointed. Curtis and Ally nodded and entered the waiting area.

"So, are you going to tell me what the plan is?"

Curtis winked at her. "Nope."

"Come on, Curtis!"

"You know when directors of films sometimes don't tell the actors what is about to happen so that they can capture a real reaction? This is kind of like that. If I told you, then this wouldn't work. But there is one thing I need from you. When you're giving the description to the sketch artist, I need you to make sure his attention stays on you."

"Why?"

"You have your role… I have mine."

Ally raised an eyebrow, studying him and trying to imagine what he had up his sleeve.

"Ally Keebum?" called a voice from across the room. "Ally Keebum?"

"Here!" Curtis yelled, waving at the officer and pointing. "She's a leaky bum."

Ally's eyes widened. "I'm gonna kill you!" She jumped to her feet and grabbed for his arm, but he had already launched forward and out of her grasp, cackling all the way to the officer and through the door.

The officer stifled a chuckle, now getting the joke, and led them through to the back of the precinct and over to a cubicle in one of the far corners. He told them to sit down at the desk where a man was sitting with a sketch pad. He didn't look like a policeman. Sometimes civilians who were formerly trained by the FBI or other agencies were contracted on a freelance basis to do composite sketches for the police. His long greasy hair and beard definitely reinforced that he was not police.

"My name is Doug," the man said. "I'm going to ask you a series of questions and what I would like you to do is just clarify any details. Let me know what areas of the sketch to adjust, and tell me anything you can remember no matter how small. Are you okay with that?" Ally nodded. "Okay, let's start with gender."

"Male."

"Ethnicity?"

"Caucasian," she said.

"Can you describe his hair for me?"

"Slicked back. He had a ponytail."

Doug kept asking questions and began sketching. Ally closed her eyes and forced the images from her dreams back into her conscious mind. Each flashing image was like pins poking all over her brain. She felt sick several times. These were not images she wanted to relive. But she had to trust that Curtis's plan would be worth it.

After several minutes, Doug held up the preliminary sketch for her. Ally told him to make a few adjustments to the hairline before nodding and being satisfied with it. Over the next several minutes, the artist asked her questions regarding shape of eyes, size of nose, lips, facial hair, and other identifiable features, each time pausing to hold up the sketch for her to make adjustments to each part of the face.

Suddenly, she noticed Curtis was positioned way over by the little room on the far wall. He had his hand on the doorknob under a sign that read: Staff Only. Ally wondered how in the world he'd gotten there without her knowing. Without anyone knowing for that matter. He caught her gaze and she tried to mouth, 'What are you doing?' but Officer Myers, who'd escorted them over to the desk, suddenly looked up.

Ally opened her mouth, pretending to yawn and stretched out her arms, lifting them to the ceiling. Myers averted his gaze and she watched helplessly as Curtis turned the doorknob.

The door made a small popping sound when it broke away from the doorframe. Officer Myers looked up and nearly turned around, but Ally reached out and knocked over a cup of coffee on the table. Apologizing profusely and flapping about the desk, she managed to distract Myers enough to forget about the sound he'd heard behind him. In fact, he seemed to have forgotten entirely about Curtis.

Each minute he was inside the server room made Ally more nervous. *What if he was discovered? How could he possibly explain his way out of something like that?* What perhaps gave her more dread was, *what if everyone noticed he was gone. What if they asked her where he went? What would she say? What could she say?* She didn't even know. She blinked hard and tried to focus on Doug.

About 10 minutes later, Curtis emerged from the room, shutting the door behind him, and pulled up next to the desk. He flashed her a wink before turning toward the sketch artist.

After what seemed like an hour, Doug held up the finalized sketch. Ally's heart began to thump in her chest again and could feel her mouth and throat go dry. She nodded quickly. "That's him," she said in a half-whisper.

Doug handed the sketch to Officer Myers.

"I'll send this up the chain of command and they'll run it through facial recognition. If we get any hits, we'll call you and see what we can do about bringing you in for a line up," Myers said.

"What are the chances of finding this guy?" Ally asked.

"To be honest, not good. If he's already been arrested, we'll get a hit. If it's his first offense, we'll get nothing, unless he gets caught committing another crime."

Ally nodded sadly.

"How long does this usually take?" Curtis asked.

"To run it through the criminal database? About 6 hours."

"What about the other databases?"

"What do you mean? Like interpol?"

"Possibly... or some other database… like if this person is a cop, or a mercenary or soldier..."

Officer Myers stared at him skeptically. "I can run it through all the databases available to us but that will take more time. Probably a few days."

Curtis and Ally nodded.

"Is there anything else I can do for you guys?" he asked.

"Would it be possible for us to get a copy of that sketch?" Curtis asked. Ally looked at him suspiciously.

"Sure. Be back in a sec." Officer Myers stood up and walked over to the photocopier, which was far too close for Ally to ask Curtis what he'd just been up to. Moreover, she didn't know why Curtis asked for a copy. Wasn't the point of this whole thing to run his face through the databases? Curtis was up to something.

When Ally turned her head, she felt her heart twitch. Myers was speaking to Lieutenant Michaels. He had the sketch in his hands and was examining it. She'd seen that expression many times before. Resignation. Like a disapproving teacher after finding out a delinquent student was in trouble again. A moment later, he followed Myers back to the desk and gazed down at her disapprovingly.

"Ally. Your therapist know you're here?"

Ally ignored him.

Michaels's eyes fell back to the sketch. "So this is Mr. Smith, huh?" He half-shook his head, sighed, and handed the sketch back to Meyers. "Let me know if you get any hits. Take care, Ally."

"Wait!" Ally cried, making him turn. "The murder-suicide… the one in South End? In the Container Park…"

"What about it?"

"I think the police have it wrong."

"Do you," he said cynically. "And why is that?"

"I knew Mr. Despotes. He'd told me that BC offered him a buyout. He joked that he would nearly be able to afford a place in Sterling Heights."

"Your point?"

"Why would he kill Sandy over money when he was about to be rich? It doesn't add up."

Michaels chuckled. "Money changes people. Sometimes people get a taste and greed takes over. Simple as that."

"But surely it's worth looking into," she insisted.

Michaels looked at Curtis, then back to her. "Thanks for the tip. I'll have my guys look into it."

Ally scoffed. "No wonder you never found my family's killer."

He reared on her, his eyes alight. But he turned and headed back toward the back offices.

Curtis reached out and took the sketch from Meyers's outstretched hand, folded it into quarters, and put it in his inside jacket pocket.

"So, I guess that's it," Officer Myers said. Curtis and Ally nodded their heads, shook hands and thanked Doug for his time before they left the station.

They exited through the entrance and proceeded back to the police barricade again. It was then Ally felt safe enough to ask. "How did you manage to disappear like that? And how did you know that cop wouldn't notice you were gone?"

"Side-effects of being in a wheelchair," he said, "Half the time you're invisible."

She couldn't tell if he was joking or serious. "What were you doing back there?" she demanded.

"Trade secrets my friend," he said slyly.

"Seriously, Curtis, what did you do in that room? What was this about? You know as well as I do that this guy isn't gonna come up on any of the database searches. What were we really doing there? And why won't you tell me?"

Curtis stopped and went quiet. He looked like he was deep in thought. His mouth opened a few times as if he were trying to speak, but couldn't find the words. Finally, he said, "I can't tell you."

"Why not?"

"Because it isn't my secret to tell," he said.

"Secret?"

He pursed his lips. "Come on. There is something else we need to do."

"And I suppose you're not going to tell me about this either?"

"No, this I can tell you. You mentioned your mother used to work for Burton Conglomerates. It's a long shot, but I thought maybe your mother's old partner might recognize the guy in the sketch. So I figured, why not pay him a little visit?"

Ally felt her heart flutter. She'd never even thought about asking Dr. Hayagawa. If he knew or recognized Mr. Smith, it would confirm his existence! That would mean she wasn't crazy! Curtis did have a plan! For the first time in a long time, she felt hopeful. And if he recognized him, it would give her the first real piece of evidence to jumpstart the investigation. She just had to hope it wasn't a huge waste of time.

CHAPTER 18

When Ally reached the outside of Burton Conglomerates, she was humbled to see the immense skyscraper looming above. It was a modern sleek building which obviously spared no expense in its construction.

Inside, evenly distributed beams of light poured from the high ceiling, complimented by giant windows which added to the room's beauty and luster. Large marble tiles spanned the floor in a sea of metallic gray and hint of cream. Even the reception desk was futuristic in its design and everything in the lobby sparkled with luxury. It was like stepping into a palace.

Curtis and Ally approached the reception desk and Curtis laid on the charm. "Hiya… Dolly," he said, leaning in to study her name tag with a pleasant smile. His eyes gradually crept up from her name tag until they were eye to eye. "You're gorgeous."

Dolly eyed him apathetically as if to call his bluff. "You're going to have to try a lot harder than that, kid," she grunted.

"Dolly is such a pretty name, isn't it Ally?" Curtis said, smacking her on the shoulder with the back of his hand and breaking her thoughts.

"It's a beautiful name," she chimed in, trying to sound convincing.

"Cut the shit, kid. What do you want?"

"We were hoping we could speak with Dr. Hayagawa."

"Do you have an appointment?"

"See, that's the thing…"

"I'm sorry sugar, but nobody is allowed to see anybody without an appointment. Company policy."

"Do you think Dr. Hayagawa would make an exception for an old friend?" Ally asked.

Dolly smirked. "Old? Girl, how old are you?"

"My mother and him were partners. About eight years ago."

"Who is your mother?"

"Sara Reid."

The receptionist eyed her a moment, then her eyes brightened. "Oh! You are Dr. Sara Reid's daughter?" Dolly asked, smiling big and Ally and Curtis both nodded their heads. Her smile fell quicker than a lead balloon, "Never heard of her."

"Look, could you please just phone him? If he doesn't want to see us, I will buy you dinner," Ally said.

Dolly eyed her again. "For real?" Ally nodded. "Ok, you're on," she said, picking up the phone and dialing the number. The phone rang for what seemed like forever. Just as she was about to hang up, the line clicked on and a man answered. "Good afternoon, sir. I'm sorry to bother you, but there is a gentleman and a lady here who have asked to speak with you."

At the mention of a *lady*, Curtis giggled and Ally punched him in the shoulder. "Shut up!" she hissed.

"I know, I told them that, but the girl says you know her. She claims to be Sara Reid's daughter."

There was a pause on the line.

"All right, sir, thank you very much. Goodbye." Dolly set the phone down and turned to face the two in front of her.

"Well?" Curtis asked.

"A security guard will escort you up to the lab," she said gruffly, slumping her shoulders.

Curtis and Ally did a mini celebration and thanked the receptionist for making the call. She nodded apathetically and went back to her work.

A few moments later, a security guard arrived and introduced himself. Ally's jaw immediately dropped. Policemen were usually about three steps away from a heart attack, but this guy looked more like a fireman. He was annoyingly handsome, the kind of handsome people need to stare at. The cliché tall, dark and uniformed. It seemed to hug his physique. He had a chiseled jawline like a Batman comic and his glasses were likely designer. Both Curtis and Ally seemed to swallow their tongues.

"Hey guys. I'm Jeffrey. If you could follow me, I'll take you up," he said and led them to the escalators which ascended to the first floor. Ally and Curtis flashed him a contemptuous look and waited for it to click. "Sorry," he said, sheepishly. "The elevator is over here."

Curtis shot Ally a duckface and rolled his eyes. She wondered how often people neglected to consider others with limited mobility.

As the elevator rose up through the floors of the skyscraper, Curtis and Ally stared wide-eyed out of the glass enclosure. The building was truly incredible and each floor seemed more expensive than the next.

When the elevator finally reached the 78th floor, the doors opened and Jeffrey escorted them through a long corridor and into a science laboratory. This room was also immaculate. Everything was white, from the cubicles and shelving to the equipment and doors. The walls were painted white, the floor was white. Even the lights were LED white. The only thing that added a little bit of contrast were the black table tops and chair cushions.

Jeffrey led them to a workstation near the fire exit where a middle-aged man sat at his computer screen busily working. When the footsteps echoed across the empty lab and reached Dr. Katsuto Hayagawa, he looked up and greeted them.

"Ally?" he asked, holding out his hand. "Oh my God… you look just like her! I can hardly believe it. You are the spitting image of your mother." Ally took his hand and smiled back. "I can't believe this. What has it been? 10 years?"

"Eight," she said.

Katsu looked at Jeffery. "Thank you, Jeffrey, that'll be all." He nodded, turned around and headed back toward the exit.

"Bye," Ally said, waving.

"Bye Jeffery," Curtis said, mocking her. She punched him in the shoulder, blushed and looked at Katsu.

"Well, this is certainly a surprise. What are you doing here? No, sorry… that came out wrong. I meant to say, what can I do for you?"

"We were just passing through," she said. "But we were wondering if we could have a few minutes of your time."

"Sure. I'll be happy to give you as much of my time as you need. How are you anyway?"

"I'm okay. Yeah. Thanks for asking."

"You know, I was just about to take a break. What do you say we go for a walk and get a coffee or something. Would you guys like a tour?"

"Sure, that sounds nice," she said. "This is my friend Curtis."

Katsu looked at Curtis for the first time. "Very nice to meet you Curtis," he said, shaking his hand and smiling.

After a lengthy walk through the facility, the three of them arrived at the snack bar.

"You guys have to try the milkshakes!" Katsu said excitedly.

"Nah, we're cool," Curtis said apathetically.

"They're the best in the city…" he added.

"Do you know where milk comes from?" Curtis asked.

"Ummm, cows?" Katsu said, confused.

"Exactly. Do I look like a baby cow to you? Do I look young enough to still be breastfeeding? I didn't think so."

"Curtis!" Ally gasped.

"What? It's weird, okay? Why are we drinking milk from an animal that has four stomachs, horns, fur, hooves, and walks on all fours? Do you see tigers drinking cow's milk? Horses? Gorillas? If anything, we should be drinking chimpanzee milk. At least they're primates…" Curtis suddenly caught on that both Ally and Katsu were staring at him. "Sorry, I, uh… I had a lot of sugar today."

Katsu shrugged and ordered a peanut-butter and banana, banana split, and one strawberry milkshake, each with non-dairy ice-cream. Then they took a seat at a table with a magnificent view of the city.

Katsu told Ally that he and her mom used to be quite close. He said they were very good friends in addition to colleagues.

"You know, I spent some time with you when you were a baby. I even saw one of your plays at your primary school. Peter Pan, I think it was."

"Was I any good?"

"Nah, the play was dreadful," he laughed.

Ally laughed too. She didn't remember any of that, but it somehow made her feel closer to her mom.

Katsu cleared his throat. "So… what brings you here after all this time?"

"We were hoping you recognized this man," Ally said as Curtis handed him the police sketch. "Have you seen him before, Dr. Hayagawa?"

"Please, call me Katsu," he said, taking a long hard look at the sketch. Curtis and Ally both studied his expression carefully for any sign of recollection. But if Katsu did recognize the man, he certainly didn't reveal it. He finally shook his head and handed the sketch back to Curtis, "Should I?"

"No, it was just a long shot," she said disappointedly.

"Who is he?"

"I think he's—"

"He's just some asshole who we think scratched up my dad's car," Curtis interrupted. He shot Ally a cautionary look. She understood. She didn't really know Katsu. Who's to say he could be trusted. She nodded and agreed he was the guy who had scratched up Curtis's dad's car.

"Why would I have any information about such a thing? I don't even know his father."

"We followed him to the parking lot. I think he might work here."

"Ah, well, in that case, I'll ask around and put the security guys on it."

"That would be great. Thank you. Well, we probably have used up enough of your valuable time. We'd better go. Thank you so much for your time, Katsu," Curtis said.

Katsu looked at Curtis, then at Ally with creased eyes. As he stood up to walk them to the elevator, he suddenly stopped. "Hey, since you're here, would you like to see what your mother created?" he asked. "I promise you, it's nothing like you've ever seen before."

"No, thank you," Curtis replied.

"I'd love to," Ally chimed in happily. Curtis frowned and silently agreed.

"Then it's settled. I'm going to give you the grand tour."

Katsu led them through the building and up to a door. Ally had been to many parts of this building before when she was younger... when her mother was still alive, but she'd never even known this particular wing of the building existed. He swiped his keycard and herded them inside.

The first thing she noticed was the absence of white so prevalent in the lab. Now it was more of a basement-type feel. The ceiling was a lattice of wooden beams criss-crossing the ceiling and hundreds of LED lights lit up the surrounding tables, shelving units, work benches, material storage, and even what appeared to be a shooting range built of concrete. There were objects and devices laid out in deconstructed parts as well as complete units of all shapes and sizes.

As Katsu led them through the space, they passed even more nooks and rooms with tech and tools sprawled out everywhere.

"Woah! You have a Batsuit?" Curtis suddenly called out, ending Katsu's tour speech.

"It's not a Batsuit," he said, chuckling. "Although, it might give him a run for his money."

Ally and Curtis admired the display. Broken apart into several pieces, was what looked like a suit Batman would wear. The torso was resting on a mannequin under an LED beam of light. She leaned in closer, studying the way the light seemed to gleam off the fabric. It was constructed out of a material she'd never seen before. It didn't look of this Earth.

Beside the display was a black helmet, partially constructed, lying beside armored plates for arms and a set of gloves. It, too, was nothing like she'd ever seen before. The helmet was sleek and resembled a motorcycle helmet, but was much more contoured.

"What is it?" Ally asked.

"It's a prototype combat suit we're developing for the marines, part of a series of major upgrades in protective gear. This baby is made of bullet-proof fabric."

"Bulletproof fabric? Like bulletproof vests?" Ally asked.

"Not even close. Traditional vests are heavy, constrictive, and taxing on the wearer. They also only protect vital organs and sometimes fail to do their basic functions. This fabric is entirely wearable. It's lightweight and made of reinforced layers of Kevlar and graphene.

"What's graphene?" Curtis asked.

"It's an atomic configuration of graphite," Katsu answered.

"That flaky stuff in pencil lead?"

"That's the stuff." Katsu smiled.

"And you want people to get shot with that?"

"Graphene is stronger than diamonds," Ally answered. "I've read your books."

"So you're the one?" he laughed. "You're right. It's harder than diamonds and about 200 times stronger than steel. And that's just one atom thick. This suit is made with a thousand layers of graphene woven right into thc fabric, so a bullet won't pierce through."

Curtis's mouth dropped open.

"The graphene will absorb some of the impact, but it'll still hurt like a sonofabitch if you get shot. It's still in beta testing, but we hope it will become standard issue soon. Imagine sending off a soldier to war and knowing he'd be protected."

"Or she," Ally clarified.

"Of course," Katsu agreed.

"But if soldiers were all bulletproof... wouldn't shooting each other on the battlefield be pointless? Like a game of NERF or paintball?" Curtis asked.

Katsu opened his mouth to answer, but stopped. He thought for a moment and laughed. "I guess I never thought of it that way before. I suppose this is just the next stage in evolution."

"So what's to stop criminals from tipping their bullets in graphene?"

Katsu furrowed his brow and thought about that last point.

"I suppose escalation is inevitable. But if we didn't do it, the other guys would. Hey! You guys want to know what else the suit can do?" Katsu asked. "It can double the strength of a human. There is a miniaturized exoskeleton under the fabric."

Ally and Curtis took another look at the suit in the display. Then Katsu moved them down several more rows. He pointed to the viewing window. "What do you see?" he asked.

Ally and Curtis looked through the glass. "Nothing," they said together. Katsu flicked a switch on the wall and instantly there was a full suit like the one they'd just seen sitting on display, only this one was clearly an upgrade. All the parts were assembled and it looked very superhero-esque. The suit looked like it was covered in scales. Curtis and Ally stared in amazement.

"So it's like a one-way mirror... like at carnivals," Ally offered.

"Nope. This is just ordinary glass," he said, tapping it with his knuckles softly. "This is just one of the lucrative contracts we've picked up over the years. We call it Quantum Stealth Technology."

"How does it work?"

Katsu turned around to a shelf nearby and picked up a piece of clear plastic-looking material. He handed it to Ally, who turned it over in her hand and examined it.

"You know those bookmarks you used to get in stationary stores that have an image inside them? And when you turn the bookmark a little cheetah runs around or a monkey dances? This is the same material, with a slight modification," Katsu said, turning back to the viewing window. He flicked the switch again and the suit was instantly translucent. "It's paper-thin material that bends light around its target to make it move or vanish when a small electric current is sent through it."

"You're making invisible soldiers," Ally said in amazement.

"I like to think of it as more effective camouflage, but yeah... I guess that's the plan," Katsu said.

"But what about infrared, ultraviolet, or thermal wavelengths?" Ally asked.

"Clever girl," he said smiling. "Actually, this material hides all of those spectrums. Even from satellite imagery. First we made objects like riot shields, coverings for machinery and other equipment, and tents, but now we can weave it right into fabric. We have a prototype suit being tested in the field as we speak," he said.

"When will the military get this suit?" she asked, glancing to the empty container where this invisibility suit must have been housed.

"Well, given that this suit will cost around half a million dollars, I'd say not for a while yet," he winked. "We'd need to get it into mass production before the price will drop. Luckily, we have whole floors full of 3D printers in this building.

"Come on, you still haven't seen the crown jewels yet."

Katsu led them through the building and at last, stopped before what looked like a fortress. It was being guarded by two armed guards in military uniforms. Marines, she guessed. Beside the door, there was a security panel with a biometric full hand scanner attached to the wall.

"Good afternoon, sir," one of the marines said.

"Good afternoon. I'm going to give the kids a little tour," Katsu said.

"I'm sorry, sir, but that's not possible. This is a highly secure area with highly sensitive materials inside. They don't have clearance."

Katsu looked up at the marine, annoyed. "What's your name, marine?"

"Gunnery Sergeant Troy Palmer, sir."

"Palmer," Katsu repeated. "Do you have any idea who I am?" Palmer swallowed and straightened his poise. "There is only one man in this building with more authority than I have. And he isn't here. So step aside."

Ally could see the sweat building on his face. Poor kid. All he probably wanted to do was be a good marine and do his duty. She wondered if he violated that duty, could he be stripped of his rank and cast out of the military? What if he didn't follow this man's orders, could he likely meet the same fate?

"Did you hear me, Marine?" Katsu asked.

"Yes, sir. Sorry, sir," Palmer said as he took a step back. Katsu looked at Ally and winked, then stepped up to the biometric scanner.

"This is where science fiction meets science," Katsu said smiling, as he placed his hand over the scanner. The panel beeped, scanned his hand and turned green. Then the door opened and they were inside.

Katsu walked them right up to a large viewing window into another adjacent room where what looked like a large Star Trek photon cannon was being assembled by a team of engineers. There were large automated robotic arms transporting sheets of metal, bolting on support beams, and welding parts in place.

"What is this?" Ally asked. Her eyes went wide. Her mouth fell open. And she gaped in awe.

"This is your mother's legacy. She was working on a theory that it was possible for solid objects to pass through other solid objects. She theorized that the key was through vibration. But early testing on… on *subjects*… was too messy."

"Eww," Curtis groaned. "You vibrated animals, didn't you?"

Katsu nodded. "An unfortunate path to the betterment of science," he said somewhat sadly. "Anyway, the solution, as posited by your mother, was to instead vibrate the barrier at the right frequency. Your mother and I designed an earlier model to this one. We called it the Quantum Tunneler. Now we just call it Quantum. Did your mother ever tell you about it?"

Ally nodded. "Quantum tunneling is when a subatomic particle seemingly disappears from one side of a potential barrier and appears on the other side without ever having been inside the barrier."

"That's right. See, we currently have no weapon system capable of stopping an asteroid once it's on a trajectory to impact Earth. The mass and velocity would be too great to stop with even our strongest weapons."

"Yeah, you've got to drill into the middle of it and blast it from the inside," Curtis said, making Katsu stop and look in his direction.

"Like in Armageddon?" He laughed. "I'm afraid that makes for good television, but unfortunately has little to do with facts. The idea behind Quantum was that if we can't stop an object or change its trajectory, then we could cause it to essentially quantum tunnel through the Earth itself and appear on the other side. Your mother and I designed the first prototype a few years back."

"And it worked?" Ally asked.

"We're here aren't we?" he smiled at his joke. "The truth is, we got lucky. Whatever that asteroid was made of, it resisted Quantum's laser. In the end, we had no choice but to use the beam of energy to try and blast it into smaller pieces. I'm sure you remember the news. They called it Project Starfall."

"Yeah," Curtis said. "It smashed up my neighborhood."

"Yes, it was terrible. But I guess it was a small price to pay for the survival of the planet," Katsu said matter-of-factly.

"A small price to pay!?" Curtis blurted. "Thousands of people died! People like my mom! I lost my legs. Some people paid a lot more than a small price."

Katsu's eyes hit the floor.

"Apologies. You're absolutely right. Forgive me, it was a poor choice of words." He cleared his throat while Curtis shook his head and turned away.

"Umm, anyway," he said, glancing back at Ally. "We're planning on launching this baby up into orbit in the next few months. Can't be too careful…"

"Wait… I don't understand something," Curtis interrupted.

"Go on," he said.

"You said the Quantum Tunneler was supposed to cause asteroids to phase through the Earth and pass through the other side.

Then you said you had no choice but to use the beam of energy to blast it to pieces."

"Yes, that's right."

"How did you know that the Quantum Tunneler would be able to do that since BC didn't find that out until after the asteroid exploded?"

Katsu's body language changed. He was no longer bubbly and excited, but nervous and agitated. It was like he'd just been prodded with an electric poker.

"What is this thing really?" Curtis demanded.

Katsu looked at his watch and moaned. "Woah! I didn't realize the time. I'm late for a meeting. I suppose I better get back to work," he said, excitement replaced by anxiety. "To be honest, I'm not even supposed to be showing this to you, but the NDAs you signed are pretty ironclad. As long as you remember not to share anything you saw today, everything will be fine. I only thought that since your mother designed it, it's your legacy too."

Ally nodded.

"Come on, follow me." Katsu walked them to the main elevators and they all said their goodbyes. Each shook hands and thanked Katsu for his time. Ally stepped into the elevator, but just as the doors began to close, Katsu held up his hands and stopped the doors from closing.

"Ally… how would you feel about interning here?"

"Interning?" she asked, surprised.

"Yeah, why not? You're obviously a bright young woman. Your mother was a legend. If you're half as bright as she was, there is a place for you here. Interning with us would be a great way to secure you a career."

Ally thought about it for a second. Katsu reached into his jacket pocket and pulled out a business card. He handed it to her and said: "Call me if you make a decision."

"I'll think about it." Ally smiled as the elevator doors closed and the two descended back to the lobby.

When they'd reached the street, Ally was still twiddling the business card in her fingers and thinking about Katsu's offer. This could change her future in a way she never thought possible. Plus, something about the whole idea made her feel closer to her mother. Like her mother was proud of her.

"You're not seriously considering taking him up on the offer, are you?" Curtis asked.

"Is that such a bad thing?"

He didn't answer. He just kept meandering down the street.

"What's with you?"

"Nothing."

Ally knew it wasn't nothing. He was most certainly in a mood. He'd gone quiet since he'd asked Dr. Hayagawa about the Quantum Tunneler and now he seemed to be retreating into his own thoughts, barely aware that she was even there.

"So what's next on the master plan?"

"I don't know. I need to think," he said.

"Curtis!" Ally called. "Seriously, what's with you?" He ignored her and kept driving forward. "Look, if you don't want to tell me, fine. But there is something going on here."

"I said, it's nothing," he snapped.

"Oh yeah? So what were we really doing up there, huh? We certainly weren't there to ask him about Mr. Smith."

Curtis removed his finger from the throttle and slowly the wheelchair rolled to a stop, but he didn't take his eyes off the path in front of him.

"What were you doing in the police station, Curtis? What did you mean about the Quantum Tunneler being launched before they knew it would de-atomize asteroids? Why were you so hostile to Barney? What did he mean about hacking into BC? And why do I get the feeling that there was more to you being at the fight club than pissing off your dad and uncle?"

Curtis turned to face her. "Can you keep a secret?"

"What do you mean?"

"I mean, are you good at keeping secrets?"

"Why are you being weird?" she asked.

"Just answer the question! If I showed you something, if I told you a secret, how do I know you wouldn't tell anyone?" he asked with a peculiar tone.

"If you are about to profess your undying love for me or something, you can just stop right now," she joked.

"Eww… no. Gross," he said, making a face. "Forget it," he said defeatedly and started rolling forward again.

"Curtis!" she yelled after him. "Come on, Curtis!"

"I said, forget it," he grumbled.

Ally rolled her eyes. She'd had enough. She was tired, she was still being kept in the dark, and she was done following Curtis around with no explanation. "Fine!" she shouted. "I'm out!"

She allowed a car to speed past her and then stomped off toward the other side of the street.

"Where are you going?" he yelled after her.

"Home!" she yelled back.

“Fine!”

“Fine!” she yelled again and stormed off in the opposite direction.

She could hear Curtis curse under his breath as he turned back around and headed toward the dojo.

CHAPTER 19

Ally marched up to the door of her storage container, still fuming and feeling let down by Curtis. She cursed herself for believing he'd actually help her. People always say they'll help, but they always have ulterior motives. She reached up, angrily fiddling with the lock in the pouring rain and shoved her way inside. Her shoulder bumped hard against the metal frame, but she ignored it and slammed the door.

Once inside, she tried the lights. Nothing. *The batteries must be dead again*, she thought. *Great.* She sighed heavily and felt her way over to the corner of the container. Removing the check from the envelope, she placed it into the removable pipe on the floor, then thumbed out a few bills, enough for basic groceries, and stuffed the wad of money into her pocket.

A loud knock sounded, echoing through the container above the sound of rain on the metal roof.

She sulked to the door expecting to see Curtis with his tail between his legs waffling some sort of apology, but instead was surprised to see a stranger. A nervous weedy man in a suit stood hunched over in the pouring rain. He was squinting and bearing his teeth like he'd just seen his mother naked. Like a frightened turtle. One look at him and Ally could tell he didn't frequent the area.

"Are you Allyson Reid?" the man asked.

"You have the wrong address." She slammed the door, in no mood for peddling.

"Erm, Miss Reid? My name is Kirkland? Sean Kirkland? I work for Klein and Beckett?" He seemed to speak in questions.

"What do you want?" she called through the door.

"I have something for you."

"I don't want anything from you, or anyone else."

"Uh… Miss Reid?" his voice squeaked through the thin metal. "I'm here at the request of Sandy Sutton?" Ally stopped and perked up her head a little. "She left specific instructions for this to be delivered to a Miss Allyson Reid in her will?"

Ally opened the door again to see Sean fumbling in his satchel. With some difficulty, he removed a dented tea tin.

"How did she put me into a will when I just met her?"

"The coroner found a note in her pocket. As part of the last will and testament for Sandy Sutton, she wanted you to have this. Are you Allyson?"

She nodded, taking the tin from his outstretched arms. Immediately she noticed the weight. Whatever was inside, it definitely wasn't tea.

"I'm sorry for your loss. On behalf of—"

Ally shut the door again and walked over to the counter.

"Than… thank you," she heard him mutter.

She set the tin down and took a half-step back, resting her palms on the counter. Why would Sandy leave something for her in her will? She hardly knew her.

She was about to open it when another knock sounded on the door. This one was slightly more aggressive and echoed through the container like a set of base drums.

She sighed, slid the tin back against the wall, and returned to open the door. A fist struck her in the nose and instantly, her eyes went teary. She stumbled backwards in surprise and a kick knocked her onto her back. Through blurred vision, she could just make out the silhouette of a man looming over her. Ally's eyes still hadn't cleared enough to fully see, but she could make out the shape of a black pistol pointed at her forehead. She smelt iron and felt warm fluid dripping over her face. She choked on a mouthful of blood that was draining down her throat and held her palms up.

"Get her up," a man with a gruff voice grunted.

Two shadowy figures reached down, gripped her by the shirt, and ripped her to her feet. They led her to the center of the container and shoved her forward onto the beanbag chair. She crashed into it face first before managing to turn herself around to face them.

Another stream of blood trickled from her nose and she wiped it with the back of her hand as she searched for anything that could be used as a weapon. Or better yet, some kind of projectile she could use to throw and distract them while she escaped. But she came up short. There was nothing in this room that she could use to her advantage.

Ally stared back angrily at the three men, cursing herself silently. She recognized one of them—Zane, the bodyguard who'd accompanied Fisher to the dojo the other day. *These must be Fisher's men.* She could see the butt of a pistol from his chest holster poking through his jacket. The other two men she didn't recognize.

Zane stood in front of her, leaning against the wall. "This place is a real shit hole," he said disgustedly.

Ally stared defiantly back at him.

"You're a hard person to track down," Zane continued. "No social media presence, no telephone, fake address... the Johnsons say, 'Hi,' by the way. Nice family," he said coldly. "Cute daughter."

Ally's eyes burned. She gripped the chair until her knuckles went white. She didn't particularly like the Johnsons. But that didn't mean they deserved to be hurt... or worse.

"What did you do to them!"

"They're fine. For now," Zane said. "Whether or not they stay that way, that's up to you."

"What do you want?"

"The only thing you need to know is that I represent a client who's lost a lot of money."

"So what, you want your money back?"

She watched as a man handed him a small wad of money. Ally felt her empty hoodie pocket and realized it must have fallen out when they'd jerked her up. Zane accepted it, made a face, and chuckled. "The money isn't my primary concern. I've been tasked with bringing you back with me."

"And if I refuse?"

"Then I'm going to have to get unfriendly."

One of the men stepped forward and pulled an envelope from his inside jacket pocket. From it, he removed a series of photographs and tossed them at her, one at a time.

Ally leaned forward and examined them. Then her heart sank. There were pictures of the Johnsons shopping, standing around near what looked like an elementary school, and eating at a restaurant. Then she saw pictures of her and Curtis. Of Maury and Lana. Of Samantha, Tyler and Anthony and some other volunteers at the soup kitchen. There were photographs of everybody she'd ever had contact with over the past several days. There was even a picture of Curtis's dad and Barney.

This was bad. She had no choice. She had to go with them.

Zane must have seen her defeated expression. "A wise decision." He tossed a black hood at her. "Put it on," he said gruffly.

Ally reluctantly obeyed. She slipped the hood over her head and immediately noticed a peculiar smell. It was some kind of sweet smelling chemical, but she couldn't quite place it. It reminded her of ether. Then she felt the room begin to spin. Panic coursed through her like adrenaline. Instinctively, her arms shot up to the hood, but rough hands held them down. Slowly, she felt herself blacking out.

Chloroform was her last thought.

CHAPTER 20

Ally jerked herself awake like she'd fallen off the bed. Groggily, fuzzy images faded back into her mind: getting home, the lawyer with Sandy's tea tin, Fisher's men. It took a few moments to remember why her brain hurt until she recalled the black hood and the state of panic she'd felt just before she blacked out.

Straining to focus, she forced her eyes open and slowly turned her head, trying to take in her surroundings. Her vision was blurry, but was improving. Though her head was spinning, she decided to try standing up, but found her arms and wrists were bound with rope and tied behind her back to a chair. So were her ankles. She started pulling, tugging and twisting.

"You ain't gettin' through them ropes," came a disinterested voice from across the room.

She tracked the voice and spied a man who looked a lot like Dopey sitting on a chair near the door. He didn't look up from his comic book, The Shadow. After a minute, he closed the comic and folded it in half before placing it inside his jacket pocket. Then he picked up a two-way handheld radio and uttered two words: "She's awake."

A few moments later, the door opened. Dopey and Darrell each lifted the chair and carried her down a corridor and into an office at the far end. They placed the chair on the floor in front of a desk where Fisher sat. He was filling out some paperwork, taking no notice of her until he'd finished his last thought. Then he placed the pen down and looked up at her.

"I apologize for the theatrics, but I didn't imagine you'd come willingly, and given the nature of your… *talents*… I thought it best to avoid any unnecessary injuries. Who taught you to fight like that? I've never seen anything like it."

"What am I doing here?"

"You're here because you have meddled in things beyond your understanding. And while these aren't my usual methods, your actions have forced my hand."

"Let me out of these ropes."

Fisher ignored her. "My men tell me that they only found $100 at your place. Where's the rest?"

"I gave it away," Ally felt relieved that Fisher's men hadn't found the hidden pipe in the floor.

Fisher glared at her. "That's okay. You're going to make it up to me," he said.

"I'm not doing anything for you."

Fisher's glare intensified. There was a strange hint of enjoyment behind his eyes. "I'm going to save both you and me a whole lot of time here. We're going to skip the whole back and forth banter where I tell you what I want and you stubbornly refuse. We're going to skip to the part where you realize I *own* you."

Ally looked at him amusedly, mocking him with every muscle in her face. "Tell me, does that little speech usually do it for people? Because—"

"Every time you refuse to do what I tell you, I'm going to kill someone you care about. Let's practice."

Practice?

Fisher adjusted himself in the chair. "Smile," he ordered.

Ally scoffed.

"That's your friend Cletus dead," Fisher said coldly.

Ally's face scrunched up. "Who's Cletus?"

Fisher turned to Zane. "What's the name of Baráo's boy? The cripple?"

"Curtis, boss," Zane clarified.

"That's your friend Curtis dead," he said again with conviction. This time, Ally dropped the act. She stared into his eyes hoping that Curtis was still okay. "Now, this is for real," he said and nodded to his men.

Ally could hear a scuffle in the other room followed by muffled cries of protest. Before her eyes, Samantha was shoved into the room. She had duct tape over her mouth and her arms were pulled behind her back. She fell hard onto the floor, landing on her chest before managing to maneuver onto her knees. She'd been knocked around but didn't look seriously hurt.

Zane removed a Glock from its holster and pointed it at Samantha's forehead, then looked at Fisher, waiting for confirmation. At the sight of the gun, Samantha began sobbing, snot and tears sliding down her face.

"Now smile," Fisher snarled.

Ally quickly observed her predicament: Samantha - terrified; Zane - in his element; Darrell - eyes avoiding Samantha; Fisher - cold, hollow eyes.

He wasn't bluffing.

Her delay caused Zane to cock the gun and press it into Samantha's forehead. Ally didn't wait any longer. She forced a smile.

"Good dog," Fisher said. He leaned in close and stared into her eyes. "There are two things you gotta know. First, you work for me now. I *own* you, got it?" —Ally glared at him. It was all she could do, given that she was hogtied to the chair— "Second, you have a fight in three days. I suggest you prepare. You win when I say, you lose when I say. If you so much as show up a minute late, someone dies."

Ally read his expression. Again, he wasn't bluffing. He spent the next minute explaining that any deviation from his instructions would result in someone's untimely death, like Sandy.

Ally's eyes filled with fire.

"Get her out of my sight."

Zane placed his pistol back into its holster, then pulled out a knife. He cut the duct-tape from Samantha's ankles, allowing her to walk. Then he shoved her to Darrell before squatting down to eye-level with Ally. He held the blade of the knife to her chin.

"Please struggle," he whispered, before cutting the ropes. He backed away a few steps and told her to follow Darrell.

*   *   *

The whole ride back, Samantha silently sobbed. Ally just sat there, contemplating the situation. She was in real trouble now. Worse, everyone else's lives were depending on her.

"Hey," Ally whispered. Samantha turned her head. "Did they hurt you?" Samantha shook her head. "Did they... *touch you*?" Samantha hesitated, processing the question before shaking her head. "Everything's gonna be okay. I'm going to get us out of this."

Samantha nodded, but Ally could tell she didn't believe her.

When the car rolled to a stop, Zane tossed Ally a burner phone. "You have three days. Wait for my call. Now get out." Darrell opened the door for her and she stepped out, expecting Samantha to be right behind her, but Zane slammed the door.

Ally turned back and smacked the glass with her palm. "What about her?"

Zane rolled down the window and smiled. "Don't worry. We'll take real good care of her."

Ally glanced at Darrell, who bowed his head remorsefully. "They won't hurt her. Just do what they say," he whispered, then he got back into the car and shut the door.

Ally looked back at Zane and leaned forward, looking him dead in the eyes. "If anything happens to her… I'll—"

"You'll what?" he interrupted.

"I'll make you sorry."

Zane smiled. "Say hi to your cat for me." He rolled the window up and the car drove away.

Ally's face dropped. She turned and rushed back into the storage container, frantically looking around, screaming Piggy's name and scanning every inch. Zane had to be lying!

She stopped suddenly when she saw a pool of blood coming from behind a pile of boxes. Her heart sank. Crawling closer on her hands and knees, her worst fears were confirmed. Piggy was lying on her side, impaled with a screwdriver through her abdomen, pinning her to the floor.

Ally shuddered. Piggy's paws were matted with fresh blood. There were bloody scrape marks on the floor where she'd tried to free herself.

Ally collapsed. She cradled Piggy's head in her hands and began to sob. She sobbed so hard she thought her veins would explode. Finally, she hung her head and her eyes went dead, her body slumping in an emotionless heap.

Several minutes passed. Then her eyes twitched and filled with fire. She suddenly knew what she had to do.

Fisher fucked with the wrong girl!

CHAPTER 21

The next morning, Ally didn't show up to the dojo. Violating her probation didn't matter to her anymore. Everyone was depending on her. She'd been working tirelessly through the night and didn't come up for air until it was nearly dawn. This was the one time she viewed her insomnia as a blessing. It allowed her to canvass the entire supply of crates stacked against the sides of her would-be apartment. She'd gutted anything electronic and began fusing together all parts required to enact her revenge.

At first light, no banks were open and Ally didn't have time to go about explaining where the money had come from or jump through hoops. Instead, she traded her cashier's check with a loan shark. She offered them 10 grand in exchange for 40 large. She stuffed the money into her bag, headed to the nearest supply store and purchased several state of the art lenses, projector materials and any of the other parts she required. It was incredible to think how yesterday, she was going to give away more money than she'd ever seen before. Now, she dropped 30 grand in less than an hour.

Before the streets started coming to life with people, Ally was already back in her container. It was another four hours before a knock made her conscious of the clock for the first time since she'd begun.

"Ally?" came Curtis's voice. "Ally! Are you in there?"

She sat still for a moment, fully prepared to ignore him. She was too busy for an apology.

"I know you're in there!" Curtis said, banging again. "Look! I'm sorry, alright? I didn't mean to upset you yesterday."

Ally reluctantly moved toward the door and pressed her forehead against the cool metal.

"Come on, Ally! I'm not leaving until you talk to me!" More banging.

She sighed and opened the door to see Curtis sitting nervously. As she opened the door wider, she saw his mouth fall open, probably noticing her bloodshot eyes and the bags that come with a tearful night.

"Woah! Are you alright? What's wrong?"

Ally tried to stop herself but she felt sobs coming on again. Tears rolled down her cheeks, her shoulders began to heave from the powerful sobs, and her legs gave way, sending her into a squat.

Curtis rolled forward and put his hand gently on her shoulder. "Woah. It's cool Ally. I'll just tell my uncle that you're ill."

"It isn't that," she said through stifled tears. Then she gestured with her head for him to come inside.

As he crossed the threshold, he stopped dead in his tracks. His hand flew to his face. "What's that smell?" He plugged his nose. "Pwuah! It's seeping into my pores," he coughed and spluttered. "Is that meth? You're cooking meth?"

Ally followed his gaze to the beakers, boiling flasks, tubing and various dry and wet chemicals littering the countertop. "What? Meth?"

"Don't even try and deny it! I know what that is!" he said, pointing to the chemistry equipment. "I've seen Breaking Bad, yo! That's a Methamphetamine distillery."

Ally smirked and shook her head. She then proceeded to tell him everything that had happened, about Fisher's men, about being drugged and kidnapped, about what they'd done to Piggy, what he was forcing her to do, and what the stakes were—the lives at risk.

When she'd finished, Curtis didn't react the way she expected. He just sat there, in silence. "We have to tell Maury about this," he said after a few minutes.

"No!" she said quickly.

"Ally, I… I…" he tried. "Look, you have to trust me, okay? This is something you need to let us help with."

"No," she repeated, shaking her head. "I shouldn't have even told you about any of this. I'm sorry. This is something I need to sort on my own."

"*Sort out on your own*?" he scoffed. "You think you can go up against the mob single handedly? Are you mental? Oh, wait… you're on meth."

"It's not meth, Curtis."

"Then what is it?"

"You need to go."

"No. Not until you come to your senses."

"Curtis, you need to leave! They might be watching us right now!"

"I'm not going anywhere," he said, crossing his arms in defiance. "Forget it! You either let me help or I'll go back and tell my uncle." He sat there staring her down until at last Ally realized she was wasting more time than she could afford. Fisher had told her that her fight was in three days. That gave her two more, and she had plenty more to do. Reluctantly she nodded and agreed.

"So… I assume you have a plan?" he asked.

"You're looking at it," she said, waving her hand over the floor. Curtis followed her gesture and studied the mess. Wires, tubes, tools, and various electrical parts were scattered about the floor beside five dissected small hover drones. Then he looked up at her and laughed. When he realized she was serious, his smile fell off his face.

"What is all this?"

"Misdirection," she replied. "I'm gonna fuck Fisher's life up."

Curtis looked at the mess on the floor, then at Ally in utter confusion. "You really *are* mental."

CHAPTER 22

Ally scaled the wall to the Bad Kitty nightclub using the drain pipe to reach the fire escape. From there, she cautiously moved across the roof, feeling the distant beat of music thump through the stone walls. Initially she'd prepared to break in, but finding the window ajar, she pried it open and lowered herself inside.

Dropping down to the floor, she looked around. No sign of life. The private bathroom was under construction. The soft glow of a heat lamp bathed the room in a warm yellow hue. The air was tinged with the scent of fresh paint and concrete. In the corner, dust and debris were swept into a pile beside an intricate web of exposed pipes and skeletal walls. Boxes of unused ceramic tiles lay stacked nearby, waiting to be laid.

Ally crept to the door and peered out. A yellow caution sign was draped across the corner of the hallway. On the floor in a haphazard pile, lay a builder's tool belt and uniform. Ally figured whoever dropped them must have popped out for a smoke given the unwashed paint supplies. Luckily for her, this meant she wouldn't need to explain her presence.

Moving down the hallway, she emerged above a dance club. A captivated crowd of mixed ages sat at various tables or were leaned up against the stage and bar. Some were tossing money onto the stage while others tucked bills into women's g-strings. One of the dancers was dangling upside down from the top of a pole by her legs, letting her torso and breasts hang toward the floor. Slowly, she slunk her way down the pole like Spider-Gwen while clients cawed and hooted in approval.

Ally scanned the crowd meticulously until finally, she spied her target: Zane. He was sitting inside a private booth facing the stage and talking to another lady of the club. She imagined girls like this were hired to chat up customers, making sure that they were being looked after by the barman before other girls invited them up for a private dance. They were just the lure. Once inside the private booths, she imagined other girls were tasked with the *pleasantries*.

Ally watched the girl lean in and whisper something into Zane's ear, then she took his hand and started pulling him up the stairs toward the private booths. It was obvious the woman was repulsed by him. Every time she turned her face away, she dropped the fake smile and sexy eyes and looked ready to vomit. But as soon as he pulled her close again, she sparkled with charm.

Ally followed at a distance through the crowd, trying not to arouse suspicion. She cursed. A bouncer was stationed near the entrance to the private rooms. She had to get in that room! Taking out the guard would definitely attract attention. And she couldn't just waltz in there either. *Think!* Then it hit her.

She watched Zane's escort turn toward a room and hold the door for him. Zane leaned in and whispered something, but the escort flung her head back and laughed with an over-the-top cackle. She shook her head and booped him on the nose playfully with her index finger, trying to be cute, then wagged it in his face like he'd just said something naughty. She gestured for him to enter, but Zane grabbed hold of her wrist. At this, the escort dropped the flirtatious act and tried to pull away, but Zane jerked her into the room and shut the door.

Ally turned and rushed back to the restroom where she'd come in. She stripped down to her underwear, slinging the Fanny pack over her shoulder and kicked her clothes toward the corner. She pulled on the builder's overalls, rolling up the sleeves and pant legs. Next, she clipped the tool belt around her waist and looked herself over in the mirror. She hoped she could pass for one of the working girls.

Racing out of the bathroom, she reached the end of the corridor. Taking a deep breath, she closed her eyes and channeled her inner actress. "Hey Mistah," she called, sounding a little too like Mona Lisa Vito. "You seen a guy come through here just now? Kinda an ugly fella with gym muscles?"

"He's in room three," the guard said. "Who are you?"

Ally feigned shock. "They didn't tell you? No, course they didn't. You people never get no respect. I'm the new girl, Tiffany." She held out her arms and did a little curtsy. "Anyways, the little pervert wants to pay double, so here I am." She shrugged, attempting to walk past him, but he stepped in front. He glared at her with beady eyes for a moment. She was about to knock him out when he turned to a cabinet in the wall and pulled out a zipped pouch. From it, he removed a purple lipstick and held it out.

"You're a mess," he said.

"Oh, thanks, doll!" Ally said, taking the lipstick. "They called me in on short notice. The guy has a fetish for role play. What do I care?"

"What's in the Fanny pack?" he asked.

Ally gasped and slapped him across the face playfully. "You can't ask a girl that! A good girl never tells!" She winked and applied the lipstick heavily, then handed it back.

The guard smiled, placed it back into the bag and gestured with his head for her to go in. She leaned in and kissed him on the cheek, then stepped past him.

The door shut behind her.

"This one's taken!" she heard Zane shout. To her left, she could see him pinning the partially clothed girl to the bed. The dim LED lighting from the ceiling illuminated her pleading and frightened stare.

Ally ducked behind a sofa and removed a hover drone from her pack. She let it flutter in the air.

"Did you hear me?" Zane yelled, standing and zipping up his trousers. Ally peered over the edge of the sofa. Zane was looking around, squinting in the dark, but turned back to the girl. The escort was breathing hard and trying to swat away his attempts to grab her arms and pin her down.

"Please! Stop!" she half-whispered, half-cried. He ignored her and instead ripped at her shirt until it tore away into two pieces. He tossed one of them aside, then he sliced through the center of her bra with a knife before working on her skirt, ripping at the button and zipper before undoing his trousers again.

The girl was panicking now. She flailed wildly and started screaming. Zane struggled for a few seconds, trying to control her arms before he got angry and struck her hard across the cheek. The girl went rigid and began sobbing and sniffling.

"No! Please!" she tried feebly.

"She said no!" Ally yelled, startling Zane. He jerked himself up again, whirling around and gazing out into the dark toward the drone.

"Hello?" he called.

Ally pressed a button on her forearm. The neon lights in the room began to flutter, fluxing between strobes of color and the pitch black. She pressed another and a drone hovered by the door, blasting loud music to drown out what she was about to do.

"What the fuck is this?" he grumbled.

"Pathetic!" Ally's voice barked from another drone's speakers.

Zane whirled and jumped back, tripping over a stool and scrambling to his feet awkwardly. Ally made sure the sound had come from right behind him. "This isn't funny!" he yelled, swiping his finger over his phone and opening the flashlight app. He shone the beam of light all over the dark until it rested on the far corner. Then he held the light still for a moment. Some kind of strange hairy creature was crouched against the wall.

It slowly stood up. It was thin, gangly and hairy. He could see its enormous hands, whose fingers were splayed out down to the razor-sharp claws. Its face was werewolf-like, with faintly glowing red eyes, big triangular ears with rounded points, and sharp visible fangs. As it stood up, its hind legs gradually straightened from its unnatural joints.

The girl shrieked from the bed and curled herself into a fetal ball.

"What the fu—" but the creature roared and lunged toward him. Zane instinctively stumbled backwards, again tripping over the stool and landed on his back. He smacked his head on the hard floor.

Zane grunted and exhaled as he tried to sit up but Ally struck him hard in the forehead, sending his skull slamming down onto the hard floor again. His phone landed screen-side down and now projected two shadows against the far wall. The light was constricting his view, but he now saw his attacker in front of him.

Still on his back, he swung his arms wildly, but Ally blocked his attempts and threw a few of her own. She broke his nose with the first punch and hit him hard enough to knock a molar loose with the second. She threw a quick 1-2-punch before striking him across the face, sending his head back to the floor. He groaned and spluttered. Immediately, Ally recognized the familiar sickly signs of a concussion.

"Watch her!" Ally barked. The hologram creature lumbered toward the bed and stopped, fixing its eyes on the escort. She couldn't afford to let the girl run and draw attention… not before she could get the information she needed out of him. She'd beg her forgiveness later.

Ally's heart was racing. She felt a spike of adrenaline pump through her veins as she stepped over his body. Her arms tingled and felt weightless. The nail gun, heavy and powerful in her hand, was the only thing anchoring her. She stared down at Zane, hesitating for a moment, then pounced upon him, straddling him. Before he could react, she grabbed his right arm and pressed it against the floor. She steadied the nail gun and as if aided by the beat of the music, squeezed the trigger, unleashing multiple thick clunks into the fabric and floor, pinning his right arm.

Zane's desperate struggles intensified, the fabric of his clothing stretching and testing the nail's hold. His eyes filled with panic, his breathing erratic. He tried to hit her with his other hand, but Ally blocked it away easily and shot a nail straight through his wrist. He shrieked in pain, thrashing and staring at his pierced arm.

He jerked and kicked wildly, but Ally had already grabbed his arm and pressed it against the floor. Again, she squeezed the trigger, unleashing multiple thick clunks into the fabric and floor. Now both of his arms were pinned.

She leaned in close and pressed the barrel to his chin. "Please struggle," she whispered into his ear, her voice firm, but laden with venom.

Zane's eyes widened with fear and recognition.

Ally proceeded to nail the rest of his clothing to the floor, effectively pinning his body down along its edge.

When she'd finished, she stood up and towered over him. Her heart raced in anticipation. She was breathing hard and panting with delight, like a cat with a mouse. She felt the dim, neon lighting paint her face. The anger that was bubbling up inside of her was stayed only by her tightening knuckles as she clutched the handle of the nail gun.

"Where is the girl?" she growled.

"What girl?" he whimpered.

Ally hovered the nail gun over Zane's thigh and pulled the trigger. The deafening crack of the nail launcher pierced the air. Zane howled, a sharper reaction than she expected.

"Where's the girl?" she repeated.

"At her house! We dropped her off just after we left the containers," he babbled.

Ally straddled him again, leaned forward and shoved the nail gun hard under his chin. "If I find out you're lying…"

"I swear! Ple... please," Zane spluttered, his voice breaking.

Ally backed off, letting the gun slide off the base of his chin and rest at her side.

"I'm going to ask you some questions, Zane. If you lie to me, you're in for a painful night." Zane's eyes darted nervously. The room's shadows seemed to deepen the lines of fear etched on his face. Ally waited what felt like minutes, then moved the nail gun towards him. "Where did you take me yesterday," she demanded.

"The old depot!" he huffed. "Fisher's got an office in the back."

"What business is he conducting there?"

Zane hesitated and Ally raised the gun, firing another nail into his left pectoral. He cried out. "Shit! Weapons! Shipments of weapons!"

Ally leaned in closer, her eyes still locked onto Zane's. "What kind of weapons?"

"The illegal kind," he hissed.

"How often does he receive shipments?"

"I don't know, like every other week, I think."

"When is the next one due?"

He snuffed. "Tonight. In about three hours."

Ally sat up a moment, thinking. The time would be tight. If she had any hope in getting to Fisher, she needed to wrap this up. Ally moved the nail gun even closer, its cold metal almost touching Zane's skin. "Tell me about his security."

Zane's face contorted. "He's got four guards, heavily armed. Two positioned near the entrance, the others are near the loading dock. I swear!" he spluttered.

Four guards was doable. She'd just need a way to incapacitate them quickly. Curtis had suggested modifying the drones to fire a tranquilizer dart. Though small, the drones should be able to account for the added weight of a dart, as they would only add a few grams. If Curtis had managed to finish by the time she returned, she could take out the guards before they had time to shoot. It was still a risk. But did she have a choice?

"Please don't kill me," he whimpered.

Ally didn't waste time with words. She slapped him across the face with a resounding crack, hard enough to shut him up. "I'm not going to kill you," she said, her voice cold. "Now, I need you to listen."

She leaned in close, her face inches from his. "You are going to leave this nice lady here, the biggest, most generous tip she's ever seen. And then you are never to set foot in this place again. Do you understand me?" she growled.

Zane nodded vigorously, blinking tears out of his eyes.

Ally's voice was a low, menacing growl. "Do I need to draw you a picture of what I will do to you if she suffers any kind of harm?"

Zane shook his head. "N...no."

"If she so much as rolls her ankle, I'm coming for you!" she hissed, pressing the nail gun hard under his chin.

"Please don't kill me," he whimpered.

Ally slapped Zane across the cheek again. "You're not listening. I said, I'm not going to kill you. But I am going to send you a little message."

She moved the nail gun over his crotch.

Zane started to hyperventilate. "No, please!"

She was about to pull the trigger, but she suddenly had a better idea. She dropped the nail gun onto his crotch, pulled out a long screwdriver from the tool belt and held it up. "So… you like to kill animals."

Zane's eyes went wide. "I'm sorry! I'll get you another cat," he whimpered.

Ally glared at him, her eyes conveying fire and fury. "Fuck you."

"What are you going to do?"

"I'm going to shove this screwdriver through your stomach."

"No... No!" Zane whimpered.

"Yes! And the next time you think about hurting another animal… I want you to think of *me*."

"Please... I'm sorry!"

"Shut up, Zane. This is happening. Are you ready? Because this is gonna hurt."

She wasn't bluffing. With calculated precision, she took the screwdriver and pressed it through his abdomen. It pierced his front and poked out through his back. Zane's agonized shriek filled the room.

Ally knew what she was doing. She knew exactly where his vital organs were and purposefully missed them. She removed a hammer and pounded the metal tip through the floor, pinning him to it.

Zane grimaced and whimpered for nearly a minute. Finally, she spoke. "Remember what I said. I'll be watching." She slammed her heel into his forehead, knocking him out. Zane's rigid body went limp. When she saw him draw breath, she turned to the escort.

She pressed a button on her forearm and deactivated the two drones. They fluttered over to her and she placed them back into her Fanny pack. Holding out her hand, she beckoned for the girl to come to her.

"I'm sorry. He had information I needed and I couldn't have you running out before I was finished."

The escort sat with her knees pulled to her chest. She was still frightened.

"Come on. I won't hurt you." The girl slowly slid toward her and took Ally's hand. Ally pulled her to the door and steadied her. "What's your name?" she asked. The girl stared blankly and continued shaking. "Hey!"

"Huh?" she grunted.

"Your name."

"Mal... M...Mallory," she stammered.

"Listen Mallory. You're probably in shock, so you need to listen to me carefully." Mallory nodded and blinked, straining to focus. "Go outside and get that bouncer. Tell him what happened."

Ally took Mallory's hand and stuffed a wad of money into her palm that she'd taken from Zane's wallet—an asshole fee. Then she handed her a robe she'd taken from the rack near the door.

"How can I thank you?" Mallory asked, shivering as she slowly pulled the robe over her shoulders.

"You can thank me by getting yourself to a safe place. Now go!" she ordered, but Mallory lingered for a moment. She threw her arms around Ally's shoulders.

"If you ever need anything… anything at all..." she whispered. "I'm yours!"

Ally had no intention of ever stepping foot in this place again, but she nodded.

Mallory let go, slowly turned and jogged down the hall. Ally watched her until she disappeared around the corner, then quickly stepped into Room 2, waiting until the bouncer went to look for Zane, then she'd dart out and make her exit.

CHAPTER 23

Sergeant Floyd Lockhart navigated through the beat cops loitering near the booking terminals. Some were holding onto suspects who looked like bikers. Some were talking to the bail bondsman. Some were arguing with lawyers or screaming mothers. He gawked at the chaos unfolding in front of him. He couldn't remember a single time when the precinct was this busy. Maybe on Mardi Gras, but never in the middle of winter so close to the Christmas holidays. Finally, he approached the center desk and stood in line behind three men arguing with Lieutenant Michaels.

"It was *his* house, John! Of course my client's fingerprints were found there!" a greasy lawyer cried. "Why should my client rot away in a holding cell while the real killer is out stalking his next victim?"

"I've already told you, your appointment with the judge is next week. I can't help you," Michaels said.

"But I've got the cash right now…"

"Listen pal," Michaels interrupted, now very cross. "I don't care who your client's connections are... and frankly, I don't give a shit if he's innocent or not. We don't play favorites around here! Now get out of my station and take Papa John here with you!"

Lockhart regarded the men as they grudgingly turned away, then caught Michaels's sour look. "What took you so long?" Michaels barked gruffly. "I called you an hour ago."

Lockhart frowned and pressed his tongue hard against the roof of his mouth, resisting the urge to remind him that it was his day off.

"You been outside lately?"

Michaels ignored him. "Come with me," he said, motioning for him to follow. "I need you to interrogate a suspect. The perp has refused to talk to anyone except you."

"Did they say why?"

Michaels stopped and scowled. "How the hell should I know? I just said he refused to talk to anyone. Now, if you're done playing 20 Questions, there's something you need to see." He led him to the back of the precinct, barging over to a computer with CCTV queued up, leaned forward and pressed play.

On the screen, the double doors burst open. A man shambled in, tripping over himself and slid on his front. He struggled to his feet and began limping forward through the lobby, grimacing with each heavy step. One arm was hanging limply at his side. He turned from left to right yelling over the precinct chaos.

“Do we have audio?” Lockhart asked.

“No, but I was told the poor bastard was babbling like a baby. Probably completely off his face from drugs.”

Lockhart watched the man shout above the commotion. He seemed invisible. Then he raised a handgun into the air and fired three bullets. The room hit the deck. On the screen, several officers drew their weapons and pointed them at the gunman.

The man looked like he was sobbing. He tossed the weapon and raised one arm just before the officers pounced on him like a fumble on the 10-yard line. They cuffed him behind his back and jerked him up to his feet, manhandling him into the cuffs with uncaring force.

Lockhart watched the officers drag the shooter away through a side door while others in the room raced out the front door, scanning the area for additional hostiles.

Michaels pressed stop on the tape.

Lockhart exhaled. “Shiiiiit…”

“Come on. There’s something else you need to see,” Michaels led him to an interrogation cell. Through the one-way glass, he saw a battered man handcuffed to the table. He looked like he’d just survived a war zone. His face was smeared with dried blood from a beating. One arm was in a sling. The other was chained to the desk. His clothes were ripped and he was still sniffling and crying, visibly disturbed. Beside him was a suit, presumably his lawyer, a beautiful Italian woman.

“Jesus! Our guys did that?” Lockhart gasped.

Michaels shook his head. “Came in like that. Covered in blood and bruises.

“What happened to him?”

Michaels ignored him. “You know this guy?” he asked gruffly.

Lockhart looked at the man through the one-way glass and shook his head. “No.”

“You sure?”

“He leaned in and took a closer look, then shrugged. “Should I?”

“We ran his prints. His name’s Tony Piciani. A low-level groupie for Andrew Fisher.”

So, you already knew who he was, Lockhart thought.

“What we *don’t* know is… why he requested to speak with *only* you.”

Lockhart shrugged. “Beats me. I’ve never seen him before.” He looked again at the man in the chair.

Michaels studied his face then turned to look through the one-way glass at the cop now entering the room. "That's Peters, a promising young detective. Been training him myself. He's a little rough around the edges, but he's a good lad. I told him to sit in until you arrived."

Lockhart looked at the detective. He recognized him. The two of them had a few run-ins over the years on different cases. He'd always felt Peters was lazy and sloppy. It made sense that Michaels was training him up. There was no way he'd make detective on his own.

"Hey Lydia," Peters said with a smirk. "Long time no see."

"Not long enough," she said with a hint of disgust.

"You look good. Been working out?"

"That's none of your business anymore."

Peters smiled and sucked on his tongue. His eyes looked her up and down. Then he sighed. "You want to tell me what I'm doing here, Lydia? This case is open and shut. Why don't you just plead him out... stop wasting our time with all these little fish."

"I don't know, Detective," Lydia said playfully. "Little fish see all kinds of things... swimming around in their bowl."

Peters smirked. "So he's a snitch. Is that why your face is all prettied up?" He leaned forward and eyeballed Tony sitting in the chair. "Ever hear of snitches get stitches, bro?"

Tony didn't seem to hear him.

"Hey!" Peters called, louder. "Hello!" He snapped his fingers but Tony only shuffled slightly in his chair, grimacing in pain.

"He doesn't speak English," Lydia said.

"What, he don't understand snapping fingers neither?" Peters rolled his eyes. He crossed his arms and slumped in his chair. "So what's Pretty Boy got to say."

"How about the location to the largest illegal weapons cache this city's ever seen?"

Peters straightened, eyeing Lydia before side-eying the one-way glass.

"As I said, my client will cop to everything, no pun intended," she said, smiling falsely. "Full confession. Even name names."

Peters looked at Tony. "Just like that, huh? You must be very popular in your line of work."

"Where's Lockhart?" Lydia demanded, smiling with animosity.

Peters turned his head as Michaels tapped the glass. "He's outside," Peters sighed, cocking his head.

"Well, then get him in here."

The door opened and Peters made a show of standing up. "Call me," he said smugly, winking at Lydia. She scrunched up her face, disgusted. "He's all yours, old-timer," Peters said, turning to Lockhart, and left the room.

"You Lockhart?" Lydia asked, eyeing him suspiciously. The sour look on her face was no doubt a remnant of her fondness of Peters and perhaps the department for jerking her around.

He nodded. "That's me."

"No offense, but can I see some ID?"

Lockhart removed his badge and showed it to her. Satisfied, she whispered something in Tony's ear. He stirred and eyed Lockhart through swollen eyes, but didn't speak.

"My client believes his life is in danger. He believes you will keep him safe in here."

"I've never seen this man before. How does he know me?"

"He wouldn't say. Just that he was told to speak to you."

"By whom?"

Lydia shrugged. "First, let's talk years. We want the maximum."

"The *maximum*?" Lockhart scoffed. "Shouldn't you be trying to keep your clients *out of prison*?"

"Look at him, Floyd. He's afraid of his own shadow."

Lockhart studied Tony. He noted his bloodstained face. His broken arm. He was visibly sweating and trembling, nearly in tears. "Look, I can't make any promises until I hear what your client's got to say. But depending on what he says, I could put a word in with the judge. We could argue that he's a danger to the public."

Lydia leaned towards Tony. "Va bene," she said.

CHAPTER 24

Peters and a dozen officers made their way into the abandoned toy factory. The light from a dozen flashlights revealed an eerie scene—an empty facility taken over by years of dust and grime, and the occasional rat. Cobwebs hung from the ceiling and layers of dust covered various discarded toys. Broken machinery and forgotten tools lay scattered throughout the facility, a stark reminder of the bustling production that once occurred within its walls.

As they made their way down the corridor, Peters's beam panned over to the loading dock. Dozens of wooden crates lined the walls, each one stamped with a military logo.

"Something smells off," Peters mumbled.

"Yeah, it's mold and rat piss," an officer quipped.

Peters frowned and kept looking around.

"Hey Detective!" Officer Bly yelled. "You better come take a look at this."

Peters looked up and stepped toward him. Six AR-15 rifles were spilling out of a broken crate near a moving truck. Bullet casings scattered the floor beside a large body lying in a pool of blood. Another body was slumped over inside a forklift with its head resting on the steering wheel. The windshield was peppered in bullet holes.

Peters glanced at the number of crates stacked in the room and pointed his flashlight toward the back of the moving truck. It was stocked nearly two-thirds of the way full. "Jesus…" he mumbled, then he stopped cold. "Everybody shut up!" It took a moment, but the officers all stood still and held their breaths.

There it was again… quiet moaning.

His flashlight spun and shone onto three men, bound together around the midsection with their heads drooping into their laps. Their arms and ankles were bound with zip-ties and their mouths were duct-taped shut.

Peters walked up to the three men, bumping a small metal canister with his foot. He bent down and picked it up. It was small, about the size of a hockey puck, but hollow.

"What'cha got, Detective?"

Peters sniffed the puck and put it into an evidence bag. "I'm not sure," he said, leaning in and lifting the man's head nearest him. The man's eyes suddenly shot open and he began shrieking in terror. Peters recoiled. Even through the duct-tape, the sound was unnatural, like a feral cat getting tortured. It made the hair stand up on the back of his neck and echoed across the dark airwaves.

* * *

Lockhart scribbled down a few notes onto his notepad and took a sip from his coffee. He looked up at Lydia with intrigue. "Alright. We'll send some people to check out the facility," he said. "Ask him what happened to the men."

* * *

Tony followed Marco through the doorway trying not to think about identifying the different smells in the stale air. Old grease, metal shavings and mildew perhaps.

"Are you hearin' me?" Marco asked, glaring at Tony contemptuously. Tony nodded. "And when you get in there, you keep your head down and your mouth shut."

Tony followed his cousin Marco through a maze of heavy machinery, wondering if asking for an introduction with the mob was a good idea. He had to keep telling himself it'd be worth it once the money was rolling in.

"And one more thing… when you get in there, the only words you'll need to remember are: Yes, Sir," Marco reiterated. "The last guy who asked too many questions was *disappeared.* His made guy, too, so don't embarrass me," he said, his voice firm, "I vouched for you. You sneeze, and I get sick."

Tony stopped abruptly, grabbing Marco and pulling him into a recess in the wall. Two cops in uniform stepped around a bend in front of them.

"What the hell are you doing?" Marco demanded.

Tony shushed him and hissed. "Cops!"

Marco laughed. He smacked his cousin in the shoulder and chuckled. "They're with us."

Tony did a double take then relaxed.

"Come on," Marco said, still smiling. "It's just through here."

As they emerged onto the loading dock, five men busily stacked large wooden crates onto pallets. It took two men to lift each one. Beside them, a man operated a forklift, loading the pallets into a moving truck at the end of the facility.

"Remember what I told you," Marco said.

Tony nodded, swallowing hard against the knot of anxiety tightening in his throat. "I got it, Marco," he replied. "I won't let you down."

"This is Mason. He'll show you the ropes."

"Wait, you're not coming?"

"I got my own shit. Just do what I told you, and you'll be fine." With a curt nod, Marco gave him a quick hug, then headed toward the dock and joined in the rotations with the other men.

Within five minutes, Tony was sweating profusely and struggled to keep up with the others. He grasped hold of the handle and together, he and Mason lifted, but Tony could feel the sweat on his palms lubricating the handle. Despite his best efforts, his grip slipped and he dropped his end of the crate. It slammed hard onto the concrete floor with a loud crunch and broke open. AR-15 Rifles spilled out onto the floor as Mason stumbled.

"Watch it, dumbass!" Romano shoved him hard in the chest, knocking him to the ground. He picked up one of the 200 pound crates all by himself and stacked it onto the wooden pallet. He gave Tony a 'fuck you' smirk and picked up a hammer.

Tony suddenly looked down. An object slid toward him, scratching against the concrete floor and tapped against his foot. Instinctively, he reached down and picked it up. "Hey, did anyone…" He glanced around but no one seemed to be missing any parts. Two men had knelt beside the wooden pallet and began to fix the crate, nailing it back together.

Suddenly, the puck in his hand released a whoosh of compressed air. It made his eyes sting and he tried to blink them clean. He shook his head, feeling dizzy and lightheaded. Then he froze. Not five meters away, two gargoyles tossed a human corpse into a mass grave while the larger of the three tortured another and was stuffing him into a coffin, nailing it shut.

Tony blinked and shook his head.

One of the gargoyles was looking at him. A large one. "You see something you like, sweetie?" it said, making a kissy face.

Tony shrieked and leapt back, tripping over a crate, and crashed to the floor.

Other creatures, hearing the commotion, started toward him. Quickly, Tony snatched up one of the assault rifles. "Get back!" he screamed, waving it back and forth as the other three growled and swatted. "Back!" he screamed again, aiming the rifle.

The chimeras stopped, but continued to growl and snap their jaws. Tony shuddered as the big one stood up and lumbered straight toward him. "Get back!" he screamed again, but it was nearly on him. He squeezed the trigger and the gun exploded. The bullets punched through the large beast's chest and thumped through the forklift windshield behind it, killing another gargoyle inside.

Tony didn't stop until the clicking sound of the empty magazine echoed through the open room. His eyes filled with panic as the other creatures roared and swatted in his direction. He was about to run when the work lamps suddenly failed, pitching the room into jet black.

Tony gasped. Something stirred in the shadows, something lean and fast. He watched in horror as something ripped one of the gargoyles into the darkness. It squealed, its cries piercing the silence. The other rounded, but was struck down hard by the monster's swat.

Tony didn't wait to get a good look at this new predator. He scrambled to his feet and sprinted out of the factory and into the night as the sound of gunfire echoed behind him.

He raced through the dimly lit streets, breathing heavily, his footsteps echoing through the alleys and across buildings. He turned a corner and tripped, crashing to the pavement before scrambling back up again. He sprinted, all the while glancing over his shoulder, severely frightened, like he'd seen a ghost and it was gaining on him. He could feel his lungs start to close and he was starting to tire.

Several blocks away, he darted down an alley, right into a chain-link fence. It was locked by a padlock and chain. "No!" he screamed, banging on the fence feebly. He looked over his shoulder, then attempted to climb over the fence, but could not pull himself up. He was too fatigued.

"HELP ME! HEY!" he screamed out into the night, still out of breath and hoping someone was near. But there was no one around. Defeated, Tony bent over to catch his breath.

Tony suddenly stiffened as a deep laugh rang out through the alley. "Did you think you could run?" a demonic voice called. It was unnatural, almost guttural. It sent eerie shivers down his spine.

Tony spun around and raised his Glock, squinting into the blackness. "Wh…who's there?" he called, mostly to just calm himself down by hearing his own voice. Then a shadow darted across the alley and Tony squeezed off five rounds.

"What's the matter Tony? You scared?" the voice bellowed.

"How do you know me?" he stuttered.

A menacing laugh that seemed to come from all directions echoed through the alley. "I know a lot about you."

"Cut the shit! Show yourself!" he cried out in terror.

"As you wish." Out of the shadows of the alley, a creature lumbered forward and stopped. It was difficult to see in the amber glow, but it had a hairy, beastly shape. It was tall and slender. Its hind legs bent unnaturally at the joints like a werewolf from a horror film. Its head was shaped like an overgrown bat and spouted red eyes, big triangular ears with rounded points, and sharp visible fangs.

Tony gasped. He squeezed off six more rounds, which punched straight into the beast's chest. Nothing. The bullets passed through it like it was made of smoke.

The beast laughed.

"What the hell are you, man?" Tony screamed. He went to fire another shot but something clocked him in the jaw. He tripped over himself from the force of the punch and the gun slipped from his hand. It skidded across the pavement and rested beside the alley dumpster.

In a panic, Tony clambered to his feet and lunged at the cloaked figure, swinging wildly, desperate to make contact, but was knocked down by a hard punch-kick combo.

In one final attempt to kill this creature, Tony dove for the gun beside the dumpster. His fingers slid into it and he swung it around, aiming where the monster stood. Instead, he locked eyes with the beast. He tried to move the gun, but something punched the side of his face and grabbed his arm. It twisted and he could feel something snap. He shrieked and fell back.

Tony now lay face up on the ground moaning until the figure reached down with both hands and jerked him to his feet. It lifted him off the ground and pulled him close. A ratty cloth concealed its face.

"Don't kill me, please!" he whimpered.

"You wanna live? Tell me about Andrew Fisher."

Tony sighed as if despair had deflated his soul. "I can't," he said distraughtly.

Ally ignored him. "Who's his supplier? How do they meet? When?"

"Look man, I don't know anything about that!"

She slugged him in the stomach. "You must know something."

"Even if I did," he choked, "do you have any idea what these people will do to a rat?"

"First you have to survive me!" Ally hissed, applying pressure to Tony's injured arm.

"Ahh!" he whimpered. "Okay! I overheard one of the guys talkin'. Said a big guy made Fisher nervous. He said from the way

Fisher acted, he was on thin ice with the guy. You want to hurt Fisher? I imagine disrupting the shipment would piss off the big guy."

"I need a name," Ally growled.

"I swear, I don't know! These ain't the kind of people you ask questions to."

"You need to go," Curtis said into her ear. *"Cops are en route."*

"Go to the police. Tell them about the guns. Offer the shipment in exchange for protective custody."

"Come on, man! If I set one foot in there, I'm a deadman. I won't last a week!"

"The cops will keep you safe."

"You ain't listenin', man! I can't go to the cops… they're in on it! Who do you think makes sure everything makes it through customs?" Tony spluttered.

"Tell him to speak to a Sergeant Lockhart," Curtis said into the mic. *"According to his file, he has the chops to be a Lieutenant, but has been passed up multiple times for promotion, which means he probably isn't dirty."*

"Speak to someone called Lockhart," Ally instructed. "You can trust him."

"Please!"

"You have about 30 seconds to start walking… or I'm going to feed you to my pet."

Tony stole a glance behind her. The beast was still lurking in the shadows. Its eyes were glowing faintly red, and as it took a slow step forward, a drop of saliva fell and hit the pavement.

"Is that a werewolf?" Tony gasped.

The hologram snarled and snapped its jaws, making like it was about to leap forward.

"No!" Ally commanded, halting the projection.

Tony swallowed and inhaled a shaky breath.

"Come on, Ally! Time to go," Curtis said as sirens grew louder.

Ally shoved Tony hard. He crashed into the brick wall with a thud and bounced off, collapsing to the pavement. He raised his good arm in defense, expecting another attack, but the figure was gone.

"Surrender yourself and confess your crimes. Or I'll find you Tony Piciani!"

Tony looked down and picked up the gun again, then he scurried to his feet and limped out of the alley. When he'd made it a block, he looked behind him, still weary that it was out there… watching him.

* * *

Lockhart rubbed the bridge of his nose impatiently. "You didn't answer my question Mr. Piciani. Who did this to you?" he demanded. "Who's responsible for what happened at the factory?"

Tony began muttering in Italian. Most of it was incomprehensible to him, but he did make out a few choice words. Something about a creature, horrible, and… something he couldn't quite place.

"He says he doesn't know," Lydia translated. "He says a creature pounced from the shadows, some kind of beast or demon." She opened her mouth to continue, but stopped herself.

"Go on," Lockhart said.

"He thinks it was a werewolf," she said reluctantly.

Lockhart screwed up his face. "A what? Has his blood work come back?"

"IT WAS A WEREWOLF!" Tony suddenly shrieked, leaping up from his seat and testing the resilience of his chains. "It was fucking real! Look at me!" His eyes were wild and his bared teeth salivated.

Lockhart flinched, but quickly regained control. "Oh, so you speak English now, do you?"

Tony slumped back into his chair, grimacing in pain and scowled.

"Alright, look... I got three of your buddies swearing that you wigged out and shot two people! This werewolf Kool-Aid? I'm not drinking it!"

A knock on the door turned his head. "Talk some sense into your client." Lockhart stood up.

"Sergeant?" Lydia asked. "Something beat up those men. Could it have been The Blur?"

He didn't answer. Instead, he exited the room and the door closed behind him. He'd never admit it, but the way Tony had just snapped chilled him to his core.

Outside, Michaels was standing beside a lab technician. "The lab came back on the contents of the canister we recovered from the scene," Michaels said before turning to the technician. "Tell him what you told me.

The technician consulted her tablet. "We found traces of a compound in his blood called psilocin, a key ingredient in magic mushrooms."

"So he was hallucinating?"

"It looks that way. The mind-altering effects of psilocin vary from person to person, but resemble those of LSD and DMT. This attacker must have found a way to reconstitute it into an aerosol, essentially weaponizing it. It's quite brilliant."

Michaels looked at the technician and thanked her. She nodded and walked away from the observation room.

"So have you checked out his story?" he asked Michaels.

"I sent a team down with Peters to inspect the facility. We'll hear back soon."

"So what do we do now?" Lockhart asked.

"Now, we find this werewolf." He motioned for Lockhart to follow and they both turned and walked away.

*   *   *

Ally followed Tony all the way to the police station before returning to the factory. *"Badass!"* Curtis shouted into the earpiece. *"That's gonna ruin Fisher's weekend."*

"Exactly. Whoever he reports to won't be too happy when they learn the shipment was confiscated by the police. I'm betting whoever Fisher reports to will make sure he focuses on *his* business, and not on mine."

"And if it doesn't?"

"We'll know if someone rings me for the fight."

"Fair enough. In the meantime, I'll send a drone ahead and scout you a clear route home."

CHAPTER 25

Across the city, atop a towering skyscraper, light from a solitary window burned brightly, like a lonely star in a black night. Inside, a long mahogany table reserved for the brass was positioned in front of a million-dollar view of the city. Hal Burton sat at the head of this table, exuding an air of untouchable elitism as his VP brought him up to speed on a matter far more important than dull finance. He listened intently, his poised elegance unwavering. "How many are we talking about?" Hal whispered.

"We estimate nearly a quarter," Mr. Duncan answered.

"Christ! What the hell happened?"

"According to our source, some kind of creature was responsible..."

"A creature?" Hal asked with indignant cynicism.

"Yes... one of Fisher's men was babbling about it. It killed two of his men and—"

"I don't give a damn about the men; I care about my shipment. I want it back in our possession tonight. Just take care of it," Hal barked. "Have you located him?"

"Fisher?" Mr. Duncan nodded. "Your guy is having a... chat... with him now."

* * *

Andrew Fisher collapsed to his knees in a bloody heap. Dully, he raised his arms in a feeble state of denial, though he knew blocking was pointless; the fight was already over. Mr. Clark had just delivered the kind of beating a person just doesn't walk away from. All he could do now was attempt to stay conscious. With every strike, his blood splattered against the dark concrete floor of the slaughterhouse, adding to the permanent stench of flesh, adrenaline and fear ingrained into each stone slab.

* * *

Hal placed his hand thoughtfully on his chin, contemplating what Mr. Duncan was telling him. "Are you confident that Mr. Overgaard will be able to absorb Fisher's assets?" Hal asked.

"Felix is young, but ambitious. He already controls the lower-east side... and with the support of our connections, I believe he could do better."

Hal thought for a moment. "I'm not so sure... he's unpredictable. A liability."

"He'll toe the line."

"And if he doesn't?"

* * *

Mr. Clark lifted Fisher up over his head with an inhuman fit of strength and hung the bloodied man on a meat hook by his duct-taped wrists. It was then that Fisher caught a glimpse of a faint reddish glow that seemed to radiate from the assassin's pores. It was even in his eyes. A person could easily mistake this to be a parlor trick or mere reflection from a nearby lamp, but the rare mineral inside the watch was pulsating radiation through his body. It was brighter the closer one's eyes got to his wristwatch. The effects of the mineral were unique and known to few. Fisher had heard whispers of rare unearthly elements, but chalked them up to be no more than urban legends. It was a mistake he'd now take to his grave.

Mr. Clark walked over to a control console dangling from the ceiling, leaving Fisher hanging nearly unconscious, blood dripping from every orifice. He pressed a button, activating a buzzsaw at the end of a long conveyor track, one which typically brought the carcasses of bulls and steers to a saw blade. The conveyor belt started to move, pulling Fisher straight toward it.

"Nothing personal Mr. Fisher. But our organization is experiencing some cutbacks... and we need to trim the fat," Felix said, enjoying his amusing play on words.

Fisher opened a swollen eye and glimpsed the saw-blade inching closer. He silently cursed, knowing the assassin had purposefully positioned him so that he'd see it all coming. He didn't even have the energy to plead for his life. He just hung there, defenseless and at the mercy of a madman. There was still a chance this was just a message, a warning meant to put him in his place. But a moment later, he screamed as the saw-blade…

* * *

Mr. Duncan shrugged with his eyebrows. "Then we'll handle it."

"Very well. Begin the necessary arrangements."

"It's already done. I'll break the news to our investors and apologize for the latest inconvenience."

Hal nodded approvingly. By now the meeting was progressing to the next matter. The room would soon require Hal's blessing to discuss the next order of business.

"What about our other little problem?" Mr. Duncan asked. "Should we help Fisher's men with their recent legal troubles?"

Hal considered his options. "Let the police do their jobs. That's what we pay them for, isn't it?"

"I'll make the call."

"And Nicholas? Find out who disrupted my shipment."

Mr. Duncan nodded.

* * *

Mr. Clark deactivated the conveyor belt and buzzsaw while Fisher's men jumped forward and began cleaning up the mess. Nobody addressed what they'd just seen. It was the most terrifying and disturbing series of events they'd ever witnessed. Watching Mr. Clark move like that… the beating he took... and still taking out a man like Fisher? It was one of those things that chilled hardened men to their cores.

As Mr. Clark turned and made his way toward the exit, Paulie nervously handed him a towel. He wiped his face and hands, then tossed it back and left without a word.

When he'd disappeared, Felix turned to Paulie. "Is it done?"

"Yes. The shipments have been intercepted on their way to the precinct. They'll be back in our hands shortly.

* * *

Tony sat in his holding cell. Everything was lime green... the walls, the bench... even the damn wall camera in the corner was green. The lights emitted an uncomfortable glow throughout the little room. Was it designed to drive people mad? Because it was doing a pretty good job. At least in here, he was safe.

For the first time in about 24 hours, he breathed a sigh of relief and thought about getting some sleep. He almost smiled at himself. Though this was not the outcome he'd wanted or envisioned, he laid there another 20 minutes feeling surprisingly grateful for everything that had just happened. Being under some oppressive mad man's thumb, like in the Mafia, didn't suit him.

Suddenly the meal slit in the door opened and in slid a food tray. Tony looked at it, puzzled. There was no way it was meal time. Was it standard operating procedure to feed inmates when they first arrived? It couldn't be the case. This wasn't a hotel. It was prison.

As he looked closer and inspected it, he noticed something set underneath a dinner roll—a picture of Tony kneeling next to a little girl... his daughter. He lifted the photo off the tray and sat up. For a moment, he just stared at the photo. Then gasped. Underneath it, lying on the tray, was a razor blade. As if in denial, he sat there and blinked. Then it clicked.

First, he just laughed, though it wasn't joyful. It was out of sheer disbelief. Then, he screamed in anger and started banging and kicking at the door until at last, he broke down and started to cry. He knew it was a message. He knew what he had to do. He knew what would happen if he didn't.

Slowly, he turned back to the tray and picked up the razor blade. He sat down and leaned his back against the cool bricks. He pulled his knees up to his chest and rested his feet flat on the floor. Through tearful eyes, he stared at the blade and took a deep breath.

CHAPTER 26

Early the next morning, like a forest with a predator in its midst, the bustling gym fell silent as a large man and two bodyguards headed straight to Maury's office. They strode past the punching bags hanging from the ceiling, passed the weight racks off to the side, and parted through a group of idle jump ropers.

Maury looked up from his desk and straightened as the men pushed into his office. He regarded the bodyguards as they perched on either side of the doorway like twin vultures. Their beady eyes pierced into his, sending a very clear message. This was not a social call.

The large man sat down in the chair and adjusted his cufflinks. "Mr. Baráo, isn't it?" the man said, more of a statement than a question.

"Yeah. That's me. Can I help you gentlemen?"

The man didn't answer. He just stared, eyeballing him. "Do you know who I am?"

"I'm guessing you're not the man I spoke to on the phone yesterday about volunteering," Maury joked.

"My name is Felix Overgaard. Have you heard of me?"

"I know your reputation."

"Good, then we can skip with the pleasantries." He took a deep breath and exhaled loudly. "I understand you had a certain, shall we say, *understanding*, with a former associate of mine… a Mr. Fisher."

Maury tried not to let his expression betray him.

"I regret to inform you that that arrangement is no longer valid."

"What happened to Fisher?"

"He split," one of the twins said, smirking like he'd told a funny joke.

Maury furrowed his brow. He didn't like the sound of that.

"I'm here to inform you that my employer desires this facility. As such, I'll be sending one of my people to buy out the remainder of your lease and arrange for the transfer. You will be compensated at twice the market value. Thank you for your cooperation. I understand this must be upsetting." Felix did not wait for a response. He stood up and turned to leave.

Maury narrowed his eyes. "Mr. Overgaard." Felix stopped and turned around. "That is not going to happen."

Felix's expression hardened.

"The lease of this property is through the bank. You have no rights to it. And as of tomorrow, I will be paying back all of the debt I owe, in full, and will be signing a new lease. I'm afraid if your employer desires this facility, he'll have to get in line."

The two bodyguards shuffled.

"I see," Felix said, turning to look out the office window. He inhaled a breath. "All these people… these kids," Felix said, gesturing to those scattered around in the dojo, "you look out for them, don't you?"

"I do," Maury said.

"It must be hard to keep your eyes on all of them in a city like this."

Maury stood. "Is that a threat?"

Felix smiled. "I'm here as a courtesy, Mr. Baráo. My employer finds your colorful history amusing. Which is why he's graciously given you until the end of the week to comply. If it were up to me," he said, his eyes like two black holes, "I'd burn this place to the ground with you all still inside it."

Before Maury could react, Felix turned and left the office. His bodyguards followed, but not before they fixed their predatory gaze on him, each burning with fierce intensity, as if daring him to make a move. Then they were gone.

When the door shut, Maury cursed and swept everything off his desk with his arm, then bowed his head and composed himself. He bent down to the floor, reset the telephone and dialed a number.

"We need to meet," he barked. "This can't wait."

"Who was that?" Ally asked when the men had walked far enough away.

Curtis shrugged. "Beats me. Never seen 'em befo—"

"Curtis! Family meeting!"

Maury had stuck his head out of the office door. Curtis nodded all-too-willingly, then assisted Maury with making the rounds and telling the remaining patrons still in the building that they were closing up early today.

"What about me?" Ally asked.

"Here," Curtis said, handing her the smart glasses she'd built for him. "Go nuts," he winked, then wheeled off toward the back.

She looked at the headset in her hands, then set it on the table beside her.

"I'll meet you down in a minute," Maury said. "I'm gonna wait for your dad."

Down? She'd been going to this place for a while now and never saw any downstairs. Is that where Curtis was going? She decided to follow.

Sneaking past the office, she peered around the corner. Curtis flipped up a hidden panel in the wall and started punching in a code on a numerical pad. Every press had a unique pitch. Ally had fiddled with enough electronics over the years to memorize all the distinct tones.

2-4-6-8-5?

She gasped as a section of the wall slid open. *What the hell?A secret door?*

Peering around the wall, she watched Curtis wheel inside and wait until the door closed before walking up to the keypad. She punched in the code and the door slid open. Her feet touched the platform and she felt it begin to lower. When it reached the bottom, she was in what looked like an underground bunker of some kind, only… it was somehow familiar. Maybe she was crazy, but the configuration of this place resembled that of the Burton Conglomerates's research lab. Glancing around quickly, it was equal in size to what she assumed was the room above, where children and young people had been learning martial arts, how to box, and generally just trying to work out. For years, they were none the wiser.

The lights from the ceiling were illuminating various sections of the room, some of which looked like workstations or storage compartments. One table was laid with soldering and welding tools, while others contained various types of electrical equipment. Cupboards and compartments housed what appeared to be non-lethal weapons—flash grenades, smoke bombs, tear gas canisters, and pepper spray. Various ninja weapons ranging from throwing instruments, swords and bow staffs were pegged up on the wall. Then she eyed the shelving units to her left and saw combat and protective gear, bullet-proof vests, and what looked like guns and ammunition.

"So what's the big emergency?" Curtis called, turning around.

He was positioned near a large bank of computers off to one side of the room beside several monitors, which were hooked up together and glowed dimly. When Curtis saw Ally, he opened his mouth like he was going to speak, but he changed his mind. Instead, he scrunched up his face. Finally, all he could manage to say was, "How did you—"

"Curtis… what the hell is this place?"

He exhaled a deflated sigh. "My dad's gonna kill me," he muttered, rubbing his face.

Ally slowly walked towards him. "Curtis…"

"Come here." He maneuvered his wheelchair about the computer system. He waved his hand over some kind of sensor and a beam of light shot onto the table projecting a digital light keyboard and trackpad. His fingers tapped the desk as if he were typing on a real keyboard and several screens came to life. The system Curtis was now accessing looked extremely expensive, like something in a spy movie or hacker's wet dream.

Curtis continued typing and in a few seconds, a video feed popped onto one of the multiple screens. It took Ally a moment to recognize it. But she finally knew what it was. It was a live feed into the police department. She saw a detective doing paperwork at his desk and a few others walking about or standing around chatting.

On a separate screen, another video feed popped up. At first, it just appeared to be a random street. Then she thought it looked familiar, but wasn't quite sure where she'd seen it before.

Curtis stopped typing and took a deep breath. "The night you had a panic attack... when you passed out in the street? What do you remember?"

"Curtis… what the hell is this place?" she demanded.

"Ally, I know you have a lot of questions. This whole thing must seem crazy. I'm going to explain it all to you. But first, answer the question. What do you remember?"

Ally stared at Curtis in frustration. Then her look softened. She could tell he wasn't going to budge. She hated not being in control and hated putting her trust in other people even more. But she thought it best to be patient and do what he said. "I was in the ring," she said. "I looked out into the crowd and thought I saw Mr. Smith. I chased after him into the street, but when I got there, he was gone. Then everything went black. That must have been when I passed out."

"You don't remember anything else?" he asked.

"No, why are you bein' all mysterious? What are you trying to say?"

Curtis tapped his fingers on the desk again. When the video feed started, Ally recognized the place immediately and realized there must've been a security camera positioned across the street with a clear angle of the building where Fisher's underground fight had taken place.

A few seconds later, a man - Mr. Smith - emerged from the entrance to the building and got into a black sedan. It drove away and out of view of the camera.

Ally felt her thoughts drift to the deepest parts of her mind. She was back in the house. She could see her mother gripping her bloody thigh, she could feel the knife to her throat, she could hear the sickening whisper of the silencer.

"Ally?"

She shook off the memory. "So he *was* there!"

"Yeah, but the plates came back fake, so impossible to trace. I tracked them for a while, until there was no CCTV."

Ally glared at Curtis. All she could think about was how long he'd known this man was real. How long she went on doubting herself. "How long have you had this?" she growled, trying not to strangle him.

"Not long. The files were just uploaded yesterday."

"What files?"

"Uh… in a minute. First…" He pointed to the screen.

Ally focused on the video and saw her digital self stumble out into the street, frantically looking every which way. Then something surprised her. An angry crowd poured out of the building led by a large bald man with rolled up sleeves. Marching behind him and in front of the rest of the mob were two mouth-breathers. The leader looked like he was calling out to her.

She watched her digital self just stand there as if in a drunken daze. When Ally didn't turn, he grabbed her by the shoulder and spun her around. He got into her face and screamed at her with muted rage.

As she watched the footage, she couldn't believe what she was seeing. An angry mob was closing in on her, shouting and screaming, but her digital self appeared completely calm and unphased, entranced even, and more concerned with looking around her than the man grabbing at her shoulder.

"No, this isn't right. This didn't happen! I don't remember any of this," she said as if watching someone else entirely. Though she had no memory of it, the footage was undeniable. It was a surreal and unsettling experience, like the stranger on the screen had taken her place in the world.

On screen, having not gotten any kind of response, the large bald man finally shoved her to the ground. The crowd loved it. It was then that a smokey haze rose up silently in the center of the crowd, covering everything in a close radius in gray mist. Then a human figure suddenly appeared on screen. She hadn't noticed it before. The video feed just seemed to reveal the figure's silhouette all at once. Its body was semi-transparent, but human in shape. Before she could ask, Curtis stopped the feed.

"This is the type of video that I let make the news," he said.

"That you *let*?" Ally asked.

"Yeah, one of my jobs is to hack into street cameras and alter the footage. That's how I got this footage of you."

Ally scoffed, doubting the skills of a 16-year-old hacker. "Bull."

Curtis shrugged. He tapped his fingers on the light keyboard, removing the glossy filter and revealing a man dressed in black. "This is what really happened," he said, and Ally turned back to the video monitor.

On screen, a man in black engaged the bald man with a running jump-kick to the chest. Baldie fell backwards and crashed into several people in the crowd, then scrambled back to his feet. The man in black turned his attention to the other thugs in the mosh pit, knocking them back and taking them on one at a time until Baldie came at him with a knife. He slashed his forearm before the man in black ended the fight in a series of impressive martial arts moves. The two mouth-breathers were taken out next in a matter of seconds and this made the crowd retreat and everyone began running away.

As the mist cleared, Ally saw Curtis parked beside a prone body. The man in black picked Ally up and carried her out of view of the CCTV with Curtis following close behind him.

Curtis tapped his fingers on the keyboard again and the video stopped.

She looked at him in disbelief. How was it possible there was a whole other part to this that she had no memory of? Then there was this man in black, who had jumped into the crowd and possibly saved her life. But that wasn't the full story here.

She glanced around this mysterious underground room. There was only one obvious conclusion. The vigilante sightings, the blurry human images and clips on the news, the witnesses—the Blur was real! And Curtis was working with him.

Ally thought back to the night she left the hospital. She remembered Maury's arm was bandaged up and bleeding. If it wasn't for the shock of this new black out, she'd have picked up on it the second she walked into the place.

"I assume the strange figure is Maury?"

Curtis nodded. "He saw you take the flier. He sent me to try to talk you out of it. But when I went to your house, your foster family said you had gone out. By the time I got to the fight, it was too late. You had already made the bet. So I called my uncle because I figured there'd be trouble."

Ally suddenly felt the need to sit down. Her brain felt like it was about to explode. This was a lot to process. Curtis sat still watching her. When she'd taken a breath, he continued. "You asked me what we were doing at the police station earlier... I installed a gateway."

"A what?"

"Okay... police and other agencies sometimes have closed networks that don't have a direct link to the web. It keeps them from getting hacked. So a gateway is like a master key. I can use it to gain access to the entire system inside the police department, from cameras and security locks to the computer files. I can even adjust and play with the lights, which I do when I'm bored sometimes. I'm pretty sure I have one of the detectives convinced the building is haunted," he laughed, but stopped when Ally didn't share his taste in play. "Anyway... the plan was to take a look at the case files. Maybe if we dig around a little... you know, read the witness statements, the forensics... the coroner's report... maybe we might be able to piece together what happened that night."

"You can access the files?" Ally asked.

Curtis studied her sullen face. "What?" he asked. "I thought you'd be happy."

"I am, but... Curtis, what is this place? There is no way you guys can afford to pay for all of this."

"Uncle Maury, my dad and I, are sort of a… well, we're… we're like a superhero team, okay? And we… umm, we pick a target. Like drug dealers. We stake them out, bust them up and take their money."

"So you rob drug dealers… and the GoFundMe page you set up is, what? A way to launder the money?"

"Well, it's not that simple… I mean, technically yes… but we don't keep the money. We invest it back into the community."

"What do you mean?"

"Like when someone can't pay their rent, or afford their college tuition. Or maybe they have a job interview and don't have the right clothes. That kind of thing. We step in. We even pay Fisher to look after our members with his own money," he said, chuckling.

Ally thought about this for a moment. Morally, did the ends justify the means? Was taking blood money and using it for good, ethical?

"Don't do that," Curtis said, interrupting her thoughts.

"Do what?"

"That look. We aren't the bad guys. We do a lot of good in this community."

"I didn't say anything."

"Yeah, well the only person who thought that Robin Hood was a dick was the sheriff. Just sayin'." Curtis checked his watch. "We can talk more later. Right now, you need to get out of here before—"

He didn't have time to finish his sentence. A sound from behind them made his face drop. The lift was being operated again. "Oh shit," he said. "Ally, hide!"

CHAPTER 27

Ally looked around. There wasn't any place to hide. The room was open plan. "Where?" she demanded sarcastically.

The doors to the lift opened and out stepped Marcus and Maury. When they saw Ally, their expressions went from surprise to anger.

"Umm, hi Dad… Uncle Maury," Curtis said with a sheepish grin like he'd been caught with his pants down. "I can explain…"

Both brothers stopped dead in their tracks and stared at the intruder now standing in their lair. For a moment, they didn't know what to say. Letting slip the biggest secret their family had ever held will do that.

"Dammit, Curtis. We agreed not to get her involved!" Marcus finally blurted, walking toward them. He ran his fingers through his hair and paced the room.

He turned to his brother. "I knew this would happen! This is how it starts."

"Calm down," Maury said.

"Don't tell me to calm down!" Marcus yelled. "We all agreed that anything major would be a group decision!" He turned his attention to Curtis. "A girl pays you a little attention and you just spill your guts? How could you be so selfish?"

"It's not like that!" Curtis protested. "I didn't tell her anything! She—"

"Do you have any idea of the responsibility you've just laid on her shoulders?" Marcus interrupted.

Curtis lifted his chin. "If I can handle it, so can she."

"But you *can't* handle it, Curtis. You've just proved it! We don't know anything about her! What happens if she tells someone? Huh? They'll use her to get to us," Marcus said.

"I trust her," Curtis said. "She's not going to tell anyone."

"I'm glad you trust her, Curtis," Marcus said sarcastically. "That will make me feel a whole lot better when she goes running to the press."

"I would never do that," Ally interjected. "You don't know me."

"You hear that Maury? She says she won't tell anyone. I feel a whole lot better," he said cruelly before turning back to his son. "What's worse, is that you've just endangered her life... and ours! What you don't seem to understand is every person who finds out about us becomes a liability."

"Help me out Uncle Maury," Curtis said, turning to his uncle.

"I agree with him," he said. "This is a responsibility that she didn't ask for. It was reckless and stupid to involve her."

Curtis frowned. "Like I was trying to say, I didn't involve her, she just… I don't know… she just—"

"I said, I won't tell anyone!" Ally interrupted, raising her voice.

"That isn't something you can promise," Marcus said. "People always think they're strong, but when the right amount of pressure is applied, we find out who we really are. Everyone cracks when they're tortured. *Everyone*! It's just a matter of time."

Ally wondered if Marcus was speaking from personal experience. There was something about the way he said it, like there was a deep regret in his voice. But now was not the time to ask if he was ever a POW.

"Look, for years we've been searching for someone to take Maury's place. You've never found anybody. Well, *I have* found somebody!" Curtis yelled.

"Wait, what? Take his place?" Ally cried.

"She's not cut out for this," Marcus grunted, ignoring her.

"*Not cut out for it*?" Curtis scoffed. "One night with Ally's tech and a truckload of guns were taken off the streets! The police said it was the largest bust in history. With those guns off the streets, that means fewer deaths, robberies, and gangs getting their hands on them."

"Yeah, and you managed to draw attention in the process," Marcus said.

"But Dad—"

"No Curtis!"

"But she—"

"Shut your mouth, boy! I can't believe you!" he screamed. "After all I've taught you?"

Curtis sat still looking like you'd expect after being shouted at for two minutes.

"And what do you have to say for yourself!?" he yelled to Ally.

"You're welcome," she replied coldly.

A flicker of anger boiled behind Marcus's eyes. "Excuse me?"

"You're welcome," she repeated.

Marcus cocked his head and made a move toward Ally like he was going to clobber her, but Maury stepped in front of him and stopped him. "Take a walk!" Maury said. "Cool off."

Marcus jerked his arm away from his brother and glared at her. He leaned against a table and gripped the edge with his hands before pacing back and forth, shaking his head.

Maury turned to Ally. "What did you mean, you're welcome?"

"When I left here the other night, your pal Fisher sent a few of his boys down to *my* place. They drugged me and abducted me at gunpoint."

"Jesus!" Maury cried. Marcus stopped pacing. He turned abruptly, anger replaced by genuine concern. His eyes were wide and his mouth hung open.

"They brought me to the old depot in the Scrubs. When I came to, Fisher blackmailed me. He had pictures of everyone I had ever hung out with. Your clients, the soup kitchen volunteers, everyone… including you three. He said if I didn't do what he wanted, he'd kill each of them, one by one. I tried to call his bluff, but he nearly shot Samantha right in front of me."

Marcus no longer cared about the breach of trust. He stepped forward, intently listening.

"I forced Curtis to help me take down the men at the warehouse so I could stop him. So I could shut his operation down. So the police could start investigating. I did it to protect everyone. Curtis only helped me because I threatened to expose you all to the police if he didn't."

Maury looked at Curtis, who quickly nodded. "No you didn't," he said, seeing right through it. "If you'd have coerced Curtis, he'd have made sure you were caught."

"It doesn't matter… everyone is safe. So yeah, you're welcome."

"Nothing is that simple," Maury said. "Your actions have altered the deal I had with Andrew Fisher. Thanks to your little stunt, Fisher's dead. And he's been replaced by someone worse. His name is Felix Overgaard."

"That must have been the big guy we saw leaving earlier," Curtis whispered to Ally.

"Now that Fisher's gone, the arrangement I had with him is no longer valid. Which means our boys are now at risk."

"And you've put a target on his back," Marcus scowled. "This Overgaard mobster just threatened to hurt everyone if Maury doesn't turn this place over to him. And then there's the police! Do you have any idea how long the cops have been waiting for an excuse to make him a public enemy?"

"What you should have done, was come to us," Maury said.

Ally bowed her head, considering what was said.

Maury turned to Curtis. "I'm disappointed in you."

"I'm sorry, okay? But I say we go after Felix next," Curtis chimed in. "You should have seen what Ally did to Fisher's men. It was incredible."

"We aren't equipped to start a war with the mob," Maury said.

"We *can* with Ally's tech. Don't you see? Now she can join us."

"We agreed to wait, Curtis! We don't even know if she's sane!" Marcus said.

"Jesus Christ." Ally sighed, rubbing her eyes with her palms, and walked toward the lift.

"Where do you think you're going?" Marcus barked, stepping in front of her and blocking her path.

"I don't need this shit. And where I go is none of your business."

"All of this?" Marcus gestured to the room. "This makes it my business."

"I have better things to do than watch you all have a domestic," she said, staring Marcus down.

"You're not going anywhere until we've finished discussing this!"

"Discussing what? How you guys sit around playing Batman and Robin?" she scoffed. "Get out of my way."

"We need to decide what to do with you. I don't trust you. We can't just let you leave."

"So your plan is to what? Kidnap me?"

"She's right, Marcus. Let her go," Maury said.

Marcus glared at her, then grudgingly stepped aside and allowed her to walk into the lift.

"Ally, wait!" Curtis called.

"You should have told me your help was conditional," she scolded, stepping onto the lift platform. It began ascending, giving her just enough time to add, "Don't worry. I won't tell anyone about your stupid Batcave."

The lift ascended into the level above and Ally stormed out of the doors and onto the street, her strides fueled by all the choice words she should have said. Her blood boiled under her skin, willing her legs to get as much distance from those idiots as possible.

As she glared at the pavement, she felt her phone start to vibrate. She ripped it out of her pocket, ready to scream, *Go to hell!*, but it was a message from Dr. Hansen:

👋 Ally. U missed R appt. □ I'm heading out of the office for a bit. 📞 me/meet me @ Flutters ☕ in an hour. If I don't 👂 from u, I'll have 2 report it

Ally stopped. Suddenly, everything was clear. She needed to tell her about the CCTV! It proves that he was there, that she saw him, that she wasn't crazy. She suddenly felt a wave of excitement. Finally, she had proof!

She checked the timestamp; the message was sent nearly 45 minutes ago. She sighed in relief and sent a reply:

On my way. Maybe 10 min.

She was only a few blocks away from Flutters, so if she hurried, she could make it. She stuffed her phone back into her pocket and headed toward the coffee shop.

*   *   *

The lift reached the top floor and the mechanical whir left the room in silence. Maury looked at Curtis, a little calmer now. "The decision should have been ours to make. Our survival depends on us making decisions as a group."

"Okay. I understand that. But you saw what she did to Terrence. She dropped him with one kick."

"Sometimes people get lucky," Maury added.

"Lucky? Okay. But you didn't see what she did to Grzegorz. She took out Fisher's undefeated champion in less than two minutes!"

Maury raised his eyebrows, conceding the point.

"Oh, come on!" Marcus interjected. "If I have to be the one to say it, then I'll say it."

"Don't say it," Curtis muttered, rubbing his palms over his eyes in frustration.

"You and I both know a woman cannot go toe-to-toe with a highly-skilled man."

"He said it," Curtis sighed.

"But even if she could…"

"She did!"

"Maybe so… but even if she—"

"It's not 'maybe so'… she did!"

“Ok… but that was still just one fighter!” Marcus said. “It’s another thing entirely to go up against multiple fighters at the same time, pissed off and full of adrenaline. Women don’t have the physical strength.”

Curtis sighed in frustration. “Multiple fighters? You want to see her take on multiple fighters? Check this out!” He rolled over to the computer array and brought up the drone footage from Fisher’s abandoned toy factory.

The two brothers watched in fascination as Fisher’s men shot wildly at various monstrous projections, then one by one got ripped into the shadows by a dark figure. The drones were creating holographic distractions to draw their fire, leaving Ally free to clobber them.

“As I’ve been saying,” Curtis said. “She’s legit.”

“I have to hand it to her, she can handle herself in a fight. And the tech *is* impressive,” Maury admitted, deep in thought. “Sure beats getting shot at.”

“Or shot,” Marcus agreed, having patched up his brother one too many times.

“So? What do you think?” Curtis finally asked. “Is she in?”

“Pull up the footage again,” Maury said.

CHAPTER 28

Ally listened to the espresso machines and steamers spraying out amongst the noisy café clatter like part of a percussion symphony. She watched baristas scurry over one another, trying to keep pace with orders, while patrons sat at tables slurping sugary drinks and stuffing their faces with muffins, oblivious to all the effort and hard work.

She'd chosen a booth which had a full view of the front door on account of her anxiety. She didn't like large crowds. Though she had every right to be here, she somehow felt out of place, like the coffee in her hand was the only reason she wasn't being exposed as a fraud.

Looking around, everyone else seemed to be in their element. The laughs, the occasional cackle, the flirtatious looks. She wondered if any of it was genuine. *Were people really this happy inside?* It all seemed like a performance to her. She'd never felt part of a group and she had only this empty table to remind her of that.

Her thoughts were interrupted when Dr. Hanson plopped down a little too hard onto the cushioned seat, letting out a little whoop as the drop startled her. "Sorry that took so long. It's a madhouse today." She slurped foam off of her latte and savored the aroma before relaxing against the seat. "Mmm, that's good." She closed her eyes and allowed herself a brief moment. "So, Ally… what happened today? Why did you miss our appointment?"

Ally took a deep breath, unsure of where to start. She felt a lump in her throat and though she hadn't had a sip of her coffee, her heart was fluttering like she'd overdosed. "Remember in the hospital when we talked about Mr. Smith?" Dr. Hansen took another sip, nodding in affirmation. "I can prove he's real."

Dr. Hansen raised an eyebrow, her eyes crinkling. "Ally…"

"Wait." Ally leaned forward, her eyes intense. "I have CCTV footage from a street camera. It captured him getting into a car!"

Dr. Hansen set her latte down and leaned back in her chair. "Look, Ally, I understand you believe what you're saying, but—"

Ally's frustration bubbled up inside her, threatening to overflow. She clenched her jaw, trying to keep her composure.

"—It's important to remember that your mind can play tricks on you."

"No! It's him!" Her words carried a hint of sharpness, a restrained anger simmering just beneath the surface. "I've been telling the truth for eight years! This proves it!"

Dr. Hansen sighed and shook her head gently. "No, Ally. It doesn't."

Ally frowned. "You're not listening. I have him on CCTV!"

"I believe you have a man on camera… but do you have any way of proving to me that it *is* Mr. Smith… and not just a random man?"

Ally stared dumbfounded. She opened her mouth but only exhaled a slight gurgling sound. Her face contorted with hurt and desperation. She groaned, feeling trapped in her own mental prison. Dr. Hanson was right. The proof was only in her head.

Dr. Hansen nodded kindly in a way that made Ally's blood boil. "Are you free tomorrow? I think we need to schedule an emergency session. We need to address these delusions."

Ally looked away in frustration. It was then that her attention was suddenly drawn to the entrance of the coffee shop—to two police officers. She was taken by an instant feeling of familiarity. She stared open-mouthed as they sauntered in, pushing their way through to the front of the line, much to the displeasure of the people who had been waiting. The thirsty patrons began making loud disproving comments, but the cops ignored them and rested their elbows on the counter.

"I know this is hard," came Dr. Hansen's voice, "but we're going to get through this. I promise you, I am going to help you. But we just need—"

Ally suddenly stiffened in her seat. Her eyes went wide and she inhaled a sharp breath through her nose. She stood from her chair, slowly, dazed, like her eyes were playing tricks on her.

"Ally? What are you—"

Ally felt something inside of her snap. She snatched Dr. Hansen's steaming cup, storming away from the table and ignoring her startled cries. She marched toward the cops, moving quicker and quicker with each step, until she was nearly in a run.

"Hey, Officer!"

Buzzcut turned, and Ally thrust the cup of scalding liquid into his face. He screamed, both in surprise and pain, and shielded his eyes. Ally quickly spun back to Beardy and slugged him hard in the nose, feeling his bones crack on her knuckles. She reached out, gripped a canister of pepper spray from his belt and booted him hard in the chest. He flew backwards and landed onto his back, blood leaking down his lips and chin.

The sudden action threw a crowd of people into surprise. They gasped and leaped back.

Behind her, Buzzcut recovered and drew his weapon, but Ally spun around and pepper sprayed him. He shrieked again, shielding his face with his hands and frantically clawed at his eyes before waving his gun blindly in her direction, desperate to see his attacker.

Ally hesitated, but counted on him not daring to fire blind into a full crowd. Behind her, she sensed Beardy climb to his feet. She whirled just in time to dodge a swing from his nightstick.

Ally bounced the canister off his forehead, and lunged forward, grabbing hold of his club. She twisted, relieving him of it, and struck him under the chin with a hard uppercut, the swung it down onto Buzzcut's arm in one fluid motion. She felt the bone crack and he dropped the gun, cradling his wounded limb.

Ally was not in the mood for mercy. She swung the nightstick across his head hard, dropping him to the floor with a loud thud. She watched Beardy whimper and cradle his broken jaw, snuffing blood from his nose and blinking furiously, all the while scooting back on his rear with his legs in pure instinctual survival.

The crowd was in complete disarray. Some had pulled out their phones and were recording the hullabaloo while others clapped and cheered. Some were cowering and trying to get away.

Ally dropped the baton, grabbed Buzzcut by the collar, and dragged him out the door.

"That's what you get for cutting in line!" someone in the crowd shouted.

"Yeah, no cuts, bitch!" laughed another.

With labored effort, she managed to shove him into the trunk of his squad car before she heard Dr. Hansen's voice.

"Ally! Stop! Ally!"

Their eyes met and Ally shot her a hardened look that made Abby take a step back. Then she slipped into the driver's seat and sped away.

CHAPTER 29

Peters felt himself begin to stir, suddenly aware that he was rocking gently from side to side, swinging like a pendulum in the breeze. He noticed the cold wind first as it rustled his hair, tickling his scalp. Something clinked together, delicate, like metal, almost white noise against the sounds of an angry city blaring in the distance. But there was something else... something familiar, like... like sirens!

Detective Greg Peters's eyes suddenly shot open as if waking from a bad dream. He gasped and blinked out into a cold darkness, into an upside-down world of open air, metal beams and unfinished sheetrock. Pain pulsed through his body, and his head pounded from the hangover he never earned. His vision hurt him, like being blinded by the sun and slowly faded into focus. He couldn't understand why the world was frustratingly upside-down, why he was hung limply from a winch hook by his ankles, or why his hands were bound together behind his back. He tried to force his brain to remember what happened, but was met with only throbbing pain.

He couldn't see himself, but he became acutely aware of the smeared streaks of dried blood that had trickled past what he assumed was now a broken nose and swollen cheekbones. The truth was, Peters had just taken a beating, the kind few were willing to give to a policeman.

As his vision cleared and he realized there was no escape, he noticed something that made his skin crawl. Sitting criss-cross on the floor in front of him, deep in meditation, was a bony undead creature out of someone's nightmare. Two soul-piercing dead eyes burned at him above a snarling and freakishly large toothy grin of porcupine quills.

His breath caught and he stifled a gasp.

*   *   *

Nearby, on an adjacent street below them, a blue sedan pulled up beside two other police cars flashing blue and red. Lockhart opened the door and stepped out.

"Sarge!" Sutko hurried up to him. "We've set up a five block perimeter and we're sweeping the area now. So far, no sign of him."

"And the girl?"

"No sign of her either, but the K-9's have just arrived. We'll find them."

"Thank you, Detective."

Sutko nodded and hustled off.

* * *

Ally sat criss-cross on the cold roof glowering at Peters. It took every ounce of strength she had to wait for him to regain consciousness. Luckily she didn't have to wait long. He began to stir just as chatter squawked over the police radio. The volume was turned down, but it was loud enough for two people on the roof of the construction building to hear: *"West side clear. Proceeding south. Over."*

"Hear that? My friends are coming," Peters said smugly.

Ally stepped toward the dangling man and spoke, her voice changer croaking ominously. "Well that doesn't give us a lot of time to chat."

She'd made some improvements to her signature projections. What used to be only independent and external distractions, was now an encompassing live-action hologram suit. The holograms continuously tracked her movements, coating her limbs and body in the desired effect. In this case, a bipedal, hominid figure with thin gangly legs, unnatural joints, hairy feet and large clawed hands. They could still operate fully independently if she wished, but now, the drones hovered around her, disguising her body in illusion.

"You think all this is supposed to scare me?"

Ally smiled, her porcupine quills spreading into a nightmarish grin. "No. This is." She picked up a small paint can and a brush and lathered a sticky glue-like substance all over the toe of Peters's boot. He squirmed, testing the strength of his bonds but came up short. "We're going to play a game, Detective..." Ally said, tossing the can and brush aside. "It's called Candle."

Peters scrunched up his face, but she could tell he regretted it when the pain pulsated through him.

"I'm going to light your boot on fire," she answered, "and as the flame begins to burn through the rubber, you'll start to feel heat in your toes. Answer my questions before you burn, and you win. Sounds like fun, right?"

Ally held up a blowtorch, sparked the tip, and adjusted the flame to a soft blueish-white. Of course, she didn't need a blowtorch. She could have just as easily lit a match. But this was for effect. She wanted him to dread every coming second. Anticipation is always worse than experience.

"Woah! Woah! Stop! I don't know who you think I am… or what you think I know, but I don't know what the *fuck* this is about!" he screamed angrily.

"Now, now, Detective... you're not playing by the rules." She waved the torch over the end of his boot and the glue ignited. Black smoke began swirling from the flame as the chemicals in the rubber bubbled and blistered. She clicked off the blowtorch, but the flame on the boot continued to dance in the breeze.

Peters convulsed, screaming and wriggling, trying desperately to get free, but it was no use. Ally had secured his bonds tightly.

"Eight years ago, you and another cop killed a woman, Sara Reid, and her daughter, Emmalee. She was 9. I need you to tell me what happened that night. And if I were you, I'd make it fast."

"You're gonna have to kill me," he said, keeping his eyes fixed on his flaming boot.

"There are fates worse than death," she said, holding up the blowtorch.

"You wouldn't."

"As I said… no time to chat." Her voice came out low and cold, like an animal's growl. Ally could tell from his expression that he believed her.

* * *

A few blocks away, Lockhart stood hunched over the hood of Peter's abandoned squad car studying a map of the surrounding city blocks. The biting wind clawed at the map's edges, but Lockhart was busily calculating distances and footpaths. By his calculations, a woman could drag a man anywhere in a half-mile radius in the assumed timeframe.

Above the sound of nearby police clatter and car horns in the distant city soundscape, he heard footsteps approaching. "Sergeant!" An officer sprinted up the street. He was out of breath for such a short run and panted beneath the flickering glow of a nearby streetlight. "Sergeant! We just got a call. Witnesses reported hearing screams near a construction site, out on 22nd," he panted, his breath visible in the cool night air.

Lockhart's face flickered as he adjusted his heavy overcoat. "I want a perimeter set up there, now! Get me SWAT! And a K9 unit," he commanded.

"Right!" the officer yelled. With a swift nod, he sprinted away.

“We’ve got you now, you son-of-a-bitch,” Lockhart muttered to himself. He folded the map, stuffed it back into his jacket and leapt back into his car.

* * *

From below, Ally heard the sound of a squad car’s pulse siren and a door slamming shut. She peered over the side of the rooftop and studied the commotion. Cops were gathering up. A German Shepherd hopped out of a squad car, growling and barking excitedly and pulling on its leash.

“My foot, man! My foot!” Peters screeched.

Ally picked up a soda bottle, which was lying off to the side, and dumped the remains over the tip of his shoe. A yellowish liquid sloshed over Peters’s face and into his mouth.

“Ugh! Was that piss?” he whined, coughing and spluttering.

Ally whirled her head toward the staircase. Voices were growing louder and the sound of drumming boots were clomping closer. She could hear excited yelping and the sound of claws digging their way up the stairs, desperate to break free of its handler.

“You’re fucked now!” Peters laughed. “I’m up here! Up h—”

Ally turned and angrily soccer-kicked him in the head, knocking him out. She made a break for the fire escape on the other side of the roof, but seconds later, the door was kicked open and five armed officers flooded through it. She was out of time. Having no choice, she ducked and cowered into the shadows of the wall half-way to her exit.

“POLICE! FREEZE!” The officers shouted, turning their guns in all directions, searching for movement or any sign of her.

Ally watched the leader direct the squad with silent hand gestures and cautiously step across the roof toward Peters. He held up a fist and he clicked the button on his shoulder mic.

“We’ve located Peters. Checking for signs of life.” The leader leaned in and checked for a pulse. “He’s alive. Send EMTs.”

“What about the woman?” a voice barked into the radio.

“Stand by,” he replied.

Suddenly, the dog began barking excitedly and dug its claws into the floor, trying desperately to leap in her direction.

“Come out with your hands up!” an officer ordered.

Ally didn’t reply. She hoped it was a bluff and they couldn’t see her in the shadows.

“Comply or we will use force!” a cop ordered.

Ally didn't move.

"Release the dog!"

Not a bluff.

Ally saw the German Shepherd break free of the harness and leap towards her. With no escape route in sight, she reached into her fanny pack, but the German Shepherd was already on her.

She recoiled, catching the dog by its chest and head. It lunged at her, its snarling jaws mere inches from her face. She tried to shield herself, but it was too strong. It writhed free from her grasp and sunk its teeth into her arm, ripping and tearing at the flesh with every shake of its head. Ally screamed. Blood spurted from the wound. The pain was excruciating, and Ally's vision began to swim as she struggled to break free. She began to panic.

In a last ditch effort, she let go of the dog, reached for the canister of hallucinogenic gas in the pocket of her pack, and sprayed it directly into the dog's snout.

As the gas engulfed it, the beast began to writhe on the ground, yelping in pain. It was a horrible sound, like it was being beaten. It pawed at its face, aggressively at first, then its movements became slow and disoriented.

Ally scooted back and examined her arm. It was bleeding bad. She wouldn't know how bad until she got out of there. But first, she had to *get* out of there!

"Over there!" the handler yelled. The dog stepped out of the shadows and stood still. "Come!" he called. The dog paced a few short steps, whined, and sat down, whimpering and shaking its head. "What's the matter, girl?"

"Worthless fucking mutt," another officer growled. "She's in there somewhere! Go get her!"

As he raised his gun, the dog suddenly leapt onto him and sunk its teeth into his arm. The officer screamed in pain and dropped to his knees, trying desperately to get the dog to release its grip while the handler struggled to regain control.

When the dog smelled its handler, it released its grip on the officer and cowered, confused by what it smelled and what it saw. Finally, it decided to turn and bolt for safety.

Ally couldn't afford to wait any longer. She raced from the shadows.

"POLICE! FREEZE!"

To her right, S.W.A.T. agents rushed the rooftop. For a moment, Ally thought she could jump, but she'd never survive the landing. There was also no way she could take on six heavily armed

S.W.A.T. agents either, not without any of her usual tricks. And her arm was fucked.

She stopped and held her hands up, but was taken aback as the agents started backing up, murmuring.

Ally followed their gaze. She must have been seeing things. In the sky, a winged creature flapped and screeched. A dragon swooped down out of the sky and breathed fire all over the rooftop. Confused officers ducked and swatted their hands, anticipating the scalding flames scorching their skin from their bodies. The ones that could, ran for cover while the handler jumped and shielded his dog from the coming inferno.

The S.W.A.T. agents shrieked and thrashed about on the rooftop. One sprinted away from what looked like a velociraptor from Jurassic Park and knocked himself out by running straight into a wall. The others were trying to get away from other creatures. They couldn't believe what was happening, and neither could Ally!

She sprinted toward the stairway of the building, but was blocked. "End of the line, sweet—" the cop yelped as a figure in black body-slammed him to the ground and struck him. Ally stood gaping. Standing right in front of her… was the blur. Maury had come for her!

"Let's go!" he shouted, sprinting to the side of the building and leaping over the edge and onto the rooftop of the next building. She didn't hesitate. She didn't have a choice. She followed him.

They sprinted to the stairway and began their descent, but could hear the sound of boots drumming in their direction. "In here!" Maury called, leading her onto another floor. They ran as fast as their legs would carry them all the way to the opposite side of the building and entered the stairway.

More cops were running up the stairs, which gave Maury no other choice. He engaged, flipping and kicking his way through the officers in an impressive display of martial arts prowess, taking them on two-at-a-time and dropping them like bad habits. He pushed some down, rolled across the backs of others, and shoved them into one another.

Behind them, three hover drones floated in pursuit, covering their retreat with decoy projections and drawing their fire. One drone fired a taser disc, attaching it to a cop's chest just as he aimed at Maury.

Maury body-slammed him to the floor and struck him with a hard punch to the face. He hit him so hard Ally thought he may have cracked his skull against the concrete. The last cop left standing aimed his pistol at Maury. Ally, despite her injured arm, struck him across the face and finished him off with a backflip kick to the chin. He fell back and landed on a pile of discarded construction supplies.

She grimaced and cradled her arm.

From there, they sprinted down the remaining flights of stairs until they were on the ground. Two drones projected two figures sprinting near the front of parked police cars, drawing the attention of officers on the ground, who dashed after them.

When the coast was clear, they silently slipped into a nearby alleyway. Maury tore at a sleeve of his shirt, ripping a strip from it, and tied it tightly around Ally's throbbing arm. The blood flow slowed to a drip.

He led her further into the shadows where Maury had stashed his bike. She hopped on the back and Maury fired up the engine. Together, they sped away to safety.

On the other side of the building, Lockhart stood by the squad cars listening to the screams and shrieks. "DAMNIT!" he shouted. "What the hell is happening up there?"

There was no answer.

"SOMEBODY TALK TO ME!"

He dropped the CB radio and took four leaps forward. He made up his mind to find out what was happening for himself, but stopped when he heard the radio chime: "Sir, you're not gonna believe this."

Lockhart picked up the CB again. "What's happening? What about the girl?"

"We lost her," an officer said.

Lockhart chucked the CB, took a swing at the air, and kicked the side of the car, nearly breaking his foot. He hopped and growled then limped his way all the way up the stairs and stepped onto the roof to see for himself just what in the hell had happened.

"Sergeant!" Detective Sutko yelled.

Sutko was helping to lower Peters's body down onto the roof. Peters was muttering and babbling under his breath. The word "MURDERER" was written on his forehead in black sharpie. Lockhart moved out of the way as the EMTs loaded Peters onto a gurney and began carrying him away.

"Is Peters bent?" Sutko asked. Lockhart didn't answer, but this whole situation was strange. Why would someone abduct a cop? Leaving him alive meant he had information. But what?

"Sergeant. There's something else. This was found lying beside Detective Peters."

Lockhart took what looked like a digital tape recorder from Sutko. On it, was a piece of paper taped to the side with his name on it. He stared at it, then clicked play.

CHAPTER 30

They rode the rest of the way in silence until Maury slowed the bike to a stop and disengaged the engine. Ally was about to say something, but he turned his head to the side. "Anything you have to say to me, you can say to the group."

Ally smirked at her own words being parroted back to her.

They stepped onto the lift and descended into the lair. Marcus and Curtis both lifted their heads from a computer array. As expected, their deflated faces lacked warmth.

"Come on," Maury said, stepping off the platform and ushering her over towards them.

Curtis clicked a few keys and brought up the security feed from the coffee shop as Ally stepped forward. On screen, she watched a black woman stand up from a table and attack two police officers. He paused the feed.

"Could be anybody," she tried.

Curtis cleared his throat and typed a few commands, calling up dozens of images from social media and recordings from patron's cell phones, all clearly showing high quality images of her face.

The gravity of the situation hit her in full force now that she was thinking clearly. By now, the cops likely knew her identity and would be searching for her. She was looking at serious jail time.

"They're calling you the "No Cuts, Bitch," Curtis giggled.

"Not helpful, Curtis," Maury growled. He turned to Ally. "Who was that guy to you?"

Ally sighed. She pinched the bridge of her nose and bowed her head while she decided where to begin. "He was there that night," she finally said, her voice empty. "He was one of the cops that worked with Mr. Smith."

"You sure about that?" he asked.

"When I was a kid, I heard his voice and I saw his face. It was him," she said definitively.

The room quieted.

"Well, I hope it was worth it. Every cop in the city's probably out looking for you right now," Maury said.

"That won't matter for much longer. I've got a lead. Peters said his former partner, Brian Davis, set the whole thing up and even knows who Mr. Smith is. We find Davis, we find Smith."

"We?" Marcus interjected. "There is no *we*. The only reason we helped you tonight was because we've seen enough people get killed by the police."

"What he means is, we're going to help negotiate your surrender," Maury said. "Safely."

"I can't. Not until I finish this."

"Ally, finding this guy could take years. Until then, you really want to live the fugitive life? Every day looking over your shoulder?"

"I don't know, Maury. But this is the closest I've ever been. Davis may be the key to the last puzzle piece. I have to see this through."

The team was still for a moment, then they asked Ally to let them confer amongst themselves.

"I can't believe we're discussing this," Marcus chimed in. "Did everybody forget that she beat up two cops in broad daylight?"

"One of which murdered her mother," Curtis reminded him.

"*Allegedly*," Marcus clarified. "That distinction is very important. We can't just go around assaulting police officers without evidence."

"The evidence is in her head," Curtis said.

"You know what else is in her head? Mental illness."

Curtis rolled his eyes.

"She said it herself. She takes antipsychotic meds! How can we really think this is a good idea?"

"She's not crazy. She just has repressed memories," Curtis insisted.

"We still don't know if any of it happened," Marcus finished.

"I heard that man confess," Maury said. "I believe her."

Marcus crossed his arms. "Well, people tend to tell you what you want to hear when you beat the truth out of them."

Maury shook his head. "He knew too many details. Beating, or no beating," he added.

"Alright. This isn't helping. Let's just vote," Curtis said. "All those in favor of helping Ally?"

Curtis and Maury both raised their hands. Marcus didn't.

"All those in favor of inviting Ally to be part of the team, assuming she's not delusional, of course."

Again, Curtis and Maury both raised their hands, and once again Marcus didn't.

"Then it's settled. If Davis knows something, we'll figure that out later. And if he doesn't, we'll negotiate her surrender."

Grudgingly, Marcus turned to follow the others.

Ally looked at Curtis, who winked at her.

"We've decided to help you find out what Davis knows," Maury said, "but there are ground rules."

"Such as?"

"One: you follow my lead. You do what the group decides. No cowboy antics. If we say walk away, you walk away."

Ally thought for a moment. "Ok, deal."

"Two: when this is all over, you turn yourself into the police. It was against the law what you did. That needs to be answered for."

Ally laughed. "And beating up crackheads and drug dealers before stealing their money doesn't?"

"I beat up criminals we caught red handed, out of the public eye. You attacked two police officers in front of dozens of witnesses."

"It was pretty cool," Curtis muttered.

Maury shot him a dirty look. "It wasn't cool. All the public sees is an unprovoked attack on benevolent public servants. To them, Peters is a victim. And you're a psychotic menace."

"Fine, deal," Ally agreed.

"And there's one more thing. No killing," Maury said. "If this man did it, we agree here and now to turn him in to the police."

Ally nodded in agreement, though she knew if things came to that, she had no intention of letting her family's killer live.

"Then let's get started," Maury said.

Across town, Peters laid awake in his hospital bed, listening to the melodious heart rhythm as it chimed and chirped. He could hear the scuffle of nurses wandering from room to room, checking on their patients and attending to hospital duties. He wasn't sure what hurt more, the embarrassment or the beating.

He could hear Lieutenant Michaels talking with a woman outside. He shifted in the bed with some difficulty and caught sight of her. She looked about 5'7" and pretty. Through the window, he could just make out her silhouette.

From down the hall, the door banged open. "Ah, we were just talking about you," Michaels called.

"Sorry, am I interrupting? I can come back," came Lockhart's voice.

"No, not at all," Michaels said. "Sergeant Lockhart, this is Dr. Hansen."

"Pleasure."

Peters watched her shake Lockhart's hand politely.

"Doctor Hansen came to us with information about the assault. She says the woman who assaulted Officer Blake and Detective Peters is a patient of hers."

Peters leaned forward, straining to listen.

"That's right," she said. "I was in the coffee shop when it happened, and as I was telling the Lieutenant here, I saw the whole thing."

"I've asked Dr. Hansen to provide a statement and help us identify the suspect."

"I'll pop to the station when I leave," she said. "It was nice to meet you."

"You too," Lockhart said.

Peters could hear the sound of her shoes as she walked away. He watched Michaels hold out a file folder.

"What's this?"

"Her medical records."

"What about doctor/patient privilege? Don't we need the patient's consent to be reading this file?"

"In accordance with HIPAA rules, medical information can be disclosed to identify or locate a suspect, fugitive, witness, or missing person," Michaels said.

Lockhart shrugged. "If you say so."

"Her name is Allyson Reid. Goes by Ally. I got to know her *real* well over the years. She used to come by the precinct every week, checking up on the status of the case.

"She's a mental case. Suffers from a type of delusional disorder. She hallucinates… sees things, I don't know. But she's certifiable. She believes her family was murdered by some kind of mystery assassin eight years ago."

Lockhart glanced up from the file.

"I worked that case," Michaels said. "Her mother died of smoke inhalation. I never told her, but the case has been closed for about six years. I didn't think she would be able to cope with the news given her fragile emotional state."

Peters could see Lockhart study the contents of the file again.

"Criminal record?" Lockhart asked.

"She's been arrested a few times, but nothing stuck. Goddamn lawyers. But, *this… this one* is gonna stick! I want you to see to that *personally*, Sergeant," Michaels ordered. "I want that girl found and in handcuffs."

"Yes, sir."

"Get some sleep. Tomorrow, I want you to give this case your full attention."

"Actually, sir. I'd like to have a word with Peters, if you don't mind.

"He's resting."

"I just have a few procedural questions. You know… damn paperwork, eh?"

Michaels's stern look softened. "Five minutes."

As they entered the room, Michaels took a few steps back and hovered over by the window.

"Good evening, Detective," Lockhart began.

"Sarge."

"How are you feeling? Can I get you anything?"

"No, I'm alright. I was lucky. If S.W.A.T. hadn't shown up when they did, she might've killed me."

"I don't suppose you can tell me what this is all about."

Peters shrugged. "If I knew, I would, sir."

"Would you mind walking me through what happened? I mean, unless you're too tired… we could always do this formally at the precinct when you're feeling more up to it."

"No, that's fine, sir. There's not much to tell, really. Me and Blake made a quick stop at Flutters to grab a coffee before roll call. Then out of nowhere, some girl just goes apeshit on us. She got the drop on me. Before I knew it, I was out."

"Did she say anything to you? Anything at all?"

Peters narrowed his eyes. "I was out cold, Sergeant."

"Oh, right… excuse me," Lockhart said. "What about after?"

He's bluffing. He can't know about that.

"After, sir?"

"Yeah, on the rooftop. Did she say anything to you then?"

Peters heard the heart monitor's rhythm pick up the pace. He prayed it wasn't enough to rouse suspicion. He risked a glance at Michaels, but his expression was stoic.

"Nah, man. I never woke up."

Lockhart followed his gaze. "Sorry, just so I can get everything straight for my report. You were out cold the whole time?"

"Isn't that what I just said?"

Lockhart scratched his head. "Look, Detective, I can help you. But first, I need to know what happened up there on that roof. If you have anything to tell me, now would be the time."

"I've just told you everything I know," Peters said. "I told you; I was out cold."

"He said he was out, Floyd. What's the matter with you? This man was just beaten within an inch of his life. What's with all the questioning?"

Lockhart reached into his jacket pocket and removed a tape recorder and pressed play.

"Say the words," an angry female voice barked.

"My name is Detective Greg Peters. I am recording this because I believe I am about to die and this recording should suffice as my dying declaration.

Peters closed his eyes and fell back against the pillow.

"Eight years ago, on the night of November 10th, I was complicit in the murder of a woman named Sara Reid..."

"You don't understand! I had to say all those things!" Peters protested, throwing up his hands, but neither cop stopped the tape.

"Talk!"

"Screw you!"

A faint squeak sounded in the background, followed by a sharp hiss of gas... then flames.

"Okay! Okay!" Peters cried. *"It was Davis! He set the whole thing up! He took me to this house and said to just play along. But Davis, he... he beat her up good. The dumb bitch wouldn't give up the passwords. He called in some mercenaries... and they tortured the woman and killed her kid—"*

Lockhart pressed stop on the recorder and placed the recorder back into his pocket.

"That bitch! She's fucking crazy! She was... she was gonna kill me! I had to say those things! She made me!"

"Save it for the D.A., son."

"Sergeant!" Michaels barked. "Outside, now!"

Once out the door, Michaels stepped up to him. "What the fuck was that?" he barked.

"Sir?" Lockhart asked, feigning puzzlement.

"If you knew what was on that recording, why the whole dog and pony show back there?"

"I wanted to see if he would tell the truth."

"What you should have done was clear it with me first. I'm your superior officer; I'm in charge! I need to be consulted."

"I thought that's what I just did…"

Michaels glared at him and stepped forward. "Has it been logged? The recording. Have you logged it into evidence?"

"Of course." He stared into Michaels's eyes to sell the lie.

"Give it to me. I'll return it back to evidence after I listen to the full tape."

"I would like to, sir, but I'm on the way to show it to the Captain. He's asked to hear it."

Michaels glared at him, as if calling him on a bluff.

"Would you like to come with me?"

For a moment, Michaels didn't move. Then he shook his head. "No. I'll get it out of evidence myself."

Lockhart shrugged. "Ok, have a good night, sir," he said before stepping past him.

He could feel Michaels's stare on his back. His own heart rate was thundering in his chest now and to try and act calm, he began humming as he walked down the corridor.

* * *

Back at the precinct, Captain Stevens sat at his desk with his elbows resting on the surface. He was listening to the tape for the second time and hadn't spoken for the past 10 minutes.

"Tell me, how much is a woman's life worth these days?"

"Screw you!"

The sound of a blow torch being sparked and flaming crackled in the background.

"Wait! Wait! OK! ... shit... 10 grand! They paid me 10 grand to recover the data."

"Who gave you the money?"

"I told you! I don't know his name."

"But you helped cover it up?"

"Yeah..."

"And?"

"And that's it, alright? HE shot her! DAVIS burned it down! HE killed the girl! I didn't do shit!"

Finally, he'd had enough. Captain Stevens clicked off the tape recorder and placed his hands over his eyes. The two sat for a moment in silence, then he looked up solemnly.

"This could really hurt the department. If the press were to get wind of this..." he shook his head. "We need to handle this quietly, clean our own house. How do you feel about that?"

"The public doesn't need to know, so long as Peters is done on the force."

Captain Stevens nodded in agreement.

"And pending the results of an internal investigation, he does time," Lockhart said.

“I agree. When he gets back from leave, I’ll ask for his resignation. The man’s been through enough and has enough to worry about.”

“I’ll start tracking down Peters’s former partner in the morning. See if Peters is telling the truth. Either way, we need to speak to Brian Davis.”

CHAPTER 31

Three hours later, Ally was still sitting on a sofa below the gym, bouncing her knees and mashing her palms together. This wasn't what she'd envisioned when the others said she could join the team. For the last three hours, Curtis had been hacking into the Grace City police files, which was a huge waste of time. The files were likely doctored and she already had the name of the person they should be going after. Every moment she spent cooped up in the dungeon was time the asshole walked around scot-free.

Sullenly, she watched the others as they sifted through the case files, trying to get a read on their faces for signs of life. But after a time, her excitement waned. None of the three showed any signs of discovery, and soon, Ally felt the weight of disappointment settle over her. With a heavy heart and unable to wait any longer, she sighed and stood up.

"Any luck?"

"Some," Maury said. "We've pieced together who the lead detectives on the case were, which officers took witness statements, and who was acting Captain at the time. We've also examined the coroner's report and looked at the crime scene photos—taken, of course, after the fire torched everything. It took a while because the case has been closed for six years."

"Wait, what?" Ally exclaimed.

"You didn't know?"

The voice of Lieutenant Michaels cycled in her head. *There isn't an easy way to say this, but I promised to update you on any changes in your family's case. I want you to know I did everything I could, but as there have been no further developments or leads, the department cannot justify allocating active resources to it. The case will remain open, but it will be moved to inactive status until new evidence or leads emerge.*

Ally smacked her fist on the table and gripped the edges. "Bastard!" She jerked herself away from it and made for the elevator, but Maury headed her off.

"Get out of my way, Maury."

"Ally... we're a team now. We make decisions as a group. That's how we stay alive."

"Move!"

"This will not end the way you think. I'd have been dead a long time ago if I acted on every impulse."

"Michaels knows something!"

"Then we'll figure out what *in time.*"

She glared at him.

"Okay, let's play this out," he offered, crossing his arms. "Say you rush out there. Say you find Michaels and you beat him within an inch of his life. What then?"

"I'm one step closer to my family's killer."

"Wrong. You go after Michaels now and there'll be questions. He'd know that we're looking into the case and he'd want to know *how* we'd gotten the files. There'd be an investigation. And *if* Michaels is dirty, he'd have a head start on destroying evidence. Game over."

Ally's angry glare softened. He was right; surprise was their advantage. She exhaled, and threw her arms down in resignation. "Ugh!"

"As far as anyone knows, the case is closed. We need to keep it that way until we have something."

"Okay," she finally said.

Maury looked at her skeptically, like she was telling him exactly what he wanted to hear and was tricking him so she could bolt.

"I mean it. You're right."

Maury nodded and relaxed, and Ally headed back to the table, catching a look Marcus sent to his brother.

"What else did you find out?"

"Well, we can forget about witnesses," Marcus sighed. "One's deceased, but their statement does say they heard a loud bang. Probably overlooked due to the major thunderstorm that night. Another is in the advanced stages of dementia. He's living in a care home up-state. Has trouble remembering his own name."

"And the third?" Ally asked.

"She isn't a credible witness."

Ally pretended he wasn't referring to her. She sighed and pursed her lips. "What about neighbors?"

"Aside from those, two others were on vacation at the time. There are passport scans and credit card receipts to prove it," Marcus finished, handing over the talking to his brother.

"The two police officers who handled most of the investigation was Greg Peters, the guy you abducted from the coffee shop. He's a detective now, first grade. His partner was a man named Brian Davis, who appears to have retired shortly after the murders," Maury said.

"How long after?" Ally asked.

He checked his notes. "Just shy of seven months. He's a construction worker now, working for BCC."

"BCC?"

"Burton Conglomerates Construction."

Ally nodded, then looked at Curtis. "What about the coroner's report?"

"The coroner was a woman called Peggy Wilcox. According to the death certificate, the cause of death was smoke inhalation. There is no mention of a gunshot wound to the leg, head, or abdomen, so from what I can tell, this is a good starting point. I think our best move is to—"

"What about my sister?" Ally interrupted.

"Huh?" Curtis asked.

"What does it say her cause of death is?"

Curtis scanned over the coroner's report, twice. "There's no mention of any other bodies," he said, scratching his head.

Ally's mouth went dry. Her legs began to wobble and she braced herself with her arms. Her throat felt like it was closing in on her and it was getting harder to breathe. Maury started over to her, but she held up her hand. "I'm fine."

She took a couple deep breaths before standing fully upright. The tightness started to dissipate and she was able to take deeper breaths.

"You OK?" Maury asked, ignoring Marcus's frown.

Ally nodded. "So my sister might still be alive?"

"I suppose it's possible," Marcus answered. "But more than likely, her body just burned up in the fire. I'm sorry."

"Bones don't burn," Curtis interjected. "In crematoriums, they grind the bones to dust and that is mostly the ashes given back to the family. I doubt the police could have missed a charred skeleton... sorry, Ally," he said, making a face and regretting how he'd phrased that last statement.

She couldn't believe it. If the coroner's report didn't mention her sister's death, then who was buried beside her mother in the Grace City Cemetery?

Ally clenched her jaw. "So what's the plan? We find Davis and go after him?"

"Actually, I'm more interested in the coroner's report," Maury said.

"But Peters said Davis—"

"We'll get to Davis." Maury interrupted. "Right now, we need to figure out what we're dealing with. If the coroner's report was doctored, then it means one of two things: either the coroner is in on it. Or they can point the finger at who is."

"This is a waste of time. Peters said—"

"Ally, this is the group's decision and you agreed to follow my lead. We go after the coroner."

Ally sighed. "Fine; at least I get to beat the truth out of someone."

"No, Ally. If we have any chance in hell of building a legal case, we need Wilcox to testify *willingly*. Any decent lawyer who suspects a witness has been coerced will get the testimony thrown out for witness tampering," Maury said. "We need her to go on the record and explain her part in this. Agreed?"

"Agreed," Ally said, sighing. The realization of this whole vigilante business was beginning to sink in. Things were a lot slower than she anticipated. She reminded herself that she'd already waited years, what was a few more days?

"Right then, Curtis? We'll need a Gateway in the mortuary. We'll track Wilcox's movements within the building. When we feel we can predict her every move, that's when we'll go in."

"No sweat," Curtis said. "But I'm going to need some help." He turned his head and flashed Ally a cheeky grin.

Ally's head drooped. "Why can't *you* do it?"

"It's too conspicuous. People would remember a wheelchair repairman."

"I thought you said one of the side-effects of being in a wheelchair was that you're invisible?"

"No, I said *half the time* you're invisible. This is the other half."

"Fine," she said. "But I need to make a stop first."

CHAPTER 32

As the door to the boardroom banged open, dozens of heads turned to see Hal's personal secretary strut past the array of monitors with effortless allure. She clicked her heels right up to Hal and leaned in close to his ear. "Sir?" Daisy whispered. "He's here."

Hal nodded. He stood and buttoned his jacket, silencing the boardroom. "Gentlemen, when I return, I expect you'll have worked out this little hiccup." Without another word, he turned and followed his secretary's clicking heels to meet with the Vice President of the United States.

Joe Russell was already waiting in Hal's office when they arrived, seated on a leather chair in one of the most elegant and fancy pieces of city real estate in the country. Hal liked to bring his clients and business associates here to hold meetings and discussions. The five, six-foot window panes offered a stunning 180 degree view of the cityscape, seemingly dwarfed by BC Tower's own height. The desk and coffee table were positioned opposite the generous-sized lounging area beside a full bar stocked with any particular drink a person could think to ask for.

To anyone else, Joe looked strikingly out of place, dressed like a cattle rancher in a flannel top, cowboy boots, dark jeans, a large belt buckle, a shoelace for a tie, and a cowboy hat—a hick from the hills. To Hal, however, Joe's connections to POTUS made him one of the most important people in the country. Which is why he was prepared to overlook his deliberate affront to decorum.

"Vice President Russell." Hal grinned warmly, walking right up to him without a moment's hesitation.

"It's just Joe," he said, shaking hands.

Hal nodded. "What do you think of the view? I imagine you don't get a view like this in Kentucky."

"I don't much care for heights," Joe replied, seemingly apathetic to Hal's attempt at showing off. "But how could I turn down an invitation from one of our top donors?"

"*THE* top donor, but we can discuss that later," Hal winked. "Can I get you a drink?" He nodded to Daisy, who poured Joe a glass of Michter's Whiskey, a liquor which retails for nearly $4,000 a bottle. She wrapped the glass in an elegant paper napkin and leaned in, handing it to Joe on an expensive coaster. A strand of her auburn hair fell over her eye and she brushed it back with a seductive smile. She stifled a giggle as she turned to leave. Hal watched Joe admiring her figure as she walked away.

"You've outdone yourself," Joe said. "I'd have been satisfied with a glass of JD. But you people are all about flash."

"I treat my guests with the respect they deserve," Hal said, helping himself to a Bowmore 1957 Scotch whisky, a drink valued at over $9,000 per glass.

"Well, guest or not, I'm only here because of what you did for my son," Joe said, taking a sip of his drink and setting it down on the glass coffee table. "So tell me Hal, what can I do for you?"

Hal took a sip from his glass and swallowed. "Very well. I imagine you're a very busy man. Perhaps we should get right to business." Hal stood and walked over to a corner of the office, accessed the wall safe with a 10-digit pin code, and retrieved a stack of documents. He handed Joe a folder and sat down.

"What am I looking at?" he finally asked, flipping through it.

"Thanks to one of my ambitious technicians, our communications satellite uncovered an active nuclear arms program in the village of Sukurlu, a small remote town in southeastern Turkey." Hal took another sip as if it was just another Tuesday. "Up until five years ago, it was just that… a remote village. But from my calculations, I would guess they're about three months away from becoming operational. Would you agree?"

Joe's face hardened. "I'll need to get a team of analysts on this," he said.

"Of course," Hal conceded. "My people will give you the coordinates."

"Looks like we're about to go to war," Joe said dryly.

"A war?" Hal asked, pretending like Joe hadn't just played right into his hands. "Surely a man of your stature wouldn't want to subject more troops to another endless war."

"I didn't take you for a *Democrat*," he spat. "What do you propose we do, *nothing*?"

Hall took another sip. "What if I told you that my company could take out this terrorist cell… or any current or future terrorist cell on the United States Bureau of Counterterrorism's watch list? And all without a single soldier on the ground or shot fired?"

"Now how could your company do that?" he asked skeptically.

"Let's take a walk," Hal suggested, standing up and buttoning his jacket.

He led Joe to the private elevator and together, they made their way to the advanced sciences lab. Hal moved through the space with full recognition. Every technician, scientist, janitor and intern they passed looked up and greeted the man like he was some kind of famous celebrity. Hal smiled and greeted each of them by name.

He'd made a point to know each and every employee who worked for him.

Soon, they arrived outside the state of the art research facility. Hal placed his hand over the biometrics scanner and the door clicked open. The two Marines recognized the Vice President and immediately saluted him as he entered.

Hal walked Joe into a small room about the size of the luxury box at a professional sporting event. At the far wall, a curtain blocked the view to the other side. It just appeared to be an empty room.

"I don't understand," Joe said impatiently. "You said you were going to show me something in the interests of national security."

Hal smiled and pressed a button on the wall. The curtain began to slide away, revealing the view below. Joe stepped forward, looking down through the now open window. He gazed at a large cannon-like device constructed out of mostly transparent material.

"What is it?" he asked.

"We call it the Quantum Tunneler," Hal answered.

"Quantum… now, why does that sound familiar?" Joe asked rhetorically. "This isn't the same Quantum that cost taxpayers billions to develop, is it?"

"Indeed it is," Hal conceded.

Joe smirked. "I seem to remember that little project nearly bankrupted you."

"That's true, but that previous model also simultaneously saved the world from extinction."

"Be that as it may, what makes you think I'd be interested in seeing some faulty asteroid deterrent device?" Joe asked.

"Quantum was never just an asteroid deterrent. That's just an idea we sold to the press. What Quantum really is, is the world's next super weapon."

Joe looked down at the device again skeptically. "It looks like a hunk of plastic."

Hal stifled a chuckle. He knew that Vice Presidents were like any politicians. They were businessmen, not scientists or scholars. Few were intellectuals and even fewer were men of vision. The specifics of this device would be too much for him to understand. Hal knew that in order for a man like Joe to get on board, he'd have to oversimplify the device's capabilities.

"Do you know how Alexander the Great, Genghis Khan, and Julius Caesar were nearly able to conquer the globe?" Hal asked.

Joe shrugged.

"They used the world's most advanced weapon."

"The catapult?" he asked.

"The bow and arrow," Hal corrected. "The bow and arrow was once, and remained, the world's most advanced weapon until the 9th century when the Chinese discovered gunpowder. Those who learned to wield it, went on to defeat whole empires."

Hal placed his hand on the window and leaned in.

"A few centuries later, someone split the atom and the first atomic bomb was created. When it was dropped on Japan, the world trembled, ending the Second World War. Who could have predicted that a short time later, someone would go on to create something even more destructive... the hydrogen bomb."

"Thanks for the history lesson, but would you mind getting to the point?"

"The point is..." said Hal through gritted teeth, "the greatest *country* on Earth, needs the greatest *weapon* to maintain its stronghold and rule."

"We already have that. We've got guided nuclear missiles that can shoot the hairs off a weasel's backside from halfway around the globe."

"Nuclear weapons wipe out your enemies, sure, but they also wipe out the available resources in the region for generations, and as we both know, what's the point of a war if there are no resources to profit from? Plus there is always the threat of retaliation."

"Okay. You have my attention. So what does it do?"

"It destabilizes the atoms in a target and causes any structure to crumble. In layman's terms, it's an earthquake weapon."

"An earthquake weapon?" Joe repeated.

"Precisely."

"And that's your plan? To load up this... this *plastic cannon*... onto an aircraft and shake this Turkish terrorist cell to death?" Joe smirked, completely missing the weapon's potential.

Hal had anticipated this.

"With this *plastic cannon* we can take out an entire city, effectively resetting them back to the Stone Age."

"A missile could do the same."

"A missile can be shot down," Hal retorted sternly. "Plus, a clever investigator could trace every piece of hardware back to us. But, if we put Quantum up into orbit and fixed it to a satellite, no one could blame the United States when a desert town in some God-awful armpit of the east suddenly crumbled to dust. How could they? No one would even know it existed. The weapon leaves no trace. It's invisible. Investigators would merely examine the rubble and find faulty engineering and poor construction. It would be completely untraceable," Hal said.

"Well, that *is* interesting," Joe said, catching on.

"Imagine China refusing to negotiate on economic trade deals. Or Russia not budging on their oil prices. Or—"

"Or those little shits in North Korea running their mouths," Joe finished.

Hal faked a smile. "Exactly. It's the ultimate sleeper weapon. Hell, the President could even call it divine wrath and keep all the Jesus freaks on their knees. And all without a single troop deployed."

There was a soft knock at the door.

"Ah, Dr. Hayagawa. Right on time. Come in!" Hal said happily.

Dr. Hayagawa left the door's threshold and walked toward them.

"Vice President Joe Russell, meet our chief scientist and the brain behind Quantum."

"It's a pleasure to meet you, sir," Katsu said, bowing and then holding out his hand.

Joe shook Katsu's hand and pursed his lips. "Tell me, Doctor, does this machine really work like Hal here, says it does?"

"Yes, sir."

"Uh-huh," Joe said, rubbing his goatee. He turned to Hal. "How soon could this gizmo of yours be up and running?"

"Three weeks. A month at the latest," Hal said. "Plenty of time to handle our, uh... little problem."

"What's the catch," Joe asked.

Hal smiled. "As we agreed, the targets would be yours to select, in exchange for the government's help in putting Quantum into orbit, of course."

"That shouldn't be a problem. I will, of course, need to run this past POTUS."

"Of course," Hal said.

Joe shook Hal's hand.

"Excellent. Let's discuss this more back in my office. Thank you Dr. Hayagawa and excellent work."

Katsu bowed his head and the two men left the viewing window.

CHAPTER 33

Curtis stopped and his mouth fell open. "*This* is where you had to make a stop?" His eyes flicked back and forth between Ally and the Bad Kitty nightclub.

She smirked and crossed the street.

"Probably best I go with you. Ya know, for moral support."

"Don't be a perv. Wait out here. I'll be back in a few minutes." She flashed her ID to the bouncer and heard Curtis wheeling forward.

"I'm with her," Curtis muttered in a deeper than usual voice.

As the bouncer returned her ID, he eyed Curtis. "How old are you?"

"18," Curtis grunted.

"You should have said 15. I'd have believed that."

Ally stifled a giggle as Curtis hung his head and crossed his arms, disappointment washing over his face.

Inside the club, crowds of patrons tossed money onto the floor or were tucking them into women's g-strings. Some were getting lap dances. Some were flirting with women they had no chance of pulling on the streets. But since her last visit, there was now a security guard posted in three places around the club. What almost happened to Mallory must have reached upper management. Girls getting raped is bad for business.

Scanning the crowd, she spied her. Mallory was serving drinks to clients, dressed to attract attention, but was more moderate than the last time she'd seen her.

As Mallory handed the last drink from the serving tray to one of the clients, she straightened up and spotted Ally. Her face fell, then she ran over and threw her arms around her. Ally winced, but politely received the hug. "Oh my gosh! I didn't think I'd ever see you again!"

"Are you okay?"

"I'm better than okay!" Mallory said. "When I told the boss what happened, he was so afraid I'd sue that he offered me a new job with a pay bump. I'm a manager now!" she said grinning and holding her arms out.

Ally smiled. "Congratulations."

"Thanks!" she said, then there was an awkward pause. "Are you here because of—" she turned her head and made sure no one could eavesdrop and mouthed: "—that cop? I saw you on the news. Don't worry, I didn't say nothin'. Bastard probably deserved it. Is that why you're here?" she asked. "Are you in trouble, honey?"

"Not exactly. You probably don't remember this, but you said that if I ever needed anything, I could come to you. Did you mean it?"

"Of course! Anything!"

"Is there somewhere we can go and talk?"

"Come on." She reached down and took Ally's hand and began tugging her through the crowd and up the stairs to the private booths. A guard was stationed at the top of the stairs and allowed them in after Mallory said Ally was a friend. She pulled her into one of the booths and shut the door. "What's up?"

"I need a favor."

"Anything."

"I need your body."

"Honey, I'm not one of the paid girls," Mallory said, looking puzzled.

"No, I didn't mean that… not like that… I…" Ally reached down and into the bag she brought. She pulled out a hover drone and tossed it into the air.

"I need a body scan," Ally said.

* * *

The next morning, Curtis hacked into a tech company's warehouse and ensured one of their uniforms was delivered to a costume shop downtown. When he arrived, the owner was arguing with the delivery driver.

"And I'm telling *YOU*, I didn't order it," the man said, sliding the box back toward the driver.

"Well *someone* did. I have the purchase order right here," the driver said, sliding the box back to him and slapping the receipt on top.

Curtis took his cue and wheeled right up to the desk. "Excuse me, sirs?"

"Just a minute!" the man grumbled, but as his eyes registered Curtis, he changed his mind. "I'm sorry. What can I do for you?" he said in a more polite tone.

"I'm looking for a unique costume. There's a party on Saturday and I really need something kind of geeky... something like a tech guy would wear if he were going to make a house call and fix your WiFi, that kind of thing."

"We don't have anything like that. Sorry kid," the owner said, and went back to arguing with the delivery driver.

"Actually..." Curtis interrupted. "I can't help but notice the two of you are having a little disagreement. May I?" he said, reaching up and taking the purchase order. "One uniform, unisex, for... EnerTech! Hey fellas, I think I might have a solution to this little debacle." He looked up and smiled.

* * *

"I look ridiculous," Ally groaned.

"You look great," Curtis said. "In fact, I'd say it's an improvement."

Ally adjusted her hat, studied her reflection, and sighed.

"Come on," he said. "Do you want to talk to the coroner or not?"

"Yes," she said sullenly.

"Ok, then put your big girl pants on and get on with it. We all make sacrifices."

"Oh really? And what sacrifices do *you* make?"

"Babysitting little whiners like you, for starters," he said. "Plus, I do all the tech stuff. You're just a foot soldier, so get marching."

"Ha... Ha..."

She dragged her feet out of a nearby alley. Anyone who set eyes on her wouldn't think twice. It was an official uniform from one of the major tech giants. She just hoped Curtis had added her appointment into their calendar.

She edged into the building carrying a handbag, her sneakers squeaking their way across the linoleum floor. She marched right up to the reception desk and gasped as she caught sight of the girl at the desk.

The poor thing must have been fresh out of high school and looked like she'd been injecting filler into her lips, cheeks, and forehead. She had no notable expression. Her face was just frozen in place like she'd just come back from the dentist. Her swollen fish lips were smeared with red lipstick, her hair was bleach-blond with dark roots, her fake eyelashes protruded well past her eyebrows, and she had on enough bronzer and makeup to service three girls. She tried to smile at Ally, but could only manage to move the corners of her mouth slightly.

"Good afternoon. How can I help?" she asked in a southern, Legally Blond sort of way.

"Hi there," Ally said, working up her charm. "I work for EnerTech. I'm here to run a speed test on your internet. We're upgrading all their clients's systems and I'm here to do a preliminary checkup."

"Oh, wow! That's so good of them!" she said overly excitedly. "The service here has been so bad!"

"I know, right!" Ally said, mimicking her speech patterns. "I mean, space is a long way up there?"

"Totally!" The girl turned and click-clacked her fake nails onto the keyboard, opening up the calendar where all the appointments were kept. "Oh dear," she murmured dramatically. "I don't see you in the appointment book. I'm going to have to schedule you in on another day, I'm afraid," she said with sad sincerity.

"Oh dear, that is a shame... see my boss told me that any companies that can't fit us in, will not be getting the Turbo Boost Speed Upgrade for free.

"I knew you were too good to be true," the girl joked.

Damn it, Curtis! You had one job!

She was about to leave, but decided to try her charm one more time. "Those are beautiful nails. Where did you get them done?"

"Oh, I did them myself. It's a do-it-yourself kit."

"Oh, well you're mighty talented," Ally said with a jealous smile.

The girl looked around her as if checking for any supervisors. "I'll tell you what. I like you! I have a feeling about people. I'll just add your name to the appointment list and let you sneak on in," she said happily.

"Really? Wow! That's so nice!"

"What's your name, Miss?" she asked.

Ally panicked. She didn't want to use her real name and hadn't prepared one. She glanced at the girl's name tag which was pinned to her revealing top.

"My name is Chloe."

"No way! That's my name, too!" she said, flashing a lot more than just her name badge at Ally.

"No way!" Ally said, feigning excitement.

"We're like twins!" Chloe giggled. "From another mother," she clarified. Then she began click-clacking her claws back onto the keyboard.

Ally couldn't help it. She widened her eyes in exaggerated surprise when Chloe wasn't looking.

"Ok, you're all set," Chloe said. "Don't forget to wear this visitor badge at all times."

"Thank you so much," Ally said smiling. "You're a doll."

She waved as she walked away from reception and rounded the corner. Proceeding down a long hallway, the walls were a faint custardy-yellow with a brown bumper padding along them. The floor was tiled with typical hospital tiles. They were an off-white color, probably eggshell with a light blue border around both edges of the floor. Rooms were found on the left and right of the hallway all the way down until it turned a corner, revealing another section of identical hallways and doors.

Ally made her way through the mortuary until she arrived outside the maintenance room. She raised her hand, ready to knock, but Curtis's voice shot through her earpiece.

"Ally, look out!"

"Where the hell were *you*?" she barked.

"Umm, getting coffee," a voice behind her replied.

Ally turned around to see a security guard holding out three cups of coffee on a cardboard holder.

"Can I help you Miss?"

Ally's eyes widened and she smiled, realizing she'd just yelled at the guard and not Curtis.

"Miss?" he asked.

"Answer him, Ally," Curtis ordered.

"Ummm, yes. Sorry. I uh... yeah, I need to get into the maintenance room? I'm here to run a speed test on your internet. EnerTech's upgrading all their client's systems and I'm here to do a preliminary checkup."

"About time. The reception here blows," the guard whined. He removed the key from the ring on his belt and inserted it into the knob. He turned the key and held the door open for her.

"Thank you," she said, but her smile quickly faded as she entered the room. Two other security guards sat at their stations watching the monitors. There were three widescreens on two different desks. Each one had nine camera feeds from a different area from around the mortuary. On the wall above them, six more monitors displayed nine separate feeds from the building.

"You're just in time!" another guard said eagerly, waving his arm. "They've just pulled the really hot chick out. She's on the table now. Look at those milkers!" He giggled and sort of bounced on his chair. "Is that my coffee?" he asked, turning around. His face froze.

Ally's eyebrows went up along with the corner of her mouth and she gave him a little wave.

The guard whirled around and quickly closed the magnified feed of the nude cadaver on the screen. He turned back and sheepishly reached for his coffee from the cardboard holder, averting his eyes, then ran his fingers through his sweaty hair and cleared his throat.

"Hi. I'm Chuck," he said embarrassed. He held out his hand which glistened in the fluorescent light.

Ally looked down at his hand, made a face, and glanced around the room, pretending not to notice. The other guard also took his coffee, then sat down in his chair and picked up a comic book called the Umbrella Academy.

"What's she here for?" he asked.

"She's here to check the Wi-Fi and network," the first guard said.

"About time! Videos take…" he coughed. "Emails take forever to load."

"Well, I suppose we'll let you get to it then," the first guard said and sat down at his station.

"What was that about?" Curtis asked through the earpiece.

"Don't ask," she whispered.

Ally walked over to an ethernet box hanging from the wall by its cable. From her bag, she removed some plastic fasteners and a screwdriver, and fixed it securely to the wall. When she was satisfied, she reached back into the bag and pulled out Curtis's Gateway, but she suddenly got a strange feeling, like something was boring into the back of her head. She checked over her shoulder and three heads moved down like synchronized swimmers.

Eww, she thought. *But better their eyes are on my ass than what I'm doing with my hands.*

She leaned forward, pushing out her rear end a little more obviously. Then she worked on attaching the gateway to the wires. Curtis had upgraded this one upon her request. It no longer needed the casings to be cut away. It only needed the clips to grip directly onto the outer wires. This meant she could install it in seconds.

One final time, she reached back into her bag and pulled out a device which resembled a sauntering iron with its metal tip but it was connected to a bright yellow box. She figured these guys wouldn't know a voltage tester from a network speed tester and just pulled it out to make herself look more official. When she placed the metal tip onto a wire, the light on the device lit up and made a buzzing sound.

"All good," she said, placing the voltage tester back into the bag. She turned around and her face dropped. She was now staring face-to-face with what appeared to be the main supervisor. He was wearing a suit, carried a tablet, and had a CB radio clipped to his belt. He did not look happy.

"What are you doing in here?" he asked gruffly.

Ally blinked away her dumbfounded and guilty expression. "I'm Chloe," she said. "I'm just checking all the network settings. Everything is good to go now."

"I checked the appointment calendar. There is no record of anyone showing up today."

"Oh, yeah… I already spoke to the receptionist about this. There must have been some kind of mixup. Management, am I right?" she giggled nervously.

A guard let out an all too enthusiastic grunt in approval and instantly regretted it when the supervisor shot him an angry glare. He turned back to Ally. "What company did you say you worked for?"

"EnerTech," she said with conviction. "We're going around to all our most loyal customers and upgrading their speed for free."

"We don't use EnerTech," he said. "We use Burton Media."

"No, I'm pretty sure it's EnerTech... I mean, why would they send me out here if you were already signed with our biggest competitor?" she asked, clinging like hell to the lie.

"Can I see some identification, please?"

"Oh, that's in the work order," she said.

"The work order?"

"Yeah, everything's online now. We're going paperless… anything to help out Mother Earth."

"You're telling me that you don't have a badge or any ID? And that it's all online?"

"Yes," she said, smiling.

"That's preposterous! I'm calling the police."

"Uhh... sir, shouldn't you call EnerTech before you embarrass yourself?"

The supervisor hesitated, then cleared the display on his phone. "Ok, Chloe. I'll call EnerTech and if there isn't a work order with us, I'm having you arrested," he said as he started typing on his keypad.

"Umm… Ally... I can't hack his phone. He must not be using the WiFi," Curtis said, his voice coming in through her earpiece. *"Stall him. I need a minute."*

"Actually, there's a faster way to check this," Ally offered. "See, if you call the service number, they'll just put you on hold." The supervisor looked up from his internet search and met her eyes.

"Yeah, so if you use your tablet, you can access the account and my name should be on the service records for today," she said.

"Good thinking," Curtis said through the earpiece. She could hear his fingers furiously typing in the background.

"Here! I can do it for you," she said, stepping forward and reaching for the tablet. It caught the supervisor off guard and he took a half step backwards. Ally grabbed the other end of the tablet.

"Let go," the man said.

"Really, sir. This is my job. I can do it a lot faster if you—"

"Let go!" the man bellowed, this time catching *Ally* off guard. She released her grip on the tablet and the man pulled it into his face. He grunted and held his hand to his nose.

"I'm sorry, but you did tell me to let go," she said, reaching her hand forward to set it on his shoulder.

He jerked his arm away from her, sniffed, then resumed typing on the tablet. The man tapped his foot impatiently. "I thought you said you upgraded the wifi?" he snorted.

"It takes up to 24 hours to recalibrate."

He huffed and stared at the buffering icon. Finally, it loaded the page and he grunted. "Right, as I suspected. I've pulled up EnerTech's current callouts. There is no *Chloe* on the page nor is there any *work order* listed to the Grace City Mortuary," he said, holding the tablet up for Ally to see. "You're some kind of imposter. Steve, phone the police."

"Done! The page is refreshing," Curtis shouted.

"Umm, sir? I saw it. It's listed right there," she said.

"You're a liar. It's not..." he started to say, but saw the latest work assignment was the Grace City Mortuary and that Chloe Henderson was doing the work.

"Sir? What's your name?" Ally asked.

"Spencer," the supervisor said.

"Spencer, are you a racist?" she asked.

His eyes nearly bugged out of his skull. "What? Don't be ridiculous! I'm not a racist! I was just—"

"Checking to see if the only black person in the room has business here?" Ally finished. "And from what I can tell," she said, glancing around the room, "not a single non-white security guard in the building?"

"That's ridiculous! Glen is uh... well he's uh…" Spencer scrunched up his face, probably trying to think of his race.

Ally imagined a dark skinned Glen, and how Spencer likely never enquired about his background or heritage. "Does Glen have dark skin like me?" Ally asked.

"Yes... well, no… not… not exactly..."

"And let me guess... he works the night shift, doesn't he Spencer?" she stated matter-of-factly. She could see that Spencer was getting agitated. His upper lip was sweating, which was draining down into his patchy mustache. He was stuttering and completely flustered.

"I am not a racist!" he protested. "I have many black friends."

"That sounds like something a racist would say," Ally said.

"It does, boss," Chuck echoed.

"Shut up, Chuck!" he yelled.

"I'm afraid I'm going to have to report this to corporate," she said, tutting and walking past him.

"Wait!" Spencer called, making Ally turn just when she got to the door. "I'm sorry, I… I… now, there's no need to report this. I think it was all just a simple misunderstanding."

"I don't know…" she muttered, looking around the room.

"There must be something I can do to fix this," he pleaded.

Ally pretended to think a while. "Well, I suppose you could pay for my bus fare, seeing as how EnerTech doesn't validate," she said.

Spencer dug out his wallet and thumbed out a five dollar bill from a larger wad and placed it into her palm.

"And I haven't had any lunch yet," she hinted. "I am pretty hungry and there is this new sandwich place down the block I've been meaning to try."

Spencer placed two more five dollar bills in her hand and waited for the all clear.

"Well, I suppose I better go. Thank you very much, Spencer," she said, turning toward the door. "And don't bother following me out of the building," she added. "I can find my own way."

Ally turned toward the door and exited the room, leaving a relieved Spencer still flapping around like he'd just been slapped.

"That was incredible," Curtis said, laughing. *"How did you know that was going to work?"*

She shrugged. "I saw it in a movie once."

Curtis chuckled. *"Well, hurry back to the lair. I'll get started while you're enroute,"* he said.

"Lair? More like a warren," she corrected just before he clicked the microphone off.

CHAPTER 34

Dr. Peggy Wilcox rubbed her right wrist and continued writing. The climate controlled room needed to be chilled to delay decomposition and it wasn't doing her wrist any favors. She'd just done a full work-up on a John Doe who rolled in four hours ago and was writing up the report. Cause of death was multiple gunshot wounds to the abdomen and right leg. She noted in the report that the blood loss would have been great and she didn't expect him to have survived more than a few minutes after being shot.

He was just a kid. Somewhere there was a mother bawling her eyes out, or a father who was waiting to take him home after work, or perhaps a sibling was walking home alone rather than with their big brother. Senseless violence in Grace City had been on a steady rise for the last decade. Mass shootings, gang violence, school shootings, accidental deaths and police shootings, they were all up. She shook her head and silently cursed the cowards in the capital who refused to take a tough stance on implementing stricter laws on firearms. She'd heard a comedian say once that after one failed attempt at a shoe bomb, all passengers must now take off their shoes at the airport. But even after more than 400 school shootings since Columbine, politicians still haven't taken any acceptable steps toward resolving the issue.

She put her head down again, wrote the final line on the report and signed it.

"Good night, Peg," Tamara said.

"Night!" she called back.

"Are you coming to Michiko's?"

"Huh? Oh, Trivia Night! Nah, not tonight. You guys have fun."

"See you tomorrow then!" Tamara called out with a wave.

Peggy walked the file over to a cabinet in the office and placed it in the unsolved drawer. She figured someone would likely come to the morgue to ID the body sometime this week after the family saw the news. Until then, the body will be here under her watch. *I'll keep you safe*, she thought.

"Doctor Wilcox?" whispered a female voice.

Peggy jumped. The room was empty. So was the office. She looked around, scanning the parts of the hallway that she could see through the office windows, but there was no one there. She furrowed her brow and shook it off, closing the file cabinet. Then she walked back into the morgue to double check everything had been cleaned and sorted for the morning shift.

"Doctor Wilcox?" came the distorted voice again, this time it whispered from multiple directions in rapid succession.

The little hairs stood up on the back of Peggy's neck. "Hello?" she called. Her voice echoed through the room but was drowned by silence.

"Doctor Wilcox!?"

Peggy recoiled, letting out a squeak. She spun around, tracking the voice behind her. Her heart was now an erratic drum inside her chest. She frantically scanned the room: high, low and around every corner. Fear clawed at her throat; it was time to get out of there.

Forcing her nerves to quiet, she inhaled a shaky breath, intending to walk out of the morgue with some dignity, but as she turned, her body went rigid. She gasped. Lying on the table, was a naked woman as if ready for an autopsy. She was of African descent, mid 30s.

Peggy was thoroughly spooked now. Slowly, she edged closer to the table and leaned over the cadaver's face, breathing in short quivering bursts. As she got close, the woman's eyes shot open!

Peggy shrieked and stumbled backwards, knocking over a tray of surgical tools and pans used to hold organs. The cadaver slowly sat upright and turned its head. Its eyes glistened with watery tears and looked right at her.

"Doctor Wilcox..." the woman rasped, hopping off the table. Wounds on her forehead, chest and thigh started oozing a dark liquid, unmistakably blood. It poured over her groomed pubic hair, down her thighs, and began pooling on the floor, flowing faster and faster with each step as she shambled towards her.

"Help me Doctor!" the woman rasped. "Help me!" she pleaded, reaching her hand out.

Peggy couldn't hold herself together anymore. She took a deep breath, screamed, and took off toward the door at full speed. She ripped it open and breathlessly sprinted into the changing rooms. At her locker, she frantically thumbed the 3-code pin, desperately keeping her eye on the door, expecting it to burst open.

"Doctor Wilcox?" the woman's voice called.

Peggy gasped, the hair on her neck standing on end. The voice hadn't come from the door. It had come from the showers. Right beside her!

Peggy jerked her head as the woman stepped out. Fear ripped through her. She shrieked in panic, desperately tugging on the stubborn lock. The woman was five steps away. Finally, the lock popped open and Peggy reached inside, gripped her handbag, and bolted out of the locker room.

Searching the bag with one hand for her phone, she sprinted down the hallway. "Help!" The security guard was just around the corner. "Help!" she shrieked. "Hel—" The soles of Peggy's shoes screeched to a halt and she fell backwards. The guard was lying prone on the floor. Standing beside him, was the woman. She turned her head and looked right at Peggy.

Peggy scampered to her feet and darted for the first office on her left. She slammed the door, turned the dead bolt, and dialed 911 before cowering in the corner in a squat.

"911 Emergency Response," said a female voice on the line.

"Help me!" Peggy whimpered. "I need the police at the Grace City Mortuary, RIGHT NOW!"

"*Why won't you help me, Doctor?*" the dead woman's voice asked on the line.

Peggy cried out and flung her phone. It bounced and skidded across the floor.

"I need to rest," the woman's voice said, this time from inside the very room on the far corner.

Peggy tried to will herself to move, but all she could do was tremble and sob, petrified in fear. She watched in horror as the woman came closer and closer until she squatted down right beside her.

"Who are you?" Peggy whimpered.

"You know who I am..." she replied.

Peggy shook her head. "Are you going to kill me?"

The woman smiled, then seemed to look off into another direction as if troubled. *"They killed me,"* she said with a chilling tone.

"Who did?" Peggy asked through choked tears and breaths.

The woman stood up again and walked slowly away. She seemed to float, like she wasn't putting any weight on the floor. When she reached the door, she turned and waved Peggy forward before walking right through the solid door. Peggy couldn't believe it, but she stood up and followed the woman out of the room and down the hallway, back to the morgue.

The woman strode up to the computer and extended an arm. The screen seemed to come to life, bypassing the password window as if she'd typed it in herself, and brought up the files. Then a blue highlighted cursor began moving down through the file names.

* * *

Curtis, on the other end of the server, took control of the screen. He pressed the down arrow until he arrived on the Rs. He stopped the cursor on Reid, Sara J.

* * *

Beside her, the printer came to life, making Peggy jump again, and when it had finished, she took the report from the printer and made a face. Her eyes widened and her mouth instantly went dry. She knew this case. She knew it well. Nothing could cause her to forget it. She lifted her eyes back up to the woman, Sara Reid.

Sara's face was burned to a crisp. Black charred skin and inflamed reddish meat clung to her bones. One of her eye sockets emptily stared back at her from a half-melted face.

Peggy gasped. The papers in her hand started shaking and she shut her eyes, pushing tears down her cheeks.

"I'm sorry," Peggy whimpered. "I'm sorry… I—"

"Help me, Doctor. I need to rest."

When Peggy opened her eyes, Sara was gone. There was no sign of her. There was no blood on the floor. No footprints. Nothing to show that any of this had happened, except for the file in her hand.

"Hi," a child's voice cried. Peggy screamed and jumped back, clutching her chest with her free hand. She didn't know how much more her heart could take. A little girl of African descent sat beside her, looking up with big almond eyes. *"Are you going to help my mommy?"*

"I can't," Peggy said shamefully. "They'll kill me if I—"

"Like they killed my mommy?" the little girl interrupted.

Peggy put her hand to her mouth. She started sobbing and the papers fell from her hands. "I can't…" she whimpered. "My family... they'll—"

"Hurt them?" the girl finished. *"Who will?"*

Peggy took a breath and regained control over her sobs. She sniffed her nose and wiped it on her sleeve. "Some bad men, honey."

"Like gangsters?" she asked.

"No… a cop," she said.

"Which cop?"

Peggy shook her head. "I can't."

"My friends can protect you," the girl said, *"and keep your family safe."*

"What friends?" Peggy asked.

The little girl pointed to an empty section of the wall in the room. Suddenly, Peggy's eyes started playing tricks on her. A semi-transparent figure was peeling itself off the wall. Its skin was changing from the custard yellow to a black. A few seconds later, she was staring at a figure in a black combat suit.

It startled her again when the figure fully materialized before her eyes. She shot a quick glance back to the girl, but she was gone, vanished like the woman. Looking back to the figure in black, she felt the hairs stand up on the back of her neck again. She felt a panic begin to rise inside of her.

"Calm down, Miss," the figure said, putting up its hands as if to say it meant no harm.

"What do you want?" Peggy choked out.

"I need your help. I need you to come forward and confess to doctoring the report on Sara Reid."

"Why?" Peggy huffed.

"Because her family deserves justice."

"I can't. They'll kill me. Or worse, they'll kill my family."

"I can protect your family."

"Who will protect them when I go to prison?"

"I'm not after you. I'm going after the corrupt cops who threatened your family, who forced you to doctor the autopsy report... who have been holding your life and the life of your family hostage. Give me the name of the policeman who did this. I'll track him down and free you of this burden."

"His name was Davis," she said after a while. "I saw his name badge the day he came in. That's all I know. I was too scared to look into it any further."

"Thank you," the figure said. "I'll call you when I've tracked down all the men responsible."

"What about my family?" Peggy asked, causing the figure to turn back. "You said you would protect them."

"As long as we keep this matter quiet, they will not suspect anything. When the time comes, I'll ensure your family is safe before we proceed. You have my word." Then the figure turned and seemed to dematerialize as it walked out of the morgue.

* * *

Inside the lair, Curtis removed the control helmet and set it on the table. He rubbed his face and eyes before turning to the rest of the group. "See? I told you it would work. Every time we send in holograms, we minimize the risk of being stopped, caught, or killed."

"He's got a point," Marcus said. "This is a game changer. Not only do we not have to be physically present all the time, but we could be at multiple locations simultaneously. All we'd have to theoretically do, is just let people catch a glimpse of one of the holographic projections lurking in the shadows. That would keep people talking and perhaps scare them enough to not commit the crime."

"And I'm all for that," Maury said. "But Davis is ex-police. He's not going to be scared by a hologram. It's going to take something more than that." He looked at Ally. "Are you ready?"

She nodded.

"Then follow my lead."

CHAPTER 35

Brian gasped and forced his eyes open. Squinting through the bright construction light, he struggled to blink away his blurred vision and the vertigo swirling in his head. He tried to move, but something was restricting him. With difficulty, he managed to lift his head. Ropes were strung across his chest and his wrists were bound at his sides. "What the hell?" he muttered, tracing the rope with his eyes. One end was tied to a piece of rebar that protruded from a wall of concrete blocks, the other to his chair's brace.

"Brian Davis!" a deep voice barked.

With a jolt, Brian's senses returned. Gasping, he felt the chair beneath him wobble and creak. He was teetering over the edge of a construction building and the rope was the only thing preventing him from plummeting to his death. Panic surged through him and he desperately started to test his restraints.

"Help me!" Brian yelled, huffing out short breaths.

From the side, a figure dressed in black stepped slowly into view and over to the rope. Brian fought against the fatigue in his neck and strained to keep the figure in view, forcing his eyes against their sockets. "Hey!" Brian huffed.

He gasped as the figure pulled a retractable knife from a pouch on his belt and flicked it open. "No!" Brian screeched. "No, wait! I don't know who you are or what you want, but I promise you, you've got the wrong guy!"

"Is your name Brian Davis?" the figure asked. Brian just blinked in shock, his expression betraying him. "Then I have the right guy," he said, tapping the rope with the knife, taunting that he was about to cut it.

"I'm going to ask you some questions, Brian," the figure said, sliding the blade up and down the rope like he was sharpening it. "So I need you to focus. Each time you lie to me, I cut a strand of this rope. I'm not entirely sure how many strands there are, so you should tell as few lies as possible. Understand?"

Brian nodded. "Ok... Ok..." he said, taking deep breaths and fighting to keep his head up. It was starting to tire from resisting the pull of gravity.

"November 10th, eight years ago, you killed a woman—"

"No!" Brian cried, "I swear, I—" The figure dug the knife into the rope and pried out a strand. "WAIT!" Brian shouted, but the man cut it. The chair wobbled and Brian could feel himself slip a few inches toward the edge.

"Eight years ago, you killed a woman and her daughter," the man repeated.

"No!" Brian cried again. "Wait!" To his horror, again the figure dug the knife into the rope and secured it under another strand. "WAIT!" he pleaded. "Wait! I didn't kill her!"

"He's lying!" a second voice cried out. This one was synthesized and gravelly.

Brian's eyes went wide. *There are two of them!?*

"Listen!" Brian pleaded, "I have a family! My son, he... he's sick... he needs these special treatments…" The figure sliced through the strand of rope. "No! Fuck!"

"You're running out of rope, Brian."

"Okay. Okay. The woman you are talking about. I didn't kill her. I swear!"

"But you were there?"

"Yes! But… please, I will tell you… but… I can't think if you keep cutting the rope!"

"Calm down, Brian." Brian nodded and took two deep breaths. "Now, tell me everything."

"Okay… I used to be a cop… my partner, Peters! He told me he had a job that would pay big. He said no one would get hurt. I needed the money. So I agreed.

"He brought me to a house somewhere in the suburbs. Peters just said play along, but as soon as the door opened, I knew something was off. Peters, he... he started asking the woman about data and passwords. He hit her hard and knocked her to the ground. I tried to stop it, but Peters held his gun under my chin and said he'd shoot me if I didn't do what he said.

"The woman, she took a beating," Brian said sadly. "But still, no matter what Peters did to her, she refused to give it up. She kept saying billions of lives were at stake, or something like that. After a while, Peters called in some help. And I mean, these were bad people. I think they were mercenaries. One of the guys came in and shot her. He tortured her."

"What did this man look like?" voice one asked.

"Maybe late 20s. White. He had long dark hair. Hollow eyes. I remember his eyebrows stuck out, almost… Neanderthal-ish. His nose was large. He was clean shaven. About 6 feet tall. And looked like a fitness freak. And Peters... he wasn't afraid of nobody, ya know? But that night, he was afraid… like a dog when you yank its leash."

"What about the other men?" the second voice asked.

"I don't know who they were." Brian gasped as the dark figure dug his knife under the rope again. "I swear! They were just hired muscle! I think there were three of them!"

"What happened next?"

"Please, you don't—"

The figure cut another strand of the rope, sending the weighted chair rocking and jolting closer to the edge. Tension tore along the rope, its remaining threads groaning.

Brian collected himself and continued. "I stepped out. I didn't want to watch them torture the woman. A few minutes later, I heard screaming. I mean, the woman was screaming before, but now she was *really* screaming. When I came back, one of the kids was lying in a pool of blood. They'd killed her. The woman kept screaming until the man held a knife to her other daughter's throat. She gave up the data and passwords."

Brian stopped talking and tried to stifle his sobs.

"Keep going, Brian."

Brian didn't answer. After a few seconds, the dark figure cut another strand of rope and the chair rocked backwards. Brian could feel the blood begin to rush to his head.

"He shot the woman," Brian said. "I knew the girl was next, so I struck her on the forehead and knocked her out. I was gonna come back for her, but they shoved a squirt bottle full of gasoline from a duffel bag at me. Peters took a bottle of alcohol from the side table and they told us to pour it all over. I knew if I didn't, they'd kill me, too, so I began pouring.

"Then everybody went outside. Peters stuffed a rag into the bottle and lit it."

"So Peters burned down the house?"

"No..." Brian whimpered. "I did it," his voice full of shame. "Peters told me if I didn't, he'd throw me in there with them. So I threw the bottle through the window and we left.

"A few days later, I learned the little girl made it out. Against all odds. I like to think I saved her, ya know? But she would never be…" He swallowed. "I tried to work after that, but I just couldn't do the job anymore. I quit... and I've worked for BCC ever since."

"Tell me about the coroner."

"What coroner?"

"The one you threatened into doctoring the autopsy report. I suppose Peters forced you to do that, too?" the synthesized voice growled.

"What coroner? I didn't threaten any coroner."

"I think you're lying to me, Brian."

"What? No! I swear! I don't know what you're talking about."

The masked figure dug the knife under the rope again. He cut another strand, leaving only two left.

"Shit! Come on man! I don't know! I don't know what you're talking about!"

"That's just not the answer I'm looking for," the masked man said as he cut another strand of rope. This left only one small thread left. Brian could hear it buckling and stretching under his weight.

"I swear!"

"The only thing that's keeping you from rocketing toward the ground, Brian, is one last thread on this rope. So think very hard about what you're about to say… because they might be your last words on this Earth."

"Wait! I can prove it! Ask him!" Brian huffed. "Just ask him! He'll tell you it wasn't me!"

"I already did. See, your ol' buddy Peters says *you* were the one who forced him into the whole thing. Says *you* were the one who shot the woman… and *you* were the one who threatened the coroner."

"Wait, you talked to Peters?" Brian asked, his confused expression slipping off his face. He laughed. "I get it," he half-whispered, letting his aching neck finally relax from holding up his head. "That's why you're doing this." He scoffed, then laughed again.

"So you're admitting that you're responsible," the synthesized voice said.

"No, but if you're going to kill me, then just do it. But do me a favor, will ya? Ask the coroner! Ask him!"

Ally and Maury looked at each other. "Say that again," Ally said.

"You say I threatened some coroner, right? Well if I really did threaten him, he would have seen my face. He'd recognize me, right? I mean, would you forget the face of someone who threatened your life? Ask him!"

Ally pulled Maury off to the side, far enough away so that Brian couldn't hear what they were about to discuss. "I think he's telling the truth," she said. "Why else would he assume the coroner was a *man*?"

"You caught that, too?"

"Also, why would he tell us to ask Wilcox? He's right. You'd remember the face of the man who threatened you and your family. We didn't think to ask her what Davis looked like. She just said she read his name tag. Peters could have worn Davis's uniform or badge."

"You might be right," he said.

"Shit!" Ally huffed. "That fucker!" Ally was royally pissed at herself. Peters had fed her a load of bullshit and she'd eaten up. Marcus was right. She was too emotional. She vowed that from now on she'd look at future matters more empirically.

"It always bothered me… the fact that Davis quit the force shortly after. Peters didn't," Maury said.

Neither of them spoke for a moment.

"It's your call," Maury finally said.

"He's not our guy."

"I agree."

Together, they walked back over to the rope again. "All right, Brian. I believe you," Maury said. Then he flicked open the knife again and held it under the last strand of rope.

"Wait! I told you everything! You said you'd let me live!"

"You don't deserve to live," Maury said, his voice unable to mask his disgust. He dug the knife under the last thread, despite Brian's frantic cries, and cut it away.

For Brian, everything happened in slow motion. He gasped as he felt the chair drop backwards. He could feel himself tipping until the inevitable fall. He knew he only had seconds to live. He remembered how strange this thought was. The certainty of death and the futility of denial. But just as he was about to crash onto the ground below, he reckoned something caught him in mid-fall, then he felt himself swing out and away from the building before descending slowly toward the ground.

The chair slowed until it rested gently on the ground with a PLUNK.

Ally and Maury floated through the air and set foot on the ground beside Davis. They each let go of a rope, and behind them, a pile of counterweights rocketed back from the roof to the ground with a crash.

"You didn't kill me," Brian whimpered.

"I said you didn't *deserve* to live... not that you wouldn't," Maury said coldly. He walked toward him and squatted down to meet his eye level. The mask on his face revealed only his eyes. "I need you to do something for me Brian. I need you to walk into the police station and confess to what you just told us tonight."

"I can't... if I say anything, those men will kill my family."

"We'll protect your family. You have my word."

"Even if I believed you, I testify... I go to prison. Who'll look after my family then? My son... he... he's really sick. He needs medicine and I—"

"Tell the police you want to negotiate a deal, one that will keep you out of prison so you can be with your family. I'll set you up with enough cash to get a fresh start somewhere safe."

"But my testimony isn't enough to bring anyone down. You need corroboration."

"That's *my* problem. You just make sure you take my call when you wake up."

Brian sighed. "Okay. I'll do it."

"I know you will, Brian," Maury said, as he shot him with a tranquilizer dart.

Brian grunted and slumped in the chair. Maury cut him loose and sheathed his knife. "You see? My way put the fear of death in him, but he lived. *AND* he'll still be alive to testify. So when this is all over, we'll have the testimony of a coroner, an ex-cop, a dying declaration from Peters, and a direct witness to the crime... *you.*"

"Okay," Ally admitted. It was a good plan. "So… what now? We go after Peters again?

"No. Peters is irrelevant. After we give our statements, there'll be no place he can hide. He'll get what's coming to him."

"So now we make the call?"

"Now we make the call," Maury answered.

CHAPTER 36

The sound of whirring gears and the faint hum of electricity filled the air as the lift slowly descended. With a soft hiss, the doors parted and Ally and Maury stepped off the platform. "Any changes, Curtis?" Maury asked as the lift doors slid shut behind them.

"Nah. He's still sitting in his office."

Maury leaned in to examine the viewing screen. Sergeant Lockhart was sitting at his desk with a drink in his hand, staring at a case folder. "He should be off the clock by now. What's he been doin'?"

"Well, for the past hour he's been sorting through piles of paperwork in his office, which has been thrilling to watch by the way. Again, thank you for choosing me for that part."

Maury rolled his eyes. "So what do you think?"

"Umm, from what I can tell. He's done a pretty good job. Everything's now organized by type of crime."

Maury scrunched up his face and lightly smacked him on the back of the head. "No, Curtis… what do you think about—"

"Oh! You meant… ah," Curtis nodded, "we're about ready." He tapped his fingers on the light keyboard and lines of code scrolled rapidly on multiple monitors, revealing a complex web of algorithms and worm codes that began to breach the online security protocols of the precinct. He initiated an encryption program with end-to-end protection until finally, an open padlock icon appeared on the screen. "We're good," he said, giving a thumbs up.

Ally reached for the phone while Curtis dialed the number and waited for Lockhart's desk phone to ring. The team watched Lockhart briefly glanced up from the file he was reading, then ignored it. Five rings. Ten. Finally, he picked up the receiver. "Lockhart," he grunted.

"Good evening, Sergeant," Ally's deep, synthesized and robotic voice growled through the receiver. "Did you get the tape recorder?"

"So, it's you..." he said, exhaling loudly. "Allyson Reid, I presume." There was a pause on the line. "You can dispense with the theatrics. I know it's you."

Ally wasn't surprised Lockhart knew about her. Her face was all over the CCTV and probably the news. Moreover, she'd abducted Peters right in front of Dr. Hansen, who no doubt would have told all the cops who she was by now. Then, there was her history with Michaels.

"Did you listen to Peters's confession?" she asked, her voice sounding soft and unsure after disengaging the voice changer.

"I did."

"And?"

He scoffed. "What, you expect me to thank you? Is that why you called?"

"I didn't do it for gratitude. And no, that's not why I called. I called because I need your help."

Lockhart laughed. "Let me get this straight," he said, taking a swig of his drink. "You assault my officers, some of which are in the hospital right now, you abduct another - torture and beat him within an inch of his life - drug over a dozen S.W.A.T. agents with some kind of hallucinogenic, evade arrest, give our K9 unit PTSD or some shit, and you expect me to help you? Why in the *hell* would I do that?"

"Because it's your job. Because you're a good cop. Because I have information on a murder case."

"Let me guess… your family's *alleged* murder?"

Ally didn't know how to answer. He said it like she was expecting him to prioritize her family over everyone else's. Like what happened to her family didn't matter.

"I'm right, aren't I?"

"What, my family doesn't deserve justice?"

Lockhart sighed. "Look, turn yourself in. Give your statement on the record and I can promise you my men will look into it."

"Men like Peters?" Ally prodded. She listened to the faint crackle on the quiet line. "You only know he's dirty because of me."

"No, what I know," he growled, "is that you obtained an admission of guilt by methods of torture. Did you really think the courts would just pretend that didn't happen? Even a rookie lawyer could get that thrown out of court."

"I also have others willing to come forward, real witnesses that can corroborate—"

"And did you torture them, too?"

Not all of them, she thought.

Lockhart laughed again. "You did, didn't you?"

"I was just trying to help."

"No, you were just trying to help *yourself*. Do us both a favor, the next time you feel like helping, don't. You want my advice? Turn yourself in, before this gets any worse."

"I am! That's why I called. I'm turning myself in tonight… but only under one condition."

"No! No conditions. Either you turn yourself in, or I will hunt you down and bring you in myself."

Ally ignored him. "My condition is, you agree to receive my two witnesses and take their statements personally. With Peters's taped confession and my statement, that makes four."

"And I'm just supposed to, what… take the word of these witnesses you probably coerced, threatened or assaulted? I'm supposed to take *your* word? The word of a *criminal*?"

Ally felt her tongue loosen. She was losing patience. "The real criminals are working alongside you, Sergeant."

"Well, I suppose it takes one to know one."

"That's ironic, coming from a cop," she sneered.

"Goodnight, Allyson," Lockhart barked, slamming the phone down.

The team stayed locked on the CCTV as a hush fell over the room. Tension lingered in the silence as all four awkwardly exchanged looks, saying more than words ever could, while Lockhart downed his drink. They watched him shake his head and pour himself another.

"Call him again," Maury finally said. "Try not to be so abrasive."

"Me? Abrasive?" Ally joked, and picked up the receiver. Curtis connected the call and the phone rang again. They watched Lockhart stare at it. He let it ring five times before he answered.

"Lockhart," he said gruffly.

"How's Tony Picianni?" Ally asked.

On screen, Lockhart stiffened and laid his elbow on the table. He looked down at the file on his desk. "If I find out you had something to do with his death, I'll—"

"Death!?" Ally cried. "He's dead? How? I practically gift wrapped him for you!"

Lockhart didn't answer. His eyes were transfixed on the file on his desk.

"Sergeant!"

"Suicide. He slit his own wrists with a razor blade. But you probably already knew that. Probably slipped it to him yourself."

"And how did he get a razor past your men?" Ally hissed.

The team watched Lockhart remove the receiver from his ear and rest his hand on his chin. He rubbed his face, deep in thought, then placed the receiver back to his ear. "I don't know," he grumbled. "But if I find out you had anything to do—"

"The only way he could have gotten a blade past your team is if there was someone on the inside, and you know it!"

Lockhart didn't reply.

"Look out your window," Ally sneered. "Those weapons would have been on the streets by now if it weren't for me. I even gave you a witness! Are those the actions of a criminal?"

"I've been at this racket a long time... and do you know what I've learned? Villains rarely perceive their actions to be villainous."

"Neither do cops, Sergeant," Ally snapped. "Eight years ago, my family was murdered right in front of me! Men in your precinct helped them and covered it up!"

"Allyson—"

"Listen! I have a city coroner willing to come forward. She'll confess to doctoring the autopsy report under threat to life. You already have Peters's confession. I have an ex-cop who will confirm the existence of the assassin who killed them, and admit to aiding him… one guess who his former partner was."

"Peters," Lockhart said.

"Are you starting to see why there were never any suspects brought forward and no charges ever filed? Why my sister wasn't even mentioned in the coroner's report?

"How did you—"

Ally didn't let him finish. "I'm willing to bet Peters can uncover a laundry list of other dirty cops and corruption. This is the kind of case that people like you dream of, isn't it? The kind that fast-tracks you up the ladder?"

Lockhart didn't answer.

"Sergeant?"

"I'm here," he grumbled, pinching the bridge of his nose. "Why me? Why not Lieutenant Michaels? It was his case."

"I don't trust Michaels. He lied to me. And he's connected to Peters—"

Lockhart's thoughts drifted back to when Michaels said he was training Peters.

"—he could be in on it. That's why I'm asking for your help. Will you help me?"

Lockhart set the phone down and poured himself another drink. He stared at it so long the team thought the feed had frozen. Finally, he cursed and downed it, then picked the receiver up again. "Okay," he muttered. "I'll help you. *If* you turn yourself in."

"Thank you, Sergeant," Ally said. "I'll surrender myself tonight at 11:00." She saw him check his watch. "Just don't tell Michaels."

Lockhart went to put the phone down.

"And Lockhart? You're my last shot. I'm trusting you. Please don't screw me. "

CHAPTER 37

It was 10:50 pm. Rain was coming down in sheets, overtaking the sounds of the city. In the shadows of an adjacent building to the precinct, Maury was crouched with a night-vision scope pressed to his eye. He'd insisted that he suit up and stay close just in case things didn't go to plan. Experience had taught him one thing: the closer to victory, the sharper the blades of fate.

"I'm in position," he said.

"Copy that."

Movement in the dim lighting caught his eye. Through the suffocating mist that obscured his vision, a man quick-stepped it through the small rivers that formed atop the pavement and flowed to the gutters.

"Peters is here," Maury said.

Back in the lair, Marcus and Curtis used the gateway to monitor the CCTV cameras in the precinct and except for a few cops and the night guard at the reception desk, the precinct was having a relatively quiet night for Grace City. They watched Peters slip through the front entrance and shake off the excess water.

"How's the weather?" the guard asked.

"Piss off," Peters growled, heading down the hall.

He made his way to the coffee pot, poured himself a cup, and headed to his desk. The moment he sat down in his chair, he dipped too far backwards, spilling coffee down his front. "Come on!" Peters set down what was left of his coffee and tried to flick away the spill with the back of his hand. "Damn it!"

"Dumbass," Curtis muttered, shaking his head.

"Peters?" Captain Stevens called over the cubicles. "My office."

Marcus and Curtis watched Peters sulk into the Captain's office and poke his head in through the door.

"How are you feeling?" Stevens asked, gesturing to the chair.

"Feeling good, sir," Peters said, sitting down. "A little sore, but ready for active duty."

"I'm glad you're on the mend. Hell of a thing that happened. I'm really glad you're okay, son."

Peters relaxed a little. "Thank you, sir. I appreciate that."

"Listen Peters, I'm gonna level with ya. I've listened to the recording—"

Peters lurched forward. "But sir! She made me say those things! I'm not dirty!"

"And that will be determined by an internal investigation," Stevens replied.

"Oh, come on, Cap! This is bullshit and you know it!"

"I'm sorry, son. There isn't any easy way to say this… I'm gonna need your gun and badge."

Peters looked at his captain with helpless eyes. "Come on, Cap…"

"It's not personal. It's just procedure."

"Yeah, well it feels pretty personal."

Captain Stevens sighed. "Detective Peters, you are hereby suspended from active duty pending the results of said investigation, whereby at which point, we will be able to determine your future here. I'm sorry."

Peters sat still, mouth open. Curtis would have felt bad for him if he weren't such a piece of shit. Slowly, Peters stood up, removed his gun and badge, and set them on the table. "You're making a big mistake here, Captain."

"I advise you not to discuss any element of this investigation with anyone so that you may receive a fair and just result. You have 15 minutes to clean out your locker."

The team watched Peters storm off through the office door and back toward his desk. He grabbed his coat off the back of his chair and marched toward the locker room.

"*Someone's here,*" Maury said.

"We copy," Curtis said into the mic. He and Marcus watched through the exterior cameras as a figure holding an umbrella headed up the steps. Dr. Wilcox entered the lobby, shook off the rain, and took her seat as directed on the phone. A few moments later, a man approached reception and sat down in the waiting room opposite her and removed his hood.

The team watched intently through the CCTV, studying their reactions. "Davis is in position. Wilcox is just sitting there. She seems awfully calm for having just reunited with the man who threatened to kill her."

"Looks like Davis was telling the truth," Maury said.

"Ally?" Curtis asked. "Are you sure you still want to do this?"

"I'm sure. Wish me luck."

As Ally walked up the steps and into the lobby with arms raised, Curtis's breaths came in shallow gasps. He sat on the edge of his seat, leaning forward and gripping the fabric of the chair tightly until his knuckles turned white, unable to tear his eyes away from the screen. The officers raised their sidearms and screamed at her, ordering her to get on the ground. Curtis watched her comply, slowly, and they cuffed her behind her back and jerked her to her feet.

Curtis sighed in relief. "She's in," he said into the mic as they took her further inside.

"And the witnesses?" Maury asked.

"Lockhart's on his way," Curtis said. "Thirty seconds."

"Received."

Lockhart walked around the corner of the waiting room and approached the seating area. *"Good evening. I'm Sergeant Lockhart,"* he said. *"I understand you two are here to make a statement?"*

Davis and Wilcox nodded, exchanging a nervous glance and realizing they were both there for the same reason.

"Please come with me," he said gently, leading them around the corner and down a corridor.

On the other monitor, Marcus checked on Peters, who was gathering up his few belongings in the locker room. He hung his head a second, then headed toward the door. It opened and Sutko brushed past him.

"Peters! There you are! Did you hear?" he gasped. *"They got the bitch!"*

"What? Who?"

"The No Cuts Bitch! She's in Room 1. She turned herself in, like 30 seconds ago."

Marcus stared intently at the CCTV monitors, his eyes flicking from one camera to the next. As he watched, Detective Peters stormed down the hallway and turned the corner towards the interrogation rooms. Suddenly, he stopped in his tracks and on screen, he seemed to be studying something.

Marcus could see Peters's face contorting in confusion and alarm. It took a moment, but Marcus finally spotted what Peters was looking at - Lockhart was holding the door open to Interview Room 3 for the coroner.

He watched Peters pace back and forth, running his hands over his hair as he glanced into the interrogation rooms. Then Peters spun around and headed for the toilets.

"I think our boy Peters just clocked Ally," Marcus said. "Stay alert. I'll let you know if he tries anything stupid."

"Received," Maury said.

Inside Room 3, Curtis watched Lockhart press record on the recording machine and let the tape go a few seconds before speaking: *"Sergeant Floyd Lockhart sitting in Interview Room 3 to take a statement, on the record, for Dr. Peggy Wilcox from the Grace City Mortuary. The time is... 23:15 on December 13th. Please state your name for the record?"*

"Peggy. Uh, Peggy Wilcox..." She cleared her throat. *"Doctor Peggy Wilcox. I work for the city. I'm a coroner for the Grace City Mortuary."*

"And you're here on your own free will? You're not being coerced into being here tonight?"

"Yes. I mean, no... I mean, yes, I am here on my own free will... and no, I'm not being coerced into giving a statement."

Lockhart made a face. *"Thank you. Go ahead," he said. "Tell me what you came here to say."*

A knock sounded on the door. Lockhart leaned into the tape recorder. *"Interview paused at 23:16 for knock on the door."* He pressed pause. *"I'll just be a second,"* he said, walking to the door.

When he opened it, two men were standing in front of him: Lieutenant Michaels and Detective Sutko. "*Sergeant, what is the meaning of this? Why are you conducting interviews?"* Michaels asked.

Lockhart looked like a deer caught in headlights.

"Sergeant, have you been drinking?" Michaels leaned in like he was inhaling the air around them.

Lockhart tried to reply, but just stammered.

"Sutko!"

"Sir."

"You'll finish these interviews—"

"No!" Lockhart objected, finding his voice.

"Unless you want me to suspend you for drinking on the job, you'll cease-and-desist immediately."

Lockhart opened his mouth to protest, but closed it. He stood rigidly while Sutko entered the room.

"Sutko, finish these interviews. And report back to me when finished, is that clear?"

"Yes, sir."

"You," he said pointing to Lockhart, *"come with me."*

Marcus's eyes flared. He gripped the mic and called out. "Maury, do you copy?"

"I'm here."

"We've got a little problem. Michaels just pulled Lockhart from the interviews. A Detective Sutko has taken over. Should we get Ally out?"

"What do we know about Sutko?"

"Curtis tried to pull up information on him, but there wasn't much."

"Well, maybe that's a good thing. Finding nothing could mean there is no indication of corruption. Is Ally alright?"

"She and her doctor are in Room 1. A detective is with them; Davis is in Room 2 with another detective. I guess Lockhart was having all three give their statements at once."

"I say we stick to the plan," Maury said. *"If anything feels wrong, tell me immediately, and I'll get them out."*

Marcus and Curtis directed their attention to Michaels's office. Michaels sat at his desk and motioned for Lockhart to sit down in front of him, their conversation audible through the CCTV.

"Listen Floyd. I think you and I need to bury the hatchet. What's done, is done. I'm sure you feel like I didn't deserve the promotion to Lieutenant and probably resent the fact that you have to remain a Sergeant. God knows, you are a brilliant officer. You'll get your chance someday. But until that day, you and I need to be able to work with one another without turning the knives in each other's backs," he said candidly.

Curtis watched Lockhart's expression through the CCTV feed, his eyes fixed on the monitor. He was clearly taken aback by Michaels's sudden attempt at reconciliation.

"So I propose you and I talk things out, like men... get a drink," Michaels finished. *"What do you say?"*

"That sounds fine, sir," he said, finally.

"Good man," Michaels said, smiling. *"Grab your coat. I'll meet you by my car in five."*

Lockhart stood up and left, passing by Interview Room 3 and glancing through the glass on his way back to his office.

Curtis checked the recording devices in the other rooms. They were still rolling. Sutko was speaking with the coroner, Ally, seated beside Dr. Hansen, was speaking to a female Detective, and Davis to a male Detective. Everything looked legit.

"Ummm... Dad?" Curtis called. Marcus stepped closer and stood behind Curtis's computer array. They both watched as Lockhart exited the precinct.

"Maury, do you copy? Lockhart's leaving the building."

"He's what?"

"He's meeting his boss for a drink. I'll explain later. Michaels just met him in the parking lot. But just before he left, he sent a text message on what looked like a burner phone. Something about this feels off. Lockhart may be in danger. I think you should—"

"OFFICER DOWN!" came a crackled radio call. *"OFFICER DOWN!*

CHAPTER 38

On screen, Curtis watched as the hallway outside the interview rooms came to life. Every available cop who wasn't occupied stampeded past the camera's view. Sutko paused the interview as police chatter squawked through on his radio.

"Wait here," he said to Peggy, and exited the room. He looked down the hallway and saw officers charging passed, ready for action.

"Let's go, Sutko!" an officer yelled as he ran past him.

"What's going on?"

"999!" the officer yelled over his shoulder.

Back in the shadows, Maury watched the parking lot fill with officers and cars roar to life. "Guys, talk to me. What the hell is going on in there!"

"Someone just called in a 999. Half the precinct just left their stations. What do you want to do?"

"What about Ally?" Maury asked.

"Ummm... so far, the three of them are still okay. It looks like Sutko left the room to check things out, but he's still hanging around. I think the call is legit, or he'd be acting strangely."

"I'm about to lose Lockhart... should I go after him?" Maury asked.

"Erm, I don't know... hang on."

"I need an answer!"

"Go. Everything looks legit. If anything comes up, we'll call you."

Maury pulled on his mask and helmet. He fired up his bike and waited.

Michaels and Lockhart looked at each other as the radio crackled. *"SEND BACKUP! SEND BACKUP! OLD TOWN! THE DOCKS! WE'RE PINNED DOWN!"* Machine gun fire echoed in the background through the walkie. All around them, cops poured out of the precinct and raced to their cars.

"Get in!" Michaels shouted.

He didn't have to say it twice. Lockhart jumped into the passenger side of the sedan and together, they sped off, following a line of flashing cars out into the city.

"You got a piece?" Michaels yelled.

"No."

"There's a spare," he barked over the noise of the sirens, "in the glove box!"

Lockhart opened the little door and retrieved the handgun. He ejected the magazine, checked to see if the Glock was loaded, reinserted the clip, cocked it, put the safety on, and held the weapon at his side.

"Looks like we're going to have to reschedule that drink!" Michaels barked with a sparkle in his eyes.

After two to three minutes of following the line of cars, Michaels suddenly turned off and headed down a side street.

"What are you doing?" Lockhart protested. "The docks are that way!"

"There's construction! Road's blocked! This is a shortcut!" Michaels yelled. "We'll get there a few minutes before they do!"

Maury followed behind them, lights off and cautious of his distance and yelled into the mic. "Lockhart and Michaels just pulled away from the rest."

"Everything is still fine here," Marcus replied. *"Be careful."*

Maury zoomed past a few alleyways at twice the speed limit to keep up with them, still careful to keep his distance. Finally, Michaels's car entered a car garage and screeched to a halt.

Maury turned the engine off, coasted silently to an alley nearby and moved in for a closer look.

Michaels slammed the car into park, removed his side arm, cocked it, and the two officers stepped out.

"What the hell are you doing?" Lockhart protested. "We're nowhere near the docks."

"You're right," Michaels replied, turning his gun on him. "That's because we're not going to the docks."

"What are you doing, John?" Lockhart asked, raising his gun instinctively.

"I don't know how you found out, Floyd... but you always were a clever son-of-a-bitch."

"I don't understand," Lockhart said.

"The girl... the coroner... Peters's old partner... don't pretend like you don't know!" he grunted.

"I *don't* know!" Lockhart insisted. "I got an anonymous tip."

"Cut the shit, Floyd. How'd you find out?"

"All right, John. Stop screwing around! Lower your weapon," Lockhart demanded.

"Or what?" Michaels asked. "You gonna shoot me? You don't have the balls."

"Drop it!" Lockhart ordered.

Michaels chuckled. "I'll bet you fifty bucks you don't have the balls to pull that trigger." He nodded. "Yeah, I'm gonna count to five." Michaels raised his gun and aimed at Lockhart's head.

"Don't!" Lockhart yelled, raising his.

"One... Two..."

"You're fucking crazy!" Lockhart shouted.

"Three…"

"Don't!" Lockhart yelled again.

"Four!"

"Goddamn it, John!" he screamed. "Enough of this shit!"

"Fi..."

Lockhart pulled the trigger. The gun went off and Michaels stumbled backwards, grabbing at his chest before dropping to his knees.

"Shit!" Lockhart screamed, turning on the spot and pacing. He ran his hand through his hair. Then he stopped. Michaels was laughing. He stared in confusion as Michaels lifted his hand and showed his chest. There was no wound. No blood. He continued laughing.

"I didn't think you had it in you," he taunted, getting up slowly and raising his gun again.

Lockhart pulled the trigger two more times which only made Michaels double over and laugh harder.

"Blanks... you put blanks in the gun..." Lockhart muttered.

"Look on the bright side, I owe you 50 bucks," Michaels said, cackling and wiping his eyes.

To his left, a side door opened and five men in balaclavas stepped out. Lockhart eyed them, then glared at Michaels. "You know, they did warn me…" he said, narrowing his eyes. "They said you were dirty."

"We're all dirty," Michaels said, nodding to the men.

Lockhart threw the gun at the first man to step forward, striking him in the chest. The other two rushed him. One slugged him in the stomach while the other kicked the back of his knees. He went down, and the first man clubbed him over the head, knocking him out.

Maury peered around the entryway and watched as one man placed a black hood over Lockhart's head, the others bound his wrists and ankles, then they dragged his limp body to the car and placed him in the trunk.

Michaels picked out his cell phone and sent a text.

"Guys? I think they're going to kill him," Maury whispered. "They've just put him in the trunk of Michaels's car. I'm going radio silent until I can get him out of this."

"No wait!" Marcus cried. His voice was swallowed by a burst of static.

Maury pressed his finger to his ear. "Say again!?"

"Smith is here! He's..." the earpiece crackled.

"... dozen officers a..."

"just... Wilcox!"

"He's going after Davis!" the earpiece crackled again.

"Maury! Get back here now!"

Maury looked at the car. He had no choice. He raced back to the bike, leaving Lockhart to his own fate, but stopped dead in his tracks as the radio crackled again.

"It's too late," Curtis called through tears. *"She's dead!"*

CHAPTER 39

FIVE MINUTES AGO…

Mr. Clark glided through the front entrance of the police station, his footsteps silent on the tiled floor. Every step was calculated, every movement clean and precise, every heartbeat a well-timed note in the symphony of the dimly lit lobby. In an instant, his trained eyes assessed every inch of the room, every dark corner, every possible exit, every potential threat. He was pleased to see that staging the emergency call had effectively thinned out the herd of loitering officers, leaving only a handful to stand between him and his targets.

Mr. Clark twisted the dial on his watch face, activating the red fragment from Project Starfall. He felt a numb shiver spread across his body like an anesthetic and enveloped his skin with a faint reddish hue. His mind quieted; his emotions, the noise of the busy streets behind him, the ringing phones ahead, the loud voices, all faded. Everything came into focus.

He moved forward, raising his gun, now just an extension of his arm, and pulled the trigger. The bullet sailed through the fitted silencer attached to the barrel and hit the woman behind the reception desk right between the eyes. The spray of bone and blood exploded through the back of her skull and splattered against the wall partition. Her body fell hard against the divider, sending it crashing to the floor.

Behind it, two officers involuntarily leapt to their feet, as if reacting to a thunderbolt. Mr. Clark watched them process the blood pooling from their colleague's open head, trained the barrel, and fired two rounds. The first struck one man in the temple. The second, split the other man's neck open in a flurry of crimson splatter before he could blink. He crumpled to the floor, choking.

As he moved deeper into the precinct, Mr. Clark found another obstacle. He squeezed the trigger, his shots ripping through an officer's chest. The man flinched and blinked in bewilderment. His arms flopped limply to his sides as he collapsed to his knees and keeled over. Mr. Clark stood over his twitching body. He stared down, trying to override the stone's aura so he could savor the disbelief and terror that swam in the dying man's eyes, but a shrill squeak turned his head.

An officer gaped in frozen shock. She let out a short grunt. Trembling, she clawed for her service pistol, but Mr. Clark exploited her hesitation and fired. The bullet tore through her eye socket and she fell limply to the ground with a thud.

Mr. Clark looked down again, but the man's eyes were dead and empty. He scowled and moved on.

The woman's scream had been enough to transform the police station into a whirlwind of panic and cries of confusion. Three more officers stepped around the corner, only to be shot dead.

To Mr. Clark's right, a barrage of bullets punched through a partition. He moved aside as if sidestepping a sports tackle and emptied his clip where he assumed the shooter was crouched. A brilliant burst of red splattered across the edge of the desk and a man leapt to his feet, recoiling in agony. The bullet had sliced through his cheek. His cries momentarily merged with the pandemonium until Mr. Clark finished him with a bullet to the back of the head.

He pressed on like a specter, stepping over fallen bodies, through puddles of oozing blood, and breathed in the sharp, coppery metallic tang lingering in the air. Then he stopped. He jerked his head to the side. A custodian, desperately seeking cover behind a filing cabinet clutched his mouth trying to muffle his sobs.

Mr. Clark smiled. He crouched in front of the man and turned the watch dial. The red hue faded and Mr. Clark shook his head in a quick flick. "Shhh…" he crooned, placing one hand on the man's shoulder. With the other, he removed a knife from his belt. He held it up, watching the man's eye sparkle in silent terror.

The cleaner shook his head, pressing his back against the wall as far as he could and begged, "No… no please!"

Mr. Clark's eyes lit up and he shoved the blade into the man's neck, slowly. Careful to savor the moment. The man's eyes widened in shock before Mr. Clark slid the blade, opening his throat. He watched the man choke and thrash, bleeding out.

When the man's eyes darkened, Mr. Clark stood up, sighing as if having just edged himself before release. He twisted the dial again before making for the interview rooms.

He knocked and waited.

As the door opened, Mr. Clark shoved the detective back through the threshold, pressed the barrel into Officer Sutko's chest, and pulled the trigger twice, sending two bullets through his heart. Sutko's back slammed against the wall and blood streaked against the cream colored paint. He dropped to his knees and fell forward, twitching, blood draining from the corners of his mouth as he gurgled. Mr. Clark aimed at the back of Sutko's head and pulled the trigger.

CLICK.

Annoyed, he ejected the magazine, inserted his last, and plugged a round into the back of Sukto's skull. His eyes then shifted to the coroner. She was already standing, back pressed against the wall, her complexion a pasty white. She was breathing quickly and her palms were splayed against the wall. "Please..." she begged.

Without a word, Mr. Clark fired two rounds into her chest and watched as she fell hard onto her face, bounced off the chair and landed on her side. He walked around the table and planted a final round into the side of her head.

Satisfied, he whirled and headed to Room 2 where he met Peters standing outside the door. "He's in here," Peters said, stepping aside. Mr. Clark placed the gun into his other hand and drew back a fist. "Wait!" Peters cried, holding out his hands. "I want to watch."

Mr. Clark hesitated, then nodded.

When the door opened, Mr. Clark saw the witness stiffen. He saw the panic fill his face and recognized the all-too-familiar resignation of imminent death. The officer conducting the interview stood up in surprise, only to be shot dead: two to the chest, one to the head. His body crashed to the floor as fast as it had stood.

"Hey buddy," Peters said, a cruel smile on his lips. "Long time, no see." He picked up the plastic cup of water on the table and slurped it dry.

"Please..." Davis begged. "I'll leave right now. I haven't told them anything yet. Just let me go, yeah?"

Peters tutted. "You've been a bad boy, Brian. You need to be punished."

"Please… I have a family."

"You should have thought about that before you decided to open your big mouth. I warned you eight years ago. You should have listened."

Mr. Clark pointed the gun at Brian's chest. Just like before, he fired two slugs into his heart, then walked up to his dead body and put another into his skull.

"Come on… I want to see the look on the bitch's face!" Peters yelled.

The door to Interview Room 1 burst open and in walked the man who didn't exist. The man Ally was told she'd made up to cope with the guilt of murdering her mother and sister—Mr. Smith. But he was real! He was just as she remembered him. Tall, strong, long dark hair now tinged with gray.

For Ally, time slowed. What was only a matter of seconds, passed as nearly half a minute for her. She couldn't breathe. She couldn't move. The assassin raised his gun. Ally sat horrified, frozen, completely paralyzed. He pointed it right at her chest. She was a child again, completely helpless.

Ally watched as the officer at the table impressively removed her gun from her holster and even raised it, but was dead before she could pull the trigger. Mr Smith put two bullets through her chest, walked up to her prone body and put another into the back of her head.

He then turned to Ally.

Memories flooded back into her mind. It was as if she were living simultaneously in the past and the present. *Mr. Smith plunged a knife through her sister's chest, her mother's tortured screams, the knife point to her throat.* Ally's eyes widened as Mr. Smith lifted the gun and aimed. Before she could blink, Dr. Hansen leapt in front of her and shielded her. She was screaming, but the sound was muffled, distant. Ally wanted to scream at her to move, that Mr. Smith wouldn't hesitate. But she was paralyzed. She watched in horror as an amused smirk spread across his lips before he fired.

No!

The shot struck Dr. Hansen right through the heart, killing her instantly. She fell a second later with an unsettling thud.

Ally watched Mr. Smith move the gun an inch to the right, still in slow motion.

Move! Goddamn it!

Suddenly, Ally felt herself slam against the wall behind her. Intense pain surged through her chest and back like she was hit by a baseball bat. She looked down. Blood spurted through two holes in her chest, right where her heart was. She gasped, but all she managed to do was choke and cough up blood. Her vision started to swirl around and she could feel the world fading away.

She fell to her knees and slumped to her side. Somehow she managed to roll to her back. The last thing she saw in her waning view was a pair of legs that belonged to her family's killer, a man who she'd vowed to find and take her revenge, a man she always knew existed, but could never prove it. Through blurred vision, she saw a round barrel slide toward her head.

Then her heart stopped and her eyes went dead. She took her last breath that night while looking into the eyes of her mother's killer.

CHAPTER 40

Maury braced himself against the concrete wall with his arm. The news of Ally's murder hit him like a punch to the gut. He felt like he was going to puke. Marcus was right. He'd failed her. He'd gotten her killed.

He grabbed the rim of a nearby dumpster and screamed in silence. He should've videotaped the confessions, saw to it that the witnesses were put into protective custody. He'd gotten cocky. And it had gotten everyone killed.

Michaels's car door slammed and the engine roared to life, snapping Maury out of his rage. He glared at the balaclava men as they jumped into the car and squealed out of the garage.

I've lost enough people tonight, he thought. *But there is still a chance to save another. Get it together old man!*

He kickstarted the bike and began his pursuit.

Ten minutes later, Maury crouched silently in the shadows of the rafters, his eyes fixed intently on the group below. His muscles were taut and his breath came in steady, controlled rhythms. From his vantage point, he watched as mob boss Felix Overgaard parted the plastic strips that hung in the archway and stepped through. Stopping beside the balaclava men, now unmasked, he casually lit a cigar. "The tapes!" he demanded.

Peters stepped forward and dangled an evidence bag with the three tapes inside. Felix took it and held the match under it until the tapes caught fire. He tossed the flaming bag onto the concrete floor and took a drag.

"That everything?" Felix asked.

"That's all the police have. There won't be any more loose ends. I took care of it," Peters said.

Felix scoffed. "Oh, you took care of it, did you? Coming from the man who couldn't take care of a little girl all by himself?"

Laughter arose from the other men.

Peters scowled. "Hey! If it wasn't for me, those three would have everyone's balls in a vice! You should be thanking me!"

Felix eyed Peters, taking a long drag from his cigar and blew out a thick puff of smoke. He chuckled, then handed the cigar to Michaels, who grudgingly took it, making a face.

As Felix stepped toward Peters, two things happened. First, Peters flinched like a deer on the highway. "You're right; my apologies," Felix said, gently placing his hand on Peters's shoulder. "Thank you, Detective. I appreciate your loyalty."

"Just lookin' out," Peters muttered nervously.

Second, Felix grabbed Peters by the throat in a movement so quick it was almost supernatural. He snarled, pulling Peters to his knees.

Peters's eyes went wide. He smacked Felix's hands and flailed, but Felix's vice grip wouldn't let go. Peters looked to Michaels pleadingly, twitching in his grasp and struggling to inhale.

Felix grinned. "Something the matter, John?" he asked, side-eying Michaels, almost daring him to stop him.

Michaels stood rigid as Peters's body started to droop. He shook his head. "No."

Felix smirked and turned back to Peters, his eyes burning into his. "Know this, you little shit. I don't give a damn if you ARE a policeman. I'd happily kill you right in front of your superior. And now you know he wouldn't do a damn thing to stop it. So talk to me in that tone again? And I'll kill ya!"

Peters's arms fell limply to his side and Felix released his grasp around his throat. He fell to the floor, motionless at first, then began choking. He began clutching his throat and taking deep, grateful breaths.

Felix took back his cigar from Michaels and moved closer to Lockhart, who was still sitting with a black hood over his head. "Get back to work, all'uh'yuh!" he screamed, sending everyone moving. "And John? I trust you'll be more careful in the future."

Paulie reached into his jacket pocket and pulled out two stacks of cash. He tossed one to Michaels and the other to the floor in front of Peters and escorted them toward the exit, Peters with his tail between his legs.

Lockhart was still out cold. His head hung limply in front of him. He was hogtied to a chair. Felix set a chair down opposite so he could look him in the eyes. "Let's get this over with…" he snapped his fingers and a man ripped the black hood off of Lockhart's head.

Maury had seen enough. He eased back into the shadows.

Lockhart opened his eyes and sucked in the fresh, cool air that he was deprived of for nearly an hour, only for the color to drain from his face. What once was a meat freezer full of animal carcasses, was now a personalized torture chamber. Clear plastic tarp was duct-taped to the walls and floor... and he was sitting right in the middle of it!

"You look nervous," Felix quipped. "What's your name?"

"Floyd," he said dryly.

Felix smirked. "Well, Floyd, you can relax. We're not going to torture you."

"So what's with all the plastic?"

"Oh that?" he shrugged. "That's just for effect. Usually people have information I need. But with you, they just want you dead."

"Lucky me," Lockhart muttered.

"None of this has to happen, you know. After all, I'm a reasonable man. I could always just offer you a bribe."

"Let's not kid ourselves. We both know who and what you are."

"Oh? And what's that?" he asked amusedly.

"For starters? A drug dealer…uh, human trafficker and arms dealer, and a…" Lockhart's voice trailed off as he remembered where he was sitting. "Well…" He gestured to his surroundings with his head.

Felix gawked, placing his hand on his chest. "Officer, you've got me all wrong."

A chorus of snickering erupted in the room from the other men.

"You know, I'm curious, how does a person get into this line of work? Daddy wasn't around? Mommy didn't hug you enough? Or were you born a sociopath?"

"Sounds like you've got me all figured out, Floyd. Perhaps you're right. Perhaps I am just a victim of culture."

"Please. At least own what you are."

"What, that I'm *the bad guy*?" He said it like he was talking to a child.

Lockhart scoffed. "You think you're not?"

"I think you need to open your eyes."

Lockhart snorted.

Felix shrugged. "Like you, I was born into this diseased world, but unlike you I was raised in the disorder, the chaos, the poverty."

"And so were thousands of others," Lockhart said dismissively. "Yet they didn't become a cancer on society."

Felix smiled. "Again, you think I'm the bad guy. Take a look around you. The ozone is full of holes... the icecaps are melting... the air and water makes us sick. There's no money for starving children but plenty for war. Politicians made this world, Floyd. They squabble over profits while bureaucrats send our jobs overseas, leaving only scraps for the rest of us. Whatever I am, I am because of my environment."

"Funny... I was raised here too… but I chose law and order."

Felix smirked. "Law and order?" He laughed. "Do you think that badge makes you different from me? I look at you and I don't see law and order." Felix shook his head. "You know what I see?"

Lockhart glowered through him.

"I see a guardian of the status quo. A protector of big business and corporate profits. A boot to squash the voices that dare to ask for a little more for themselves."

"That's bullshit."

"Is it? I think all those protestors outside your precinct might feel differently. Who do you suppose they feel is *the bad guy*?"

"People have a right to protest," Lockhart answered. "That's what democracy means."

"A right to protest?" he parroted. "Then why do your people gas, club and kill so many when they do?"

Lockhart searched for an answer, but he couldn't come up with a suitable one.

"You're all twisted pal. There is no law and order in this world. There's no such thing. There are haves, and have-nots. We're all just pawns on a board," he said, snapping his fingers. "You just don't know it yet."

One of Felix's men pushed in a wheelbarrow full of construction supplies. He lifted out a wooden box, a bag of dry concrete mix, two shovels, and a bucket of water from the tray. Another man set the box on the floor, cut open the bag and dumped the powder into the wheelbarrow. He poured the bucket of water into the tray and together, they started mixing. When it was the right consistency, the men grabbed Lockhart, lifted him to his feet, and stood him up inside the wooden box.

One took out his gun, cocked it, and pointed it at his head while the other continued to shovel concrete into the box and over his shoes. The mixture was now up to his ankles.

"This is a little cliché, don't you think?" Lockhart gestured condescendingly.

Felix shrugged. "What can I say? If it ain't broke."

Lockhart watched the men empty the last of the concrete over his shoes and fill the box. He tried not to think about what was coming next. He had to hope he'd be able to overpower the men before the end. Sooner or later, they had to leave just one or two to keep watch.

"For what it's worth," Felix said, "I'm really sorry about all this. The offer to buy you off still stands, but we both know who and what *you* are. So let's not drag this out any longer. Now, if you'll excuse me, I've got other business to attend to."

Felix motioned to Paulie and the two of them took two steps before the lights to the whole building shut off.

"Is business struggling?" Lockhart quipped.

"Shut up!" Felix barked. "Somebody go check the fucking breaker!"

A menacing laugh echoed through the slaughterhouse. It came from the left… then from the right. Then seemingly from all directions, but far too quickly for it to be a person running around. It was impossible to tell which direction it was coming from.

"What the hell is that?" Felix yelled.

"That's him... that's the Blur," a man whimpered.

"Oh, for Christ's sake!" Felix scoffed. "He ain't—"

"LET LOCKHART GO…" rumbled a deep, synthesized, and robotic voice from out in the darkness.

Everyone turned their guns toward the sound.

"…AND I'll MAKE THIS QUICK," the voice boomed, causing everyone to turn again in the opposite direction, tracking the sound.

"That's a neat trick..." Felix said.

"DROP YOUR WEAPONS…" the voice growled, making the men turn and point their weapons to the right.

"...AND LET HIM GO!" the voice ordered from above them.

"That ain't happening!" Felix yelled, signaling for his men to track the voice. Felix's men adjusted their grips on their weapons and obeyed, circling up and forming a large ring in the center of the main room frantically searching with their eyes for the source of the sound. "How does this end? You pummel me with your bare hands? Drag me out into the street? Take me to the police?"

"NO. I'M GOING TO KILL YOU."

"6 to 1? I'll take those odds."

"WHAT MAKES YOU THINK I CAME ALONE?"

Felix flinched. From the ceiling, seemingly from every dark corner, multiple red laser beams burned through the blackness and billowing smoke. One at a time, they aimed at Felix's men in the center circle, painting their chests. Seconds later, loud reverberating sounds echoed through the building as multiple weapons were cocked.

"THIS IS YOUR LAST WARNING! DROP YOUR WEAPONS. ANYONE WHO CHOOSES TO STAY AND FIGHT WILL DIE TONIGHT."

"If any of you cocksuckers move, I'll kill you myself!" Felix screamed.

No one moved.

"SO BE IT," the voice growled.

The rafters above exploded in synchronized gunfire from each laser source. A second later, all the henchmen in the facility dropped to the ground, leaving Felix standing alone.

Suddenly, Lockhart stepped forward through the archway carrying an AR-15. Felix dashed toward the exit, bullets whizzing overhead and clapping into the walls until a clicking sound echoed through the room.

Lockhart threw down the AR-15, raced up to another downed man, picked up his rifle, and readied himself for another assault.

It never came. Felix was gone.

He turned the gun on the Blur. "Get on the ground!" Lockhart shouted, waving the rifle in all directions anticipating more gunfire from above.

Maury stepped forward and raised his hands. "Really?" he asked. "I just saved your life."

"Do it!" he yelled. "Or I'll shoot!"

Maury kept his hands up and took three slow steps forward. "Listen to me. We need to get out of here before more of them arrive. I'm not your enemy..."

"Tell that to my squad you beat up. Tell that to the dozen lying men dead on this floor! There's no way I'm letting you go anywhere!" he snarled.

"Check them," Maury said, hands still raised.

Lockhart cocked his head.

"Check 'em," Maury repeated.

Lockhart lowered himself down, keeping his gun and eyes fixed on the figure in black. Then he looked down and examined one of the downed men. Something was protruding from his neck. He plucked it out and looked close. "Tranquilizers?"

"I told you, I'm not your enemy. Now come on. Let's get out of here and get you to safety. You can call it in on the way."

Lockhart thought about his options. He didn't like them. But he supposed that under the circumstances, he didn't really have a choice. He lowered the rifle.

"What about the others?"

"No others. Just me."

Lockhart glanced around the room full of bodies. "How did you—"

"Come on!" Maury shouted and jogged past him.

Lockhart ducked as several objects flew past his head and followed the man in black. He leapt off of the front steps and followed Maury across the street to an empty lot. Maury ran to a motorbike stashed in the shadows and kick-started it, then motioned for him to get on the back.

"You're not serious," Lockhart said.

CHAPTER 41

The lair echoed with the weight of shock and grief. Maury had gotten Lockhart out safely, but the devastating loss they now felt overshadowed their small victory. In the interests of his safety, Maury elected to bring Lockhart back with him. He couldn't think of anywhere else to stash him, but he knew that in doing so, it meant the end of the Blur.

Lockhart stepped off the platform and took in his surroundings. He first noted the futuristic computer arrays and electrical equipment near a boy and what he assumed was his father. It was high tech and looked far beyond what a master at a dojo could afford. To the back was what looked like an arsenal of weaponry and combat gear, everything from odd-looking footwear, specialized goggles, body armor, suit attachments and various stealth weapons. Lockhart recognized the look of a few gas canisters, which he surmised could contain anything from smoke bombs, tear gas, or other agents used for crowd control. There were tranquilizer darts, round marble-looking orbs housed beside slingshots, hover drones, and handheld weapons like bow-staffs, Katana swords, sais, and arnis sticks.

"Who *are* you people?" he finally asked.

"I'm Maury. This is my brother Marcus and his son Curtis."

Lockhart regarded their stoic expressions. "Why are you doing all this?"

"Doing what?"

"*This*," he gestured, "this vigilante nonsense."

"You aren't from around here, are you Sergeant?" Maury replied.

Lockhart furrowed his brow. It wasn't the response he was expecting, but as soon as he said it, he realized that he didn't really care to get into it now. He needed to see Captain Stevens.

"You shouldn't have brought him here," Marcus muttered.

"It doesn't matter now," Maury replied. "It's over."

"He's right. I should go." Lockhart took a few steps toward the lift.

"Mr. Lockhart," Maury said. "I brought you here for your own safety. Someone wants you dead. Until we figure out *who* and *why*, you need to stay here."

"That won't be necessary."

"Oh, I'm afraid it's very necessary. You think whoever just tried to have you killed is going to stop looking for you?"

"I appreciate your concern, but I can look after myself."

"Look, aside from your Lieutenant with *actual* mob connections, there are dozens of other cops at your precinct you can't trust. Not to mention the assassin that just shot up your police station."

"Wait, what!?" Lockhart barked.

"Chloe, unmute!" Curtis called apathetically, and a large TV on the wall turned on. Gail Robbins and her news crew were perched outside the Grace City Police station.

"... that's just what some people are saying," Gail said. *"The man's identity is unknown. The police are now reviewing the security tapes so we hope to get a visual ID out to you, soon.*

"For those of you just tuning in, a horrific scene has unfolded here at the PDGC when a shooter, identified only as a lone white male, stormed through the police station and opened fire indiscriminately.

"The number of casualties is unclear at this stage, but the rumor is that the toll is staggering, with multiple casualties and as of yet, no wounded. The motive behind this brazen attack remains unknown, and has left this community reeling in shock and disbelief.

"Our hearts go out to the brave men and women of law enforcement who put their lives on the line to protect our community, as well as to the families and loved ones of those affected by this tragedy."

"When did this happen?" Lockhart shouted.

"Less than an hour ago."

Lockhart gaped in horror as the news kept replaying images of the shooting, of body bags being stacked on the pavement. "I need to go!" Lockhart said.

"Did you hear what I just said? Whoever tried to have you killed is just itching for another chance."

"I can't just hide out here! I need to help!"

"Maybe we *should* let him go," Curtis yelled.

"Curtis!" Marcus scolded.

"No, Dad! Ally's dead. She's DEAD! And it's all his fault!" he yelled, pointing to Lockhart. "If he wants to run back to the people who just tried to kill him, then I say his stupid ass gets what he deserves."

"Curtis—"

"If he hadn't run off to grab a drink, then maybe she'd still be alive!"

"That's enough!" Marcus shouted.

Curtis crossed his arms and turned his head in frustration back to the TV. Gale pressed her finger to her ear and tilted her head. *"This is breaking news… we are told the shooter has been identified! We are putting an image on your screen now of the man we are being told may be responsible for the attack."* On screen, a picture of Sergeant Lockhart with his name plastered underneath it appeared. *"This man's name is Floyd Lockhart, a sergeant for the PDGC. We are being told he has been suffering from a complex interplay of mental health challenges and environmental stressors over the last few months."*

"Horseshit!" Lockhart barked.

"If you see him, police are advising you NOT to approach. He is armed and dangerous. Please just call the—"

"Mute!" Curtis yelled, and the TV was silent. He wiped his eyes and crossed his arms.

"You see? If you leave here, you'll be shot on sight," Maury said. "And trust me, if Smith can shoot up a station full of cops, he'll have no trouble killing *you*."

"You know who the assassin is?"

Maury exhaled. "It's a long story. A man we call Smith just—"

"HOLY SHIT!" Curtis suddenly yelled, watching a medical team rush a gurney toward an ambulance. The headline read: WOMAN SURVIVES SHOOTING.

"Chloe, unmute!"

"As you can see," Gale said, *"the footage shows one of the survivors of the shooting being wheeled to an ambulance. We can confirm that she is a young black female, perhaps in her twenties. She has suffered two gunshot wounds to the chest and is in critical condition. Police have not yet confirmed her identity, but rumor is that this IS the same woman from the incident at Flutters Coffee House, the No Cuts Bitch."*

A side-by-side image of Ally hit the screen. Pictures of her attacking the two cops from different angles.

The team looked at each other. There was no explanation for what happened. But Ally was alive! They let out a little hoot in celebration and their stoic expressions sparkled with a glimmer of hope.

"Thank you, Gale," Robert chimed in. *"Our sources are telling us that as many as two other witnesses were also shot and killed, execution style…"* he paused and pressed his finger to his ear as the video switched back to a live view of the precinct. A door had just opened and a group of officers shielded Detective Peters from the

press and escorted him toward an ambulance. He was holding an ice pack on the side of his head. *"...an officer who survived the attack is being taken to the hospital, where I'm sure he will be well looked after. We will get the ID of the wounded officer as soon as we can."*

"That's Peters!" Curtis yelled, as the press zoomed in on his face.

"Stay tuned, as more details to this horrible shooting continue to pour in. I'm sure our viewers will join the studio in wishing the lucky woman and the brave officer a speedy recovery, though we are told the woman may not survive the surgery." On screen, the camera followed the gurney and zoomed in as it was loaded into the ambulance. *"Our thoughts and prayers are with them.*

"I'm Robert Gamble. We'll be back after this commercial break."

Maury, Marcus and Curtis peeled their eyes off the screen and looked at each other. Then the room burst into action.

"What? What's wrong? What happened?" Lockhart demanded.

"The cameras! They just broadcast to everyone where they're taking her!" Marcus yelled. "The hospital name was right on the side of the damn ambulance. If these guys are willing to shoot up a police station, they won't think twice about going to the hospital to finish the job. We've got to get to the hospital!"

"I can help," Lockhart cried.

Curtis pulled something from the computer and tossed it at Maury, then he and Marcus made for the lift. Maury caught it and turned to Lockhart.

"Mr. Lockhart. Give us a couple days. Lay low. When we get back, we'll figure this whole thing out together. In the meantime, there is a cot in the corner. Here!" He tossed the device at him and dashed off toward the lift to join the others.

"What's this?" he yelled, catching it in his palm.

"Proof!"

Lockhart watched the lift platform disappear into the floor above. He sighed, then looked down at his palm. In it was what looked like a digital drive.

CHAPTER 42

With a twitch of her head, Ally's consciousness sparkled back to the living. Light battled its way through her eyelids. She tried to open them, but they felt heavy. She could feel a subtle coolness of crisp sheets against her skin. Sounds, vaguely familiar, began whispering in her ears. A faint rhythmic beep. Muffled voices. Coughing and wheeled carts. Then the bustling sounds registered. A hospital floor, and voices outside the room. She groaned and winced as she finally opened her eyes.

"Hey! Look who's back from the dead!"

Ally peeled her eyelids open. Marcus and Curtis were leaning over her. She tried to sit up, but pain rocketed through her body. Her chest itched. "What happened?" she croaked, lifting her fingers and feeling the new sutures.

"The EMTs gave you CPR." Curtis chuckled, his eagerness to share the details overwriting decorum. "A lot of people don't know this but they actually have to break your ribs in order to—"

"Curtis, maybe we should skip the details for a bit... let Ally wake up first, yeah?" Marcus said to the annoyance of Curtis. "You're lucky to be alive,"

Ally's eyes narrowed. "How did I… I mean, why am I not—"

"Oh! That's the crazy thing!" Curtis blurted. "You ha—"

"Ah, you're awake. I thought I heard voices in here," came a voice from the doorway. A man in surgeon's scrubs walked forward and approached the bed with a kind smile. "My name is Dr. Patel. How are you feeling?"

"How do you think I'm feeling?" Ally's raspy voice croaked again.

"Just ignore her. That's how people say 'thank you' in *asshole*. You get used to it."

Dr. Patel's lips subtly smirked. "Like someone stood on your chest with a steamroller?" he asked. "Unfortunately, that tends to happen. The good news is, we've reset the bones and removed the bullets. If it wasn't for the dextrocardia, you'd be dead."

"What's dextrocardia?" she rasped.

"Oh! Can I tell her?" Curtis tapped Dr. Patel on the hip. "It's when your heart is on the opposite side of your body! Or being shot point blank would have split your heart into like a million pieces, wouldn't it?"

Marcus gently placed his hand on Curtis's shoulder, silently signaling him to give it a rest.

Dr. Patel smiled, pulled out a syringe and injected its contents into the intravenous drip. In a reflexive surge, Ally's arm shot up, grabbing him by surprise and causing him to recoil. "What did you just give me!?" she choked, the heart monitor revving up into overdrive.

"It's just a sedative. Just something to help you rest," he assured her.

Ally looked into his eyes, then released his arm. "Sorry."

"It's okay. I should have told you first. You've been through a lot. You can rest easy now. I can assure you, you are quite safe. There are armed guards outside this room, and more downstairs. You're perfectly safe."

Ally felt the sedative dull her senses and she began to relax.

"I'll inform the police you're still resting. Give you a few more hours before they inundate you with questions." He winked.

"Thank you, Doctor," Marcus said.

"I'll come check in on you in an hour," he said before turning and exiting the room.

CHAPTER 43

A few miles from the hospital, Lockhart picked up his phone and dialed a number. He was breathing harder than he'd care to admit after a light jog, but willed himself on. He pressed the phone to his ear.

"I'm here," Captain Stevens answered, approaching the entrance to Trudy's Diner.

"Go inside. You'll see me at the back. Baseball cap. Dark jacket," Lockhart said.

Stevens ended the call. Lockhart watched him place the phone into his pocket, and head inside.

Tom Stevens approached the table at the back of the diner like he was instructed and sat down. "I hope you have a good explanation for this," he grunted.

The man sitting in front of him looked up and Stevens gasped. It wasn't Lockhart. The chilling sound of a handgun hammer being thumbed back made him freeze. He saw a hand toss down a twenty dollar bill and the homeless man sitting in front of him palmed it, stood up and left. Lockhart stepped around and sat down at the booth, holding the gun under the table.

Steven's eyes narrowed into cold slits. "Michaels was right. You really *have* gone rogue."

"I could say the same about you," Lockhart deflected. "How much did they pay you?"

"What the hell are you talking about?"

"How much did they pay you to allow the precinct to get shot to hell?"

"What?!"

"Look me in the eyes and tell me you didn't have our boys killed for money!"

"Me?! You're the one on the run!"

"How much!" Lockhart yelled, loud enough to turn heads.

Stevens banged his fist on the table top, rattling the cups and plates. "YOU SON OF A…" He stopped himself. A nearby waitress gawked at him, clearly frightened. He clocked multiple heads staring in his direction. His eyes wandered. Some of them were children. He forced himself to take a deep breath.

Slowly, he seated himself back into the booth's cushion and scowled. "All right, Floyd. If neither of us did it, then would you mind telling me what the hell's going on? Why am I here? And put the goddamn gun away for Christ's sake. There's kids here."

Lockhart tried to read Stevens's poker face and knew he had to make a choice. He too noticed the room full of gawking strangers and agreed it was best to put away the gun. "I'm sorry, but I needed to be sure," he said, slipping the gun back into his pocket.

"Sure of what?"

"That you weren't involved in any of it."

Stevens studied his expression. "Any of what? What the hell's going on, Floyd?"

"Yesterday, I got an anonymous tip that there'd be three witnesses coming into the station to make a statement about an old murder—a cold case. Around 23:15, I took the three witnesses to the interview rooms.

"Michaels interrupted me just before the place was shot to hell. He pulled me away from conducting the interviews… I'd been drinking… well, my shift was over. That's why I'd been drinking… but—"

"Floyd… slow down. You're not making any sense."

"Okay," he sighed. "I got a call from the girl who attacked Peters in the coffee shop."

"Jesus Christ, Floyd! You spoke to the—"

"Listen!" he growled. "On the phone, she said there'd be three witnesses coming to the station. She warned me about Michaels… said he might be dirty. At first I thought it was bullshit. It's no secret that Michaels and I have had our differences, but I never took him for *bent.*

"Anyway, shortly after the witnesses arrived, Michaels must have gotten wind of it. He pulled me out of the interview room. He knew I had been drinking and ordered me to turn over the investigation to Sutko.

"He said we needed to bury the hatchet, that we needed to find a way to work together. He asked me out for a drink to discuss the matter. I thought he was being sincere.

"Just as we got to his car, the Code-999 rang out on the walkies. Everyone rushed out. He and I jumped into his car and we engaged, following a convoy of squad cars.

"But shortly after, he left the convoy and pulled a gun on me, muttered something about the witnesses and demanded to know how I'd figured it out. But I honestly didn't have a clue what he was talking about."

"What do you mean? You didn't know why the witnesses were there?"

"I knew they had information about a murder. But it's a lot more than a murder. We're talking police corruption, coverups, bribery, witness tampering—"

"Jesus Floyd. Do you really expect me to believe this?"

"Michaels pulled a gun on me. His men jumped me. I woke up hogtied to a chair, where a mobster was gonna… it doesn't matter… if it weren't for that vigilante the media's been banging on about on the news—"

"The Blur?"

Lockhart nodded. "If it weren't for him, I'd be at the bottom of the river. *Literally*. He saved me."

Stevens's eyebrows went up and he sighed, scrunching his lips in a judgmental glare.

"I've still got concrete on my shoes," Lockhart said, holding out one of his feet with the crusty mixture still clinging to his ankle and laces.

"Okay, let's say I believe you. Can you prove any of it?"

Lockhart removed his phone from his jacket and unlocked it, then slid it across the table to Stevens.

"What's this?"

"It's a video recording from the slaughterhouse. A mobster named Felix Overgaard operates out of it. And it's the real CCTV from the station.. not that doctored shit on the news."

"Jesus, Floyd! You could have led with this!" He watched Lockhart get dragged to a chair on the screen. Soon after, the faces of Michaels and Peters appeared. They each received a stack of money.

He swiped his finger, then glanced at Lockhart in horror. His eyes danced back to the screen, where he watched an assassin take out a dozen officers and move toward the back of the precinct.

"How in the hell did you get this footage? The station's tapes were missing."

"The Blur," Lockhart replied.

Stevens's eyes suddenly went wide and he sat bolt upright. His face went white.

"What?"

"I just sent Michaels to the hospital to make sure there was adequate security!"

Lockhart jumped up. They didn't have to say anything; they both knew. Both men sprinted out of the diner, rushing past the patrons and staff in their haste.

* * *

Captain Stevens screeched to a halt near the front entrance of the hospital and he and Lockhart quick-stepped it inside. On the way in, Lockhart surveyed the room. The hospital staff seemed to be proceeding as usual. Patients were seated in the lobby calmly waiting to be called. Doctors and nurses were going about their duties—checking on their patients, sliding charts in and out of the wall cubbies, and drumming the floor with the sound of their footsteps. There was no indication anything was unusual or suspicious.

"Miss? I'm Sergeant Lockhart. I'm here to see a patient… Allyson Reid, gunshot victim."

"One moment, sir," the woman said. "Do you have ID?"

Lockhart fumbled through his pockets before turning to Stevens. "They must have taken it," he said.

"Well, I've been instructed not to let anyone through without valid ID," the woman said.

"Those were *my* instructions. I can vouch for him," Stevens said, holding up his Captain's shield.

"She's in room 513."

"Thank you," Lockhart said, turning to walk away.

"Wait, sir!" the receptionist called. "What did you say your name was again?"

"Lockhart."

"Hey Susie!" the receptionist called to a woman in the back. "What was the name of that sexy cop you spoke to a little bit ago? The one with the funny name?"

"Floyd Lockhart!" Susie called back, smiling from embarrassment.

"Call for backup!" Lockhart shouted and bolted for the elevator.

"Call security!" Stevens ordered. "I want this place locked down."

The receptionist snapped out of it and quickly picked up the phone.

CHAPTER 44

Above them, Mr. Clark stepped into the SICU wing of the hospital and made his way through the corridors until he neared Ally's room. Two guards were stationed outside.

"Woah!" a guard shouted, raising his hand. "Sir! You can't be here. This is a restricted area. You need to turn around, now!" But Mr. Clark did not slow down. He reached for his wrist and twisted a dial on the watch face. It opened like a skylight and a shimmering red stone seemed to activate. It grew brighter and seemed to spread over his exposed skin like a force field. His eyes fluttered with a faint red glow, and he kept walking.

"Stop!" the guard ordered, drawing his gun, but Mr. Clark lunged forward and punched him in the throat so fast the man could hardly blink. The strike broke his windpipe and he collapsed onto the floor, choking on his own blood.

The second guard raised his gun and fired a round, which clipped Mr. Clark's shoulder. He spun round and employed a disarming strike, removing him of his weapon. Then he struck the guard across the face with the butt of his own gun.

The huge guard winced in pain, but quickly shook it off. He reached forward and grabbed Mr. Clark with both hands, lifting him into the air. Not able to feel the ground beneath his feet, he head-butted the guard hard enough to crack his skull. Blood spurted out of the man's nose and mouth and he instinctively let go to cradle his face.

Now back firmly on the ground, he didn't hesitate. Mr. Clark kicked the man's leg at the knee, bending it sideways and causing the big man to collapse onto the ground. He wailed, until his neck cracked from the force of Mr. Clark's boot.

He started to turn, but another cop had charged from inside the room and struck him with a lowered shoulder, slamming him into the wall. The woman drew her nightstick and clubbed him hard across the head and stomach. The third strike he caught and grabbed her by the throat. He snarled, pressed her against the wall and used the nearest door frame to hyperextend her elbow. She shrieked as he jiggled it, forcing her to drop her nightstick. Then he reached forward and snapped her neck.

Mr. Clark thrust his head, searching for more threats. All he saw was an audience of hospital staff and patients, gasping and frozen in shock. Angrily, he ignored the startled cries and stepped forward, entering Ally's room like nothing had happened.

Inside the room, a man leapt towards him and tried to block his path, but Mr. Clark booted him in the chest and sent him reeling backwards. The man crashed into the corner of the bed, bounced off the frame and hit the wall. He could tell by the way the man struggled to climb to his feet that the collision gave him an instant concussion. He recognized the signs of vertigo kicking in, followed by the muscle fatigue that would cause his limbs to buckle.

To his right, he heard someone fumbling with a zipper and looked over. A boy in a wheelchair shakily raised some kind of gun and aimed it at him. Instinctively, Mr. Clark neutralized the threat, backhanding the tranq gun out of his hand. He then kicked the boy hard in the chest, launching the chair backwards into the concussed man, sending him back to the floor.

Removing his gun from his underarm holster, Mr. Clark cocked it, and aimed it at his target—the one who came back from the dead. He stared into her groggy eyes, wondering how she'd managed to escape him twice. *Perhaps it should've been you*, he mused. *Pity*.

He squeezed the trigger, but something rammed him hard from the side. He missed!

Whirling angrily, he reached down and ripped the right side of the wheelchair up into the air, spilling the boy out of it and pinning him underneath it. The move put him off balance, which is why he couldn't stop the concussed man from ramming him against the wall.

Mr. Clark recovered. He shoved the concussed man away from him and swung a brutal upper-cut to his chin, knocking him to the floor. He fell hard and didn't move.

He raised his gun to shoot but felt a firm grip pull on the barrel. A cop had joined the fight.

Mr. Clark was now extremely pissed off and through playing around. His target wasn't these bystanders, but enough was enough. They were interfering with his mission.

NOTHING interfered with his mission!

"You have the right to remain—"

Mr. Clark ripped at the cop's extended arm and dislocated his shoulder. The man howled and released his grip, but he took no mercy. He slammed his head into the cop's nose, breaking it. He punched him hard in the face, then delivered a high kick across his cheek and followed through with a spinning hook kick to the head. He went down hard, falling next to the other man and didn't get up.

Turning his head, he glared at the boy crawling on the floor.

He's not a threat. Finish the mission!

He bent down and reached for the gun on the floor. His fingers managed to touch the smooth handle before he was suddenly jerked backwards. He was thrown so hard that he couldn't get his footing, effectively running backwards until he crashed into the wall of the hallway.

Slowly, he rose to his feet.

Before him stood a large man, fit and fearless. He recognized a fighter when he saw one and took a small side-step, eying up his opponent. The man did the same, and the two men slowly began to circle each other, each sizing the other up. It occurred to him then who this man was.

He was older than he remembered. But it was definitely him—Mauricio Baráo, the Chameleon. A legend in the underground fighting world. He was the only man who held an undefeated record in the ring. Legends about this man were still whispered amongst the crowds of people, like he was some kind of god. All Mr. Clark saw was a man.

"I don't know who you are… or who you take your orders from… but you don't have to do this," Mauricio said. "I don't want to hurt you. But I will if I have to."

Mr. Clark didn't reply. Without hesitation, he marched forward and engaged, going at the Chameleon with everything he had. He threw punch after punch, and kick after kick, some of which he landed, but most he missed as Mauricio expertly dodged or blocked them.

Every strike he attempted, Mauricio countered with its mirror image like he could sense his moves, almost like he was telegraphing them. It was like he was watching one of the Chameleon's fights back in the ring.

When Mr. Clark swung his fist, instead of making contact, he was met with a hard punch to the face. When he tried a combo, Mauricio landed two punches and a devastating spin-kick to his face, sending him down hard from the force.

He was losing control of the fight. He had to try something different.

Maury cocked his head. Mr. Smith got back up immediately, completely undeterred—like someone who'd slipped on a wet floor and jumped up hoping no one had seen, and attacked again. He seemed totally immune to the pain he must have been feeling. The hits this man was taking were enough to drop even the most seasoned fighters. Yet he acted as though he'd been slapped!

And he kept coming!

Nurses, doctors, and patients cowered as these two delivered one hell of a martial arts show. Each man executing expert moves to the other, and each man deflecting them with expert skill. They were evenly matched.

After a long minute, a trickle of fear began to creep into the back of Maury's mind. He could feel himself tiring. And the fact that this man wasn't letting up began to seriously worry him. But he shook the feeling away. He didn't have time to be tired. He knew he couldn't let up, or people would die.

Mr. Smith faked a punch and struck with his other, but Maury saw right through it. He knocked the assassin onto his back with a devastating uppercut.

"Stay down!" Maury yelled, panting.

But the man kicked-flipped up and stood tall. His face was bleeding and his jaw was dislocated and hanging unnaturally crooked. Maury watched as the assassin reached up and reset his jaw without the slightest flinch.

Maury swallowed hard. That uppercut alone would have cracked even the toughest man's jaw. But somehow, defying all logic, the man looked unfazed, as if he were fully refreshed.

He began circling Maury again, his black eyes scanning his opponent for any potential weakness. Then, as if fired from a gun, he bolted forward and tackled him with both hands. Too tired to deflect, Maury tried to absorb the force, but Mr. Smith hit him so hard he busted through the wall.

The blow dazed him. It took him several seconds to climb to his feet. He was now exhausted. He was pretty sure his shoulder was dislocated. It would explain the incredible pain. He sucked in a labored breath. *Punctured lung*, he feared. *Broken rib, too. Damn.*

Thinking desperately, he kicked a chair and sent it sliding into Mr. Smith's shins. He stumbled, but it only bought him a second. Frantically, he searched for anything he could use as a weapon, finally grabbing a lamp. He threw it at him, but the man was unstoppable. He swatted it away like it was a minor annoyance, kicked the chair away, and kept advancing.

Desperately, Maury grabbed an intravenous fluid pole and held it up to keep him back. It bought him another second while Mr. Smith attempted to go around it, until he grabbed the end of it and jerked with all his might. Maury was launched forward and knocked down by a hard clothes-line to his neck. His head and body hit the floor and he could feel the fight leave him.

He was down, he was hurt, and he knew it.

Mr. Smith ripped him to his feet with both hands and dragged him back by the collar, ripping him through the door and into the hallway. Maury feebly attempted to strike him, but his movements were so slow and telegraphed that the man just batted his arm and fist away. In desperation, he reached up and tried to shove his thumb into Mr. Smith's eye, but he was slugged in the gut so hard it took the wind out of his lungs and made him vomit up blood.

For the first time in his life, Maury started to feel true panic. He knew that if he didn't do something—and fast—Ally would be dead. So would Marcus and Curtis. Everything was riding on him!

Mr. Smith spun and leg-swept Maury, putting him onto his back. Then he grabbed his ankle and began to drag him across the floor into the room opposite. Weakly, Maury tried to grab and kick his way free, managing to do so once, but Mr. Smith spun with great ferocity and punched him several times in the face, chest and stomach.

Maury was barely conscious. His nose was broken. His eye socket was cracked. He could hardly breathe and his good arm felt so heavy he didn't know if he could lift it. Panic swam in his eyes now. He had to do something!

Mr. Smith continued dragging him until they were in the middle of the next room. He let go of Maury's ankle so he could shove an elderly patient out of his way.

Maury knew this was his last chance. He forced himself to his feet and slammed his shoulder against the doorframe, grunting as the ball slipped back into its socket. He watched Mr. Smith pick up a chair and hurl it out the window. It crashed through it and shattered the glass.

Maury rushed the assassin, but Mr. Smith kicked him in the chest and swept his legs, sending him crashing back to the ground. He stomped on his chest so hard it made his ribs crack. Blood spurted out of his mouth as his lungs punctured.

Mr. Smith again ripped him to his feet and lifted him up with a fit of inhuman strength.

With his last ounce of strength, Maury clung to the sides of the window frame. Mr. Smith snarled as he tried to shove him out the window, then let go and upper-cutted him. He punched the inside of his right forearm three times as hard as he could.

Maury's grip on the window frame finally failed. Weakly, he clawed at Mr. Smith in a desperate attempt to cling on, but only managed to scrape his fingers against his wrist. The assassin pulled him close, looking right into Maury's defeated eyes as if to say—I beat you—then pushed.

Maury tried to scream as he hurtled down to the pavement below, but he had nothing left in his lungs except blood.

Mr. Clark didn't even bother to watch his body hit the ground. He knew just from the sound of splattering meat against the concrete that the man was dead. Satisfied, like an itch finally scratched, he turned and headed back towards Ally's room, passing a dozen frightened hospital patients and staff.

He took a step, furrowing his brow as he felt himself start to limp. His furrow became a grimace, then his face contorted and he doubled over, nearly collapsing. He squeezed his eyes shut, his mouth opening in a silent scream as pain shot through his nerves and branched out like jagged tendrils. He thrust his palms over his throbbing ears to drown out the tinnitus overtaking his senses.

The mission!

Desperate for relief, he reached for his wristwatch, but felt only skin. He scowled. It was no longer attached to his wrist. He now understood why pain was coursing through his body. The bastard must have ripped it off him as he fell!

His eyes shot open in disbelief, in shock, as his body went into convulsions. He struggled to breathe, saliva hanging from his lips, as the pain worsened with each heartbeat, clawing its way into his senses.

The mission!

Through sheer force of will, he forced himself on, futilely attempting to suppress the electrifying jolts that ricocheted through his shattered jawbone, but each step was a battle through waves of anguish that pulsed through his body. His brain was in a vise-grip.

He entered the room, grimacing as he reached for the gun he'd dropped earlier. The two men were still out cold.

Labored, he picked up the gun, positioned himself and aimed the weapon at Ally's head with difficulty. The bullet wound in his shoulder was so painful he could barely lift his arm. He had to stabilize it with his other and lean against the wall to keep it from shaking. He took his time, breathed in deep, then…

THUNK! THUNK!

Mr. Clark winced. He felt something puncture his leg. Even stranger, his vision began to blur. He shook the dizziness from his head, then looked down. Two tranquilizer darts were sticking out of the back of his upper thigh. He growled, plucked out the darts and turned around. The boy was propped up against the wall beside the door trying to cock a tranquilizer gun for a third shot.

Mr. Clark howled in frustration. He suddenly felt like he hadn't slept in a week, but he shook it off and shambled toward him. He could no longer hold the gun in his hand. He dropped it and fell to his knees. He crawled forward, reaching for the boy's throat until he gripped it tightly, fighting away the coming unconsciousness, and squeezing with all his strength.

Curtis tried to free himself but the man's grip was like iron. Mr. Smith's eyes were burning and his mouth was foaming around a vicious snarl. Curtis started to panic as darkness swirled around in his eyes. He was desperate to suck in a lungful of air. It was then that it struck him; the last thing he was going to see on this Earth was the ugly look on the assassin's face—what a way to go. He would have laughed if he could spare the oxygen.

Curtis felt the edges of his surroundings fading into darkness. His limbs grew heavy, and dizziness overwhelmed him. Futility, he made one final empty gasp like fish out of water and let his head slump over.

Light returned.

He felt the man's grip loosen and air found its way back into his lungs. Curtis shoved away the man's arm and gasped. He coughed and sucked in deep, grateful mouthfuls of air while his vision slowly returned. The assassin was slumped over beside him.

Curtis took in one more full breath and managed to choke in a raspy voice, "Uncle Maury!?" He coughed again. "Uncle Maury!?"

For the first time all shift, the place was silent.

CHAPTER 45

Ally sat propped up in the bed, staring blankly. She could hear the dull buzz of commotion all around her. Police, like little insects, busily swarming around looking for any possible connections to the incident. Curtis told her what happened, that Maury had sacrificed his life to save hers. For the last 10 minutes, she'd been grappling with that realization. She shut her eyes, feeling the weight of her head on the pillow. She didn't feel worth the trade.

Glancing over to the corner of the room, Curtis was sobbing quietly. If she hadn't been high on pain medication, could she have done something? Even in her condition? She clenched her fist, squeezing the life out of the paper sheets. *Poor Marcus*. He was out in the hallway speaking to an officer and giving his statement.

The door clunked open, interrupting her thoughts. Lockhart's arm was in a sling, his nose looked broken, his neck was braced by a foam pad, both of his eyes were purple and swollen, and he had a nasty bruise on his cheek. He looked roughed up enough to be lying in a hospital bed next to her, but somehow, despite the pain he must be feeling, he was still managing to do his job.

"I'm sorry," he said in a raspy voice obscured by the gauze in his nose. "I can't even imagine what you two must be thinking right now. What happened is an absolute tragedy and you have my deepest condolences."

His empty words just had a dull hum to them. They didn't register and just rolled off Ally's shoulders as she continued to stare off into space.

"I suppose you've worked out that the case you hoped to build against your mother's killer won't be moving forward. With Mrs. Wilcox and Mr. Davis dead, I'm afraid there just isn't enough evidence to bring against this man… what did you call him? Smith?"

Ally looked down sullenly. She'd already realized this and was too out of it to feel anything.

"But you can be damn sure we're going to prosecute him for *this*! That's the only good news I can offer you. Thanks to Curtis, my men are taking that bastard away as we speak. He'll get the death penalty for what he did. You can count on that!"

Ally and Curtis didn't say anything.

"Look," he shut the door behind him, "we don't have a lot of time. Maury saved my life. I'll do whatever I can for you, Ally. I owe him that. But your situation is complicated. You assaulted two cops - crooked or not - and your face is all over CCTV for Peters's abduction. There is no way we can just drop the charges. But I promise you, I will try and negotiate the best deal I can for you. I wish I had something better to offer, but my hands are tied. The good news is, this will all be over soon. We—" Lockhart stopped short. His eyes narrowed and Ally saw his hand move to his gun. She followed his gaze out the window into the hallway. Lieutenant Michaels strutted past the glass and was now speaking to an officer outside.

"I'm sorry. I need to go."

Lockhart exited the room and blocked the door, shutting it behind him.

When the door clicked shut, Curtis snapped out of it. He rolled up to the bedside exhaling long breaths through his nose, his teeth clenched tight. When he looked up, Ally saw fire and rage.

"Whoever did this, they're gonna pay. I'm gonna find them. I'm gonna kill them. Then I'm gonna burn their playhouse to the ground. When you get better, we'll—"

"No, Curtis…" she said distantly.

"What? Oh, right… your injuries. "A few years back, a client we helped out gave us something as a thank you."

"Curtis…"

"Nanobots," he whispered. "One injection puts billions of nanobots into your bloodstream and they can speed up healing."

Ally tried again, but only managed to gurgle his name. "Curtis."

"I thought maybe we should give 'em a try… see if we can get you back on your feet."

"No, Curtis!" she coughed. "I'm done."

He stopped and crinkled his eyes. "What do you mean? Don't you want to get the bastards who did this?"

Ally swallowed. "Michaels has been arrested. Peters has been exposed and is on the run. He'll be found sooner or later. And Smith is in police custody. It's over."

"But Smith isn't working alone. He's just a henchman! There has to be someone else pulling all the strings!" He leaned in close, pleading. "We can still take them down!"

Ally adjusted herself slightly in the bed, grimacing as pain shot through her chest. She took a breath and looked at Curtis's big brown eyes and admired the fiery spirit behind them. She knew she shouldn't, but she felt completely at peace, like a weight had been lifted from her shoulders. A part of her knew she should be sad about Maury. About Peggy and Brian. But for the first time in a long time, she no longer felt this unquenchable urge to drive forward. For once, she was content with just laying low and powering down.

"We are so close! How can you just quit?"

She sighed wearily. "This was always the end game, Curtis. I never planned on getting away with all of this. I'm okay going to prison if it means that Smith finally faces justice. All I ever cared about was him paying for what he did. Even if he won't face justice for my family's murder, he'll face it for what he did to those cops… and for what he did to Maury."

"And what about me, huh?"

Ally cocked her head. "What *about* you?"

Curtis's eyes filled with pain. "You owe me!" he snarled. "If it wasn't for me, you'd be dead!"

"Curtis…"

"They killed my mom, too!"

Ally opened her mouth, but no words came.

"What? Because you got justice for yours, mine doesn't matter?"

"Curtis…"

"Forget it," he grumbled. He looked at Ally through teary eyes, then maneuvered his wheelchair carefully out the door and into the hallway. "See you around." He was out the door before she could muster the strength to call out.

Michaels stopped dead in his tracks. The color drained from his face like he'd just seen a ghost. "What are *you* doing here?" he barked.

"*Alive,* you mean?"

Michaels smirked and eyed him carefully. "Did you even *try* blocking?"

Lockhart narrowed his eyes and clenched his jaw, ignoring the intense pain.

"Get out of my way. I need to talk to the girl."

Lockhart removed his firearm from its holster.

"And just what do you plan to do with that, Sergeant?" he asked softly.

"Whatever I have to. But you're not getting in this room. You're done. I'm gonna make sure of it."

Michaels smiled. "I wonder what the Captain will say when checks your desk drawer. He'll be wondering why you have a phone linked to organised crime hidden there."

Lockhart narrowed his eyes. "Ask him yourself."

Michaels turned his head. Captain Stevens was pointing in his direction and two cops moved forward like they were on a mission. Michaels chuckled and stepped aside. "Show him to the penthouse, boys."

"John Michaels. I'm placing you under arrest for conspiracy to commit murder, bribery, and conduct unbecoming of an officer."

"What!?" Michaels's gloating expression was slapped off his face as two deputies placed him in handcuffs.

"You do not have to say anything…" the officer continued, reading off his Miranda rights.

Michaels did his best to protest, shouting his rank and threatening the two officer's careers, but it did no good. He finally shut his mouth and glared at Lockhart. "Watch your back," he whispered as the two officers led him down the hallway.

Lockhart watched Michaels disappear, then holstered his firearm. Like a switch had been flipped, he grimaced and began to feel the extent of his injuries. The adrenaline was slowly leaving his body.

"What are you doing here? You should be resting!" Stevens said.

He braced himself against the wall. "I've got to look after the witness," he wheezed.

"I've got three guards on their way up right now. They'll keep her safe."

"With respect sir, we can't trust anyone."

As if on cue, three guards with assault rifles and tactical gear stepped through the elevator and approached them—two men and a woman.

Lockhart studied them. The woman had a pretty face, but her stare was ice cold. One look at her told him everything he needed to know. That this woman was tough.

The other two men were what you might expect. Large, tall and 'roided out. Big guys with beards, the 'not to be trifled with' type. But even with all this muscle and gait, it was still no match for the determination and raw power they'd all witnessed. If anyone did make any more attempts on her life, he was confident these three could take a pounding, but they were still no match for a bullet.

Stevens must have felt Lockhart's unease. "These are good cops. I'll stake my life on it."

"But sir—" he started.

"Go get some rest. That's an order. If it makes you feel any better, you can have the room opposite."

Lockhart turned his head and eyed the room directly across the hall. It offered a clear view to hers. Reluctantly, he nodded.

When Curtis reached his dad, he heard him ask the officer if there was anything else he needed. The officer shook his head and handed him a card, which had the police station's telephone number on it, and told him not to go anywhere in case they needed to get a hold of him for further questioning.

Marcus put the card into his breast pocket and the two of them made their way down to the lobby. Against the advice of the hospital and the police, Marcus signed the discharge papers and together they left the hospital. No one spoke the entire drive back home. It wasn't until Curtis made his way toward the secret lift that Marcus finally spoke. "Where are you going?"

"To figure out who this guy worked for."

"No, Curtis. That's it. We're done. It's over."

"Maybe it's over for you…"

"Don't! He was your uncle, but he was *my* brother. I've been saying for years that this business would get us killed. And now it has."

"Great! So now you get to say: *I told you so*."

"That's not it and you know it."

"No. It's that you don't think I can do it! Uncle Maury was the only one who ever saw anything in me. All you see is someone broken. Something weak."

"That's not true."

"Yes it is! You didn't tell me the truth about mom! About what happened to me! You didn't want me to find out about the van—"

"I was trying to protect you!"

"No! You thought I was too weak to handle it."

"Curtis…" He stopped and sighed. His eyes fell and his shoulders slumped. "I can't do this now."

"Just leave me alone!" Curtis yelled. He got into the elevator and descended to the lair below. He felt bad about not being more supportive of his dad. But he knew that he would never let him do what he was about to do.

CHAPTER 46

Lockhart entered the interrogation room holding a cup of coffee in his teeth and used his only functioning arm to open the door. He took the cup in his hand, careful not to let the file folder in his armpit drop. As he approached the table, he set the coffee down gently and caught the folder as it slipped from his armpit. He set it down and grimaced as he eased into the chair.

The assassin, Smith, was chained to the steel table next to a state-appointed lawyer. He sat contorted. His spine was hunched and his hands were curled as if he were suffering from cerebral palsy or extreme arthritis. With difficulty, he was holding himself up with his forearm. Lockhart stared at him. The medical examiner informed the police that his injuries were significant, that they were not even sure why he was still conscious. They said the amount of injuries and pain he must be experiencing was unlike anything they'd ever seen. But in each attempt to offer him pain medication, the man had become belligerent.

Lockhart mused at Ally's description of the man in her file. The lighting showcased his Neanderthal-like features: high cheekbones and eyebrows, large nose bridge, strong angular jaw, only now, his long dark hair hung loosely over the sides of his face, amidst swelling, bruises, and dried blood. The left side of his jaw was visibly off-kilter, bulging unnaturally, the skin stretched taut like an overfilled balloon. As he took each labored breath, Lockhart could have sworn the man drew a subtle wince, a flicker of strain that even he couldn't mask entirely.

His eyes, though half-lidded with exhaustion, remained sharp like they could still track everything in the room.

Lockhart took his eyes away and stared at the pages, thumbing his fingers through the file. Every once in a while he'd look up, flashing shock or disbelief, but resumed reading. Finally, he returned the file to the first page and left it open. "So what do I call you?" he asked, breaking the silence.

He didn't respond. Not with words. He just sat there, jaw hanging loose, every muscle in his face clenched in silent rebellion.

Lockhart looked at the lawyer. "He speak English?"

The lawyer shrugged. "He hasn't said a word."

"Well, I'm going to call you Smith," he said as he scooted the chair forward. "Would that be okay with you?"

The man didn't move.

"Okay, Smith… I thought you'd like to know we've run your fingerprints through our databases. You've been a busy boy. Your prints match those found in over a hundred cases: murders, assassinations... I bet the Feds or Interpol would be very interested to know we have you in our custody."

"But before we tell them, we're going to sort out a few things. Is there anything that you would like to say?"

Lockhart thought that would shake something loose, but the man was unfazed.

"Mr. Smith, I just told you that we have you dead to rights. Don't you care? If you talk to me about what happened at the hospital, maybe I could convince the others to go a little easier on you given that you were cooperating.

"Tell me about the girl. Who was she to you?"

For the first time, the assassin turned his head and stared directly at Lockhart. His hollow, black eyes gave him the creeps. There was no feeling or emotion in those eyes. Lockhart saw only death. The assassin kept his gaze fixed on his.

"Okay. What about this? You want to talk about this?" he held up an evidence bag with a wristwatch in it.

Like an explosion, Smith leapt off his chair, reaching for the bag, but the chains around his wrists clunked tightly and restrained him. His eyes flinched and he grimaced at the pain that must be surging through his entire body.

Lockhart couldn't help but flinch. Thus far, Smith hadn't shown even the slightest resistance or form of aggression. But at the mere sight of his watch, he nearly broke the table.

"Interesting," he said. "What's so special about a watch?"

Mr. Clark smiled and almost laughed. His breath hissed between his teeth as he exhaled slowly, eyes half-closed as if trying to remember how to speak. "You really don't have a clue what this is all about, do you?"

"I'm a fast learner. But maybe you could save me some time, and tell me."

The man scoffed.

Voices rang out behind the door, loud enough to hear through the wall. Before Smith could utter another syllable, the door flew open, and in barged a man in a government suit. "This interview is over!" the man yelled. "I'm taking this man with me where he will remain in my custody."

"Wait a minute," Lockhart shouted. "Who the hell are you?"

"This man, on orders of the President of the United States, is hereby offered a full pardon as stated in Article II, Section 2 of the United States Constitution." The man handed a document to the lawyer and Lockhart."

"You can't do this!" Lockhart yelled.

"Sit down, Sergeant," Stevens ordered.

"Actually, I can. In addition, I am hereby enforcing, under Title 18: Section 2709, of the United States Penal Code, a federal gag order which forbids any and all parties from discussing this matter to any inside or outside agencies. Failure to comply with this order will result in a federal warrant and prosecution under the full power of the law as dictated by the Counterterrorism Bureau of the United States," he finished.

"This is horseshit!" Lockhart yelled. "That man killed police officers! He threw a man out of a fucking window! Captain!"

Stevens stood still, hands at his side, a defeated expression on his face.

"Not according to this, he didn't," the man said, handing out a third document.

Lockhart snatched it and scanned it. It called for the turnover of all records pertaining to the arrest of [redacted]. The name was redacted.

"Officially, he was never here… and neither was I."

"Who are you?"

"Who's *who*?" the man asked as two other men in suits walked over to Mr. Clark. They unlocked his cuffs and stepped back.

Mr. Clark stood up and casually rubbed his wrists like he were adjusting suit cufflinks. He flashed Lockhart a smug expression.

The man in charge reached out and took the evidence bag from Lockhart's hand, retrieved the watch, and handed it to Smith. He smiled and slipped it over his wrist, twisting the watch face. Lockhart could have sworn Mr. Clark's whole body relaxed. He walked out almost looking refreshed. The three mystery men followed.

Lockhart rushed out of the interrogation room and stared wide-eyed at a panel full of confused officers.

"What the hell just happened!?" he yelled. "How could you just stand there and—"

"They had a document signed by the President! What do you want me to do? We lost!"

Lockhart growled and shook his head. "Somebody get me the mayor!"

CHAPTER 47

TWO AND A HALF WEEKS LATER…

In the penthouse of Burton Tower, Hal looked out amongst the faces of select members of the presidential cabinet congregating around the room. It was important to him that they were enjoying the view and that their glasses were full.

He noted the US Vice President, Joe Russell, standing near a few senators and congressmen chatting about whatever men like them chatted about. At another corner, key military generals—Colonels like Frank Kirby—and other leaders from the United States military ranks stood in tight groups sipping their hard liquor and casting nervous shadows. Near the hors d'oeuvres and sample platters sat advisors and government officials eager to celebrate the launch of Burton's new satellite.

As far as the public knew, Burton Conglomerates was launching this satellite to provide better internet and phone capabilities to their customers. However, the real reason for the launch was to put Quantum into orbit.

"Ladies and Gentlemen? It's time," Hal said, "If you would please follow me." He directed them to the far side of the room where two white projector screens hung on a wall. One device projected a live feed into Hal's launch control room, while another to the launch site of Hal's rocket. He'd arranged for both to be set up and ready for today's demonstration.

On screen, around 12 technicians scurried about while others sat in cubicles. Via telecommunications, Hal and the group of spectators observed supervising agents talking through the launch procedures in the control center at the Space Launch Complex 40 at Cape Canaveral Air Force Station in Florida. They double and triple checked the specifications, each checking in as their supervisors called out their station. The rocket was nearly ready for launch.

When the final station had given the go-ahead, Launch Control radioed the tower and got the green light. The countdown started until finally, the rocket ignited.

Plumes of smoke and fire blazed from the rocket boosters until the whole unit reached Earth's upper atmosphere, ushered by the sound of clapping and cheering from within the control room. Soon, the boosters and nonessential parts of the rocket gradually broke away and fell back to Earth. Then the remains of the rocket burst apart, allowing Quantum to poke its head out and stretch its legs.

"All right people, let's show all these nervous faces their money wasn't wasted," Hal quipped, sparking murmured chuckles.

The flight controllers activated consoles and began running diagnostics.

"Running full systems check."

"All systems go.

"Awaiting your order, sir," a technician said.

"Input coordinates," Hal ordered.

The sheet which had previously documented the launch of the rocket now switched to a live feed of Sukurlu in southeastern Turkey.

"Confirmed; implementing coordinates," a technician said.

"Verifying," said another.

"Coordinates accepted," a computerized voice purred.

Hal's guests gazed upon the crystal-clear aerial view of the nuclear facility, at a truck hauling something on a trailer covered by a tarp. The tip of a missile could just be seen poking out of it.

"Gentlemen, you are about to witness the power of the world's next super weapon. Light 'em up!" he ordered.

The technician typed a few commands and talked through the status. On the screen, everything appeared to be calm and normal. The people of Sukurlu carried on about their work, completely oblivious to their surveillance. The supply truck positioned itself and reversed into position where a robotic arm was ready to place the missile onto a wheeled cart. Men scurried about on either side locking straps underneath it.

"I don't see anything," a congressman muttered.

Hal smirked, knowing whichever weasel just said that would be shaking his hand and groveling in just a few seconds.

As predicted, the invisible blast from above struck the Earth's crust. The ground began to shake violently and cracked open, warping buildings and crumbling them to dust. Trucks and vehicles crunched and exploded while the missile facility burst into flames, taking the bombs with them into a massive fireball.

Hal smiled as gasps erupted in the room. His invitees watched in utter fascination as the human features of the town blew away in the wind, leaving its former self nothing more than a dusty wasteland. The area was completely destroyed.

When the smoke cleared, the room fell silent, eyes gawking at the incredible destructive power they just witnessed. "Did the... uh... the nukes... did they?" a Colonel struggled to find the words.

"No, sir. We hit them before they acquired the uranium," Hal reassured him. "The devices were not nuclear."

"And the explosion was still able to do *that*?"

"Quantum is more than just an earthquake weapon gentlemen. It destabilizes the atoms in its target. With continued exposure, the molecules become more and more unstable, generating immense heat. When the atoms rupture, the heat creates an ignition source. This sets off a chain reaction and the details get a bit technical, but… suffice to say, this is what accounts for the magnitude of the explosion."

"They won't know what hit them," a congresswoman murmured.

"Yes; our enemies will be so busy attacking each other, that they will not even think to look for us," another whispered.

"Most impressive," came a voice over the intercom. POTUS was viewing the live demonstration from the Oval Office in the White House. "Joe? I want you to go over everything we discussed with Mr. Burton. Brief me after you've ironed out all the details."

"Yes, sir, Mr. President."

The President ended the call.

As the room began discussing the implications of the device, Joe motioned for Hal to speak to him in private. "I've got to hand it to you, Hal... that was quite the demonstration," he said with a grin. "I look forward to briefing our guys in Washington. I trust that you'll make yourself available for the exchange?"

"*Exchange*?" Hal asked, feigning puzzlement.

"Yeah, the handover... the transfer of the controls."

Hal chuckled. "No, no, Mr. Russell... I believe you've misunderstood our arrangement. We agreed that you'd be able to use Quantum as you see fit, in exchange for your help in getting the device safely stowed in Orbit. But only the first target is free. The next one is going to cost you."

"That wasn't the deal!" Joe growled. "You said *we* would have control!"

"I said you would have control over the *targets*, and I am a man of my word… you point, we shoot. After a relatively small service fee of course," Hal said. "We can discuss figures later."

"We can't leave this weapon in the hands of a corporation!" Joe protested. "It needs to be in the hands of the government, where its use can be properly monitored."

"On the contrary, the weapon will be far safer in *my* hands than in those of some political puppet who wins a popularity contest every four years."

"You son-of-a-bitch! We'll shoot that thing out of the sky long before we let you have control over it."

"Mr. Russell, let's save both of us a lot of time here. Quantum is invisible. It can't be tracked or detected with any special equipment. It is as I told you, completely untraceable. It would be a shame if we couldn't come to an agreement."

"The United States government does not respond to threats."

"I don't make threats, Mr. Russell."

"Well, I do. And I say, what's to stop us from just killing you?"

Hal scoffed. "Mr. Russell, I believe you know whom I work for. You know what they're capable of. If you wish for the US Government to be the new USSR, then… simply kill me and take your chances."

Joe narrowed his eyes.

Hal smiled. "Look," he said, placing his arm around Joe's shoulder gently and ushering him toward the exit. "I understand you're disappointed. But let's not take this personally. It's just business."

"We'll fight you on this."

"I'm sure you'll try. Now, run along and tell Daddy what a naughty boy I've been. Once you realize you can't track my satellite, you and I can have a more civilized discussion."

Mr. Russell scowled and stormed out of the room.

"How long before we can fire again?" Hal asked the technicians once the room thinned out and the political and military personnel retired back to their prior engagements.

"It'll take some time for it to position itself over the new coordinates," a technician said. "Maybe 30 minutes?"

"Call me when it's ready," he said, turning back to attend to his guests.

CHAPTER 48

For Ally, the days in the recovery wing blurred together. She wasn't exactly sure how long it had been since Maury was killed. A few days, perhaps. Or was it a week? She'd lost track. She knew she slept through the first three days, barely conscious. So far, no visitors had come to see her. She wondered if they were even allowed. The guards outside her room might as well have been statues. She imagined the boredom they must have been feeling, the effort it must take to remain alert. Her only company had been the hospital staff: physical therapists, doctors and nurses prodding and testing her like a lab rat, doing checkups and delivering pain medication.

She was feeling a little better, but she was still in a great deal of physical pain. Moving was a struggle. Today, it took her forty minutes to get herself dressed for the funeral. She made several attempts to do the simplest of tasks, like pull clothing over her head or brushing her teeth.

She hadn't spoken to Curtis since that day in the hospital. She'd resigned herself to the idea that they'd just been friends of convenience. Now that they no longer had a mutual objective, the friendship had likely unraveled. She expected this. It was something she knew would happen. No one ever stuck around in her life. Over the years, she'd learned to look out for herself, and this never disappointed her. Still, sitting on the hard pew and seeing Curtis sitting alone, did make her feel a pang of guilt and sadness at their now waning friendship.

Maury's casket was a light colored wood with a glossy finish. A bouquet of white flowers rested atop the lid which hung delicately over the sides. Six men in black suits began carrying the coffin down the center aisle. Marcus was in front trying to be strong. His eyes were full of sorrow and he was struggling to keep it together for Curtis's sake.

The choir boys were singing a beautiful hymn, which set the mood somewhere between inspiration and tragedy. The soft music made the whole room feel the loss of a great man and member of the community who had died before his time.

This community was not a stranger to untimely deaths. So many young people were put into the ground way before their time. Mothers had buried sons, sons had buried fathers, neighbors had buried neighbors, and friends had buried friends. It was a community which had no choice but to come together. They were the only support any of them ever had.

The men carrying the coffin were nearing the end of the aisle. Every pew was full. Mauricio Baráo was a beloved man of the community. For the past 10 years, he'd single handedly kept things afloat in the worst of times. But now, the community had to face the reality of tough times ahead without his help. The people would now have to rely on each other more than ever.

As the pallbearers set the coffin down in the front of the altar beside a tasteful headshot of Maury smiling, they respectfully took their seats. Ally tried not to make eye contact with anyone. Their expressions were too haunting to look at. She hadn't been to a funeral in over eight years. All of this was bringing back too many painful memories and it felt like a betrayal to mourn her own losses when she should be mourning his. She felt a wave of emotions building inside of her like an explosion and tears began rolling down her cheeks. She almost wished that the police hadn't allowed her to attend the funeral and kept her in the hospital.

The choir suddenly stopped as the minister stood and walked to the front to say a few words.

"It is a sad day," he began. "Another one of God's children has been taken too soon from us through violence. Mauricio was a great man. He was loved, respected, and looked after this community. When someone couldn't afford to pay their car repair bill, Mauricio was there. When a family needed to clothe their children, Mauricio was there. When someone was a little short on their rent, Mauricio was there. He was there for all of us... any one of us when we needed him. It is truly a sad, sad day for this community."

* * *

When the celebration of Maury's life had ended, the armed guards escorted Ally back to the hospital. She insisted on attending the funeral despite the hospital advising against it. Maury had given his life for her. For all of them. She couldn't just hide away. She had to pay her respects. They wouldn't allow her to be present for the burial though, so she was taken back shortly after the minister's speech. Now back in her room, Ally grimaced as she laid her aching body back into her hospital bed. She let out an exhausted sigh, her eyes fluttering open to the cold, sterile tiles of the hospital room ceiling.

The dull throb in her chest that burned with each inhale almost made her wish she'd listened and stayed in to rest. Beside her, the nurse took her arm and quickly reinserted the needle, letting the heavy painkillers once again drip into her veins. She shut her eyes, listening to the rhythmic beeping of her heart monitor that seemed to lull her to sleep. That, and there was a faint rumbling, like a distant hypnotic hum. Her room must be near the water heaters, laundry or air conditioning systems.

A loud shriek like warping metal echoed from outside her window. As she drifted in and out, all she could remember was how odd that bird sounded. Suddenly, she jerked, feeling as though her bed had shifted. Man, she must really be tired. Already phantom twitching only moments after laying down. But then her bed shifted again. She forced her eyes open. Now, the faint rumbling was more like a heavy truck passing outside, only it wasn't fading. It was crescendoing.

She turned her head. The machine tracking her vitals started to tremble. The cup of water on the side table tipped and clattered to the floor. She found herself gripping the side of her bed as a low, thunderous roar seemed to build above her. It felt as if the whole building was shaking. The screech rang out again. The lights overhead suddenly flickered, then went dark. Red emergency lights blinked on, casting the room in a reddish tint.

Something groaned loudly and the window shattered, showering her with bits of glass. She gasped, then jerked her head. The hospital intercom blared some kind of loud pulse siren.

Beeeeeep.

Beeeeeep.

Beeeeeep.

The low hum became a full-body vibration. Ally could feel it in her teeth. Dust fell from the ceiling and landed on her blanket. As she tried to catch her breath, only one word flashed through her mind: earthquake.

Before she could react, her door burst open. "We have to go! Now!" barked the female guard. Behind her, the two male guards barreled in, wide-eyed but alert, and rushed to Ally's side.

"What's happen—"

"We don't have time; get her loose!"

The big bearded man locked eyes with hers and removed a knife. For a split second, Ally thought he was here to kill her, but he cut the wires that fed her pain killers, then ripped off the heart monitoring cables. Quickly, he placed his hand on her back and lifted. Ally gritted her teeth as he sat her up, pressing into the exit wounds in her back. She swung her legs over the side. Her chest felt like it was being pried apart with a crowbar. She gasped, vision blurring.

"Let's go!" the woman ordered, placing Ally's arm over her shoulder and dragging her toward the door. "I'm gonna need you to be brave for me, kid; can you do that?"

Ally didn't answer, but she gritted her teeth and forced her legs to move. They felt like wet rope beneath her.

"Easy now, easy," the guard muttered, half-dragging, half-lifting her into the hallway. They headed down toward one of the emergency exits. Ahead of them, the two men cleared the way, helping people to their feet and ensuring Ally's path was clear.

Five steps later, she felt the building buckle and a large crack formed in the ceiling. It split it in two like a jagged fault line, racing across the ceiling like a lightning bolt and sending down sprays of white powder and flecks of paint. Loose ceiling panels popped free, one by one, flipping and crashing to the ground like heavy dominoes. Lights sparked and exploded into fragments of fine dust.

Ally stumbled as a chunk of plaster the size of a briefcase crashed against the floor, narrowly missing her foot.

One of the men spun on his heel and ran toward them. "Get cover!" he shouted, eyes wide with panic.

Ally and the woman skidded to a stop just as the whole ceiling buckled. Metal supports groaned in protest as a grinding, horrible shriek cried out like nails on a chalkboard. The center of the ceiling bulged downward, swelling like a balloon before it burst.

"GET BACK!" he bellowed.

BOOM!

A section of ceiling the size of a minivan plunged to the floor, pulverizing a hollow tunnel right through several floors below. The shockwave knocked Ally off her feet and she hit the ground hard, landing on her hands and knees. Her chest flared with sharp, fiery pain as her ribs strained under the pressure.

"Ally!" The female guard yanked her up with one arm, eyes wild, nostrils flaring. The dust was so thick it hung in the air like fog, choking them. Ally coughed, spitting dust from her mouth, her throat raw and burning. "Are you hurt?"

"I'm fine, I'm fine!" she croaked, wiping the grit from her eyes, only to see the mess in front of them.

What was once a hallway was now a disaster zone. Jagged chunks of concrete, ceiling panels, and exposed steel beams had imploded. Sparks were shooting from shredded wires hanging from the overhead cavity. A water pipe had burst and was spraying a fine mist over the glow of the emergency lights, turning it into a shimmering haze.

"This way!" one of the men yelled as he doubled back down the corridor. "The stairwell!" He gripped Ally's other arm tightly and tugged her along. "Move it, girl! Now!"

They shifted course, weaving past nurses, patients, and doctors clambering in every direction. Ally watched a nurse push a gurney down the hall with a terrified child wrapped in blankets.

BOOM! The alarm overhead spluttered in a synthesized wane like it was being strangled. The floor below their feet plummeted and smashed onto the level beneath them. Everybody lurched, tumbling onto the angled floor and sailing across it in a slide.

Ally hit the wall and winced as the three guards barrelled into her. Before she'd opened her eyes, she felt a hard tug on her arm and was jerked to her feet. Two of the guards hopped to what was left of the floor beneath them. The other stayed behind and lifted Ally down to them.

Ally looked up, expecting to see the man hop down, but what happened next was difficult to describe. She felt it before she saw it. The molecules in the air were suddenly somehow tangible, like dry water, and as people above tried to hop down, what could only be described as an invisible wall slid across the floor, one at a time shredding people into red mist. Ally watched in horror as the guard who'd just lifted her down vaporized into a mist of blood and chunks of flesh that exploded, hitting the walls like paint splatter. She flinched, a high-pitched squeal piercing her ears. Her vision speckled and tunneled. Her lungs strained for air.

She felt a hand pulling her through the half blocked doorway and she stumbled, nearly pulling them both down. "Stay with me! You hear me? Stay with me!" the female guard screamed as she directed her forward by guiding her shoulder blade.

CRACK! The ceiling above exploded and a support beam rocketed down. Once again, Ally found herself sprawling on her hands and knees. Her chest screamed with sharp, searing pain. She coughed, tasting copper, but fought to turn over. The beam had hit the other guard square in the back, driving him face-first into the floor and killing him instantly. Blood was pooling and coagulating in the thick ceiling dust. His arm twitched once, then stopped. Ally froze in shock. Her breath caught in her throat and her heart felt like it would burst. She couldn't look away.

Someone shouted at her. "He's gone!" the woman's voice snapped her back. "We have to go!" She pulled Ally to her feet. "We're almost there. Stay with me!"

They moved faster. Ally's legs trembled, every step more painful than the last. Her chest felt like churning glass shards. They rounded the corner to see the Exit sign ahead, flickering like a beacon.

BOOM! The whole hallway tilted. The ceiling caved in just feet from the exit. Chunks of concrete and metal beams fell, crashing with deafening force. The guard cried out as a large slab of debris struck her shoulder, spinning her off balance and sending her to the floor. Before she could stand, a larger piece slammed down and crushed her left thigh. She let out a guttural, animalistic scream.

"NO!" Ally stumbled toward her, managing to stagger around falling debris and grip the concrete slab. She pulled with all the strength she could muster. Her muscles burned. Her chest felt like it would split open.

"Get out of here!" the guard screamed over the screeching metal, pain contorting her face. She was pale. Dust was starting to cling to her face. She locked eyes with Ally. "Run!"

"I can't leave you!" Ally grunted, trying again to lift the concrete block. Her feet slipped in the dust and she fell forward, hitting her forehead. "Don't be stupid!" The guard grabbed Ally's wrist, squeezing tight. "Run!" Her eyes were sharp, blazing with adrenaline. "RUN!"

Ally's heart shattered. Her eyes welled with tears. The woman threw Ally's hand away. "I'll get help!" Ally promised, backpedaling slowly. She didn't know if the guard heard her, but she turned and ran.

She shambled through the exit, bursting into the open air. Gasping, coughing, she fell to her knees, her eyes burning from the smoke. Her lungs seized, every inhale felt desperate like she'd been pulled from the depths of the ocean.

"Help!" she choked. "HELP!"

A firefighter sprinted up to her. "Are you okay, Miss?" His eyes darted over her, checking for wounds. "Are you hurt?"

Ally shook her head feebly. "She's trapped!" she gasped, pointing to the entrance.

The firefighter didn't hesitate. "Jim! We got a live one inside!" The two of them ran for the hospital entrance without another word, disappearing into the swirling dust.

Another firefighter helped Ally across the street where people were gathered, gawking, their faces pale and shocked. Nurses, patients, survivors—all of them watching in horror as the hospital groaned, creaked, and slowly began to collapse in on itself. Floor by floor, the structure crumpled like a stack of cards, each level slamming into the one below. The air filled with dust clouds so thick, it turned day into night.

Ally's heart sank. Her lips quivered as the building became nothing but rubble.

She stood in a daze, unable to fathom what just happened. Her legs were shaking. Her gaze locked on the burning husk of the hospital. She didn't move. She couldn't. Blood dripped from superficial wounds where she'd scraped her skin.

"Ally!"

She spun toward the voice. Curtis was waving from the back of the crowd. "Over here!"

Her mind was too fried to argue. She staggered toward them. She barely noticed the tremors still rumbling beneath her feet.

Barney threw his jacket over her shoulders, ushering her toward a black car. He helped her into the seat and together, the three of them sped off.

CHAPTER 49

Barney hovered a moment at the door. "I'm sorry about the mess," he said.

The door opened and Barney shuffled inside. Ally followed, instantly struck by clutter and grime. The house was in terrible condition. Wallpaper was peeling in several places, showing they hadn't been painted in years, maybe decades. There were a few pots and pans around the floors where the roof had obviously been leaking for some time. Stacks of newspapers—hundreds of them—some of which were still bound with their twine lay in untouched piles. They'd never even been read. Beer cans and alcohol bottles littered the floor and every available surface.

As she passed the kitchen, piles and piles of used plates and eating utensils not only filled the sink, but also covered most of the counter surface. *At least he doesn't have cats,* she thought.

"Catch ya later, Barney," Curtis called.

Barney raised a hand dismissively and kicked some debris away from the door to the basement.

Ally leaned in to whisper, "You're not staying?" She turned her head to make sure Barney couldn't hear her. "Don't leave me with him."

"Don't be an asshole. His place is disgusting, but you really need to hear what he has to say. "

"Where are you going?"

"Back to the lair. Meet me there when you're done," he said.

"You mean, warren," she corrected.

He smirked and left.

Ally turned back to Barney, or where he had been moments ago. The door to the basement was open wide and she could hear his steps retreating, each stair creaking and threatening to collapse from the additional weight.

Ally tried to ignore all the stories where young girls entered creepy basements like this and never returned. Reluctantly, she followed, the stair nails squealing in protest as she made her way down.

The condition of the basement was no better than the top floor. As she walked over to the far wall, she noticed newspaper clippings, photographs, printed out screen-grabs, and pretty much every type of paper media you could think of pinned to the wall like some kind of conspiracy board. The only thing missing was the red string.

She looked closer at the photographs. There were collapsed buildings, rubble, massive amounts of debris like the area had been bombed—and bodies, some of which were scorched like they'd been burned with a flamethrower. But there was one thing that made her legs go weak. In one of the photographs, there was a figure standing in the distance. She squinted and stepped closer. *It couldn't be.* She stared at it long and hard. *It was! It was Smith!* She was sure of it.

"You've seen him before, haven't you?" came Barney's voice from behind her. "I've spent nearly a decade searching for this man. Except for this photograph, he doesn't exist. But then I saw his face on the news when he was arrested at the hospital. I was on my way to the police station that day to show someone these, but as I approached the front entrance, three men in suits escorted him into a black SUV. The police just let him walk right out of there."

"Wait, what?" Ally swung her head.

He looked at her inquisitively. "You haven't heard? Lockhart said the order came from the President of the United States. There wasn't anything he could do. Even telling Curtis that could land him in federal prison.

"Curtis is off running surveillance on a mobster named Overgaard. If they can get him to talk, it might help them track down who this man is."

Ally clenched her teeth, finding no words to express her dissatisfaction with the police. She was too exhausted to lose her shit. Instead, she turned back to the wall of pictures.

"What are all these? I recognize some of them."

"Those," he said referring to photographs on the board, "are what's left of some old neighborhoods, businesses and companies in Grace City. "And over here," he continued, "these sites are from other cities around the world."

"And you still think there's a government conspiracy behind this?"

"I know there is. See, prior to 15 years ago, not a single earthquake had ever been recorded at most of these global locations, Grace City being one of them. The same month BC launched Quantum into orbit, they were hit relentlessly from devastating earthquakes. Over the next few months, the number of earthquakes reported abroad skyrocketed, and Grace City became one of the most seismically active places on the globe.

"Look again at the photographs. What do you see?"

Ally looked again. She saw all the devastation one would expect from a natural disaster: debris, destruction, piles of rubble. Finally, she turned her head and shrugged.

"Look carefully."

She scanned from one photograph to the next for several minutes before her mouth fell open and she laughed. It was so obvious."

"You see it now, don't you?" he asked.

"The ruins are all BC's competition. These places were economically targeted!" she cried.

"Yep, a building here, a building there… and rarely ever larger than a city block. Earthquakes don't do that. They devastate whole regions." He tapped a print out that looked like annual stock prices. "And this one is BC's profit margins over the years."

"Holy shit!" she huffed.

He laughed. "Then one day, they just stopped. The earthquakes, I mean. They just stopped."

"Why?"

"A more important question is *when... when* did they stop?"

Ally shrugged impatiently.

"After Burton Conglomerates blasted a giant asteroid out of the sky and meteorite fragments peppered parts of the world, they claimed that their satellite was destroyed. That was November 8th. Two days later, your mother was killed."

Ally's eyes narrowed. "What are you saying?"

"I'm saying that after your mother's death, all these unexplained earthquakes around the world, and here in Grace City, just stopped. Hell of a coincidence, isn't it?"

"You're suggesting that my mother invented a superweapon and used it to slaughter millions of people?" She shook her head and stepped back. "No. She wouldn't."

"Ally…" he started.

"No!" she cried. Her eyes welled up with tears and she swallowed the lump in her throat. "You're wrong about her! Her work would have helped emergency support workers… firefighters, police, EMTs… it would have allowed them to… to pass through physical barriers and get to people faster, to save people! To pull them out without the need for doors. My mother would've never done something like this!"

"You sure of that?"

"I watched her die telling Smith to go to Hell rather than let people get hurt."

Barney nodded thoughtfully and took a step away. After a moment, he turned back. "If that's true, then there is only one possible explanation.

"In the '40s, when the US started the Manhattan Project, the recruited scientists thought they were going to save lives. When the weapon was completed, Oppenheimer and Einstein approached President Truman in the Oval Office and suggested they drop a bomb in the ocean off the coast of Japan, rather than on the mainland. They reasoned that the Japanese would surrender after seeing the devastating effects of the weapon and end the war without any lives lost.

"President Truman kicked them out of his office and ordered the military to drop both bombs on civilian targets. The devastation was beyond imagination. Oppenheimer had to live with the fact that he'd created a doomsday device and caused the suffering of millions for the rest of his life. He said afterwards, "*I am become Death. The destroyer of worlds*."

"You're forgetting one thing. We've been having earthquakes for years well after the satellite was destroyed. And BC didn't put a new satellite into orbit until this morning. So what you're saying is impossible."

"See this?" he said, tapping one of the photos and pointing to a white van off in the distance. Then he pointed to three more photographs with what looked like the same van. "After the last time we met, I began looking through all these photos. When their first satellite was destroyed, I believe they were forced to use their prototype weapon, and they fitted the device into this white van."

Ally thought back to the night she was arrested. The night she saw the white van slide up in front of her, how the whole world around her began to shake. She remembered her car vibrating and bouncing out of control, then it overturned and she crashed into the barricades.

"I think when your mother realized what Burton Conglomerates was doing, she sabotaged the satellite. That's what really caused it to explode eight years ago. And they killed her for it."

Tears flowed freely down Ally's cheeks. Her legs felt heavy and she collapsed into the chair, lowering her head. Her mind just went blank. For at least a minute, time stopped and she couldn't even bring herself to breathe.

"I told you I recognized your face," he said, referencing their first meeting at the soup kitchen. "You look like your mother."

"So this man," Ally said, tapping one of the photographs. "This Smith… you think he works for Burton Conglomerates?"

Barney nodded.

"So he must work for Hal Burton."

Barney nodded again.

"And this Smith killed my mother, my sister, and Maury."

Again, Barney nodded.

"And you're telling me they have another one of these satellites?"

"It was launched this morning. Already, within hours of the launch, on the news, a small village in Turkey suffered from a major earthquake. And then, there is what happened today in Grace City not 30 minutes later. You saw what happened… they levelled the Grace City hospital. Curtis thinks that since their assassin failed to kill you, they used it to try to bury you."

Ally's eyes flinched. She hadn't thought of that. *Could she really have been the target? Was Hal really capable of killing hundreds of innocent people just to get to her?* The thought made her sick and she shook her head to clear it. Of course he was. He was behind all of this.

"Why are you telling *me*? Shouldn't you be telling the police?"

Barney smiled. "I'm an alcoholic hoarder who writes for a tabloid. Who's going to listen to me? Besides, the police can't stop men like Hal Burton. There was only one person who could." His voice dipped and became sadder. "Sometimes what the world needs is somebody who can operate outside the law, someone with special skills and the technology to do what the law can't or won't."

Ally cocked her head.

"Relax, I know Maury was the Blur. I've known that for about three years. I've been following the reports on the dark web. Since you've been around, the dark web has been blowing up with all kinds of crazy sightings. But behind each of those sightings, is what I have been paying attention to. The unexplained sightings at the mortuary? The police station being shot up… and the hospital... and Maury… well, it doesn't take a genius to put it all together. You don't have to pretend. Your secret is safe with me."

Ally didn't reply.

"With this satellite, BC is now the most powerful entity in the world. They can bend entire nations to their will. They can demolish their corporate competitors, bolster economic trade deals, and send anyone considered a threat back to the Stone Age. What can anyone do against something like that?"

* * *

As the lift descended, Ally approached Curtis with a faraway look. He glanced up at her from one of the tables. She sat down and sighed.

"Did Barney tell you?" he asked.

Ally nodded. "This is all my fault. My mother died because she found out that BC used her research to build a weapon. She tried to destroy it, but they came for her, and used me and my sister as leverage to get access to her research."

"Ally, don't be stupid. It's not your fault!"

"Maybe," she said dismissively. "But thanks to my sister and me, they've built another one. And there are only two people who know about it."

"Three," came a voice from the back. Marcus walked forward and approached them.

"He got here just before you did," Curtis explained.

"I didn't take you for the 'change of heart?' type," Ally said coldly.

"Burton Conglomerates is responsible for the deaths of countless innocents. Including your mother, and my brother. They've got to be stopped."

Ally eyed him as if waiting for the catch. "I suppose you are about to suggest we call the police?"

"No. Men like Hal are too big to fail. Curtis and I have been talking… we need to get you back to work," he said, gesturing to the device in Curtis's hand. It was a silver cylinder and syringe.

Ally eyed the canister and large needle. "What's that?

"Nanobots, remember?"

"So these nanobots… they work?"

"In theory. We never actually tested them. My brother was never a big fan of needles. The big baby," Marcus laughed.

Ally looked at the large needle doubtfully. "Could this kill me?"

"Honestly… I'm not sure," Marcus said. "I don't think so." He turned away to look at the computer screen.

"Thanks for the reassurance," she muttered.

"It's either we wait around for another six weeks for your wounds to heal, plus the years of physical therapy, or we inject these into you and hopefully get you back out there in three weeks," Curtis said. "It's your call."

Ally thought for a moment. With Burton Conglomerates leveling entire city blocks and blasting foreign nations, she didn't really have much of a choice. Her mother gave up her life protecting the world from a doomsday device. If she were alive, she wouldn't hesitate; she'd finish the job. Now, it was her turn. Sandy was right. She finally did find her fight—she had to finish what her mother started.

"Okay. I'll do it," she said.

"Are you sure?"

She nodded.

Curtis pricked her finger with a lancet and slipped the blood sample into the device, waiting for it to analyse and align to Ally's DNA. Then he picked up the syringe, carefully inserted the needle into her arm and slowly pressed the nanobots into her bloodstream.

Ally gritted her teeth and tensed her whole body.

"What are you doing?" he asked.

"I'm waiting for the surge of pain that's about to rip through my body," she said, squinting her eyes and still gritting her teeth.

"Dude, this isn't the movies," he said smirking and set the syringe down.

Ally opened her eyes and eased off of the tension. "Oh."

Curtis chuckled.

"So what do we do now?" she asked.

"Now, you heal," Curtis said. "In the meantime, we'll continue to keep tabs on Felix's operations and collect evidence so the department can build a case. The footage we gave him was enough to take Michaels down, but Felix's face was never on camera."

"You mean the charges against Michaels are actually going to stick?" Ally asked sarcastically.

"Michaels pleaded guilty to conspiracy to commit murder. He was offered a lighter sentence in exchange for fingering other bent cops in the department."

"Of course he was."

"Thanks to him, four others were suspended pending an internal investigation, including Peters, who is in the wind after the incidents in the hospital. He must have managed to slip out when Smith…" he stopped and took a breath. "Part of the deal that was offered to Michaels was to give evidence against Felix."

"Don't tell me he's getting out!"

"No, he refused. He said no amount of time off his sentence was worth a shanking in prison."

"Why don't *they* just do it?"

"He says Felix is a person of interest to the department, but a judge won't sign off on a surveillance warrant without cause."

"But Felix is a scumbag!"

"Yes, but a scumbag with privacy rights. The truth is, putting Felix out of business and behind bars would mean safer streets. It would also mean one fewer gang leader attempting to recruit young people in our community. And it also means we can renew the lease to the dojo without the consequences. But mostly, it's what Maury would do."

"Then let's nail the bastard," Ally said.

CHAPTER 50

THREE WEEKS LATER…

Stevens and Lockhart watched Felix intently through the one-way glass as an officer cuffed him to the table. Any run of the mill crook would display the tell-tale signs of nerves in his position, but Felix was a hardened criminal. He looked more inconvenienced than nervous.

"Why hasn't he lawyered up?" Lockhart asked.

Stevens shrugged. "Pride? Ego? Who knows with these psychos. But for now, he's waived his right to counsel. Think you can get the name of his supplier?"

"Yeah, no sweat," Lockhart quipped.

"We *need* that name." Stevens handed him a manilla folder. "He doesn't know that we got this from that damn vigilante, so use that. Christ, Floyd, what the hell happened to us? If the public found out where we got our intel..."

Lockhart nodded. He slipped the file folder under his arm, grabbed his coffee and opened the door.

"Hey Felix! How've you been, buddy?"

Felix screwed up his face. "Better than you. Rough couple of weeks, Sergeant?"

Lockhart smiled, but instantly regretted it as pain shot through him like a migraine. That damn assassin left him looking more raccoon than man.

"I hope you like the color," he joked, sliding his fingers against the stone wall. "I'm gonna find you a cell just like it."

Felix chuckled.

"So they tell me you've waived your right to counsel. Are you sure that's what you want?"

"Only guilty men need attorneys."

Lockhart set down a file on the table and opened it. "Funny you should say that. You've been a busy boy, Felix," he teased, thumbing through several documents with photos paper-clipped to them, one after the other, making a big show of the size and scope of the evidence.

Felix didn't even blink.

"Well, I've been busy, too. I made a new friend. And this friend knows quite a lot about you."

"Really… see, I think if you had anything on me, you'd have charged me already."

Lockhart shrugged, removing a photograph from the folder. "We've got you for extortion… bribery..."— he continued slapping down three weeks's worth of drone surveillance photos, wanting Felix to feel each metaphorical coffin nail, so he took his time— "profiteering... procuring… Oh, uh... that last one is what we boys in the business call *pimping*."

Felix smirked, admiring his handiwork.

"We know you're calling the shots in the mob... we know about the drugs... the weapons..." he continued, slapping down a series of large photographs of street pushers, full crates of product, and rolls of money. "And it seems you're even involved in human trafficking. Nasty business. Takes a special kind of psycho to prostitute young girls." He laid down photos of young women huddled together beside a dockside shipping container.

"Ya see, Felix, I *am* charging you. And from where I'm sitting, you're in a world of trouble. You're looking at death by lethal injection. But if you cooperate with me, I'll see to it personally that your sentence is reduced to life in prison."

Felix shook his head. "You think all this is supposed to scare me? This isn't my first arrest, and it probably won't be my last. These charges will never stick. The world is a very dangerous place. Witnesses have accidents all the time, sometimes evidence can just…" — he made a popping sound with his lips — "disappear, rats have short lifespans, and in my experience, police officers aren't always model citizens, *hypothetically,* of course."

Lockhart tried not to let his face betray his thoughts. He knew Felix was right. Corrupt networks use their contacts in the police to ensure key evidence is tainted, lost or destroyed, and witnesses removed or threatened before they can testify. They get their whole crew to round up every single person who worked for them and through a long, grueling process, find the rat and gut him in front of everyone to show what happens to people who cross a man like Felix Overgaard.

Lockhart needed to act fast.

Felix leaned in closer. "So let me tell you how this is gonna work. In about five minutes, you're going to let me go."

"Now, why would I do that?"

"Call it a feeling," he said smugly.

Lockhart remembered Stevens's comment, about how the source of the evidence was unknown to Felix, and had an idea. "Oh, you think..." Lockhart dramatized his movements, glancing at the door, then back at Felix. "You think someone's gonna come in and save you?" He laughed, leaning in closer. "I thought you were supposed to be a smart guy, Felix. You still don't get it. See, I think the person you expect to walk through that door... the person who you're protecting? I think it's the same person who's handing you over to me on a silver platter.

"Take a good look at the table..."

Felix stared coldly at Lockhart, then grudgingly looked at the orgy of evidence against him. Lockhart could see his seed growing. As he looked at the photographs, his hard expression changed. His eyes flickered up like someone who just realized the only way someone could have gotten this amount of evidence was if they were being thrown to the wolves.

"Ah, there it is," Lockhart said, watching Felix's eyes. "The moment of clarity."

"I want full immunity," he demanded.

Lockhart laughed again. "Felix, I've got you dead to rights. I don't need to make a deal with you. This case is a slam dunk. I'm only here to gloat and rub it under your nose."

"You been watching the news lately?"

"I don't watch the news. Too depressing. Although, I might make an exception when your special report hits prime time."

"Well, you're gonna want to hear the story I've got…"

Lockhart started packing away the evidence on the table, placing everything back into the file folder and stood up.

"What are you doin'?"

Lockhart stared Felix in the eyes. "May your concrete shoes sink you to the bottom of the river." He winked and made for the door.

"I'd sit my ass down if I were you, Sergeant. That is, if you want this city to go on breathing."

Lockhart stopped and looked at Felix. If he were lying, he was doing a pretty good job. "What the hell are you talking about?"

Felix pointed to the chair and Lockhart rolled his eyes. He sighed as he sat down.

"Ever heard of a place called Sukurlu?"

"What am I, a geographer?" Lockhart asked.

"It's a little village in southeastern Turkey. It suffered an earthquake about three weeks ago."

"So?"

"So before that, it was an active nuclear weapons site. Burton Conglomerates orchestrated the whole thing. They funded that village, arranged for the transport of materials, financed their nuclear program, and supplied them with the resources to begin constructing the weapons."

"Oh they did, did they? Why would they do that?" Lockhart asked apathetically.

"They used 'em... to get leverage on the government. To get their satellite up into orbit."

"Enjoy prison, Felix."

"Wait. It ain't just a satellite."

"No? Then what is it?"

"What do I look like, a physicist?"

"Come on, Felix. You're wasting my time."

"Whatever it is, it took out that village in Sukurlu, demolished countless buildings all over Old Town, and collapsed the Grace City Hospital a few weeks back. I hear they did that just to get to one person."

Lockhart rolled his eyes. "You mean to tell me that the CEO of Burton Conglomerates has some kind of space-age ray gun? Is that really what you're telling me?"

"I don't know what it is... but it acts like an earthquake weapon."

"Weapons like that don't exist."

"Don't they?" Felix smirked. "The device inside one of my warehouses says different."

"I thought you said it was a satellite."

"I said it ain't *JUST* a satellite. Before they put the device up into orbit, they had one fixed to a van. And for the past decade, that assassin who rearranged your face has been using it to take out any target Hal ordered."

"Bullshit."

"You give me immunity... and I'll give you the address. You can have a look for yourself."

Lockhart scoffed. He sat back in his chair and wiped the corners of his mouth, staring at Felix for a good while. Why would he offer up the device if it didn't exist? Was it some kind of trap? Or was he telling the truth?

* * *

Hal Burton exited his Rolls-Royce and strolled leisurely inside an opulent gentlemen's club. The room was magnificent, styled with the best that money could buy. Old money. The walls were decorated with mentors and heroes of old beside the portrait of the current US president. An expensive plaque fixed to the center of a large mahogany table bore the capitol building logo: a dome spire resting atop a blanket of patriotic stars and stripes, sun rays of gold and yellow glowed out from its rear.

As Hal stepped through the room, he passed several old white men sitting in lavish lounge chairs smoking cigars and sipping expensive liquor. Servers in white gloves attended to them. He walked casually into the lounge, took his seat opposite two distinguished men and adjusted his tie.

"Sorry I'm late. My grandson has the flu... he's been up all night."

"Let's get right to the point, shall we?" Mr. Santos said unsympathetically. "We've decided to move up the timetable."

Hal cocked his head. He narrowed his eyes, reading the expressions of the two men. They were sphinxes. Impossible to read. "Why? Everything is proceeding as planned."

"Are they?" Mr. Santos asked.

Hal waited for what felt like an eternity, resisting the urge to beg for scraps.

Mr. Santos continued. "Your operation has been exposed. This vigilante character... this Blur—"

"That's not the name I hear," interrupted Mr. Yang. "Some say he's some kind of shape-shifter. They're calling him The Chameleon."

"I don't give a damn what his name is. He must be eliminated, or we risk further failure," Mr. Santos grunted.

"Failure! You are mistaken, gentlemen. I've solved that little problem," Hal said as he accepted a drink from one of the servers.

Mr. Santos looked at Mr. Yang. "He doesn't know."

"Know what?" Hal asked, not used to being a step behind.

"There have been sightings. A cloaked figure at the old depot."

"When?"

"Several times over the last few weeks. We believe he is supplying the authorities with details regarding Felix Overgaard's operations."

"Not possible. My guy broke him and threw him out a five-story window. He's dead."

"And yet, Felix Overgaard has been apprehended."

"What are you saying? That a ghost is watching our men? I stopped believing in ghost stories when I was nine, Mr. Santos."

Mr. Santos removed an envelope from his briefcase and handed it to Hal. He squinted and saw a strange image spray painted onto a stone wall nearby. He couldn't identify it. It looked like it had two clawed fingers on one side, and three on the other. It reminded him of that facehugger creature from the movie Alien, the one that lays eggs in people's throats.

"What am I looking at?" he asked.

"We think it's a symbol of the vigilante. A marker. Found all over the city… in places where people claimed to have seen some kind of… *creature*."

"What the hell is it?"

"We think it's a footprint," Mr. Yang said. "A *chameleon* footprint. That was Mauricio Baráo's fighter name, was it not?"

Hal looked right at Mr. Yang. "Your men are mistaken. The Blur is dead. My man killed him. Whatever it is that your men saw, it was something different."

Mr. Yang exchanged a glance with Mr. Santos. "You're suggesting there are two of them?"

"If what you are saying is true, then yes. It's possible."

"Then this copycat must be eliminated."

"Very well, gentlemen. I'll have Mr. Clark bring you the Chameleon's head."

"It may not be that simple. Word on the street is that this chameleon has… *abilities*."

"That's what people said about the last one. Now he's dead," Hal grunted.

Mr. Santos looked at Mr. Yang. "Perhaps it would be wise to bring in another specialist. Someone more... *tailored*... for such a task."

"Not necessary," Hal boasted. "My man can handle it."

Mr. Santos ignored him. "With respect, Mr. Burton, your man has already failed twice. I'm afraid, I'm going to have to insist. We'll send another asset over to you tonight."

"Very well," Hal replied, trying to hide his irritation. "Your man can intervene if mine fails. Otherwise, he'll just get in the way."

"This is… agreeable," Mr. Santos said.

Mr. Yang nodded.

"And what of the girl?" Mr. Yang asked.

"Killed. As you requested. Courtesy of our new weapon. Now, if you'll excuse me, gentlemen, I—"

"There is one more matter that we find troubling," Mr. Yang said. "My contact on the inside says Felix is singing like a canary." He flashed an intimidating stare at Hal. "Bad news for you, I'm afraid."

Hal subtly shifted his weight. "Let me worry about Felix. He doesn't even know you exist."

“Be that as it may,” Mr. Yang said. “The Guild is in agreement. We’re beginning Phase Four.”

Hal glanced at Mr. Santos, hoping for confirmation that Mr. Yang was joking. Instead, all he saw was a stoic mask. He turned to Mr. Yang, his face hardening. “We’re nowhere near ready for that. Give me more time to—”

“You misunderstand,” Mr. Yang interrupted. “This isn’t a discussion. The decision has been made.”

“I have served The Guild for over 10 years,” Hal growled. “When have I *ever* missed a mark?” He looked into the eyes of both men. “The answer is *never*. Because I never have.”

The men exchanged glances. Then Mr. Santos nodded. “Very well. I will speak to the Guild and request a prorogation.”

“Thank you, gentlemen,” Hal said. He stood up and buttoned his jacket. “You can tell the Guild I’ll handle this new vigilante. Everything is under control.”

* * *

Lockhart resumed the interrogation and slid Felix a document. “You sign that, you’re a free man, assuming we can verify the rest of your story.”

“I need a pen,” Felix said, holding out his hand.

“You get your pen when you have told me the rest, assuming your device checks out.”

“I’ve told you already.”

“Tell me again.”

Felix glared at Lockhart. Finally, he shook his head and sighed. “For the past few years, the shipments have been coming in at various places throughout the city, like at the old depot.”

“The drugs and weapons...”

Felix nodded. “But some of the crates had a strange stamp on them. Looked like hieroglyphics. We were told not to open them.”

“But you did…”

Felix smirked. “The crates were full of some kind of rare mineral. I don’t know. I never had time to analyze them. My guys just unloaded the cargo and I handled the payoffs of various individuals... cops, officials... a long line of people.”

“I’m gonna need a list of their names.”

Felix nodded again. “Once the shipments were unloaded, my guys pushed the weapons and the drugs in the streets.”

“I know all this already... skip to the part about the earthquakes.”

"My operation is only Phase One... to make the streets so unsafe that the people would either voluntarily relocate, or be enticed by Burton Conglomerate's financial incentives."

"What's Phase Two?"

"To forcibly remove people who have refused all incentives. He's after those minerals."

"And Phase Three?"

"The satellite. To remove any obstacles still standing in his way. Threats against his company or to ensure specific land acquisitions."

"And Phase Four?"

"That, I don't know. But I do know that that village in Turkey and the neighborhoods in Grace City are just the beginning. Hal Burton plans to level Old Town."

"When?"

"I don't know that either. But before your men arrested me, my instructions were to get the hell out of Dodge and shut everything down. To move all product and operations out of Old Town. Which means, optimistically… maybe 36 hours?"

"I assume you can prove all this?"

Felix nodded. "The device is in one of my warehouses. And I can get you the names of the key players. But first, I'd like my pen, Sergeant."

"If I find out you're holding out on me... or that you've concocted this story to embarrass me or the department, I'll make sure this document gets lost in transit and you never see the light of day. I'll personally ensure that everyone inside the state pen knows you're a rat," he said, sliding him a pen.

Felix scowled and signed the document, then slid it back.

"All right, boys, show Felix to his new home."

Felix's eyes flinched.

"Just until we verify your story," Lockhart assured him.

Felix didn't like it, but he nodded and let the three officers return him back to his cell. When he'd left, Lockhart headed to the phone to speak to the mayor.

*   *   *

Inside the holding cell, two police officers escorted Felix to his temporary quarters. The door opened and they shoved him forward. The bolt slid shut with a loud CLACK, locking him inside. Felix immediately met eyes with a massive prisoner who was unchained.

“I thought I was supposed to be alone!” he called out to the guards, one of whom laughed and shut the viewing window. “I want to speak to Sergeant Lockhart!” Felix screamed, banging on the door. But he could hear nothing. No motion coming from outside. “HEY!”

Behind him, the prisoner stood up and glared at Felix. He towered above Felix and lifted his massive arm. A shiv sparkled in the fluorescent light.

CHAPTER 51

Down in the basement below the dojo, Curtis was sitting unusually quiet. He was staring at a bare section of wall, only moving to breathe. Occasionally, he closed his eyes, like he was focusing his mind and tuning out all sounds and distractions. It wasn't until Ally cursed that he snapped out of it.

"What?" he asked.

Ally pointed to the CCTV monitor screen and Curtis rolled closer. Lockhart was standing above them in the dojo, looking around for signs of life. When he didn't see any, he made his way to the lift and waved at a camera impatiently.

"What does *he* want?" Curtis muttered.

"Me..."

Curtis looked at her. "Should we pretend like we're not here?"

"No. Let him in."

He shrugged, then pressed a button. The secret door slid across, allowing Lockhart to enter.

"Look…" Ally began when he approached them. "I know I shouldn't have just walked away, but—"

"According to the media, you're dead. I'm not here for you," he interrupted.

"Thank you for agreeing to see me," he said, shaking Marcus's hand.

"Wait, *you* called him? Why?"

Marcus threw Curtis a disheveled look.

Over the next several minutes, Lockhart relayed what Felix had told him during the interrogation, about the weapon he claimed Hal Burton had been using to demolish buildings around the city, about the dirty money trail, about Hal's plan to level Old Town in search of some rare mineral, about the imminent disaster headed their way in less than 36 hours.

"That was two days ago."

"If Felix went on record against BC, why didn't you just get a team and roll up and arrest Hal Burton?" Curtis asked. "You've got Felix's taped confession."

Lockhart looked down at him. "No. What I've got is a lunatic raving about nuclear weapons in the desert, ray guns and corporate conspiracy theories."

The team acknowledged all that had been said and sat quietly for a moment. Finally Marcus spoke. "So what do you want from us?"

Lockhart looked taken aback. "Isn't this… I don't know, kind of your thing?"

"We're more like *local* vigilantes. We're not James Bond," Curtis said, smirking at his own joke and looking to the others for reinforcement. None came.

"Please tell me you can do something… I came here because, legally, we have no options. I pressed as hard as I could in the department until my Captain told me to drop it. So there won't be any help from the police."

"There's a shock," Curtis said.

Lockhart flashed him an annoyed look, but ignored him. "I've gone as high as the Mayor. Dead end. The department can't afford to go after someone like Hal without rock-solid evidence. Believe me, if I had any other options, I wouldn't be here. We're on our own."

Curtis scoffed and muttered: *we,* under his breath.

"What's your problem?"

"My problem? By problem, do you mean witnesses mysteriously committing suicide or being straight-up executed while in police custody? No… no problem at all."

"Not all cops are dirty," he barked.

Curtis scoffed again.

"Yeah, that's right. Badmouth the police if it makes you feel better, but we're always there to answer the call when you need us."

"That's a very white person thing to say, Floyd."

"Oh come on! That's leftist horseshit! Any criminal can run around in a rubber suit and punch people in the dark. I serve a higher cause than myself. I wear a badge, not a mask, and I'm accountable for my actions."

"A cop being held accountable for his actions? That'd be the day!"

"That's enough!" Marcus yelled. "This isn't why we're here. We've got a serious problem and a ticking clock. Table the politics for another time!" Lockhart and Curtis scowled, but both agreed. "All right then. Any ideas?"

"I say we go after Dr. Hayagawa. He has to know how to shut it down. He built it," Ally stated.

"I agree," Marcus said. "If there's anyone who can tell us more about this satellite, it's him."

"I can't go near him without a warrant."

"Who said anything about a warrant?" Curtis said ominously.

"What if this doctor isn't forthcoming?" Lockhart asked.

"Then we persuade him," Marcus said, handing Ally a tranquilizer gun.

Lockhart couldn't believe what he was hearing. "So that's the plan? Kidnapping?" He looked at the faces in the room, hoping for some kind of reassurance. Instead, all he got was a wink from Curtis. "Jesus…" He sighed and ran his hand through his hair.

Marcus cleared his throat. "I've deluded the solution. It should only knock him out for 15 minutes. Aim for a meaty area." He checked his watch. "Lockhart, you go with Ally. Bring back Dr. Hayagawa."

"What? Me? No, I can't be a part of this."

"What do you mean?"

"I'm a cop. I can't just go *kidnap* someone."

"Technically, it's abducting," Curtis interjected.

"Look, I don't like this any more than you do. But we have to find out how to shut this thing down, *now*! We don't have time to invite the guy out for coffee."

"Yeah, but this… this is too much… I can't..."

"You came to us because, as you said, legally, we have no options. This is why we do this. Trust us. We'll get Hayagawa and bring him safely back here."

"We're wasting time," Ally interrupted.

Marcus looked at Lockhart and shrugged. "Look, you're in it now, like it or not."

"Look on the bright side," Curtis muttered. "You've already broken a dozen laws tonight… why not add abduction to the list?"

Lockhart sighed heavily.

"That's the spirit," Curtis said.

CHAPTER 52

It was a full moon. If not for the street lights, the ocean of stars above would've been quite the spectacle. Ally thought about the irony of superstition. She wondered what the chances were that on this night, there'd be such an ominous sign floating above her head. Of course, she didn't believe in that sort of thing. It was just mildly amusing. In truth, the night was bright and beautiful.

By the time she and Lockhart arrived in the BC parking lot, the streets were winding down and most people were half-way home. This left the lot quiet and empty.

Since they didn't have time to properly surveil him, their only chance was to catch him on his way out of the building. Ally had parked the van close to the entrance and had the hood propped open.

"You sure you disabled the cameras?"

"What do I look like?" Curtis replied sarcastically through the earpiece. *"I looped the feeds. You're all clear."*

"Shut up."

"I know, right? The parking lot cameras are not part of BC's security system. It must have been cheaper to hire out to a third party than to incorporate a full time staff—"

"No, shut up, Curtis!" She smacked Lockhart on the shoulder. "That's him!"

"Rude..."

As Katsu left the building, he reached into his coat pocket and fumbled for his keys.

"Excuse me, sir?" Lockhart called, poking his head around the hood. "You any good with engines?"

Katsu looked up from his phone. "You need a jump?"

"I don't know. The damn thing won't start."

Katsu took a step toward him. "Does the engine turn ov—"

THUNK!

Ally shot a tranquilizer dart into the back of his thigh and Katsu yelped and hopped. He reached down and plucked the dart from his leg. He stared at it, confused, then he stumbled and braced himself on the side of the van. Slowly, he fell into Ally's arms, who caught him to avoid injury. Lockhart rushed out from the front of the van and together, they carried him to the rear door and tossed him inside.

"Well, that was easy," he said, as they hopped into the front seat.

Ally started the engine and they drove to the back of the dojo. Carefully, they carried Katsu's limp body down into the basement. They strapped him to a chair, binding his wrists behind his back and did the same to his ankles.

Marcus handed Ally a unit of smelling salts.

"You guys better stand back," Ally said, activating her holotech. Her apparition enveloped her, morphing her into a disfigured creature. The others stepped back behind Katsu, out of sight.

She cracked the smelling salts and held them under Katsu's nose. "How long does it take to—"

Katsu suddenly inhaled a deep breath of air and jerked his head as the strong ammonia shot through his airway, into his bloodstream and straight to his brain. He began sucking in fast, deep breaths and his eyes shot open. His head twitched from side to side, scanning the unfamiliar room, and noticed his arms and legs were bound.

Testing his restraints, he twisted and pulled, jerking his body in confusion, then desperately tried to free himself until a deep, synthesized voice made him gasp.

"Dr. Hayagawa…"

Katsu jerked his head, trying to get a look at his captor, but they stood just out of sight.

"I have taken you against your will," it continued. "For that, I apologize. But you have information I need. Lives are at stake and time is running out."

"What is this? Why am I here? What do you mean running out?"

"I don't have time for 20 questions, Doctor."

Katsu flinched as a figure stepped into view, cloaked in a tattered hood riddled with rips and tears that obscured their head. The fabric draped to the floor.

"I need you to tell me how to shut down or disable the Quantum satellite you built."

Katsu's eyes nervously shifted. "Shut it down? It can't be shut down."

"I don't believe you," the voice said, turning to face him. Katsu gasped. Staring back at him was some kind of creature. It was grotesque, not man, not beast. Its hands were furry, and from them jutted predatory claws.

The creature turned to the table in front of him and set a leather bag onto the surface. It clunked and heavy metal tools banged together. Katsu watched as bony fingers tugged the string, unwrapping a set of instruments like the ones used to torture people in crime dramas—knives, sharp pointy hooks, bone saws, and others he was too afraid to contemplate.

Katsu inhaled sharply. Fear took hold of him. It pulsed through his veins, leaving his breaths shallow and erratic. He felt his heart kick into overdrive.

"I don't take pleasure in hurting others, Doctor," the creature said as it picked up a set of mini bolt cutters. "So I'm going to ask you again." It's face turned, revealing a set of dead eyes and scarred skin from under the hood. "How do you shut it down?"

Katsu gulped. "I… I told you. It… it can't be—"

The creature's eyes hardened and it snarled. It held up the cutters and took two steps toward him.

"Wait!" Katsu cried. "Wait! You don't understand! It's not that I'm unwilling. It's that it cannot be done!"

"Explain!"

"After BC lost their first quantum satellite, Hal took more stringent precautions. He made sure he was the only one with the means to access it."

"Are there any backdoors to the programing? Any fail safes? Any way we can hack into the satellite?"

"No. That's what I mean… the first quantum satellite was sabotaged, hacked. This one uses PQE."

"PQE?"

"Post-quantum encryption. You'd need a supercomputer to crack it. This one was designed to be impenetrable… untraceable."

"If Hal Burton can access it, then there must be a way."

"It's not that simple. This is really hard to explain—"

"Try!" the creature growled. "And make it quick. You're testing my patience… and my restraint."

"Okay," he huffed quickly. "Mr. Burton has a shard of a rare mineral. It acts like a unique ID drive. It powers the control console in his penthouse. Without it, the satellite won't respond."

"So anyone who has that shard can access the control console?"

Katsu nodded. "Yes, but if you're thinking of taking it off of him, he's too heavily guarded. He has the US Army at his disposal. You wouldn't get within 10 yards of him."

The creature snarled and pawed at its face. "How long would it take you to make another one of these shards? Like the one Hal has?"

"It's made from a unique mineral, one almost impossible to find. But even if we could find one, only one person was smart enough to bypass the encryption firewalls and hack the satellite."

"Who?"

"A former colleague of mine. Sarah Reid. But she can't help you. She's dead. She was the one who disabled their first satellite. It burned up on reentry—"

Katsu stopped suddenly.

"What, Doctor?"

"Well, Sara must have known BC would try again. She showed me once—"

Showed you what?" the creature barked impatiently.

"She created a worm… a-uh, an algorithm that could… could counteract the satellite's cloaking technology. Make it visible to weapon detection systems. She infused it into another rare stone, a black one, but it disappeared when she was killed. Whoever killed her must have taken it."

Ally stiffened. Her hand rose instinctively to her necklace. She felt the rough edges against her fingertips. Slowly, she tapped her wrist and the holographic projection enveloping her body fizzled out and disappeared. "You mean this stone?" she asked, holding out the black stone from her neck.

Katsu blinked in confusion. "What is this? *Ally*? Where did you get that?"

Ally's gaze drifted to her necklace. "My sister and I took it the night my mother was killed." She rubbed her thumb against its rough surface. "After what happened, I didn't think anybody cared about a missing lava rock."

"This's no lava rock," he gasped, glancing between her eyes and the stone. "If this is what I think it is… then we just found out how to disable Quantum! I'll need to get it to my lab to be sure."

Ally slipped the rock around her neck and rejoined the others.

"Right, you heard him," Curtis said. "We have what we need. Let's go shut it down."

Marcus held up his hand. "Curtis, stop. I need to think."

"We don't have time to think! Felix said they're gonna level the city in a matter of hours. We can't just stand here!"

"It isn't that simple, Curtis!"

"Sure it is! Don't you get it? We have Ally's stone. We give it to Katsu, he inserts it into the console and voila! System failure."

"You're forgetting about the soldiers," Marcus said.

"And the guards… and most likely the police when they catch on to what we're up to," Lockhart added.

"So we fight our way in," Curtis said.

"I can't take on a platoon of soldiers," Ally snapped.

"Maybe *YOU* can't, but the Blur can."

"Shut up, Curtis! This is serious!" she hissed. "We don't even know if the stone has the algorithm."

"All right; everybody just stop. Curtis is right," Marcus said. "We have to find a way."

Ally scanned the faces in the room, long and heavy, full of dread. They knew, just as she did, that stopping Quantum meant they must first infiltrate a military controlled building.

"I think I might be able to help," Katsu offered.

Lockhart jerked his head. "Help?" he shouted. "If it wasn't for you, we wouldn't be in this mess! How could you build something like that for a madman?"

Katsu's face hardened. "Do you have a family?" he asked.

Lockhart's lips closed and he narrowed his eyes. He didn't reply. He understood. A person would do anything for their family.

"What do you mean *help*, Doctor?" Marcus asked.

"I can get you into the building. If we can get to my lab, I can verify the stone's algorithm. Then we'd at least know if we can attempt a takedown."

"The second we let him touch that stone, he'll erase it," Lockhart protested.

"I won't."

"How can we be sure?" Lockhart demanded.

Katsu did his best to look up at him. "Sara was my partner. My friend. She came to me for help once… back when she'd learned what Quantum really was. I didn't believe her. It wasn't until after she died that I understood. After they threatened my family. I *owe* her."

Ally took a deep breath. "Can you really get us in?"

Katsu nodded. "I believe I can."

"Then I'm in."

Marcus held up his hands. "Ally, wait—"

"My mother died trying to stop Quantum. I have to finish what she started. This is *my* fight now," she insisted.

Marcus took a deep breath. "Then I'm going with you," he said. "If Maury were here, he wouldn't let you go alone."

"I'm in, too," Curtis said. "You'll need someone to watch your backs and operate the drones."

"Umm… guys?" Katsu called, straining his head to see them. "You think maybe you could untie me now?"

Lockhart was about to protest, but Marcus stepped forward and cut the restraints. Katsu rubbed his wrists and ankles a while, then stood up. He cracked his sore and stiff joints, joined his abductors somewhat hesitantly, and stood shoulder to shoulder with them.

"Katsu, my name is Marcus Baráo. This is Sergeant Floyd Lockhart, my son Curtis, and you already know Ally."

Katsu nodded.

"Okay," Marcus said. "The way I see it, after we enter the building, I'll make my way down to the servers. From there, I'll install a gateway so that Curtis can access the building's network remotely from inside the van, which will be positioned outside the tower. From there, he'll watch our backs and give Ally every possible advantage."

"Game on," Curtis said.

"Katsu, you'll go with Ally and get her to your lab. Verify the algorithm. If it's legit, you'll both make your way to the control room. I'll meet you there."

"What about the soldiers? Security guards?" Ally asked.

"Hopefully you and Curtis can distract them long enough for me to slip into the control room and upload the algorithm into the console," Marcus said.

"I'll walk you through how to upload the algorithm," Katsu offered.

Marcus nodded. "If that fails, maybe I can rig something up to fry the circuits."

"What about my family?" Katsu interjected.

"I can pick up your family on my way back to the precinct," Lockhart offered. "I'll put them in a holding cell. They should be safe there."

Katsu nodded gratefully, happy to put his faith in Lockhart's police protection.

"Yeah, that's not gonna happen," Curtis scoffed. "Take them back here. They can hide out in the dojo."

Lockhart opened his mouth to protest, but must have understood. Too many had recently died on his watch. He nodded. "I'll bring them back here," he agreed.

"There's one more thing…" Marcus said. "We need to try and minimize the collateral damage in case we fail tonight."

The room hung their heads on that last statement. They knew the stakes, but hearing them spoken aloud made it real and highlighted that their chances of failure greatly outweighed their chances of success. In all likelihood, this was either going to end in death or prison.

"Lockhart, after Katsu's family is safe, I want you to go to the precinct and round up a few officers you can trust. Send them to the residential buildings on this list," he reached his hand out to Curtis, who slapped a piece of paper into his palm. "These are known sites Burton Conglomerates has been pressuring with eviction. Start with those. Try to evacuate as many as you can."

"I'll call Barney," Curtis said. "Maybe he can spread the word through social media."

"Good idea."

Lockhart grabbed his coat and slipped it over his shoulders.

CHAPTER 53

Katsu swiped his access card and entered the parking lot. The van navigated the underground network of concrete pathways below Burton Tower. The stone pillars of the building's structure stood sentinel among the shadows, their porous surfaces absorbing the harsh fluorescent lights. Ally imagined the employees rushing to and fro during operating hours, like ants scurrying beneath a colossal, man-made mountain. She wondered how many of those who bustled beneath this tower were aware of the corrupt activities their employer was entangled in. How many of them would truly care?

Ally's thoughts were cut short as the van screeched to a halt. She scanned over the faces seated around her. They looked rattled. Her own heart was fluttering and her mouth was dry.

Marcus cleared his throat. "Remember everybody. Stay in contact." Three sets of nervous eyes stared back at him. "Curtis, you're our eyes and ears."

"Thanks, Dad," he said sarcastically.

"Remember to—"

"Dad! I got it!"

Marcus nodded and jammed a few rough sketches and notes that Katsu had given him into his satchel while Ally slung her Fanny Pack over her shoulder and patted the drones with her hand. Marcus opened the rear door of the van, then hopped out.

Ally went to follow, but Curtis stopped her. "Ally, wait. You gonna be alright?"

She rubbed her chest, feeling the scar tissue and rolled her shoulders to test her mobility. "I'll be fine. Just watch my back." She, Katsu and Marcus ran to the entrance of Burton Tower. Katsu swiped his pass over the security panel and they moved inside.

"We're in," Ally said into the earpiece.

"According to the digital schematic, the servers are in the sub basement, Level 4. Take the door to your right."

"You and Katsu get to the lab," Marcus said. "Verify the algorithm. I'll meet you there after I take care of the servers."

"Be careful."

"You too," he said, dashing off toward the basement servers.

Katsu grabbed Ally's arm, nudging her to follow him to the elevators.

Up in the control room, high above the street, Hal Burton stood waiting for the team of technicians to awaken the satellite.

"Sir?" a technician asked. "There are multiple intruders flagged in the lobby of the building."

Hal turned and walked closer to the monitors. "Show me," he said, watching as three people entered the lobby. "Rewind that," he barked. "Play it again."

The technician rewound the feed. Hal watched the group separate, one man heading for the basement while two other figures dashed toward the elevators.

Beside him, Mr. Clark stepped forward toward the door. "No! I need you up here. Send him." Hal gestured toward a darkened corner of the wall where a figure in a black combat suit stepped forward. Two Katana swords were magnetized to his back—one short, one long. "Bring me that man!" Hal barked, pointing to the one heading toward the servers.

The figure nodded, turned toward the door, and drew a Tanto sword from his back.

"Alive!" he barked.

The figure hesitated, then walked out.

"Pull up that camera feed," Hal growled, pointing to one of the monitors.

As the elevator door to the 78th floor opened, Ally and Katsu rushed into the lab. Sadly, she slipped her mother's necklace over her head. She hadn't anticipated how naked she'd feel without it, like a part of her was missing. Taking one last look at it, she handed it to him and Katsu headed for his computer.

Ally was about to follow but a picture frame drew her attention, like it was calling to her. It was a group photograph of no significance, yet she felt an instant connection. Stepping closer, she saw why. Amongst a crowd of technicians and people in lab coats, were two figures raising glasses to the sky like a retro Star Wars poster. Leaned elegantly against a desk in a long flowing white dress, champagne in hand, was her mother. She looked so strong and proud. Ally guessed that this photo must have been taken to celebrate the Quantum Tunneler's successful test.

"Ally?" Katsu called. "In that cupboard, there's a suit. Put it on. I have a feeling we're about to run into some trouble. It'll keep you safe."

Ally nodded. She opened the cupboard door and stared at the black suit. It appeared to be the same one she'd seen the day she'd had the tour. She picked up the suit while Katsu turned back to his computer and suited up.

* * *

"Pretty cool, huh?" Katsu said, startling her. She hadn't heard him approach. She was too busy admiring her feminine curves in one of the reflective panels. She felt like a superhero, strutting around in black spandex. The suit was almost made for her. It fit her body like a glove, contouring to her shape and yet somehow concealed her form. The suit was astonishing.

Katsu held up the necklace. "The algorithm is there," he said smiling.

Ally breathed a sigh of relief, then notified Marcus through the earpiece.

"Excellent! I'm nearly finished here. Head to the penthouse. And be careful!"

Ally turned to Katsu. "Come on."

"Wait, I want to show you something. There's a trigger mechanism fitted into the gloves."

Ally looked down and saw that there were two small buttons, one on either hand between the thumb and forefinger. "What do they do?"

Katsu held up his index finger. "First things first." Katsu inserted what looked like a quartz crystal into a compartment hidden on the suit. "In the aftermath of Project Starfall, scientists discovered various meteorite fragments capable of generating large amounts of energy. This stone is one of many we discovered, each with a unique energy signature. This one is one of the more common ones and powers the… well, it's easier if I show you. Slip the helmet on."

well, it's easier if I show you. Slip the helmet on."

Ally picked up the helmet, feeling its sleek and form-fitted casing. It resembled a motorcycle helmet, but was more contoured like an extra layer of skin made of glass. She slipped it over her head and immediately a glass shield slid over her face and locked into place. The fit was tight. It was designed for a person with a short military cut, not for hair like hers. But now wasn't the time to dwell on this. Almost as if it were self-aware, the helmet booted on, immediately enthralling her with a visual spectacle. Her vision had never been more clear. It was like every object was somehow real for the first time, like they were more specially present. It was difficult to describe, but if before she was blind, now she could see.

The helmet auto-adjusted to the new lighting and she instantly saw far more than she ever thought to. "Woah," she muttered. "It's like God-Vision. Is this what the stone does? Makes you see all visible light spectrums?"

Katsu chuckled. "No. That's just the optics tech. Press the button on your left thumb, then touch the wall," he said.

Ally touched the wall and her hand turned translucent as if it were made of glass, seemingly matching the color and texture of the wall. "Woah!" she exclaimed.

Katsu smiled. "Pretty cool, huh?"

Ally stared at her arm. 90% of her silhouette was concealed by the suit's cloaking device. The other 10% looked like the surface of a bubble when it partially catches the light. You'd have to really look to see it.

She touched the table and the suit morphed again, creating a different translucent optical illusion. "This is incredible!"

"Umm, guys? They know we're here. They're calling 911!" Curtis called. *"Move your asses! Oh shit! Ally… th…oms…"* the radio crackled and went quiet.

"You hear that, Katsu?"

No answer.

"Katsu?" She turned around just in time to see Katsu back up toward the doorway.

"I'm sorry…" he whimpered, then disappeared around the threshold in a dash.

Ally raced out the door after him, digging in with her new footwear but gasped as she shot into the hallway at twice her normal speed and crashed into the wall of the hallway. She bounced back and landed hard on the floor. Turning her head, she saw Katsu sprinting toward the elevators and kicked herself up.

Again, she bolted towards him, but it was too late. The doors were closing. Inside the elevator, Katsu clutched Ally's black stone to his chest, his lungs heaving. "I'm sorry," he croaked again. "I'm sorry."

"Katsu!" Ally screamed, as the doors slid shut and began ascending. "NO! Damn it!"

The earpiece in her ear crackled again and Curtis's voice rang through it. *"Ally! Come in! Ally!"*

"I'm here!"

"Sorry, the coms rebooted when Dad connected the gateway. Why is Katsu in the elevator?"

"He double crossed us!"

"What do you mean he double crossed us?"

"He has the stone," Ally growled, looking up and watching the elevator floor numbers. "Do you see where they're taking him?"

"Shit... looks like the penthouse. What do we do, Ally? Without that stone..."

Ally bowed her head and closed her eyes. "I don't know… I need to think." She forced her heart to slow and her breathing to normalize. Curtis's voice rattled on in her ear, but she wasn't listening. It was just a distant hum to the realization surging through her. Their mission had just failed. Above her, Hal Burton was in control of a super weapon taking aim at hundreds of thousands of people, Katsu had betrayed them and was probably giving Hal the only thing capable of destroying the satellite, and standing between them was likely a squad of soldiers, and most probably… Smith. And the worst part about it was that if she didn't think of something, and fast, Marcus was about to die.

"Oh shit! Shit shit shit! Ally! We've got a serious problem!" Curtis cried. *"They've got my dad!"*

CHAPTER 54

Ally threw her eyes open. *"Someone in an identical suit to yours just roughed him up! They're taking him to the penthouse... what are we gonna do?"*

Ally began pacing, racking her brain for a way to win. For a way out of this. But none came. The mission had seemed impossible enough when it was just soldiers and one assassin - Smith, the man who killed Maury, the best fighter she'd ever read about. But now there was a second assassin. In a suit, which meant whoever it was, they had skills. And they had a hostage, so even if she could manage to survive two assassins, it would never get that far. She couldn't fight her way out of this. Not this time. Maybe it was time to admit they just lost.

"Ally!"

"Shut up, Curtis! I hear you!" Ally headbutted the wall. This wasn't a mission anymore. She was in over her head.

Above her, a squeal from a PA system squawked. Then a moment passed before a voice broke the silence. *"Whatever it is you think you're doing, by now, you must know you've lost. It's over. Surrender now, or your friend will suffer the consequences."*

Ally stiffened, tracking the voice to the loud speaker above her head, and stared into a camera lens. She did her best to throw her angriest face, even though she knew the visor blocked her scowl. "Is this what it means to be a patriot now?" she snapped. "Killing millions of your own people?"

"You wouldn't understand," Hal's voice replied.

"No, I get it; you're a genocidal psychopath."

Hal tutted his tongue. *"How short sighted. People like you live in a world men like me allow. To you, freedom and democracy are just words you parrot in history class. I live in the* real *world... a world run by resources. Oil... metal... lithium... water... cheap labor. That's what wars are about. Controlling resources."*

"This isn't war!"

"Not yet. But before this night is over, after this city is reduced to rubble... the American people will again have another invisible and nameless enemy to fight... one that can take on any face, ideology, religion, or philosophy seen as a threat to the State. And they'll once again unite behind a new cause and be stronger for it."

Ally glared into the lens through her helmet.

"What?" he scoffed. *"You think this country rose to power by playing by the rules and being the nice guy? The Mexican-American War, The Gulf of Tonkin, Pearl Harbor, 9/11...*

narratives, all orchestrated so that one day people like you can have an iPhone and sneakers with lights in them!"

"You're insane. Trust me, I know a thing or two about insanity."

"I'm necessary. Without men like me, countries would tear themselves apart. Men like me facilitate a country's access to resources to keep it flourishing, and I'm going to make sure the future generations are provided for."

"Not if I stop you."

"Please... don't be pathetic. Take the stairs to your left. If you're not up here in 10 minutes, you can mop up what's left of your friend." The speaker clicked and fizzled as he ended the call.

Ally opened the door to the staircase and looked up at the infinite spiral. She could hear Curtis sniffling on the other side of the earpiece. Ally knew taking on soldiers was going to test her limits. She wasn't even sure the suit was capable of repelling that many bullets. One gun, maybe. But several? And what caliber? She tried not to think about it. But there was only one way this was going to work... and that is if she did exactly as Hal instructed.

"Curtis?"

"Yeah?" he sniffed.

"It's gonna be OK."

"How? You heard him. We try anything, and my dad's dead."

Ally took one step. Then another. Then another until she was sprinting up the stairs, two at a time. "What do you see in the penthouse?"

"Soldiers. Four of them. The figure is bringing my dad in now. Hal is in the control room. And Ally? Smith is there, too."

Ally slowed and hesitated before taking the next stair. Though she'd like nothing more than to rip Smith's throat out, she needed to focus on getting to Marcus. On getting him out of this.

A few minutes later, she reached the top of the stairs and stood in front of Hal's penthouse. "Give me the layout of the room."

"Okay, I'm connecting your helmet to the CCTV cameras."

Ally's visor flickered and she now saw a bird's-eye view of the room. Directly in front of her, the room appeared to be open plan. There was what looked like an R&D area to the right with lots of partitioned off nooks and heavy equipment. To the left, there were some stairs which led up to an elevated platform with four large, round pillars holding up the upper floor. The control room was at the top left corner and south of that, was Hal's private elevator.

"Do you see the seven soldiers beside the pillars? There are two in front of the elevator doors. And directly in front of you, there are five more." She confirmed it in her visor. *"And Ally, Smith is—"*

"I know… I see him."

Smith was standing near the entrance to the control room. Hal was inside leaning over a control panel. On the platform, Marcus was kneeling down and the figure in black was holding a sword at his side.

"Ally, don't let them kill my dad," Curtis said sullenly.

"Wait for my signal, then hit the lights." She could hear Curtis's fingers frantically typing in her earpiece over an occasional sniff. All she needed was to create the right distraction. "Open the door, Curtis."

"Wait Ally, I don't think—"

"Open. the. door!"

She heard a sigh and the door lock clicked. Ally took a deep breath and entered the penthouse. Immediately, two soldiers aimed their rifles at her. She held her hands up and interlocked her fingers behind her head.

"Bring him here," Hal ordered. "Don't get too close."

The soldiers obeyed and cautiously escorted her up to Hal's level, being sure to stay a few paces behind her. Ally marched forward and lowered her arms to her sides. "Let them go," her synthesized voice ordered.

Hal smiled. "No, I don't think I will."

"Forget about me! Complete the mission!" Marcus yelled.

"You're wasting your breath. He's not going anywhere," Hal said. "Are you?"

Ally stood still.

"See?" he gloated. "Besides, you're too late, isn't that right, Dr. Hayagawa?"

Katsu stepped out of the control room. His eyes cast to Ally, his face laden with shame, then quickly shifted to Hal. "It's done, sir."

"And the algorithm?"

"Neutralised and destroyed." He handed the black stone to Hal. "The satellite is now invisible to targeting systems, as you requested"

"Excellent!" Hal said smugly.

Katsu looked at Ally. "I'm sorry," he muttered.

"Why, Katsu?"

He didn't answer. His eyes hit the floor.

Hal chuckled, then waved his hand and behind her, five soldiers stepped up and pointed their weapons at her back. Ally stiffened. She watched in horror as Hal stepped up to a console and typed in a passcode.

"Coordinates confirmed," an automated voice chimed.

The satellite was activated!

CHAPTER 55

Lockhart stood in the dimly lit alleyway beside the patches of graffiti-strewn walls and checked his watch for the third time. He took one last look out into the darkness that stretched into obscurity, its mouth concealed in the shadowed corner of a dingy street, and sighed. The officers he'd contacted were not coming.

He jammed his hands into his pockets, ventured out of the murky passage, and stepped into the feeble, intermittent light cast by a solitary, flickering streetlamp. The soles of his shoes echoed on the cracked cobblestones as he kicked aside discarded cardboard boxes and crumpled newspapers, all remnants of urban decay that littered the alley's cold, damp pavement.

Then his heart almost stopped. Several shadows stepped toward him and he recoiled. "Didn't think you'd show," came a familiar voice.

Lockhart scanned the dark faces and his fear eased. Officers Nancy Hensley, Patricia Short, James Arroyo, Mikey Barron, and John Samoset were five officers he trusted, by reputation. He'd asked to meet them in the alleyway beside the precinct rather than inside the building to avoid potential eavesdropping. Convincing fellow officers to disobey direct orders and risk their pensions was not something he wanted others to get wind of, especially after the recent shooting.

"You mind telling us what we're doing here?"

"Thank you, everyone. Over the past few years, I know you've heard rumors about me. Some of them are true. Some of them are not." A few eye rolls and snickers told him he was right. "But none of that matters right now. I've brought you here because you are all good cops. The best. And I need your help, but what I am about to ask you to do goes directly against the orders of Captain Stevens. You could lose your pensions."

"Why the hell would we do something like that?" James asked.

"Because if you don't, millions of people are gonna die."

Everyone froze. Their faces shifted uneasily to one another and the alley began to murmur. When he figured they had time to process those words, Lockhart began again.

"I don't have time to get into the specifics, but there's a weaponized satellite taking aim at the city right now, ready to send Old Town back to the Stone Age."

Everyone began talking at once. "Weaponized? What do you mean weaponized?" "Is it nuclear?" "He's lost his mind. Are you guys hearing this?"

"What kind of weapon?" John asked.

"Come on, John," James yelled. "You're buying this?"

"Floyd and I trained at the academy together. He's a good man. If he says there is a weapon, then it is so." He turned back to Lockhart. "What do you need us to do?"

"I need you to lead a discrete, full-scale evacuation."

"Evacuation!?" Nancy cried. "Of *Old Town*? In one night?"

The alley erupted in a series of gasps and scoffs.

"So why us? Why not go to the Chief?" Mickey asked. "Or the Mayer?"

"I have."

"And?"

Lockhart shook his head. They either didn't believe him or couldn't risk the public panicking, but he didn't have time to explain this.

"That's because they know what you're saying is bullshit," James barked.

"I know what it sounds like," Lockhart admitted. "But I can't just sit on my hands and wait for what's coming."

"So you want the *six* of us to evacuate Old Town? That's not possible. We'd need an army!" Nancy cried.

Lockhart didn't reply. He stood stone-face and stared Patricia down. "You'll need to head to the center of Old Town and each of you pick an apartment complex on this list."

He held up a piece of paper.

"Start at the top and work your way down. Try and get each resident to tell at least one person they know in the city to evacuate."

"You want to evacuate 15 million people through a game of whispers?" Mikey asked.

"You guys can't possibly be buying this, right? He's out of his fricken mind," James growled, pointing. "First you tank your own career. Then you frame Michaels. Now you're asking the five of us to risk our pensions by trying to somehow evacuate over 15 million people? You've officially lost it!"

"Believe it or not. That's up to you." He looked at his watch. "But in 57 minutes, there's gonna be a lot of dead people lying in the street. Will you be able to look the survivors in the eye and tell them you could have saved their loved ones, but chose not to?"

"What's your source on this?" James demanded.

"The Blur."

The alley fell silent.

"The Blur is dead," Patty finally said. "I helped peel him off the pavement."

Lockhart's stoic expression stared back at them. "The decision is yours. Please don't wait too long. I'm leaving with, or without you in two minutes." He stepped aside, allowing them some space to discuss the matter, but not too far that he couldn't still hear.

"What do you think?" Patricia whispered.

"He's full of shit!" James groaned.

"What if he's not? All those people…"

Suddenly, John stepped forward and stood next to Lockhart. He took the list from his hand and began reading it.

"Where the hell are *you* going?" James asked.

"Old Town," he replied.

"You can't be serious!"

"If there's a chance I can save people, then I will go."

Nancy was the next to step forward. Followed by Mikey. Patricia sighed and rolled her eyes, but followed in suit. "You better be right about this," she said. "Move your ass, James," she grunted.

"This is so stupid," he grumbled before stomping out after the others.

20 minutes later, in the epicenter of Old Town, the five officers arrived and split up, each heading into a different apartment building. As instructed, they made their way to the top floor of the residential towers and began knocking on doors, working their way down to the ground floor. Each time, Lockhart knocked and flashed his badge, warning the occupants to get as far away from Old Town as possible, and to tell at least one other person before leaving, and to tell them to do the same. As one might expect, the residents asked too many questions, slammed their doors in their faces, and attempted to resist, but they had already made their peace with the fact that they wouldn't be able to save everyone.

By the time the others arrived, residents were already riled up from the crowd of protestors now gathered in the streets. They took one look at the cops and believed they were there to remove them so Burton Conglomerates could snatch up their property and evict them permanently. Before long, there were hundreds of people outside the building ready to march in protest of BC's Homes Reclamation Project. Inside, several residents outwardly refused to leave and slammed their doors.

Lockhart partnered with James. He felt the others were more receptive to the idea and needed to keep an eye on him to ensure the message was delivered properly. As they moved on, he noticed

James becoming more and more uneasy and began to fear a physical altercation was imminent.

"You can't do this! We have rights!" a voice in the crowd yelled. This sentiment was echoed by the crowd and more began to take notice of him.

"Listen, on any other day, you and I could hash this out. But we don't have time! Do what I say!" Lockhart ordered.

"Fuck that, pig! I'm not doing shit! I'm gonna film yo' ass." A boy took out his phone and began live-streaming the situation to his social media account. He began commentating on what was happening. When Lockhart ignored him, he shouted, "Why don't you take off your helmet and mask and show the world who you are? Because you're a coward! That's why! You know what you're doing is illegal!" He began calling out to others in the hallway, who had now gathered behind him. "You can see for yourselves! These cops are forcibly removing us from our homes! I say we fight back! Everybody get—"

Lockhart suddenly grabbed the boy by the collar with both hands and slammed his back into the wall. He got right into his face. "Listen to me goddammit!" His tone was desperate. "If you don't do what I say right now, thousands of people are going to die!"

The boy held up his hand, keeping the other residents at bay.

"Get your family! Get your friends! Tell everyone you can in the next five minutes… and get the hell out of here!" Lockhart released his grip and let the boy slump down again. "Just go! Okay?" His eyes were glistening with real tears.

James ran to the next door and knocked, only to be attacked by a woman with a spatula and had to retreat a few steps before shaking it off. Before he reached the next door, he received a hard shove to his back that nearly sent him to the floor.

Before them, a crowd of residents filled the hallway and began shouting. Some threw cans of food or spit in their direction, screaming for them to leave.

"That's it," James snapped. He whirled around, pulled his nightstick from his belt and went to clobber the first person he saw.

"James, don't!" Lockhart tried to yell, but his voice was drowned out by the crowd. They shoved Lockhart aside and rushed James.

James reared back to swing, but something caught the stick in mid-descent. Angrily, James jerked his head just in time to see a large man swing his fist into his jaw that sent him reeling down the staircase.

A moment later, an angry mob poured from the entrance and out into the street. They kicked James hard and sent him onto his hands and knees. Behind him, a crowd of protesters headed his way. They gathered around him in a large semicircle, yelling and screaming with rage for him to leave and chucking whatever was in their hands at him.

James slowly climbed to his feet, his right hand hovering over his hip, and his fingers unsnapped the restraint on his 9mm. He slid the gun out of its holster, making the whole crowd roar even angrier. The crowd seemed just seconds away from rushing him.

Like a cornered animal, James frantically began pointing the weapon at anyone who seemed to step forward until a man with a bat lunged forward. He squeezed the trigger a little tighter and his finger tightened.

The gun went off, forcing the crowd a step back.

"That's enough, James!" Lockhart yelled, holding his wrist into the air.

James seemed to be relieved he hadn't actually shot anyone. The loud roar softened into a dull one as Lockhart released his grip on his wrist.

By now, John and Patricia arrived, drawn over by the gunshot, and stood staring at him in disgust. As John scanned the crowd, he caught sight of a boy with a phone and had an idea. "Is that thing on?" he asked the boy, who nodded. "How much social media influence have you got?"

"Enough to get you both fired," he said, smirking.

"Come here; record this!" he shouted.

"John! No!" James yelled, but it was too late. He'd already taken off his helmet and removed his mask. He got down on one knee and waved the boy closer.

"My name is Detective John Samoset. I've been a cop on the force for 25 years. My ancestors were Algonquin. Their blood… of the first Americans… runs through my veins. Long ago, my ancestors were systematically exterminated by foreign invaders. I know what it feels like… the betrayal of authority… broken promises. Long ago, I became a policeman to be a bridge between two peoples. Seeing the way you all look at me tonight, I know that I have failed. But I came here tonight to warn you. In less than 30 minutes, a weapon will come from the sky. The ground will open and swallow up Old Town."

The crowd gasped and incessant murmuring whispered through their bodies.

"I ask you, not as a policeman, but as a son… as a father… and as a resident of Old Town… please trust me. Leave your homes and get to safety."

The boy holding the camera phone dropped his hateful glare and for the first time, really looked around and saw the forest through the trees. "What do you mean *the skies are going to open up*?"

"We don't have time for this, kid. It's time for you to make a choice."

The boy stood still, as if studying him. Then he blinked, glanced around unsurely, and slowly lowered the phone and clicked it off. "You heard the man! Everybody, get out of here!"

The crowd hesitated, then one by one, started to move. John nodded and began shouting for everyone to get as far away as possible. Together, they gently ushered some people from the stairway, occasionally taking the hand or arm of an elderly person and helping them to the street curb.

"What do you need me to do?" the boy asked.

"Get out of here, kid!"

"No, sir," he said. "I'm not going anywhere. This is my home."

"You stay here, you die. You wanna help? Get your family to safety. Get on your live stream and warn as many people as you can."

The boy lifted up his phone and once again started recording. When he'd delivered his message, he turned toward the building.

"Kid!"

The boy reached up, pulled the fire alarm, then stood on the street while dozens of people began leaving through the front entrance.

Lockhart shook his head. He hadn't thought of that.

"Take only what you can carry!" a woman with a megaphone cried. Then she stopped. The deafening roar of the crowd began to wane while a rumbling sound replaced it.

Lockhart could feel the street beneath his feet shaking and could even see pebbles bouncing on the surface. Then, in the distance, multiple car alarms began to blare, echoing all around him. An awful crunch exploded to his left and glass shards began raining down, pinging against the asphalt like falling icicles. The whole street vibrated. Bits of concrete, rock, and debris began plummeting down onto the street. Screams rang out into the night, haunting screams that put up the hairs on the back of your neck.

Cars started to explode and soon, the entire block was engulfed in smoke and flames.

Fire trucks and emergency vehicles raced into action, but were forced to screech to a halt as debris rained from the sky. The streets filled with the screams of survivors echoing through the air. A moment later, one of the residential buildings that James had just managed to clear began crumbling and crashed toward the ground. It landed right on the firetruck and smashed it to pieces.

Then, like someone had flipped a switch, an adjacent building began to crack and crumble. The very structure of the building seemed to be eroding away as if a demolition team had set off explosives. This building had not been fully evacuated and as the building collapsed into its own footprint, above the crumbling sounds, were the screams of people crying out in one last desperate breath for help. Those already on the street turned and ran for their lives.

CHAPTER 56

"Coordinates confirmed," an automated voice chimed. The satellite was activated!

"Now that you've lost, it's time for you and your band of annoying meddlers to end." Hal nodded and one of the soldiers positioned himself behind her, cocked his rifle, and waited for the command.

"Wait!" Katsu cried. "You said you wouldn't harm them!"

"I lied," Hal grunted. "Do it."

The soldier fired a round, dropping Ally to the floor.

"No!" Katsu whined.

"Him too," Hal said, pointing to Marcus, but something turned his head. Ally stood up, making the group of soldiers recoil and take a step back.

"I said, kill him!"

This time, the soldier switched to fully auto and shot a handful of rounds. Ally twitched as the bullets punched through her, but this time, she didn't fall. The soldier cocked his head, then all the soldiers emptied their clips.

Moving stealthily, the real Ally, cloaked by the suit's optics, saw her opportunity. "Now, Curtis!"

The lights suddenly clicked off, shrouding the room in total darkness, but her God-Vision lit up the room like daylight. She leaped off the wall behind Hal and shoved him, sending him crashing into the soldiers. She grabbed Marcus's satchel and launched Marcus toward the control room, taking fire in the back. She screamed, her voice synthesizer growling like a demented beast. The suit was bulletproof, but the impact felt like two hits with a sledge hammer. They knocked her off balance and nearly made her fall to the floor before she managed to lunge behind a large machine.

Marcus slid into the control room and tossed two gas canisters at the technicians's feet. He removed a breathing mask from his satchel and dove for cover as the canisters erupted into a thick fog. Everyone inside began coughing and spluttering, one by one retreating out and away from the suffocating mist as tear gas burned their eyes.

He slammed the door shut and locked it. "I'm in! Curtis, lights!" He could hear Curtis typing furiously and a vent above started sucking the gas into the ventilation system. He watched Hal peer inside through the window, pausing to wipe his eyes and banged on the door.

"Get that door open!" he heard him yell and two men began hot-wiring the access panel.

"Ally, wait!" Katsu yelled, but she slammed her fist into his face, knocking him to the ground.

She knew Marcus didn't have long, and hoped she could give him enough time. Just then, clicking sounds from the empty magazines reverberated. She lunged forward, grabbed the first man's gun, and yanked him down the stairs behind her. She uppercut the second and smashed his head against the concrete pillar, and kept advancing.

The third hesitated, watching her whip through two of his comrades and seeing their limp bodies roll down the stairs. He screamed, rushed forward, and dove toward her in a football tackle, but she ducked and stood up, launching him into the air and heard him crash down onto the first soldier.

The fourth grunted and tried to strike her head with the butt of his rifle, but missed. Ally's God-Vision in her helmet revealed every movement like it was being telegraphed. She grabbed his rifle and slammed the barrel into his face. As he flinched, she used the weapon's strap to pull him close and fling him over her shoulder, once again sending him down hard onto the first soldier, who'd just managed to climb to his feet. The force of the landing hyperextended his knee and he fell to the floor, cradling his leg and wailing in pain.

Ally heard two puffs of compressed air shoot from the drone behind her and she heard two dull thuds as soldier two and three collapsed. *"I'm out,"* she heard Curtis cry. *"You're on your own."* She turned to the last man standing.

He unclipped his rifle, removed his body armor, and chucked them aside. Then he walked forward, completely undeterred by the fall of his fellow soldiers, and threw his best punch combo. Ally ducked and dodged, and repositioned herself. The man shook it off and tried again. This time, he swung harder, but Ally sidestepped, and his fist went right into the concrete wall. He grimaced, clutching his hand, and Ally didn't hesitate. She boxed him in a series of rapid punches, grabbed his fist midair, and slammed his head onto the railing, knocking him out with a sickening crack.

When the last man fell, she turned to face Hal, smirking under her visor—though he wouldn't know it—just in time to see Smith raise some sort of futuristic rifle and fire at the control room door. A loud, shrill chirp pulsed through the room and the door panel exploded in sparks and died. A few emergency lights flickered ominously nearby, while others, now dead from the blast, left eerie shadows hugging the corners of the room. She heard a loud click and the door to the control room popped open. Marcus barely had time to turn before the second assassin rushed in and grabbed him by the throat. He ripped him through the doorway, threw him to the ground and kicked him hard in the stomach. Ally stood horrified as several technicians scurried back inside over the sound of Hal's barking voice to try and resume control.

She was about to charge, but flinched as Smith whirled and fired again. Blueish-white energy rippled throughout her suit, disrupting her earpiece and helmet. Frantically, Ally clawed at her head, screaming as the suit began to reappear like pieces of a jigsaw puzzle. Her synthesized scream rang out again as electricity sparked, forcing her to rip off her helmet. She threw it to the ground and pawed at her face.

"Well, well, well... this is what has been terrorizing Grace City?" Smith sneered, stepping forward. "What took down Andrew Fisher? A little girl?"

Ally glared at him. Following him with her eyes and feeling the sting of his words.

"End this!" Hal barked.

The two assassins stepped forward and a sinking feeling in Ally's stomach lurched. She suddenly realized she'd have to fight both. Masking her fear, she slowly raised her fists and stood tall, studying the two assassins as they moved closer, desperate to identify something, anything that she could exploit. But as they took another step, Smith turned to the other figure and held out his arm, stopping them.

"I got this," he declared, tossing the EMP rifle aside. The figure in the black combat suit looked at him, then took a few sideways steps, staying well back and out of the way.

Ally did her best not to look relieved.

"Don't worry, I won't hold back on account of your gender." He unsheathed a Japanese Katana sword, holding it low near his hip. "After I kill you, I'm gonna track down all your little friends... anyone and everyone you've ever cared about and run them through... starting with him." He pointed his sword toward Marcus.

Ally glanced at Marcus and a flicker of worry fluttered through her. "Marcus… if I don't make it—" she started.

"Kick his ass!" he yelled.

Ally smiled. This was the moment she'd been obsessing over her whole life. She reached her hands back and removed two metal rods from the magnetic hold on her back and whirled the dual metal batons almost tauntingly, feeling the scar tissue in her chest stretch to its limits. Her mind quieted and all distractions slid away. She was ready. *Bring it on!*

Smith's eyes narrowed. His grip tightened on the katana sword and he lunged toward her, swinging down hard. Ally barely had time to deflect the strike, the loud clash making her flinch.

He stepped sideways, a wry smile playing on his lips. He circled her, then attacked in three purposeful and targeted strikes, sending her reeling. She barely managed to deflect them. His smirk grew wider, as if killing her too quickly would spoil all the fun. He was toying with her! Each swing was a deliberate invitation, a challenge, a subtle game of cat and mouse.

Patience! Ally willed herself. *Make him tire.*

Over the next few seconds, they each exchanged a series of high and low blows. Ally blocked the first strike with her batons and ducked the second. But he booted her hard in the stomach and sent her stumbling backwards. Pain shot through her chest, making her cry out. She gritted her teeth and steadied herself, bracing for another attack. She spun left and struck right, then spun right and struck left, but he blocked each advance with his sword.

She swung high with one of the batons and swung down hard with the second. Mr. Clark blocked the strikes and their weapons met in an X. She pushed hard with all her strength to send him off balance, but he smiled back, knowing his strength was greater than hers. He thrust her backwards so hard she almost lost her footing.

A flicker of worry suddenly pulsed through her. She knew what he was doing. He was testing her skills. He had to be. She knew if she wanted to beat him, she'd have to start attacking, and being unpredictable, so she gritted her teeth and lunged forward, slicing at him with one baton and waiting for his sword to connect before striking his leg with the other. It worked! His balance dipped as she made contact, and he hobbled back a step.

This was it! Now! She kicked off of the pillar, doubling her attack speed and power and reared back for a hard blow. CRACK! Smith jerked upright, dropping the act, and backhand-punched her in the face. She fell to the ground, dazed, and quickly rolled, leaping to her feet as he twirled his sword in a taunt, smirking.

He was faking it. This was a game to him.

She shook off the pain coursing through her face and skull and forced her arms to comply.

"Awww, did that hurt?" he asked, grinning. Then he rushed her. When Ally blocked the strike with one of her batons, he spun quickly and in a double move, slammed the hilt of the sword into her stomach and elbowed her in the face. She winced, trying to blink away the tears.

"At least make it a challenge for me," he taunted.

Ally wiped the blood from her nose and glared back at him. Her grip tightened on the batons and she lunged forward. He tried another downward strike, but she deflected it, shoving his sword to the side and counter-punched his face. She felt the bones in his nose crack and allowed herself a moment of triumph as it started bleeding.

"Awww... did that hurt?" she parroted, but watched dumbfounded as Smith showed no emotion whatsoever. No grimace. No pain. Not even a shake of his head. *Who could do that?*

If he had meant to terrify her, it worked. Fear crept up inside of her again, but she didn't have time to process it. Undeterred, Smith stepped forward and swung his sword. Ally leapt back, feeling the wind of the blade graze her face, but she spun and struck him with a reverse turning kick to the back of the head. His face slammed into the concrete pillar, splitting his eye socket. Blood flowed heavily over his eye, stopping him a moment. He wiped his face with his hand and stared at the crimson blood on his fingertips with a set of dead eyes.

"Enough of this!" Hal yelled, his voice shattering the moment. "Stop toying with the bitch and finish it!"

Smith tilted his head, acknowledging the order, and cracked his neck. He gritted his teeth and flew forward. With inhuman speed, he disarmed her, swiftly knocking away one baton and then the other.

Defenseless, she took her signature fighter's stance, not that it would do any good against a sword, but hoped to find a way to even the odds. She felt the sharp blade of the katana slash against her arm, then against the back of her leg. Had it not been for the suit, it would likely have cut straight through. She grimaced, the pain forcing her to her knees, and froze as she felt the tip of the blade slide under her neck. She sucked air in through her teeth and let him lift her chin.

"I made a mistake with you twice. Once when I killed your *whimpering, bitch* of a mother. And again when I shot you in the police station." His dead eyes flared and chilled her to the bone. "There will not be a third! This time, *I'm going to remove your head!"*

Ally felt tears well up. *I'm sorry, Mom*. She glanced at Marcus, his horrified expression haunting what was left of her soul. She was frozen. She had nothing left. This was it.

Smith turned and looked at Marcus. "I'll be right with you!" he cooed cheerfully. Then he raised his sword high.

"No cheating death this time, I'm afraid," he muttered, blood oozing over a toothy smile

Ally thought about shutting her eyes, but she didn't want to give the prick the satisfaction. She sent all the hatred she had left burning straight through her eyes and watched as Smith sliced down hard.

She winced.

Warm blood splashed her face.

She heard a guttural scream and saw an arm, still holding a sword, drop to the floor and clang loudly.

Her head whirled. The figure in black was standing beside her, sword drawn, blood still dripping from the blade. She had severed his arm!

"What the hell are you doing!" Smith screamed, gripping his bleeding stub. His scowl meant he could feel everything now that the effects of the red stone had been cut from his arm.

The figure who'd once held Marcus captive, now towered over the fallen assassin. He did not answer. Instead, he drop-kicked Smith hard in the chest, sending his back slamming hard against the pillar. Seeing the floor fill with his own blood, Smith removed his belt and tightened it as best he could around the gushing wound.

The figure, however, kicked the man's severed hand away with the toe of his boot, flicked the sword up into his own hand, and threw it like a javelin, spearing Smith through the chest and pinning him to the concrete pillar. He howled in both pain and fury, looking up with fiery eyes just in time to see a sword blade decapitate him. His head sloshed to the floor and rolled forward until it rested near Ally's knees.

Ally forced herself up and turned to face Smith's attacker, struggling for the resolve to rejoin the fight. But her mind was somewhere else. She dared not utter the words. She just stood there, gasping in disbelief, her mouth gaping, her eyes stunned.

"Emmalee?" Ally half-whispered.

The figure turned his head, slowly reached his hands up to his helmet, removed it, and lowered his arms, dropping the helmet to the ground. Standing before her, was a woman she recognized. How could she not? It was like looking into a mirror—or more accurately, at her *twin!*

Ally's voice caught in her throat. Her lungs caved. Tears bubbled under her eyes and her mouth shook. "Emma?"

Suddenly, the control console began sparking and humming. Hal sprinted toward it, but it was too late. The whole system was down. "No, no! You told me the algorithm was deleted!" Hal cried.

Ally looked at Katsu, still rubbing his jaw where Ally had struck him, but he was clearly smirking.

"What did you do?" Hal screamed, eyes burning.

"The stone didn't delete the algorithm," Ally whispered, mostly to herself. "It activated it…"

"I tried to tell you. I'm sorry. He had to believe I double crossed you," Katsu said.

Ally understood. The double bluff gave the satellite enough time to cease firing on Old Town and…

Suddenly, a low hum rattled around the room, vibrating loose debris and downed rifles that had fallen to the floor. They bounced and trembled beside them. The ground shook beneath their feet as glass cracked on two of the large windows.

"You bastard!" Hal rushed towards Katsu and swung his fist, but Marcus stepped up and struck him with a hard blow to the face that sent him flying to the ground.

Hal turned, clutching his jaw.

"I'd stay down if I were you," Marcus said coldly. "Who do you think trained The Blur!"

Hal didn't move. He glared up at him and smiled. "Kill them!" Hal ordered.

Ally's head flew back to her sister, back from the dead.

Emma stood limply, staring back at her.

"Emmalee?" Ally said again, her eyes tearing up and her voice breaking. She stepped forward, but Emma recoiled and stopped her.

Behind them, the ceiling to Hal's penthouse buckled and an entire section of roof smashed down onto the console floor.

"Move! Now!" Marcus shouted, his voice barely audible over the roar of destruction.

Ally whipped her head back to her sister, but she was gone. She'd disappeared. The helmet too. "Run!" Marcus yelled, grabbing Ally by the shoulder and shoving her as another large section of roof smashed down, nearly on top of them. The team dashed towards the staircase, their only hope of escape thanks to the EMP frying the elevator circuits. Debris continued to rain down around them, covering them with clouds of dust and fragments of concrete. The building groaned and shuddered, and the whole stairway felt like it was moving.

"Come on!" Ally yelled, shoving Hal on as the others descended, floor after floor, leaping down the stairs two at a time. Above, the ceiling groaned and sagged, threatening to give way at any moment. Dust hung heavily in the air, obscuring their vision and stinging their eyes. The acrid scent of melted concrete mingled with the metallic tang of warping metal. The walls around them began to crack, sending more dust and debris over their heads. The ceiling groaned again, threatening to bury them alive.

"We're not going to make it!" Katsu cried.

"Keep going!" Ally's voice cut through the rumble. Eyes blazing with determination, she urged them onward as the building fought back with a vengeance. With a thunderous roar, the ceiling collapsed, showering them with a fury of torrential debris as they fought their way down the stairs. They still had twenty floors to go!

With a massive crash, a huge section of the staircase gave way, sending chunks of concrete and steel hurtling to the floors below them. "Go!" Ally screamed, urging Katsu and Marcus to jump across to the adjacent section still intact. One at a time, they both jump. Katsu landed hard, his back foot slipping over the edge but Marcus grabbed his shirt and pulled him to safety. Another large chunk of debris smashed down, destroying the stairway just above them.

"Jump!" Ally ordered.

"You first!" Hal said.

Ally didn't have time to argue. She could see him wrestling with the distance in his head. With a leap, Ally jumped across and turned. "Jump!" she called again.

"I can't make it!" Hal screamed.

"You stay here, you're already dead!"

He nodded. Then he bent his legs, secured his footing, and leaped. Reaching for Ally and Marcus's outstretched hands, Hal missed his mark and crashed into the remains of the staircase with his chest, and slipped down, clinging on to the side with his fingers. Something bounced and hit Ally's boot. It was a black stone, only it was glowing faintly. Instinctively, she grabbed it and slipped it into one of her pockets.

"Help me!" Hal screamed.

Marcus and Katsu reached down and grabbed Hal's wrists, pulling him together, but Hal wriggled and his grip slipped. He screamed and plummeted into the abyss below, disappearing in the mist of dust.

Another section of concrete smashed onto the platform where he'd just stood and crunched the section of stairs to bits. Above them, the loudest, most thunderous explosion echoed through the shaft and they knew the building was falling, floor by floor, pancaking into its own footprint. The three of them turned and ran.

As they reached the ground floor, the three of them dashed through the lobby, choking on dust and debris, and barreled toward the exit. A second after hitting the front steps, the entire column that used to be Burton Tower hit the ground in full force, knocking them all to the concrete in a massive shockwave. They rolled down the stairs, the ground still trembling beneath them, and crawled their way towards flashing blue and red lights.

Figures scrambled towards them. Whether they were police or firefighters, Ally didn't know. Their shouts were drowned out by the cacophony of destruction, but they were alive. Bruised and battered, but alive. As they were led away to safety, Ally felt her knees buckle and the last thing she remembered was slumping over and the world going dark.

CHAPTER 57

Ally sat still on the uncomfortable aluminum chair trying to ignore her numbing leg, the handcuffs that were starting to pinch around her wrists, and the flickering fluorescent bulb on the ceiling that seemed to flash in no particular numeric pattern. She wondered if it hadn't been fixed on purpose. How long could a person sit in this room before they'd do anything to escape?

In the time she'd spent here, she'd learned pretty much everything there was to learn about this room. The teal wallpaper was peeling in the corner below the air conditioning unit, the wood trim circling the room at waist height was caked in a layer of dust, the white paint beneath it was scuffed and dirty. The bold blue skirting boards didn't match any of the other colors in the room. On the floor, there was one teal tile that had slid to the right, leaving an off-white crack. The smell was somewhere between bleach and mildew.

She wasn't sure how much longer she waited until Mr. Chamberlain was let in. He was wearing the same suit he wore last time, the faded blue one with the dark stain under the left breast pocket. "Hey Ally, long time no see," he said smiling before setting his coffee down on the table and sitting opposite..

"How are you Mr. Chamberlain?" Ally asked, returning the smile. "How's the little one?"

Mr. Chamberlain cocked his head in surprise. It occurred to her in this moment that not only was this the most he'd ever gotten her to speak, but he'd probably never seen her smile before. She couldn't help it. She was happy. For the first time in a long time.

"Are you OK? Have they been treating you alright?" he asked, sitting down opposite.

"He's good. Doin' real good. We just started introducing solid foods and he's getting ready to talk. Any day now," he chuckled.

"That's wonderful. Congratulations."

"Thanks," he replied, but cocked his head again. He pulled out a yellow notepad and a pen. "Ok, so here is the situation, Ally." She leaned forward in the chair. "I'm afraid I've got bad news for you. I, uhh, … well, I wasn't able to get any of the charges dropped this time."

"I'm sure you did your best, Mr. Chamberlain."

"Yeah. Well, as it stands now, you're being charged with… well, there has never been a case where one person destroyed a whole building before… I mean, without explosives. Or an airplane. Or… well," he shook his head, "there isn't really a word for it. So for now, you're being charred with egregious unlicensed structural decommissioning." Ally shrugged with her eyebrows. "And…"

"Go on," she said.

"I'm not gonna lie, Ally… it's bad."

"It's ok. Please continue."

"Uh, okay… there's also criminal trespassing, possession of stolen property, egregious criminal damage and destruction of property, reckless endangerment to the public, possession of a deadly weapon, armed assault, multiple counts of aggravated assault, vigilantism, obstruction of justice, domestic terrorism… and second-degree manslaughter."

Ally didn't flinch. She nodded, expecting most of it.

"You know, as your lawyer, I will fight these as best I can, but given the circumstances… is there anything else you can tell me that will help?"

Ally shrugged. "I'm guilty Mr. Chamberlain. Of everything except the murder. I didn't kill anyone."

"But, what about the soldiers? And let's not forget, Hal Burton is still missing. Presumed dead. You expect the court to believe none of that was your fault?"

Ally leaned back and exhaled. "Well, I would hope the courts would weigh the alternative."

"Which is?"

"Had I not intervened, hundreds of thousands of people, in Grace City alone, would have lost their lives. And countless more thereafter. I stopped it. I never intended for anyone to die. But they did. The way I see it, it's a Trolley Problem."

"Kill the few to save the many?"

"Exactly. Society may not agree with me… but it was a no-win scenario. I took the lesser of two evils."

Mr. Chamberlain scratched his chin, considering her words. "Okay. Let's say I make that argument in court. But that still leaves us with a problem: if you didn't kill Hal Burton or those soldiers, then someone else did. The prosecution will try to pin it on you unless we give them someone else."

"I can't do that."

Mr. Chamberlain narrowed his eyes. "So there was *someone*. If you tell me who did—"

"It isn't that simple," she replied.

"Are you in danger? Did anyone threaten you? Are you being blackmailed?"

Ally shook her head.

"Then what?"

"For eight years, I believed that an assassin killed my mother and sister. My doctors told me I was delusional; they put me on anti-psychotic medication. Can you imagine how that feels?"

Mr. Chamberlain pursed his lips.

"But, the man responsible has faced justice. And I'm not crazy. I feel like a huge weight has been lifted off my shoulders. I don't expect you to understand, but I'm content and happy for the first time in eight years. And right now, I'd rather die than put this person in danger."

Mr. Chamberlain looked into her eyes. He nodded slowly. "Okay. Well, that's great, Ally. I'm glad you've found closure." He leaned forward. "Are you sure you can't tell me?"

"I can't, Mr. Chamberlain; I just can't."

Arguing turned their heads. Raised voices were getting louder on the other side of the door. Finally, the door burst open.

"Hey! You can't be in here!" Mr. Chamberlain barked. "I have a private meeting with my client!"

"You're gonna want to see this!" Lockhart said as he pushed his way into the room. "Turn on the news," he ordered.

Mr. Chamberlain picked up the TV remote from the Velcro strip on the wall and pressed the power button. He thumbed through the channels until at last, he stopped on a live news feed. The title below the news anchor read: Robbery in Progress.

The news anchor read from the teleprompter as an image from a CCTV camera appeared on the screen. It froze on a woman looking right up into the camera. It was Emmalee!

"When was this taken?" Mr. Chamberlain asked, eyes fixed to the screen.

"About twenty minutes ago," Lockhart said.

"But she couldn't have—"

"I know."

"That means—"

"Yes, it does. Ally, we're dropping the charges against you. You will be released from custody as soon as the paperwork is signed."

Mr. Chamberlain looked at Lockhart and almost smiled. "But what about all the other charges?" he asked.

"Footage recovered from a nearby building shows this woman," Lockhart pointed to the screen, "parachuting down a few blocks away into a parking garage. She was wearing a black combat suit like the one Ally was wearing when she was arrested, which backs up the testimony from the other hostages. As it stands, there's enough reasonable doubt to drop them." He turned to Ally. "It appears you are just another victim in this whole debacle. You have my, and the department's, sincerest apology."

Ally looked at Mr. Chamberlain, Lockhart, and the open doorway, not sure how to feel. Until this moment, she was so certain she was going to prison. But now, with the charges dropped, she had the rest of her life ahead of her. A life without her past dragging her down. Her journey through darkness had come to an end, and a new chapter, one filled with possibilities, awaited her beyond the confines of that uncomfortable aluminum chair.

"Thank you," she finally whispered, her voice soft and grateful. She smiled. "I guess I'll see you around."

*   *   *

He stood leaned against the wall beside the wardrobe, out of reach from the gaze of the fluorescent light. The tingling in his feet and the pressure in his spine was getting worse. Standing in one place was now an act of sheer will. He knew exactly how long it had been because the clock on the wall was still ticking. It had been three hours. *Three hours…* and she was still in there! She hadn't come back.

Remember your training.

He rubbed his hand over his dark brown hair, buzzed short enough to feel like stiff bristles. His palms were slick with cold sweat. His heart was racing, beating in tune to the quiet hum of electricity surging in the walls. He closed his eyes and focused on slowing his breathing.

Remember your training!

Footsteps! He opened his eyes and strained to listen. They were coming his way, getting closer and closer. He tried to quiet the panic swelling inside him. They'd kill him for sure, if the others found him here. He knew that. They'd make an example out of him. AC19 swallowed, forgetting about slowing his heart and leaned back, pressing himself flat against the wall of the cell. His Neanderthal brows furrowed and he stared at the door, watching as AC5 and AC11 passed. He breathed out as their muffled voices drifted well beyond the door.

She should be back by now. If they hurt her, I will make them pay! I'll make them suffer! Long and slow! I'll—

More footsteps. Softer. Singular. It was her!

A moment later, 24 stepped into the room and shut the door behind her. God, she was beautiful. The light seemed to caress her skin, kissing it with tiny radiant sparkles. What he wouldn't give to just pause time so he could admire her for just a little longer. But as the rigidity and hardness of her pose wilted, he snapped out of it. Her arms collapsed. She gasped as she saw him, fear in her eyes wide like the stars. Then she breathed a sigh of relief.

"19!" she hissed. "What are you doing here? Did anyone see you?"

AC19 shook his head. "I was careful."

They rushed toward one another, throwing their arms around each other and embracing tightly. He felt her grip tighten and warm tears touched his cheek. "Hey, you're okay. Shhh… you're okay. I've got you." He hugged her tighter. "Do they know what happened?"

She shook her head. "I think they suspect."

"That's good! It means they don't have any proof."

"Not yet."

"There won't be any proof! You said it yourself, the building collapsed. Quantum destroyed it."

"What if they find out? What if they find out what we're planning?" she whispered.

"Then we die, together."

She pulled away and turned, her arms wrapping around herself.

"What is it?"

"She called me Emmalee."

"Emmalee… the girl from your nightmares?"

She nodded. "Yes. But it was more than that. In that moment, I was her. I was back in that house… watching them kill her… a mother I never had. A sister I never knew. But in that moment, it was real."

"Is that why you did it?"

24 didn't answer.

AC19 reached forward and pulled her toward him. "None of that was real. That wasn't you. Those are not your memories."

"They felt real."

AC19 bit his tongue. He wished he could unburden her. The torment she felt. He only knew of it, but he could not understand it. He wasn't cursed with memories of the host.

"You still think it's worth reaching out to her?" he asked.

"I don't see any other choice. We can't fight them by ourselves. And we can't leave… not without the children. With her help, maybe we've got a chance."

"What if she learns the truth?"

24 sighed. She looked right into his black eyes. "Then I'll kill her." She slipped into his arms and pressed her cheek to his chest, feeling the warmth of his skin and the lull of his beating heart.

THE END

Extras

If you enjoyed

PROJECT STARFALL

look out for

PRIMAL

a disGrace City spin-off
also by

Colin Ross

Here's a taste:

PRIMAL:
A *dis*grace City Novel

CHAPTER 1

He turned and headed back through the poorly lit street. There was no need to conceal the sound of his footsteps anymore. She wouldn't hear him. His heart-rate was already returning to normal and he no longer took care to quiet his breath.

As he turned the corner, he noticed lights flickering from a few elevated apartments and the sounds of a cheering crowd spilling into the street. He remembered there was a boxing match tonight. Couldn't remember who was fighting. But from the sounds of the people inside, the favorite was losing. He stuffed his hands into his pockets and quickened his pace, eager to avoid any interactions with disgruntled hooligans. Grace City was rough enough already without the added vandalism and street brawls sporting events bring. The news last week said that whenever there's a game, domestic violence increases by 26%. And that's if they win. It jumps to 38% when the team loses.

He'd made it another few yards before he heard whimpering and a shrill voice crying out in pain.

"Please! You're hurting me!"

There was another voice. A man's voice. Screaming back in anger. In hatred.

"Please! Stop! What did I do wrong?"

Few sounds in this world are as unforgettable as an animal in pain. It's a sound that melts your heart and makes your blood boil at the same time. This one was a dog. He could tell from the high-pitched squeal and the desperate yelp. Judging from the pitch, it was a young one, probably only 6-8 months old.

The stranger gritted his teeth, his feet dragging him against his will and drawing him toward the screams. Before long, he found himself at the edge of an adjacent alley. He was about to walk right in, but at the last second, he caught a glimpse of a man with long, thinning hair and faded blue jeans staring at the floor. Quickly, he ducked behind a debris chute and overflowing dumpster, peering around the obstruction, careful not to divert the man's attention. He was nursing a beer and upon closer inspection, he was glowering at a small animal lying on its side. It looked like a Dogo Argentino, a large mastiff type dog with a pearl-white coat. The poor thing was lying on its side and taking labored breaths, begging for the owner to stop.

The stranger winced as the man chucked his bottle at the dog's head, missing it by mere inches, and kicked it hard in the ribs. The pup made a sickening shriek that pulsed the stranger's ears.

"Clint!" a voice called from inside the bar. "Fight's about to start!"

The man sucked air through his teeth and scoffed before stumbling back inside, leaving the dog wheezing and trying to drag itself along the filthy ground.

The stranger eyed the door, then hurried over to the injured animal and bent down.

"Please don't hurt me," the dog pleaded, wriggling and trying to pull away.

"Shhh… save your strength," the stranger whispered. "I'm not going to hurt you." He cast his eyes over the dog's body. There didn't appear to be any gaping wounds. A few superficial bites and scrapes, but nothing that appeared too serious. "Can you walk?"

"Walk?"

"We need to get out of here. That man will be back any minute."

The dog struggled to sit up, but groaned and laid still, panting. *"It hurts. It's hard to breathe."*

"May I?" the stranger asked, waiting for an affirming blink before touching the dog's ribs gently. He felt over the bloody fur and tested each rib with the tips of his fingers. The dog winced, confirming what he suspected. A few broken ribs. Probably internal bleeding. The skin around the roots of the fur were dark, indicating an arterial bleed. This was serious.

"How bad is it?"

The stranger hesitated. There was still time to stop it, if they left now. "You have a few broken ribs. You're having trouble breathing because the fractures have caused some swelling. You're gonna be okay," he said. "But we need to get you to a vet, now."

A glass bottle shattered behind them, turning their heads, followed by dissatisfied screams and boos spilling from inside the bar.

"Come on. We need to go." The stranger reached down and gently picked up the dog in his arms. "What are you called?"

"Called? Before I got here, they called me Snowy."

"Well, Snowy, my name is—"

"The hell you doin' with my dog?"

The stranger turned. Clint edged from the bar with three men following in toe. One was wearing a faded red baseball cap, the other a denim jacket, and the third a muscle shirt.

"I said, the hell you doin' with my dog?"

"Run!" Snowy whispered.

The stranger hesitated. He thought about running, but Snowy's injuries would likely worsen if he did. "He's hurt. There's a vet clinic not too far from here. I was just—"

"He don't need a vet," Clint grunted. He lifted his index finger. "That, there, is a *bait dog*. Can't fight for shit. Needs toughening up. He'll heal in a few weeks. Now, put 'em down."

The other three men started to fan out, bawling their hands into fists and readying themselves for a brawl.

"Look, Mister, I—"

"You hear what I said, boy?"

"Do as he says," Snowy whispered. *"They'll hurt you if you don't."*

The stranger ignored him. "How much is he worth to you?"

Clint laughed. "He ain't for sale."

"I've got about $200 cash in my pocket—"

"You deaf or stupid? I said he ain't for sale."

"Come on, guys, I'm sure we can work something out."

"Please, just go. These men are real mean."

Clint exchanged a glance with his buddies. His lips pressed into a pursed frown. Then, with a resigned sigh, he gave a slight nod and shrugged. "I suppose… for say, $2,000… I could let you take him off my hands."

The stranger stiffened. "I don't have that kind of money."

"Then you ain't got a dog, neither. Now, put 'em down!"

The stranger scanned each of their faces. He knew then that negotiations were over. They weren't going to let him take the dog. Again, he thought about running, but there was no way he could outrun the four of them with Snowy's added weight. His arms were already aching.

"It's OK," Snowy whimpered. *"Go."*

The stranger sighed and placed Snowy delicately onto the pavement. He stood up slowly. *One more try,* he thought. "What if I pay you $200 tonight and the rest by the end of the week?"

"I don't think this half-wit's gettin the message," the owner said. "What do you think, fellas?"

"I think he needs to be taught a lesson," Baseball Cap said.

"Run!" Snowy pleaded.

"Well, go on then! Get on with it before we miss the whole fight!"

"RUN!"

The stranger felt his senses heighten. He started to back up, slowly, trying to maintain the distance between him and the three approaching men. Every instinct screamed at him to run, but he couldn't leave Snowy. His breath became shallow and rapid, like he'd just finished a hard run. Sweat formed on his upper lip. Blood rushed to his ears, his pulse thumping like a bass drum.

"You picked the wrong night to be out alone, buddy," Muscles chuckled, stepping forward.

"Please don't do this," the stranger said. "I don't want to hurt you."

The three men exchanged amused glances and chuckled. "Kid, it's us that's gonna do the hurtin," Baseball Cap said.

The stranger retreated further toward the shadows, the amber glow of the lights gradually fading until darkness enveloped him. He felt his back touch the cold, rough bricks behind him. There was nowhere left to go. He knew what he had to do… but he also knew what would happen if he did.

"Dead end!" Baseball Cap laughed.

Both men snickered, then paused.

"Who are you talkin' to?"

Their laughter stopped short as a deep, guttural growl rumbled within the alley. Something was pacing back and forth. Something big. Something with glowing eyes.

Suddenly, Baseball Cap screamed, but his voice was drowned out by a deafening roar that exploded into the night. The force of the sound blast sent Denim Jacket and Muscles jumping backwards.

THUD-THUD-SPLAT!

Denim Jacket looked down in horror as Baseball Cap's severed head rolled toward his shoes. He barely had time to gasp before the roar returned, louder this time. A vicious frenzy of claws lunged from the shadows, slashing Muscles across the chest and painting the brick wall with blood. Denim Jacket turned and ran, but the beast leapt an impossible distance, tackling him to the ground and sinking its teeth into his shoulder. The man howled. He managed to turn over, jutting up his good arm in defense, but the beast bit down and tore his forearm clean off with one rip. It then went for the throat, silencing him with a loud crunch.

The beast whirled and roared so loud Clint fell onto his back. It edged closer, crouched low on the pads of its enormous paws. Clint frantically scooted back, panting and staring wide eyed as the bloody jaws inched forward until its whiskers were touching his face. The creature moved slowly, basking in Clint's fear as if toying with him. Then it opened its mouth and crunched down on Clint's head with its powerful jaws, bursting blood and brain matter through his popped skull.

The alley fell silent.

Dozens of spectators gazed out from their windows in horror at the bloodbath that had just ensued. Another roar sent them scattering away and out of sight. Seeing the alley was empty, the beast grunted and shook itself, dematerializing and fading into the air, leaving behind the stranger, now crouching on all fours.

Slowly, he stood up, surveying the blood soaked alley and strewn body parts. He sighed, hanging his head a moment. Then he stepped forward and leaned over Snowy.

"What are you?" Snowy huffed, shaking like a leaf, his breath coming out in short labored rasps.

The stranger kneeled down, sadness in his eyes. He looked at Snowy. He was paler. Weaker. His breathing was raspy, coming in and out in a watery wheeze. He didn't have long. "Snowy, I lied to you before. You're hemorrhaging internally. You're not gonna make it. I'm sorry."

Snowy blinked, still processing the words.

"But there's still time for you to make a choice. I'd like to make you an offer."